pretty ugly promises

C.W. FARNSWORTH

PRETTY UGLY PROMISES

ALSO BY C.W. FARNSWORTH

Four Months, Three Words

Kiss Now, Lie Later

First Flight, Final Fall

Come Break My Heart Again

Left Field Love

Famous Last Words

Winning Mr. Wrong

Back Where We Began

Like I Never Said

Fly Bye

Fake Empire

Heartbreak for Two

Serve

For Now, Not Forever

Friday Night Lies

Six Summers to Fall

Real Regrets

Truths and roses have thorns about them.

HENRY DAVID THOREAU

CONTENTS

PRETTY UGLY PROMISES

C.W. FARNSWORTH

PROLOGUE

LYLA

Most people probably can't point to one moment from their past and recognize it as the second the trajectory of their entire life changed.

I can.

Life is an intoxicating mixture of scenarios we can't control and decisions we make.

Chance and choice.

Predictable and uncontrollable.

I promised myself I'd learn from others' mistakes.

Promises are easy to make.

Problem is, they're also easy to break.

CHAPTER ONE

LYLA

As soon as we step from the porch's slatted floor inside, past the red front door, I know this is the wrong house. A rap song is blaring, loud enough that I can feel the beat pulsing against my skin and rattling my bones. The hardwood floors, stained with spilled drinks and muddy shoes, are vibrating beneath me.

It's crowded and hot inside. Loud and smelly. Sweat and smoke swirl in the sticky air, adding substance to the intangible. Each time I breathe, I have to suppress the urge to cough.

I glance at Kennedy, who looks as shell-shocked by the scene we're standing in as I feel. Her tawny skin is flushed, her eyes wide as she takes in the throng of people packed in the room. My wildest college experience so far was passing around a bottle of cheap merlot in Pembrook Hall's common room late on a Tuesday night, knowing I had an eight a.m. interviewing skills class on Wednesday.

I've never attended a party like this.

I didn't even know parties like this existed in real life. The term *rager* seemed like a product of Hollywood and its unrealistic expectations about…basically everything.

But here I am, awkwardly standing and experiencing it firsthand.

There's an honest-to-God disco ball attached to the ceiling at an awkward angle, sending glints of light spinning around and dancing off the bodies filling the room.

Kennedy mouths something to me, but I can't catch a word of it. Reading lips has never been a strength of mine, especially when I'm already overstimulated and overwhelmed.

I shrug in response, then wave a hand toward the door we just entered, silently asking if we should head back out into the cold. There's no way to pinpoint exactly where the music is coming from. It seems to be emanating all around us, pressing in and making conversation impossible.

My wave whacks a passing football player's arm. The one and only reason I have any clue he's on the football team is his attire. His backward ball cap, sweatshirt, and sweatpants all have *UPenn Football* embroidered on them. He looks like a football player too, tall and broad.

And he's clearly used to taking hits packing more force than my hand is capable of. There's no acknowledgment of the contact or of the apology that gets lost in the high decibel of the music before he keeps striding forward, unbothered.

The crowd parts for him in a way I haven't seen it do for anyone else. Kennedy nods toward the opening, and this time, unspoken communication works.

We follow the path that's been carved before it disappears, through the first room and into the kitchen, whose cabinets are painted the same garish shade of red as the front door. It's quieter in here, but not by much. The music is audible, just slightly muffled.

"I'm going to find somewhere quiet to call Ellie and find out the right address. Be right back." That's all Kennedy says before she disappears in a swish of curly hair, leaving me alone.

It's not as crowded in here as the living room was, but it's far from empty. I'm standing between the fridge and the dishwasher, amid a small sea of strangers. A few of them eye me curiously, although at a school this size, I know I'm not the first unfamiliar face they've seen.

I glance anxiously in the direction Kennedy disappeared, but there's no sign of her. I'm confident she'll come back, but unsure how long she'll be gone for. Kennedy could make conversation with a brick wall while I struggle to hold a conversation with an extrovert. If she runs into someone she knows—or wants to get to know—this could take a while.

Kennedy was my randomly assigned freshman roommate. Well, not entirely random. We were supposedly matched by some commonality discovered on the housing questionnaire, an elusive one I have yet to find.

I go to bed early; she stays up late.

Her family consists of still-married parents and a younger brother; mine is entirely absent.

There's no telling why we were paired together, and maybe there's a reason for that.

Tonight, Kennedy talked me into accompanying her to a small get-together Mark, a cute guy in her marketing class, had invited her to. Except Mark's attractiveness apparently erased some key information shared during the interaction—like *where* exactly the party was being held.

After wandering down Birch and Maple, we ended up on Oak Street, which hosts most of Greek Row. Cold and confused, we walked into this party that appears to include most of campus.

I don't think I've ever been in close proximity to this many people at once before, and I've already decided I don't like it. Not even the warmth seems worth it. The air in here feels heavy and hot, like the steam of an indoor pool. Except instead of chlorine, it's weighted with sweat and smoke.

Chatter continues around me, making me feel like I'm marooned on an island of one.

I walk over to the fridge, open the door, and stare at the inner contents. The word *mess* doesn't even begin to cover the disaster inside. Cardboard takeout containers, half-full sports drinks, an apple with a single bite taken out of it.

I shut the door, eyeing the counter to the left of the fridge. It's covered with an assortment of alcohol and a few cans of soda. Most opened, a few not. I angle toward the uncracked can of ginger ale, but two guys are blocking most of the countertop.

The song playing ends, and I take advantage of the brief pause in noise. "Excuse me, could I just..."

The guy closer to me turns around, and the question dies in the back of my throat.

I'm not sure why.

I'm not shy, really, more antisocial. Not bubbly or gregarious or up for any adventure. If I have something to say, I have no issue shouting it.

But words are hard to find right now.

The blanket of heat and unpleasant odors in the air fade away as my gaze scans the tall figure leaning against the kitchen counter while he studies me right back.

I've never seen him before.

I know—not because I'm registering details about what he's wearing or what color his hair is, but because I've never felt this pull before. It feels like the moon and the tide.

The moon minds its own business. It rises and sets while the tide is powerless to do anything but shift in response.

His lips twitch as he watches me observe him. Not quite a smile and not mocking either. He's amused by my appraisal, it seems. Dark green eyes—the same shade as evergreens—dart down and up.

It doesn't feel like he's checking me out. There's nothing predatory or sexual about the quick inspection. Just curious.

I've never been the girl that guys notice when she walks into the room. I like observing people more than I enjoy interacting with them. But I want *him* to notice me. The uncomfortable itch that scrutiny and attention usually elicit is wholly absent.

I hold out my hand. The guys I went to high school with usually looked at me with a mixture of pity and superiority. The damsel in distress and the butt of the joke.

But this dark-haired stranger doesn't look anything but contemplative when he grips my offered hand. His palm is callous and warm. The second our skin collides, I feel the touch everywhere, pinpricks of awareness racing down my spine and spreading through every nerve ending.

A new song starts in the living room, the beat as heavy and constant as the last melody that was blasted.

"Hi."

Details begin to register. His eyes remind me of marbles in the sun. So many swirls with shades of colors that whirl and shift. Mostly green, but with the occasional glimpse of blue or gray.

I clear my throat, feeling flushed and uncertain as I repeat the simple greeting. "Hi."

A small smile plays across lips that are full and look unaccustomed to amusement. He makes no further effort at conversation, but he doesn't seem annoyed I'm standing here, staring at him. Mostly intrigued.

I've never expended this much effort into reading a stranger's body language before. Never been so fascinated by someone whose name I don't even know.

It's weird. And somewhat thrilling.

"I'll see you at home, man." The second guy glances between me and the stranger still looking at me. Raises one brow and smirks.

"Bye, Alex." The green-eyed stranger doesn't look away from me as he replies to his friend.

The friend leaves without saying anything else.

We're not alone, far from it. Bass continues to pound, punctuated by loud chatter and the occasional shout. But it's easy to ignore the sounds. All background noise, literally.

"Um, I'm Lyla."

"Nick." The melodic rumble of his voice is soothing and certain.

"Nick," I repeat. "Like Saint Nick?"

If fumbling through the fridge and the way I'm dressed for winter—unlike every other girl here—weren't enough to clue Nick in on the fact that I'm the furthest thing from seductive, I'm certain that comment did the trick.

This would be a perfect moment for the fire alarm to go off, finally registering the smoke hovering in the air.

I'd rather face Philadelphia's freezing temperatures than stick around for the aftermath of saying *that* to the most attractive guy I've ever seen—in person, on television, covering a magazine, anywhere. I have no idea where the confidence to spark a conversation with him came from, but it's fading. Fast.

Nick's grin is unexpected. Blinding. A blast of sunshine after days in the dark. "I remind you of Santa Claus?"

I'm too mortified to reply. His smile fades as he seems to register that fact, ramping up the awkward factor even higher. I can't come up with anything close to resembling a witty reply. My mind is blank in the worst way.

"I've never met anyone named Lyla before. Including a mythical deliveryman."

Goddammit, I think.

He's charming and nice and trying to put me at ease. I thought men acting like that in real life were the myth.

"I was supposed to be named Layla," I tell him. "My mom was so hopped up on drugs, she forgot the *a*. It stuck, I guess."

"Sounds like the hospital's mistake."

He's looking at me like it's a charming anecdote, something my parents probably joke about to this day. And rather than let him keep that innocent assumption, I say, "The hospital didn't give her the drugs."

Something shifts in his expression in response to the confession I had no intention of making.

It's not pity or the uncomfortable edge most people get when they don't know what to say. That look that's half sympathy, half *how the hell do I get out of here*. It's understanding. It complements the intimidating angles of his face and the intensity radiating off him.

I'd bet my nonexistent savings Nick didn't have a picture-perfect childhood either.

"Did she get clean?" he asks instead of assuming a happy ending.

"No." An unfamiliar compulsion presses me to expound—to share details I don't usually express to anyone, let alone a stranger. Especially not a hot male one. "She overdosed when I was fifteen."

"Your dad?"

I shake my head as I play with the rose charm on my necklace. A nervous habit I've never managed to lose. "Never knew him."

Nick's eyes drift to the necklace I'm wearing, the one I should have taken off a long time ago. Everyone around us is laughing and smoking and kissing, and I'm standing and sharing details about my life that I've never told anyone.

He leans closer. "You know, the last year I believed in Santa, he brought me a stuffed lion for Christmas. Carried that toy with me everywhere. I loved it so damn much. I named him Leo."

My lips quirk. Both because I can't picture the muscular, six-foot-something guy in front of me ever carrying around a stuffed animal and because I can't believe he's trying to cheer me up. I can't believe he's making me feel less vulnerable by sharing a piece of himself. "Leo the lion. Clever alliteration."

Nick smirks. "Just saying. I'm flattered I remind you of the guy."

I groan. "I'm sorry. I say stupid stuff when I'm nervous."

"Don't apologize."

"Um, okay."

Nick's cheek twitches with the ghost of another grin.

"Why are you nervous?" he asks.

My cheeks heat with a blush. Hopefully, it's hot and dim enough in here, he won't notice. "I'm bad at this stuff."

"What stuff?"

"Flirting."

"You seem to be doing just fine to me."

I raise both eyebrows. "Which part turned you on more—the St. Nick comment or the dead-mother bit?"

He rubs his jaw, but his hand doesn't completely cover his smile. "The honesty. I appreciate honesty."

"Usually, I'm bad at that too. I hate talking about my mother."

I realize after I've spoken that I've said too much again.

"Not talking about something and lying about something are two different things," Nick replies.

I consider that and decide he's right. "Do you lie a lot?"

He studies me with those mysterious eyes. "Why do you ask?"

"The things we value most are the things we know we want. We know what we want based on what we know we don't. If you value honesty…I'm guessing you've heard a lot of lies."

Nick is silent for long enough that I regret every word I said.

"Never mind. I just—"

"You're right. I've heard a lot of lies."

He holds my gaze, and the pull between us has somehow strengthened in the short time I've been standing here.

"Do *you* lie a lot?" I ask.

"Yes."

"Have you lied to me?"

"No."

Maybe I shouldn't believe him, but I do. I've encountered plenty of people who lied about being trustworthy. None of them ever admitted to lying.

"Do you promise?" I mean it as a tease, but Nick's expression doesn't lighten.

"I don't make promises."

"Lyla!" Kennedy reappears beside me. Her cheeks are flushed, and the messy ponytail she spent a half an hour constructing before we left the dorm has fallen apart. "Ellie isn't answering. But they moved to that house where Dylan lives! He just posted a photo, and Mark is in it. He could have made it easier to find, but whatever."

I glance at Nick. I can't be certain, but I think he's fighting a smile. Maybe he's contrasting Kennedy's exuberance with my awkwardness.

"Great," I manage.

"*Great*? We don't have to wander around, freezing anymore. Let's go!"

I look at Nick again, silently admitting I'm more interested in staying here and talking to him.

This time, Kennedy notices where my eyes wander. Her eyebrows fly up somewhere in her hairline as she swipes curls out of her face. "Uh, hi…"

She glances at me. *Who is he?* Kennedy mouths.

Her surprise isn't surprising. She's never seen me so much as talk to a guy before, and she had to drag me out tonight in the first place.

I shrug in response to the silent question. Even if Nick wasn't standing right here, I don't think I could verbalize an answer.

"Who are you?" Kennedy doesn't have much of a filter in any circumstance, but the lack of one is exaggerated right now by the amount of vodka she downed back at the dorms.

"I'm Nick," he says in response to Kennedy's brazen question.

"Kennedy." She looks him up and down, admiration written all over her face. Then, she glances between us, as if she's trying to figure out what I'm doing. Why I'm not as eager to leave as I was when she left me. "Come on, Lyla. Let's go."

I should feel grateful to her. Kennedy is giving me an easy out before we run out of things to talk about or another girl approaches Nick.

I glance at him. "It was nice to—"

"Stay."

That's all he says, just one word. No *please* after it. No *I wish you would* before the four letters. But it sounds like more than one syllable. It sounds like a request he means, from someone unaccustomed to making them at all. For some reason, I decide not to analyze. I listen.

And that's *the moment*.

The moment my whole life changed.

NINE YEARS LATER

CHAPTER TWO

LYLA

There's always a second immediately after you're hurt when there's no pain yet. Before the reflexes and the panic set in. It takes longer than the time for a rush of red to reach the surface of the skin. But it's slower than the spill of blood turning crimson as it leaves the body and reacts with oxygen.

"Lyla? *Lyla*!"

I turn to watch Michael enter the kitchen. His tone changes from questioning to panicked as soon as he spots the drops of scarlet I can see swelling, then starting to drip down my hand.

I can *see* it.

But I can't *feel* it.

Not yet.

Michael becomes a blur by my side, herding me over to the sink. Grabbing the white towel from the dish rack and pressing it to my palm to stanch the flow of blood. "What happened?"

I ask myself that question a lot, usually late at night, staring up at the cracked plaster of my bedroom ceiling, and I never have a good answer. They're just words that bounce around in my head.

Life choices aren't what Michael is wondering about though. He's asking why I'm bleeding.

Michael's grip tightens around my palm, holding the cotton flush against the cut. I wince at the heavy pressure. His anxiety and the strained clasp are erasing the numbness I was enjoying. Shock and adrenaline are ebbing away.

I'm aware of it all—the pain, the metal tang to the air, the dizziness.

"The knife slipped. It's not that bad."

"*Not that bad*?" Michael's expression is dubious, his voice anxious and incredulous. "There's blood everywhere!"

I pull away the towel and turn on the tap, letting the cool water flow over my hand. Liquid circles the drain, tinged with a pinkish hue.

The water keeps running. Clear keeps turning a distorted shade of red.

"I'm taking you to the hospital," Michael states, dashing off to grab his keys, I assume.

I don't argue, knowing another *it's not that bad* will be met with the same disbelieving response.

Michael is an attorney. We met when I got a job as a secretary at the law firm where he works.

And I knew long before we started dating a couple of months ago that he likes his life black and white. No shades of gray. No crimson. It's why I was so shocked when he asked me out.

I'd like my life to look clear-cut.

And maybe it does, from the outside. Maybe that's what Michael saw.

I focus on my hand, peering closely at the cut. It isn't deep. The flow of blood is beginning to slow and clot, my body's natural draw to survival kicking in.

I'm relieved.

Too often, survival has felt like a reflex I might lack.

The ten-minute drive to the hospital is filled with Michael's nervous chatter and Christmas carols. It's January, too late for holiday music. I don't bother asking about the music selection, just stare out the window and pray I'm not dripping blood on the leather seat.

Usually, I find Michael's optimism and proclivity toward chitchat endearing. Right now, I wish he'd just stay silent.

My hand is starting to throb.

My heart is racing with residual adrenaline. Or maybe it's trying to spread the blood I haven't lost.

I close my eyes and lean back against the headrest of Michael's Mercedes.

It helps for a minute—until I hear Michael calling out my name again. I open my eyes to his nervous expression.

"Did you pass out?"

I smile, trying to reassure him. "No, I'm fine. I'm just tired."

He gives me another worried look but continues driving. After circling the hospital's parking lot twice, he finds a spot close to the main entrance.

Harsh fluorescent lights and the sharp scent of antiseptic greet us inside. The receptionist gives me a tired smile and a form to fill out. Michael and I take seats in one corner of the waiting room, next to a girl who looks to be six or seven and her worried mother.

The little girl waves at us as we sit. I wave back at her with my uninjured hand.

Michael gives the little girl an uncomfortable smile. Another reason I didn't think he'd have any romantic interest in me: he values his career over having kids. A viewpoint I shared until I sat, staring at two lines on a plastic stick in the student center bathroom.

After a forty-minute wait, a nurse calls my name. We're brought back into the main section of the emergency room, a bustling mess of activity, and I'm instructed to take a seat on one bed lining the far wall.

The nurse tells me someone will be by to look at my hand shortly, then swings the curtain around so there's a temporary wall blocking off the rest of the room.

"Well"—I take a seat on the bed—"this is not exactly the romantic night I was envisioning."

Michael lets out a low chuckle, rubbing one palm across the light dusting of stubble on his jaw. He seems to have relaxed now that medical assistance is imminent. "As long as you're all right. That's all that matters."

"I'm fine. This"—I wave my uninjured hand around at the sterile surroundings—"was totally unnecessary."

"Let the doctor be the judge of that, Lyla."

I roll my eyes but smile so Michael knows I'm not actually annoyed.

His worry feels nice even if it's exaggerated. For most of my life, it felt like no one cared.

The curtain swings open. The metal circles holding it up screech as they're yanked to the side. "Hello. I'm Dr. Ivanov. How are you doing, Miss—" The male voice stalls, and I realize why when I look over.

"Alex?" I gasp.

Alex looks impassive. He was always good at schooling his emotions in the limited time I spent around him.

Just like—

I stop that train of thought in its tracks. But Alex's silence is saying everything his expression isn't. So are his eyes, which are taking in everything about my appearance, narrowing in on the hand I rewrapped in a bloody dish towel for the drive here.

"Lyla." He finally speaks, stepping forward and jerking the curtain shut behind him with a second screech.

Michael glances between the two of us, clearly confused. "You know this guy, Lyla?"

We haven't reached the stage in our relationship where we know each other's friends or family. Tonight was the first time he'd even been over to my apartment.

"Yeah. We, uh, we went to college together. I knew him freshman year."

Until he disappeared along with the person I thought I'd spend the rest of my life with.

"Oh, really?" Michael looks mildly intrigued. "You went to UPenn?"

"For a bit," Alex responds, glancing at the clipboard in his hands. Probably the form I filled out.

"Where did you transfer to?"

"Harvard." Alex's tone is short.

He drops the clipboard down on the bed beside me, revealing the paper clipped to the front is, in fact, the form I filled out.

A metal tray and short stool get rolled over. Alex perches on the stool, carefully unwrapping my hand from the towel and inspecting the cut across my palm.

"What happened?" he asks, pulling on a pair of latex gloves.

I wince as he prods at the skin around the shallow slice. "The knife slipped. I was chopping cucumbers for a salad."

Alex says nothing, just tears open a packet of gauze.

"This didn't seem necessary, but Michael thought I should get it looked at."

"Your kitchen looked like a crime scene, Lyla," Michael tells me.

Alex stands. "This will heal faster if I give you a few stitches. I need to grab some supplies. I'll be right back."

"Okay," I say, but he's already gone.

Michael raises a brow. "Friendly guy."

"We only had one class together. I'm surprised he remembers me at all."

Only the first sentence is a lie.

I could count on my fingers the handful of times I met Nick's best friend.

Michael laughs, then shakes his head. "I'm not."

I roll my eyes. "Whatever." I glance toward the curtain, which is still closed. "Would you mind getting me a soda? I'm sure there's a vending machine around here somewhere."

"Yeah, of course." Michael pushes off the counter he was leaning against. "I'll be right back."

I nod and smile. "Thanks."

As soon as the curtain closes, I slump.

My head is spinning so fast that I feel dizzy. There's no shortage of sound outside the flimsy wall. I can hear shouts and a din of commotion.

But all of it is muffled by the reminder that Nick exists. Right after he left, I tried to preserve the memories I had of him. I'd run through them in my mind like a favorite movie, pausing on the best parts. Looking for some warning, some clue, that we weren't headed toward the happy ending I hoped for. Eventually, reliving it all just hurt too much. I'm surprised to realize I can still recall it all perfectly, years after I stopped playing them.

The noise surrounding me dulls the sound of his approach. I'm startled when Alex suddenly appears in front of me again. He settles back on the stool, dropping more gauze and a bottle of solution on the tray.

There's a different energy between us now that we're alone.

"Michael went to get me a soda." I offer an explanation he didn't ask for.

"He squeamish?"

"A little. He's a lawyer."

Alex's lips twitch as he dabs my hand with something that makes the exposed skin sting. "The fuck does that have to do with a weak stomach?"

"Nothing, I guess. Just…he mostly looks at paperwork."

"If you say so."

"So…you've been good?" I ask awkwardly.

I'm in that uncomfortable stretch of space where too much time has passed to blurt something out with shock as my reasoning. But I've had too little time to fully come to terms with Alex's appearance. To think through what I should say—what I shouldn't.

All the amusement has been erased from Alex's face. He seems tense and on edge, and it's obvious why.

We have one person in common.

He's waiting for me to ask about Nick, and I'm not sure if I should. Which will haunt me more—a happy update that he's married with kids or never knowing what happened to him after he left?

"I've been good."

"Did you really transfer to Harvard?"

"No."

Everything about his answer surprises me. If it was a lie, I expected him to stick to it. Now, I'm wondering *why* he lied. Why he *admitted* it was a lie.

My hand is numb. I barely notice the tug as Alex sews up my skin, more focused on analyzing any small shift in his expression. On waiting for some further explanation.

A tiny line forms between his eyes as he snips the thread and spreads some ointment over the three stitches. "Was this an accident, Lyla?"

I blink. It takes a minute for his words to settle and make sense. "You think I cut myself *on purpose*?"

"I'm asking if you cut yourself on purpose."

I forgot how blunt Alex is. *Just like—*

Again, I cut myself off.

"I *didn't*. I was chopping, and the knife slipped. I'm tired, and I haven't been sleeping well, and I just…everything is fine."

Michael reappears with my soda. "Here you go." He hands me the cold can and kisses my temple, hovering next to the bed I'm sitting on.

"Thanks." I muster a weak smile.

Alex watches our interaction closely. Uncomfortably so. There are other things I want to ask him, and I'm both grateful and resentful Michael's reappearance prevents me from doing so.

Finally, he bends back over my hand and finishes wrapping the gauze over the cut. He stands and yanks his gloves off with a *snap*. "The stitches will dissolve on their own. Change the dressing once a day and avoid getting your hand wet too often. Any swelling or discoloration, come back in. Otherwise, you should be good to go."

Michael holds out a hand. "Thank you so much, Doctor."

Alex hesitates before shaking it. Michael doesn't seem to notice.

“Take care of yourself, Lyla.”

Then, he’s gone. I’m left staring at a gray striped curtain as it flutters shut.

My hand no longer hurts, but my heart twinges like it sustained an injury.

CHAPTER THREE

LYLA

When I wake up, my eyes feel like grit was poured inside of them while I was sleeping. I'm not sure I slept at all actually. I tossed and turned all night after Michael brought me back to my apartment. He offered to stay with me, but his face had a greenish hue when we walked into the kitchen. It did look like a crime scene.

I pulled on a pair of rubber gloves and started scrubbing as soon as he left, then went to bed and stared at the ceiling all night.

It's a random coincidence Alex Ivanov became a doctor. That he works at the nearest hospital and happened to be on call last night. I stopped believing in destiny or fate a long time ago. I've endured plenty that I never want to think I was *meant* to.

Curiosity is a constant aggravation though.

It prickles my skin and interrupts each thought.

I never got any closure with Nick. I made peace with that fact a long time ago—because I had no other choice. He left without a word, and his best friend disappeared right alongside him. He unenrolled in the middle of the semester and just…vanished.

There was no one to ask questions to.

Until now.

Nick and Alex were close. They often acted more like brothers than friends. I have no doubt Alex knows why Nick left, and I'm betting he has some way to contact him now. That's more of a possibility than I've ever had before.

My mind spins in answerless circles as I bustle around the tiny apartment, cleaning and running a load of laundry, until there's a knock on the door. I peek through the peephole, then swing the door open.

"Hey, Lyla."

"Hi, June," I reply, smiling at the woman I consider my best friend before leaning down to hug Leo. "Hey, sweetheart."

"Hi, Mom." My son grins before humoring me with a brief embrace. "Can I show AJ the Lego set I got with my allowance?"

"Yeah, sure."

The two boys are gone in a flash, down the hall toward Leo's tiny bedroom.

"Come on in," I tell June, shutting the door after she steps inside. "Coffee?" I ask.

"That would be great," she says, pulling off her winter coat and folding it over one arm as she follows me into the kitchen.

I pour some hot coffee in a mug and hand it to her. "Milk? Sugar?"

"A splash of milk, if you have it."

"I do." I open the fridge door and pull out a carton, pouring a small amount into the mug.

"Did you and Michael have a nice time last night?" June asks, a sly expression appearing on her heart-shaped face.

I've always thought that June looks like a '50s Hollywood actress with her petite stature, curves, and dark curls. I met her at a playgroup one of the other receptionists at the law firm recommended to me.

Like me, she's a single mom. She married her high school sweetheart when she found out she was pregnant with AJ. Her husband died before I met her, in a random shooting at a supermarket. Another instance to be chalked up as nothing you were meant to endure.

"Not exactly." I wave my left hand at her so she can see the bandage on my palm. I removed the gauze wrapped around my whole hand this morning, not wanting Leo to see it.

June gasps. "What happened?"

"It was stupid. I was chopping a cucumber for the salad, and the knife slipped. It looks worse than it is. Michael took me to the ER for a few stitches."

"Oh my God, Lyla. Are you sure you're okay?"

"I'm fine. It was stupid. I was just tired."

June sips her coffee, studying me over the rim of her mug. "Did you quit working for Marshall yet?"

I sigh at the mention of my second job—data entry for a freelance company. I do it at night mostly, once Leo is in bed. "No. They offered me a raise."

June clucks her tongue disapprovingly. "You can't keep this up, Lyla."

I lift and lower my right shoulder, looking down at my own coffee cup. "I need the money."

"I could—"

I cover her hand with my right one. "I'm *not* taking money from you, June."

She's raising her son on a single income, same as me. I know she's trying not to touch her husband's life insurance money to have as a cushion.

I soften my tone, knowing she has the best of intentions. "But thank you."

The boys burst back into the kitchen.

"Mom!" Leo exclaims. "Check this out!"

I squint at the tiny action figure he's holding up to me. "Who is it?" I ask after a few seconds of squinting and failing to figure out its relevance.

"It's the Indiana Jones one I couldn't find last week, remember?"

I nod, pretending to. For living in such a tiny place, it's amazing how many toys Leo manages to misplace each day. Luckily, they all seem to turn up eventually. Or maybe it's more of an inevitability than luck, based on the square footage of this place.

June smiles at Leo before ruffling AJ's hair. "We should get going." She glances down at her son. "We've got Sunday brunch at Grandma and Grandpa's this morning."

"We do?" An excited smile spreads across AJ's face as he beams up at June.

My chest squeezes as I glance at Leo, who's happily fiddling with his recovered toy.

As challenging as it was, growing up without a father and with a drug addict for a mother, it's nothing in comparison to how I feel about the fact that Leo has no one else.

No grandparents.

No aunts or uncles or cousins.

No family at all, except for me.

If something happened to me, he'd end up in foster care, same as I did when I was only a little older than he is. The thought chills me to the bone—a possibility I torture myself with on a daily basis.

"Yep," June answers, distracting me from my dour thoughts. "Say good-bye to Leo."

"Bye, Leo."

The boys hug, and June and I do the same.

"Take care of yourself, Lyla," she tells me.

Alex told me the same thing. I must look as bad as I feel.

"Thanks for watching him last night," I say.

"Of course. Anytime. Soon, whenever you're feeling up to a do-over of last night."

I smile. "Thank you."

June and AJ leave. Leo heads back to his room to play with toys and unpack from his sleepover.

I'm left in the kitchen by myself.

CHAPTER FOUR

LYLA

Sunday night is another restless sleep. I wake up on Monday morning with dry eyes to the heavy patter of rain hitting the window. I make breakfast and pack lunch before waking Leo up, then change into my workday uniform of slacks and a blazer while he's eating his eggs.

I force him to bundle into a jacket, then hustle him out the door and into the elevator. The drive to Leo's school usually takes about ten minutes. There's more traffic today, drawing the trip out to fifteen.

I drop him off just before eight, then continue driving.

Usually, I head straight to the office. Sometimes, I stop for a coffee. Today, I end up in the parking lot of Philadelphia General.

Inside the hospital, I head straight for the nurses' station. "I'm here to see Dr. Ivanov."

The nurse eyes me. "Do you have an appointment?"

"No."

"Is there some sort of emergency?"

I swallow. "No."

"Then, I can't help you."

"Please." I lean forward. "He treated me yesterday. I just came to say thank you."

The nurse hums, typing on the keyboard. "Yes. A lot of Dr. Ivanov's female patients return to request follow-up care."

I flush. "It isn't like that. We're…old friends."

"Really?" She leans back and looks up. "Which is it? Are you a patient or an old friend?"

"Both," I insist. "Please, just let him know I'm here. If he doesn't want to talk to me, he doesn't have to."

The nurse sighs, but she picks up the phone and dials. "Dr. Ivanov? Yes. No, we're fully staffed down here." She pauses. "There's a woman here, insisting to see you." There's a pause as Alex responds. The nurse looks to me. "Name?"

"Lyla Peterson."

"Lyla Peterson," she relays. Her expression shifts from annoyance to curiosity as she listens to whatever Alex is saying. "Okay." She hangs up the phone. "He'll be right down."

Based on her tone, it's as much of a surprise to her as it is to me. A large part of me expected he wouldn't see me. Showing up as a patient to treat is one thing. This—me seeking him out at work because of our ancient association—is another. He has to know the only reason I came here is for answers.

Answers I can't decide I really want, but can't seem to walk away from the possibility of receiving.

I clear my throat, nerves creeping up my esophagus and stuffing it with anxiety. "Thank you."

The nurse nods, still studying me like a puzzle.

I turn and take a seat in one of the stiff chairs. My knee bounces as I play with a stray thread on the hem of my blouse. Every time I look up, the nurse is watching me. I'm relieved when the phone rings, and she turns to answer it.

The longer I sit, the more my nerves spread. This is a lark. A fool's errand. Likely a mistake too. My past isn't a pleasant place to revisit.

Leo is what keeps me rooted in the chair. Ghosting your girlfriend isn't the trademark of a great guy. Isn't who I thought Nick was. Isn't anything I thought he'd ever do.

But he didn't know about Leo. I didn't even suspect I was pregnant when he was suddenly just…gone. Unenrolled from his classes. Disconnected phone. Empty dorm room. Alex disappeared just as suddenly and completely.

Until now.

He appears, and I blink at him. Seeing someone I never thought I would again is just as surreal of an experience the second time as it was last night. Unlike the cut on my palm, Nick leaving isn't a fresh wound. It's one I thought scabbed and healed. But it throbs now, like it's waiting to rip back open from the slightest provocation.

Alex's face is smooth and blank as he approaches, hands tucked in the pockets of his navy scrubs, but his tone is urgent when he stops in front of me. "Lyla? Is everything okay? Did something happen?"

I stand on shaky legs, taken off guard by his genuine, immediate concern. It's more than what I'd expect to extend toward a person you briefly knew nearly a decade ago.

"Everything is fine," I assure him. But the edge to his expression doesn't disappear. "I just wanted to…thank you."

"For what?"

I hold up my bandaged hand in answer.

His brow creases with confusion. "My job?"

I laugh nervously. God, this is stupid. I should turn and walk away. I feel pathetic and ridiculous.

Alex doesn't know I have a son. To him, I must look like a pathetic ex, clinging to a guy who clearly was only after one thing from me. But I think of Leo. Who's getting older and gaining more questions.

I take a deep breath and forge ahead. "Do you ever talk to him?"

The edge hardens. Sharpens.

He had to anticipate the question coming. Nick is our only connection. Yet Alex plays dumb. "Who?"

"Nick."

His name lands between us with all the subtlety of a grenade.

Alex reaches out and grabs my hand. I'm towed out of the waiting room, around the corner, and into a supply closet, lined with medical supplies.

I lean back against some boxes of gauze, studying his worried expression. "The nurse at the desk already thinks we might have some torrid affair going on. This will really get the gossip going."

Alex ignores me as he closes the door behind us and spins around to face me. "Why are you asking about Nick?"

It's embarrassing how much hearing Alex say his name matters. If not for Leo's existence, I could almost convince myself Nick never did. His disappearance was the cleanest cut a relationship could have. But he's still a living, breathing person somewhere out in the world. Alex's question is proof of that.

"He left," I answer.

Is it really so unexpected I'm wondering about him? Maybe if I'd gotten any closure at the time, it wouldn't still feel like such a gaping hole.

"Nine years ago." Alex's tone is harsh and unforgiving. As cold as the temperature outside. *Get over it*, he's saying. *Move on.* Phrases I've told myself many times.

"He left," I repeat. "One day, he was there; the next, he wasn't."

"He did things his own way."

"What does that mean?"

Alex exhales, looking angry. But not *at me*. He just looks mad. And worried. "It means you should stop asking questions, Lyla. It's in the past. Leave it there."

"I just…he's okay? Alive?"

If every part of his existence hadn't been so thoroughly—so *carefully*—wiped clean, I would have worried something happened to him at the time. It's a question I've asked myself many times over the past nine years, knowing there was a good chance I'd never know the answer.

"He's good."

That's all Alex says in response. But there's a dry, droll undertone that says more than the words. It speaks to a familiarity, to some inside information.

"So, you talk to him." I state the sentence, not bothering to ask. "Do you know where he is?"

"Yes." Alex's blunt response shocks me.

I came here so the fact that I hadn't wouldn't haunt me. I didn't actually think anything would come of it. Talking to someone who knows where Nick is wasn't supposed to happen. It's diminished the many degrees of separation that seemed permanent.

"You—you do?" I trip over the words.

Alex nods. He's studying me closer than before, shrewd eyes taking in my work clothes and my clenched fists. What I'm sure is a shocked expression.

"You—right now, you know where he is?"

Another nod.

My breathing becomes fast and jagged. It's a struggle to remember to pull air in, paired with hasty, rushed exhales.

The corners of the closet start to turn blurry around the edges. I'm dizzy and hot and nauseous. I slide down against the shelves, knocking some items onto the floor before I hit the ground myself. At least the linoleum feels cool.

Alex swears. At least, I think he's swearing. It sounds like a swear. He's literally speaking another language.

I glance up. "Where is he?"

Alex crouches down beside me. "I can't tell you that."

"You mean, you won't." I close my eyes, enjoying the dark respite from the world.

Worse than a waste of time, this is an utter disappointment. I don't think Alex is lying about knowing where Nick is. I wish he *had* lied about knowing it. Then, maybe I could have left this conversation with some dignity intact. With the closure of knowing I'd never get answers, which has to be better than holding out hope.

"Lyla."

My eyes open, focusing on Alex's serious expression.

"If you're ever in trouble, you can always come to me. You know where I am now. But not for answers about Nick. Nothing involving Nick. *Forget him*."

Alex stands. I watch him walk toward the door, and I can feel it slipping away. My one and only chance for answers.

He must think I have a stalker-level obsession with his friend. He must know Nick has moved on and won't want to hear from me.

But I'm not seeking Nick out for *me*.

I want to be able to tell Leo where his dad lives.

"I have a son, Alex," I say.

Alex freezes halfway to the door.

"Want to know how old he is? How old *I* was when I got pregnant?"

I push myself up from the hard linoleum, buoyed by his hesitation. "Would Nick care? If he knew? If he knew that *you knew*?"

When Alex turns back around, his expression is pained. Worried. Panicked. He stares at me like he wants to rewind the last few minutes and avoid having this conversation altogether.

I don't understand it. Don't understand anything.

"Would he?" I prompt.

Alex nods. "Yes."

"Well…now, you know."

I walk past him and out of the room. Past the nosy nurse and head outside.

I'm not sure if I handled that the right way. If I should have said more or if I should have said less.

All I know is, I would have regretted saying nothing. That certainty quells a little of the panic that the thought of Alex sharing the conversation we just had with Nick prompts. Saying Nick will care isn't exactly *write down your number so he can call you.*

Enough time has passed that I shouldn't be angry with him. We were eighteen when we met, basically kids ourselves.

He didn't mean to leave me to raise a baby on my own. But he did. He disappeared with no way for me to contact him, knowing I was completely alone in the world.

I reach my car and climb inside, turning it on to blast the heat. Back in familiar surroundings, it's easier to shove thoughts of Nick away.

Luckily, I'm used to being alone.

CHAPTER FIVE

NICK

I'm standing in front of panes of pristine glass, staring out at New York's distinctive skyline when Alex calls. The naked woman sprawled out in the silk sheets stirs, but doesn't wake up.

I walk into the attached living room of the hotel suite, taking my phone and empty glass with me.

"Yes?" I drawl, answering the phone and tucking it between my ear and shoulder so I can pour more bourbon into the crystal tumbler.

"You're awake." Alex sounds displeased by that fact.

"You were hoping to wake me up?"

"Figured I would. It's the middle of the night there."

I take a sip before I speak, savoring the smoky burn before I sprawl out on the couch. "I'm in New York. Mecci is stirring up some shit I had to handle in person."

"*What*?"

I chuckle. "Nothing I can't handle. But Pavel is pushing to make things official with Anastasia. I won't be able to leave the country once I've signed the agreement."

Silence.

Complete and total silence.

Unease trickles down my spine like a melting ice cube. "Alexei?" I hear the shift in my voice, from friend to superior.

"I have to tell you something."

Something he doesn't *want* to tell me, based on *his* tone.

My mind spins with possibilities. He's in Philadelphia for an ER residency. A residency he convinced me would pay off—he'll be able to save men he wouldn't otherwise be able to, learning techniques he couldn't anywhere else. What the fuck could have gone wrong? No one else knows he's there.

"So, tell me."

Alex inhales, the sound rustling through the phone's connection. "She still lives here. And…she has a kid now."

I focus on breathing, nothing else. In and out. Down the rest of my drink. The pronoun *she* could apply to millions of women, yet I know exactly who he's talking about. There's only one *she* whose name isn't spoken between us because I shut that subject down a long time ago.

"You shouldn't have gone back there."

That's all I can think to say. I swore when I left Philadelphia that I'd never look back. Never *go* back. Letting Alex return didn't break that promise, but it opened up possibilities—this possibility—that I could have prevented.

Alex is silent.

I battle curiosity and lose. "Where did you see her?"

"She came into the ER this past weekend."

I thought I'd succeeded at shutting down sappy emotional responses a long time ago. But my heart races, and my fists clench.

"Did she die?" I force the question out.

"What? No, she's fine."

I exhale with relief, then annoyance. "Don't fucking make it sound like she's not then. And if she's fine, then what the fuck are we talking about? Did the baby die?"

"Fuck, no, the baby didn't—" There's a pause, then some muttered Russian I don't catch. "There is no *baby*. Lyla showed up at the ER on Saturday night. She sliced her hand and came in for stitches. I hadn't decided if I was going to tell you or not. Then, she came here again this morning. I figured it was about you, that she had questions. I shut them down the best I could, but then she tells me she has an eight-year-old son. I got her address off the forms she filled out and went to her place as soon as I got off my shift. She lives in an apartment in East Falls. And the kid…she wasn't lying. He—well, there's no question."

"No question about what?" My mind feels like it's moving through sludge, overwhelmed and underprepared.

"He's *eight years old*, Nikolaj. No question about paternity. Kid couldn't look more like you if he was cloned. It's fucking crazy."

I'm a father.

I have a son.

I have an eight-year-old son with Lyla Peterson.

Finding out my father and brothers were murdered in cold blood and I was inheriting a position I didn't want wasn't this shocking. Mafia life is dangerous and unpredictable. There's always a strong possibility someone is trying to kill you. It's a more primitive life, Darwinian almost. Only the strongest survive.

I locked down any softer emotions a long time ago. This revelation rattles the cage for the first time. Memories I haven't allowed myself to recall for a long time flash through my mind. All featuring a brunette with a shy smile.

I try to picture it—a kid with some mixture of our features. Although, based on what Alex just said, he looks more like me than her. There's been a miniature version of me walking around the world, and I had no fucking idea.

"Lyla knows nothing, Nikolaj. *Nothing*. She thinks you're just a shithead who split on her. She just wanted to know if you'd care you have a kid—"

I hang up on him. Drop the phone on the floor and hurl my glass against the wall. It shatters, spraying splintered crystals and bourbon everywhere.

A shadow appears in the doorway before the blonde from my bed staggers in. I can't remember her name. There's a chance I never asked for it.

She blinks at me sleepily, taking in my heaving chest and the mess on the floor. "What's going on?"

"Get out," I snap.

"But I—"

"Get. Out."

The blonde scurries out of sight. She's a model I picked up during my dinner meeting earlier. She has no idea who I really am or what I do for a living, and yet me raising my voice was all it took for her to scamper away like a scared mouse.

People are naturally intimidated by me. Their instincts tell them I'm dangerous, tell them to shy away from me, even when their mind hasn't conjured a good reason for the fear.

Lyla never looked at me like I was a monster. My list of sins was much shorter back then, but my hands were nowhere near clean.

Around her, I softened. Lightened.

I didn't *want* to scare her.

I wanted to pretend I had choices. I wanted to pretend getting wait-listed for a class or not getting my first pick of summer internships were the biggest of my worries.

I didn't anticipate how hard it would be to walk away from that glimpse of normalcy.

From her.

It turns out, I walked away from even more than I realized.

And now, I have to decide what to do about it.

CHAPTER SIX

NICK

Rather than get any work done on the drive to Philly, I stare out the window.

I'm lost in thought. In memories. In regrets.

It's a lapse I could never indulge in back home. An indulgence I shouldn't allow now, considering I still have business to take care of on this trip.

But I do it anyway. I'm selfish plenty, but it's rarely in my own interest. It's the expected sort you're supposed to flaunt like a crown to signify your spot in the pecking order. Beautiful women and flashy cars and expensive liquor are all things I'm *expected* to indulge in, so I do. They're not unique in any way. None of them are meaningful to me at all; they're not vices or possessions I'd struggle to live without.

The memories of Lyla's laugh and eyes that would often turn haunted? They're mine—and mine alone.

A painful indulgence.

A masochistic relief.

I should have asked Alex more questions before making this trip. But I couldn't do so without displaying vulnerability. And the dynamic between me and him is very different now than it was in college.

Back then, I'd occasionally ask Alex for advice. Now, my role has changed. Uncertainty is weakness in my world, even among those closest to me. *Especially* among them.

Slowly, the scenery turns familiar. Nostalgia pricks at my skin, irritating yet reassuring.

We enter East Falls and stop in front of an eight-story apartment building.

"Stay in the car," I instruct my driver before I slide on a pair of sunglasses and step out onto the sidewalk.

I study the exterior of the apartment building as I cross the street. It's clean and well-maintained. But bland and lifeless, like a chain hotel.

From a security standpoint, it's a goddamn nightmare. Balconies and wide windows face the road. There's a keypad next to the front entrance, but someone has propped a rock in place, keeping it open. There's no doorman. No alarm system responding to the open door.

I don't take advantage of the easy access.

This—getting here—is as far as my plan got. I have no idea what to do now. Being the boss is a lonely job, but it's never felt more solitary than right now. Anyone I tell about Lyla and her son could become a future threat to them.

I walked away from her because I had no other choice. I walked away from her without saying good-bye because I was worried what else I might say. It would have been tempting—too tempting—to tell her the truth. To make her hate me a little less. But it would have been selfish. It wouldn't have changed our ending. And it would have put her in danger.

I shouldn't make contact. I should pretend Alex never told me anything. I can set up some secret account, route it through a few shell companies, and make sure they're well taken care of with an anonymous windfall.

Lyla was always proud and prideful. When we were in college, she never wanted to accept my help and certainly not my money. But I think she'd take it for her child.

Leaving Lyla the first time was challenging. If I'd known she was pregnant, I don't know what I would have done. Seeing her—seeing my son—opens them both up to risks.

Risks they'll face their whole lives regardless…because of me. If anyone ever put together my association with them, they'd be in danger. Any attempt to keep them safe would double as an admittance.

Word would spread fast that I have a child.

A son.

An *heir*.

I stand on cracked pavement and feel similar fissures break the heart I thought couldn't be affected.

Protect or pretend?

It's been nine years since I left. Since I stepped up to my rightful position as *Pakhan* of the Morozov Bratva. No one has come after them.

If I marry Anastasia the way I planned and have more children, they'll be the family that my enemies will target. They'll be the ones with round-the-clock protection, who I'll eat dinner with each night.

I vacillate between an impossible choice, already knowing what my decision has to be.

My feet don't move.

My decision is made.

But I fight it. Struggle with it. Mourn what could have been.

I keep staring at the building where Lyla Peterson lives with my son, trying to picture their existence. Have they always lived here? Did she finish school after she found out she was pregnant? Did she consider not keeping the baby? Was Alex right? Does he look like me?

Fuck. Fuck. Fuck.

This time, she'll know I abandoned them both. Either she'll lie to our son or he'll know I chose not to be involved in his life.

I heave a sigh, knowing I need to leave. My men are undoubtedly wondering what the hell I'm doing, just standing here. It was reckless and impulsive—two adjectives no one would use to describe me—coming here. I should go straight back to New York, settle my business there, and then return to Russia, as planned.

Feeling unsettled but resolved, I turn to leave.

And realize I took too long to make a choice.

Lyla Peterson is walking toward me. She's on the phone, tugging the end of her dark ponytail with her free hand and chewing on her lower lip as she listens to whatever is being said on the other end.

I can't think. Can't move.

I just soak in the sight of her.

Time hasn't dulled any recognition. I could pick her out of a crowd of thousands.

Lyla looks tired, but not unhappy. She's wearing slacks and a puffy coat, her cheeks and ears pink with cold. No makeup. Aside from her face, the only glimpse of skin are her hands, one palm bandaged from the injury that has me standing here.

Even exhausted and bundled, she pulls all the oxygen out of the air. My heartbeat stutters as my gaze ghosts over her high cheekbones, long lashes, and full lips. I've seen a lot of beautiful women. Most of them knew *exactly* how attractive they were. I always got the sense Lyla didn't, even when I'd tell her—and show her—and her slumped shoulders suggest she still has no clue.

Lyla says something and then hangs up the call, slipping the phone into the pocket of her jacket.

Then, she spots me and freezes. All the color drains from her face like rain sliding down a windowpane.

Neither of us blinks or breathes. This feels like a moment suspended in time, impenetrable to any outside force.

For a second, it's just me and her. Nothing else matters or even exists.

I never thought I'd see her again. Not in this life.

Everything about Lyla screams she thought the same about me. Her frozen posture. Her bloodless face.

And as fucking stunned as I am to actually be seeing her, as panicked as I am about what this will mean—what lies I'll have to spin or what promises I'll be tempted to make and possibly break—I smile. A sensation that feels strange—I don't do much smiling these days.

It's good to see you.

I think it; I don't say it. Because surprise hasn't altered reality. I'm about to be the asshole who lets her down—again. Who offers a fat check and takes zero responsibility. I won't preface that with a nice-guy act even if it isn't fake.

Doing what's best for someone else and doing what you want often diverge.

My smile seems to be what jolts Lyla out of her shock at finding me standing outside her apartment building.

"Hi."

Déjà vu hits. This is exactly how our first conversation started. It was also prefaced by lots of staring and silence.

"Hi," I repeat.

Lyla fiddles with the strap of the purse slung over one shoulder. "I guess Alex was downplaying how much you two talk."

I study her closely, trying to gauge how much Alex told her. He's loyal. He'd never disclose any details about my family or business. But I could hear the sympathy in his voice last night. The same tone that questioned my choice to leave this city in the middle of the night nine years ago.

I should have asked Alex a few more questions about their conversation before I hung up on him. I planned to after I'd gained some distance. Done some processing. "He called me last night."

"You live nearby then."

"No. I just happened to be in New York when he called."

She doesn't ask where I *do* live. "Do you visit New York often?"

I wasn't expecting this…civility. It feels a little like a job interview—tiptoeing around small talk. "A few times a year."

"Do you visit Philadelphia?"

"No. This is the first time I've been back."

Lyla nods once, absorbing that. "I would have told you sooner, if I could have. If you *had* ever come back before now." A trace of the anger I expected her to lead with appears, leaking into the words.

"I know." I watch her fiddle with the strap of her bag again. "Lyla…me leaving? It didn't have anything to do with you."

Hurt and annoyance flash across her face, hardening elegant features. "I figured. I wasn't much of a factor at all."

I reconsider my words. I'm out of practice, considering others before I speak. "That's not what I—"

"Do you want to meet him?"

Usually, I appreciate straightforwardness. Right now, I'm wishing we could revert to discussing my travel schedule.

More than anything. "I'm not sure…if I should."

At that, she scoffs. "Fine. We've done just fine without you. Walk away again, Nick."

"Things are complicated, Lyla."

Knowing she must hate me was hard to stomach. Seeing it on her face is a form of torture more effective than any I've experienced before.

"Complicated." She repeats the word with a heavy dose of scorn. "Sure, your life is complicated, but being a single mom has been a fucking walk in the park. Highly recommend getting knocked up by a guy, only to have him disappear without so much as a *see you later*."

I wince. "I didn't know you were pregnant. If I had, I would have…"

"You would have *what*, Nick?"

"I don't know," I admit. "I have no fucking clue what I would have done."

She snorts, the sound dripping with disdain. It's been a long time since anyone spoke to me this way. I should hate it. Part of me loves it.

I'm not a dangerous man to Lyla. I'm just Nick.

"This was such a mistake. I saw Alex, and I thought—I thought you deserved to know. Now, you do. Go back to your *complications* and leave me and my son alone."

"*Our* son," I correct.

Lyla's eyes flash like they're reflecting flames. If they were, I'd be a burning pile of ashes.

"Accidentally getting me pregnant does *not* make you his father. You've never even met him."

"I didn't know he existed, Lyla!"

"And whose fault is that?" she snaps.

I let out a long exhale, trying to keep my temper in check.

"Look, I need to go to a meeting. Can I come back in a couple of hours?"

"A *meeting*?" Lyla repeats incredulously. "What, do you have another baby mama to explain complications to?"

I level her with a hard look, but I want to laugh. Lyla referring to herself as my baby mama is amusing and surprisingly arousing.

Most of the women I've slept with have known exactly what I do for a living. Any of them would have come crawling to me for money and protection after getting pregnant.

"I don't have any other kids."

"That you know of," she replies pointedly.

Again, I swallow a chuckle. It's been nine years since anyone spoke to me like this. Alex will occasionally tease me, but he's my subordinate. He'll never take things too far. You respect your *Pakhan*, or you pay for your insolence.

But to Lyla, I'm just the asshole who upended her whole life. Who broke her heart and left her to raise a kid without a father—the same way she grew up.

I wonder if she'd treat me with the same wide-eyed insolence if she'd seen me washing my bloody hands before dinner last night. If she knew the things I've done to keep my family—my men—safe.

"My meeting is for business. I wouldn't have scheduled it for now if I…I'll be back as soon as I can."

"Business, huh? What do you do?"

The question I don't want to answer. "That's also complicated."

She scoffs. "Of course it is." Then sighs. "It's 613. You can come right up. The buzzer is broken."

Of course it is. Once again, I keep my thoughts to myself. I just nod. "Thank you."

I turn and walk toward the waiting car. I want to stay longer, but I can't justify it. The same way I can't characterize coming back as anything but selfish. Once I conduct this meeting with Luca Bianchi, the one I only set up to explain this trip to my men, I should leave this city as soon as possible.

Or I could tell her the truth.

She won't want me around them once I do.

Part of what drew me to Lyla was her morals. Her resilience and belief in systems that failed her. She wanted to become a social worker and help kids like herself. I should have asked if that's her job now. Her mother died from an overdose. If she had any idea the business I'm involved in, I doubt she'll take my money even if it's for…*fuck.*

I didn't even ask my own kid's name.

I've never given any thought to myself as a father, even since the arrangement with Pavel to marry his daughter has materialized. It's always been abstract. Unimportant.

Knowing I am one doesn't make me feel like one. I've never met him, like Lyla said.

Meeting him, knowing his name, will make it feel real.

There is a fleeting chance that I can make that happen. I won't risk another visit here—ever.

I'm not sure which I will regret more. Knowing exactly what I'm missing out on or knowing he's out there, but nothing else.

The door slams as I climb back into the waiting car. I'm exhausted by uncertainty about what to do, of being paralyzed by indecision. It's completely uncharacteristic. Usually, I pride myself on my decision-making. It's an essential trait of an effective leader.

I pull out my phone and call Grigoriy, who's in the car behind me.

He doesn't ask questions when I tell him to stay behind with

Viktor and watch the building. Accepts the directive to let me know of anything suspicious without hesitation.

It helps calm some of the chaos in my head as I give the signal to Andrei to start driving.

There's no right or wrong decision.

There's just *my* decision. That's been the case when it comes to everything else.

This will be no different.

CHAPTER SEVEN

LYLA

The phone rings fifty-four minutes into Nick's two hours. I drop the sponge and dry my hands.

Having the afternoon off is a novelty. Most of the attorneys were out of the office today at a legal seminar in Pittsburgh. Mary, the head secretary, sent us all home after lunch. I called June and asked her if she wanted me to pick AJ up from school when I go to get Leo. My afternoon was supposed to be a few hours to myself and then surprising Leo by picking him up instead of his usual after-school care.

Instead, I'm cleaning. Stress cleaning.

Leo's school is calling.

I answer the phone. "Hello?"

"Hi, Miss Peterson. It's Mrs. Gables. How are you?"

"I'm fine, Mrs. Gables. Is everything okay?"

"Everything's fine. But there's a cold bug floating around, and Leo says he isn't feeling well. He asked to go to the nurse, but I hate to have him sit there the rest of the day. Is there any way you could come pick him up early?"

Crap.

Concern mixes with stress. I don't mind picking up Leo early. It ruins the surprise of getting him after school myself for once and my plan to take him to get ice cream. But I'm most concerned by the realization that means Leo will be home when Nick comes back. *If* he comes back.

"Miss Peterson? Are you still there? If it's an issue, I can send him to the nurse's office for the afternoon."

"It's no issue. I'll be there shortly," I say.

Under other circumstances, it would be ideal this happened on a rare afternoon off. Otherwise, I'd have to panic call Mrs. Hudson, the elderly woman who lives a few floors down and babysits when June isn't available, and ask her to get Leo so he wasn't stuck in the nurse's office for hours.

"Oh, perfect." Mrs. Gables's voice is all relief. "I'll see you soon."

"See you soon," I echo, then hang up the phone. I pull on my jacket and grab my keys before leaving my apartment.

Nick didn't say a specific time. I forgot that about him—how he lets the rest of the world fall into place around his plans.

I'm the exact opposite. I schedule my life down to the second. I don't have much of a choice as a single mom working two jobs, but still.

Nick was always carelessly composed, completely comfortable with assuming everything would work out the way he wanted.

I'm sure he could have shown up to his meeting—if there really is a meeting—hours later and convinced everyone the delay was their fault.

I try and fail to care this outing might mean he could show up while I'm gone and think I changed my mind about continuing this conversation. If he's dissuaded that easily, he doesn't deserve to be part of Leo's life anyway. I'm not sure he deserves to even if he does show up. A reply to a question about meeting your child for the first time shouldn't include the word *complicated.*

But I know what growing up without a father is like. It's not something I want for my own child. The second-guessing, the self-doubts, the what-ifs. It was one thing when Leo was younger and easily accepted it was just the two of us.

AJ is his best friend, and he only has a mom as well. But June has photos of her late husband holding her son. Has extended family bursting with stories of what AJ's father was like to help keep his memory alive.

I have none of that. Leo has none of that. And the older he gets, the more gaping of a hole in his life that will become.

Unlike me, conceived out of my mother's desperation to access drugs she couldn't afford, Leo was created from love. He doesn't have a deadbeat drug dealer who accepts questionable forms of currency for a father.

Nick is cultured. Charming. Smart. Wealthy.

I never considered whether or not he would be a good father when we were together. But he's the guy every young kid dreams of having as a dad—effortlessly good at everything. Cool and charismatic.

I want that for Leo, more than anything. Enough that I'll swallow my pride and make it as easy as possible for Nick to be a part of his life.

He showed up less than a day after learning Leo exists.

That means something—I hope.

It starts to snow right as I park in front of Leo's school. I zip my coat all the way up before stepping out of the warm car and hurrying across the lot, trying to move fast enough to temper the chill in the air.

Leo is sitting in one of the plastic chairs that line the far wall of the office when I enter. Hot air hits me in a dry puff, washing away the remnants of cold air clinging to my clothes. I smile at Mrs. Nelson, the receptionist, before crouching down next to his chair.

"Hey, buddy. How are you feeling?"

"I'm okay. I told Mrs. Gables not to call you at work."

Something twists in my chest as I scan his worried expression. Worried about *me*, not himself.

I hide my burdens from him the best I can. He's a kid. He shouldn't have to worry about rent or car payments or insurance or anything that keeps me up at night.

But he's a *smart* kid. He notices anyway.

"I'm glad she did," I tell him, knocking my shoulder against his. "I have the afternoon off. I was going to pick you up after school. Now, we get extra time together." I stand. "Let me just sign you out."

I make small talk with Mrs. Nelson as I sign the sheet, and then Leo and I head out into the parking lot. For a second, the cold feels good, before it turns frigid.

We rush across the asphalt, over the light layer of white that's already coated the gray.

Leo sniffles a few times as I drive home, but otherwise seems to be in good spirits. I park in the lot at the end of our block that charges half as much as the landlord does for one of the building's spots, praying the snow doesn't accumulate too much. If Leo is too sick to go to school in the morning, I'll have to coordinate the logistics of his care. Having to clear off my car will only make my morning more hectic.

A black van and a red Mini Cooper are parked directly in front of the building, flouting the *No Parking* sign posted, but there's no sign of the SUV Nick got into the back of earlier. The back—because he has an actual *driver*. I knew he was well-off. He told me his parents were wealthy, but I can't picture Nick living off a trust fund.

Once we're back in the apartment, I send Leo off to wash his hands and change into pajamas. I bustle around the kitchen, making hot chocolate and putting a bag of popcorn in the microwave, stealing glances at the clock on the stove.

It's been more than two hours.

That shouldn't disappoint me. It should be the expected outcome. A relief, free from complications.

The microwave dings, indicating the popcorn is ready.

A second later, the sound of gunfire erupts. It's been years—decades—since I've heard a gunshot, but it's impossible to confuse with anything else.

Sharp and horrific.

Loud and final.

I drop the milk and sprint down the hall and into Leo's room.

He's huddled near the bed, green eyes wide and surprised, wearing the striped pajama set with dancing elves he got two Christmases ago.

The set is too small for him now, the hems exposing a couple of inches of his wrists and elbows. I rush over to Leo and pull him against me, berating myself for leaving my phone in the kitchen.

Just as quickly as the gunfire began, it's stopped.

I need to call the police.

"It's okay," I tell Leo, squeezing him tight. "I'll be right back. I just need to get my phone so I can call the police and make sure they know what's happening. Everything will be fine."

I look down. Protecting him is my only instinct. I haven't—can't—let myself absorb any fear.

Leo nods, his expression serious.

I've always known Leo looks a lot like his father. The similarities have grown more pronounced as he's gotten older. But I didn't realize just how alike they appear until I saw Nick again earlier.

There are moments Leo resembles me, but the hair, the eyes, his nose, his expression right now? All Nick.

There's an eerie silence around us, like the calm after a storm.

It's broken by a noise even more terrifying than the gunfire. A slam that sounds like a front door being forced open, followed by footsteps so close, they could only be inside this apartment.

Fear freezes my blood. The past twenty-four hours have been a riotous emotional roller coaster. My body has burned through a lot of emotions. But I feel the fear everywhere. It wants to bind me in place, but I can't allow it to.

"Stay here," I say, then rush toward the door.

I have no idea what I'm going to do.

This isn't a ritzy neighborhood by any stretch, but the crime rate is low. Gunfire at four on a Tuesday afternoon is nothing I ever expected to experience. But I'm not going to hide under the bed with my son. I'd do anything to protect him. They can have anything they want in the apartment—including me. But not Leo.

There are two men standing in the living room. One is broad with closely cropped black hair. The other isn't as big, but is still muscular. His hair is longer, hanging past his chin.

My heart takes off in double time as they watch me walk down the hall toward them silently. Neither of them is visibly armed. They're both dressed in heavy, dark clothes that are simple yet look expensive, far from the starving or desperate who might attempt armed robbery as a last resort.

There's a rapid stream of a foreign language between them as I approach. Russian, if my binge-watching of *The Americans* is an accurate indication.

"You're trespassing," I say once I reach the end of the hall.

I'm proud of the fact that my voice is even and strong, no trace of a waver.

"Fuck. I sure hope this is the right apartment." One of them speaks English.

The other man, the burlier one, takes a step back to study my front door, which is now hanging crookedly on ruined hinges. "This is 613."

The man who spoke first sighs. He has blond hair and a scruffy beard, which he scratches at. "Goddamn Italians. Dramatic about everything."

A response is spoken in Russian. I can't understand a word of it, but I think it involves me based on how they both glance my way.

"I'm going to call the police," I state, hoping it will scare them off.

"That would be a mistake," the dark-haired man says. "We're supposed to be in New York, which is why this is a clean sweep."

The blond scoffs. "Clean sweep? They'll know it was us."

"Knowing and proving are two different things."

"I'm sure that's how Bianchi will see it," the blond man responds, lifting a phone to his ear.

I take a step closer to the kitchen island, where my phone is, and their attention snaps back to me.

"He's not answering?" the dark-haired man asks the blond.

"No. I'd hate to be Bianchi when the boss finds out what went down here."

Black eyebrows bunch together. "We should see if—"

"Mom?"

I close my eyes and mentally shout a long list of swears before turning to watch Leo walk down the hallway in his pajamas. I'm not sure what these men want. I can't tell why they're here or gauge how dangerous they are. That's not a situation I ever wanted Leo walking into.

"Go back to your room, Leo."

He doesn't listen, stopping next to me and glaring at the two strangers.

There's a rapid flurry of Russian. The men look between Leo and each other, their tones sharp and urgent. Worried and confused.

They know Nick. I'm not sure why that's the first thought that occurs to me, but it's one that sticks. It's the only logical explanation for the recognition on their faces as they look at my son. For the appearance of awe I saw aimed at his father many times.

I'm not sure if it should ease some of the panic building inside of me, but it does.

I might no longer know Nick. I definitely don't trust him. But I don't believe he'd ever promote any ill will toward me or Leo. He's still the guy I lay in bed next to, describing my chaotic childhood and recounting the night I found my mother's lifeless body. If these men know him—respect him, it seems—it makes them far less of a threat in my eyes.

I pull Leo behind me, just in case.

The stream of Russian continues.

I eye my phone. If I run for it, I have no idea what they might do. It's an action I might have attempted before Leo appeared. If I move now, he'll be completely exposed. Either of the men could easily grab him, and that's not a chance I'm willing to take.

"What do you want?" I ask.

The Russian stops.

"*Want*? Nothing," the dark-haired man says. "I've been dying to kill an Italian *krysa* for years. This was better than attending the meeting."

"Grigoriy." The blond adds something in Russian, then

smirks. The other man glares. Amusement still covers the blond's expression when he turns to me. "I'm Viktor."

"I don't care what your names are. I want you to leave. *Now*."

Grigoriy smiles. "I'd expect you to feel differently if more Italians show up."

His phone rings, and any humor drops off Grigoriy's face as he glances at the screen. He answers immediately and starts speaking—in Russian.

I'm getting very tired of not understanding what is being said. Viktor is nodding along to whatever Grigoriy is saying.

They're both distracted.

This is probably the best opening I'll have to call 911.

But I can't move. Can't accept the slightest risk when it comes to Leo's safety even if it will increase our odds overall.

Grigoriy hangs up the phone and looks at me. "Let's go."

I laugh, and it's an unhinged sound. I *feel* unhinged. Grigoriy says it like it's a reasonable request after barging into a stranger's home to the tune of gunfire rather than knocking on the door like a civilized person.

Aside from that, he seems…normal. No crazy eyes or brandishing a gun. But this is *not* normal. It's insane. *He's* insane if he thinks I'm going anywhere with him.

I'm very aware of Leo's presence behind me though. Everything I do or say needs to be thought through. Everything feels surreal, like I'm watching this unfold from a distance. But it's really happening. Real actions with real consequences.

Viktor walks over to the window that overlooks the road and glances outside, down at the street. "Company."

"How many?" Grigoriy asks.

"Si—eight."

"Fuckers."

"Are you going to hurt us?" I hate asking the question in front of Leo, but I don't know what else to do. Sending him back to his room alone sounds even riskier than keeping him here with me.

Grigoriy and Viktor exchange a look, appearing genuinely confused by my question.

"Hurt you? Of course not." More of an accent creeps in than before, somehow adding to the sincerity. Grigoriy sounds genuine, and it soothes a little of the terror.

I have no reason to trust him, aside from the fact he hasn't hurt us yet. He—or Viktor—could have shot me the minute they entered the apartment.

The suffocating state of fear I've been in since I heard the first gunshot eases a little more.

Viktor has walked back over to the window. He glances outside, then says something in Russian. I can't understand a word of it, but I have no issue reading the tone.

Urgency.

"We need to go," Grigoriy states.

I'm running on adrenaline and confusion. I have no idea who Grigoriy and Viktor are or why they're here. But I can't come up with any reason why they'd be lying about more men coming. I'm already at their mercy.

There's a gun in Grigoriy's hand all of a sudden.

Adrenaline spreads, mixing with fear. I refuse to let it paralyze me though. There's too much at stake right now. I can freak out about anything and everything that could happen later.

One of mom's boyfriends when I was in sixth grade had a gun cabinet. His name was Eric, and he'd been honorably discharged from the Army. He and Mom crossed paths at an AA meeting during one of her attempts to get sober.

Their relationship ended once she started using again—and stealing from him to fund her habit. But for a few months, it was the closest I felt to having a complete family.

When we were briefly staying at his house, I'd sit and help Eric clean his guns, silently enjoying when Mom would fuss about me touching them. It felt like she cared, for once, although I'm pretty sure it was more about impressing Eric with her parenting skills than any actual worry about my safety.

Sixth grade was the last time I saw a gun in person—until now. Viktor is holding one as well now. They're not pointed our way, providing a flimsy illusion of defense.

I know that can change very quickly.

"You ready?" Viktor asks.

It's an honest question, not a demand. But I know it only has one correct answer.

I have no idea what these men want from me. At the moment, they appear protective. I have no confidence it's not another illusion and no choice but to trust it.

"One second." I help Leo into his coat and zip it up all the way, as if that will protect him from whatever might come our way. And I manage to slip my phone into the pocket of my down jacket before I pull it on, which alleviates a little of the weight that's crushing my chest.

I can call for help. I'm not helpless.

Grigoriy stops me before we reach the door, tugging on the sleeve of my coat. "Cover his eyes," he tells me, nodding to Leo.

I stare at him in shock, uncertainty. My mind is racing with what the implications might mean. It also provides me with more assurance we'll be okay than anything else he's said.

I do as he says, guiding Leo so he's standing in front of me and his movements mirror mine. "It's going to be okay." I whisper the words to him and hope they're true.

Before we step into the hallway, I cover Leo's eyes. His body tenses, but he doesn't protest as we step onto the carpet I've trodden a hundred times before.

The rapid thud of Leo's heart against my palm is the only reason I swallow the gasp.

There are two men in the hallway. Two *dead* men. I can't see either of their expressions. They're both facedown, bodies so still, it's obvious they're not breathing. The gray carpet around them is darker than the rest of the hallway, coated with more blood than anyone can lose and survive.

I heard the gunshots earlier. But there's a large part of me that hoped it was a mistake or a misunderstanding.

One of the bodies is only a few feet away from my front door. These men were coming for me, and Grigoriy and Viktor stopped them. *Killed* them. And I have no idea why.

"Keep moving." Grigoriy's tone is urgent, but not unkind.

Until he spoke, I didn't realize my steps had stuttered and slowed. Pulled to a pause by a morbid fascination.

It's been a long time since I saw a dead person. I'm yanked into memories of that night without warning, trapped in a different time and place.

A rough sound—unmistakably a swear even if it's said in another language—is spoken behind me. "Take the boy."

Leo is pulled away from me, and that is enough to jerk me from the past back into the present. "No!"

"The boy will be fine," Grigoriy says as Viktor takes over on guiding Leo down the hall. He keeps his eyes covered until they're past the second body, and it's the main reason I don't struggle more.

"If anything happens to him, I'll kill you."

I've never threatened anyone in my life. I try to take the high road. When someone cuts me off in traffic, I assume they're late for work or just having a shitty day. But when I speak the warning, the words don't sound ridiculous.

At least, I don't think they do. I sound deadly serious.

Grigoriy laughs. But then he says something I'm not expecting. "You'd have to get in line."

And before I can ask what the hell he's talking about, he's hustling me down the hallway, and I have to focus on not tripping over my feet and ending up in a puddle of blood.

CHAPTER EIGHT

NICK

My pacing might wear a hole in the tarmac. Snow falls in uneven patterns, melting as soon as it hits the black asphalt.

All of my men, most of them standing in a loose circle around the plane, are uneasy. I see it in the quick, darting glances my way. The occasional twitch. Uncertainty thickens the crisp winter air with a different type of chill, exacerbated with silence.

Today was supposed to follow the same format as yesterday. Meetings with lawyers in high-rises. Meetings with suppliers in back rooms. Dinner at a fancy restaurant. Instead, it's been a trip to Philly, a short, frigid meeting with a *capo*, and now, we're leaving two days earlier than planned.

No one questions the changes.

They know better than to ask questions.

I should know better than to show any emotion.

But there's a clawing, tearing sensation in my chest that writhes like a living thing. It makes it impossible to stand still and stoic. My jaw clenches and unclenches in some attempt to alleviate tension that doesn't work.

I always travel with a dozen men. There are plenty of times that's felt excessive. This is the first time it hasn't felt like nearly enough.

If anything happened to them...

It's panicky—this feeling. Thrashing around in my chest in a heavy coil of dread. No matter how quickly I move, I can't shake it.

I've always felt the responsibility of my position. The weight of having to make decisions that are often life or death. That can save or end lives. That ripple far beyond affecting just me.

I've been in dangerous situations. I've stared death down and haven't flinched. I might not have an appetite for this way of life, but I'm good at it. My DNA is embedded with the tools to not only survive this life, but to thrive in it.

This is different. Lyla and her son aren't just innocent lives. They mean something to me. They matter—in a way no one ever has. The only immediate family I have left is my mother. If something happened to her because of this life, I'd mourn. I'd torture those responsible.

But I wouldn't feel this fever. This helplessness.

My mother chose to marry my father. Chose this life, knowing exactly what it could entail.

Lyla didn't. Neither did my son.

I knew I'd have kids one day. I knew they'd be exposed to the same horrors I accepted from a young age. But I thought I'd have years to prepare for that moment. Ease into it. I didn't think a fully formed person would just appear, thinking he's a normal child but facing deadly threats because he shares my blood.

"They're two minutes out."

I nod, acknowledging the update. Ivan opens his mouth like he's considering saying something else, then quickly closes it. It's a wise decision. My temper is on a short fuse right now.

I'm furious—mostly with myself.

This is my fault. I should have stayed far away from Lyla and her life. I make nothing but reckless decisions when she's near, and it's a pattern that has to stop.

I'm not sure if it can be halted though.

Not now.

Bianchi's men were curious before. I should have anticipated that he would have *soldatos* tailing me as soon as I crossed into the city. I was too consumed by what to do about Lyla to think anything through about my impulsive visit.

Bianchi wasn't expecting me to have left men, or he would have sent more to investigate Lyla's building. If I hadn't, I don't know what would have happened.

There's a chance they would have poked around and left. A chance I wasn't willing to take. As soon as Viktor told me there were Italians there, I made my orders clear.

By now, Bianchi will know what took place after our meeting. Know I left men. Know I authorized them to fire first. And the fact that I did says everything I never would have voluntarily shared with the Italians.

He'll dig into Lyla's life. Learn she has a son. Connect the two dots.

Walking away now isn't an option.

A black SUV squeals its way onto the tarmac.

Everyone around me jumps into action, ensuring we're ready to take off.

I finally stand still, staring at the tinted glass like I've developed X-ray vision and can actually see a damn thing inside.

The headlights of the black SUV light up the puddles lingering from earlier rain that turned to snow. Grigoriy steps out of the driver's seat. Viktor climbs out of the passenger's side. They avoid eye contact with me, setting about unloading the bags from the back of the car and removing the license plates. They both know there will be consequences for what happened earlier. The Italians shouldn't have made it inside the building in the first place.

Lyla appears next. She's dressed the same as she was when we talked outside her apartment earlier. The only thing that's changed is the expression on her face. She's not just angry—she's scared.

The unrest in my chest is gone, but something tightens in its place.

I fucked up.

Lyla shuts the car door and strides straight toward me. With each step, more of the fear disappears, crystallizing the fury on her face.

When she reaches me, she shoves me. Hard. Years of training are the only reason I stay upright.

If she were anyone else, she'd no longer be breathing.

"I know you're upset—"

"Upset?! UPSET? There are two *dead men* in the hallway outside my apartment, Nick. I'm a witness to murders! Leo was home from school! He could have been injured! *Killed*! I don't know what the fuck you're involved in, and I don't want to know. I want no part of it, Nick. Crawl back to wherever you came from. We're better off without you."

She stares at me, chest heaving and dark hair flying.

I should reply. I had a response ready. Explanations. Apologies. I can't allow her to stand here and berate me in front of my men. It's bad enough she touched me without my permission, which is ordinarily a fatal offense.

But I'm stuck on one word. "You named him Leo?"

She stares at me, and I stare back, and for one brief second, I'm eighteen again, watching a stranger blush.

Lyla nods. I exhale, dreading what I have to say.

"I'm in charge of a powerful organization, Lyla. It's why I left so suddenly back then—I had to take over unexpectedly. It's why I didn't say good-bye. I didn't want to lie about why I had to go, and the less you knew, the better."

"You're a criminal." In her even, quiet voice, it's somehow the harshest insult I've ever heard.

"Technically, yes."

"Technically? We're having this conversation, surrounded by men with guns."

"Fine. Yes, I'm a criminal."

"Jesus fucking Christ." She exhales, then shakes her head. "Alex could have been more specific."

"What did he say?"

Sharp, intelligent eyes lock on mine. "Why?"

"Because he shouldn't have said a thing."

Lyla pales. "He's involved? In your…organization?"

"He works for me."

"He's a doctor."

"Yes."

"What the hell kind of company needs a doctor?"

"A dangerous one."

Lyla's eyes widen, letting me see the resolve in them harden. "The only reason I'm here is, I was worried more men would come back, and I had no idea who to trust. I'm going to leave with my son now, and I'm going to go to the police. I won't mention your name, but if you come near me again, I will. I can't—"

"You're going nowhere, Lyla." I give a nod to Viktor, and then men start boarding the plane. I don't want them witnessing this, and I'm hoping it'll relax Lyla some, having them out of sight. "I'm sorry you're involved now. I really am. But this is a matter of life and death. If you stay here, if you go to the police, you'll be killed. And so will Leo."

I stutter over my son's name, but Lyla appears too horrified to notice. "You're—I don't—"

"I'm a powerful person. Powerful people have powerful enemies. They'll torture you and dump you in a ditch to die." I state it matter-of-factly, trying not to scare her, but impress on her the seriousness of the situation. Especially since I know full well Bianchi will do worse than that.

"You're lying."

"I'm not. I *wouldn't* lie to you about this, Lyla."

I watch her face crumple. Watch her try to hold it together. If I were a different man, I'd step forward and hug her.

But if I were that man, we wouldn't be having this conversation to begin with.

"Get Leo and get on the plane, Lyla."

Her eyes dart around, wide and worried. "I—I have work in the morning. Leo has school. He wants a dog, but our apartment won't allow them, so I'm supposed to pick up a cat from the shelter next week. I'm dating someone. I have bills, rent. They'll repossess the apartment and tow my car, and I don't—"

I step forward and grab her shoulders. Her nervous babbling stops.

"Lyla. *You don't have a choice.*"

"Why should I trust you?" she asks.

The only one of my men not on the plane is Viktor, who's now standing by the car. No one can hear us.

I meet her anxious gaze. "Because up until I found out I had a son, I was certain you'd be the only person I ever loved."

Her lips part, but no sound comes out.

I never said the words to her. I didn't know how suddenly and unexpectedly I'd leave, but I knew I *would* leave. Saying those three words seemed selfish.

But I would have meant them. I felt them.

"I am the *only* person that can protect you. And, yes, I get that's ironic since I'm the reason you're in danger. But it's the truth."

"Well, *that's* ironic. Because as far as I can tell, all you've ever done is lie."

"I never lied to you."

"You're lying about loving me. If you ever did, you never would have come near us, knowing this could happen."

She already shoved me. Yelled at me. And then Lyla does something else no one has dared to do in years.

She turns her back on me and walks away.

One last comment is hurled over her left shoulder. "I don't want him to know who you are."

CHAPTER NINE

LYLA

Leo's worried face peers at me from the backseat as I open the car door. I watch him try to school the fear from his expression, and it feels like a fist is squeezing around my heart.

He's trying to be brave for *me*.

I blame Nick for getting us into this situation. Alex too.

But I also blame myself. If I'd been more careful, chopping cucumbers—if I hadn't gone back to that hospital in some pathetic attempt to track down a guy I should have forgotten about years ago—my son wouldn't be looking at me like this.

"Come on, sweetheart," I tell him. "Time to get out of the car."

Leo climbs out of the fancy SUV. Glances at Viktor standing outside, who makes no attempt to hide either of the two guns he's carrying. If he hadn't possibly saved my life earlier, I would glare at him.

The fact that I'm even thinking that tells me I'm buying into Nick's story—at least a little. For all I know, those men in my apartment could have been undercover cops, trying to arrest him.

Accepting Nick's version of events means acknowledging Leo

and I really are in danger. That people want to kill us now because Nick stood on the sidewalk outside my apartment for a few minutes.

It's too terrifying to comprehend, so I focus on the more pressing matter at hand—introducing Leo to his father.

"Where are we going?" Leo whispers to me as we walk across the tarmac with Viktor trailing a few feet behind us.

"I don't know," I admit as we approach a plane just as sleek and luxurious as the car we rode here in.

Whatever illegal activity Nick is involved in, it's obviously lucrative. People don't risk their lives for what they could achieve otherwise, I suppose.

We reach Nick. He's not looking at me. He's staring at Leo like he's trying to memorize every detail about him.

There's a pang in my chest that rattles around like spare change. I imagined this moment—pictured it in my mind—many times after I found out I was pregnant. It's a fantasy that's faded over the years, worn out like an old photograph folded too many times, as Leo grew older and my memories of Nick became less vivid.

The similarities I see in myself to Leo pale in comparison to seeing him next to his father. They have the same color hair. The same eyes. The same proud profile. It's mesmerizing and emotional.

I worry Leo will see it right away. But he's only looking at Nick with curiosity, not recognition.

"Leo, this is my friend, Nick."

Nick's eyes flash to mine, only for a second, before returning to Leo. I can't tell what he's thinking, if he's noticing the resemblance between them or if he's annoyed that I'm not telling Leo the truth about their relationship.

Nick squats so he's at Leo's height. He holds out a hand,

which my son hesitantly shakes. "Hi, Leo. It's really nice to meet you."

"Is this your plane?" Leo asks, looking at the behemoth shadowing this interaction. It's even bigger up close.

"Yes."

"Can you fly it?"

"Yes."

I side-eye Nick, not sure if he's lying. But his face is still smooth and expressionless, impossible to read.

"Are more men going to chase us?"

My lips press together into a tight line. Grigoriy's and Viktor's sensitivity only extended to keeping Leo from seeing dead bodies, apparently. They spent the drive here discussing the men who attacked us. And not much gets past my son's sharp ears.

"Those men are never going to get anywhere near you again, Leo." There's no emotion on Nick's face, but his tone is flooded with sincerity as he straightens.

Viktor says something in Russian behind me, and Nick responds with another flurry of words I don't understand.

"We need to go," he tells me, then looks at Leo. "Have you been on a plane before, Leo?"

"No."

"Go explore before we take off."

Leo looks at me, and I nod. He bounds up the steps and boards the aircraft.

"Where are we going, Nick?"

"My home. Russia."

Russia.

It feels like the ground beneath me just became less stable. "*Russia*? That's…far."

"I don't have time to explain everything now, Lyla. We need to leave."

Nick turns and takes the stairs.

And I follow him.

CHAPTER TEN

NICK

I can't stop staring at him.

Every time I tell myself I've looked my fill and force my eyes to focus on something else, my eyes dart right back to Leo.

Each time I get another glimpse of him, I feel like I was just punched in the stomach all over again.

Alex wasn't exaggerating when he said the boy looks like me. There's a photo I keep on my desk of myself with my father and two brothers from a hunting trip we took years and years ago—one of endless efforts by my father to toughen his offspring up. I was ten or eleven at the time it was taken. We came home with plenty of animal carcasses, but the only memento I kept was a rare picture of the four of us smiling together.

Looking at Leo is like staring at myself in that framed photograph.

But beyond just the physical similarities, he *acts* like me.

This has undoubtedly been the most tumultuous and terrifying day of his life, and yet there's a focused expression on his face as he takes in the armed, stoic men and the luxurious leather interior of the private jet. His back is stiff and his chin set as he fiddles with a small toy he pulled out of his jacket pocket. A figurine wearing a cowboy hat.

I might not know much about kids, but I'm pretty sure this isn't a typical response to trauma.

Without training, without knowing what he was born into, my son is tough. He has Morozov blood in his veins. *My* blood. Pride blooms in my chest, a thousand times more intense and powerful than it's ever been when any of my men manage an accomplishment.

Occasionally, Leo looks at me. I'm careful to never let our gazes collide and that my jacket covers my gun. I don't want to scare him, and I'm trying to honor Lyla's decision not to reveal our relation.

For such a thoughtful kid, I'm surprised he hasn't noticed the resemblance.

He's the only one on board the plane who hasn't. The men I brought on this trip have spent the flight exchanging a lot of loaded looks. None of them dare to say a word—but it's obvious what they're thinking.

As we cross the Atlantic, all my half-formed ideas about telling everyone Lyla and Leo are under my protection as a favor to a friend and stashing them in a safe house vanish. Their connection to me is too obvious, and it fills me with equal parts pride and panic.

I don't have a plan—about any of this. Ever since I answered Alex's call last night, my entire world has been upended, thoroughly and permanently.

The two events I've spent the better part of the past year concerned with—my feud with Dmitriy and the arrangement with Pavel—have both just become infinitely more complicated.

But I can't worry about hunting down my cousin or my impatient future father-in-law right now. My main priority needs to be Lyla's and Leo's safety. Everything else is secondary.

And the safest place is my private residence. It has the security of a bank vault and the layout of a fortress. There's a mixture of relief and dread as I acknowledge the decision I knew I'd made as soon as I made the call for the plane to be flown to Philadelphia and then back to Russia.

They'll be close to me. I know why I'm experiencing dread. The relief is harder to explain.

I like my space. Like my privacy.

And I don't really like kids.

Except...mine.

I glance at Lyla. Unlike Leo, she's not looking around at anything or anyone. Her gaze is focused out the window at the fluffy clouds we're hovering above. Anxiety is sketched into the lines of her face and is echoed in the way her arms are wrapped around her middle, like she's physically holding herself together.

I spent months purging Lyla Peterson from my system. Years accepting that I'd never see her again. The fact that she's sitting no more than twenty feet from me right now is a complete mindfuck.

As soon as the wheels hit the runway in Moscow, I begin barking orders. All the cargo is loaded into the convoy of armored vehicles already waiting.

More of my men are waiting outside of the plane as I disembark into the winter air, inhaling deeply. It smells like home, but I've never felt more out of my element.

Leo and Lyla are the last to descend the stairs. I focus on Lyla instead of our son, attempting to pretend he's just *a* child. Not my child. The same way he thinks I'm no one important. Not to him at least.

"Viktor will drive you to where you'll be staying," I tell her, nodding toward the line of SUVs parked and waiting.

My car is first. When I'm home, I prefer to drive myself. That's never been truer than right now.

I need a second to think, some time to process. A minute to plan. For the first time in my life, I have no idea what to do.

I turn and head toward the line of vehicles, only pausing to instruct Viktor on the plan. He nods in response to the directive, a flash of apprehension crossing his face. Without me admitting a word, he knows what I'm entrusting him with. Knows me flying them there and bringing them into my home means if anything happens on the trip, the torture he's seen me inflict on others won't look as severe.

The car is running and waiting. I climb inside and press on the accelerator. The expensive engine lunges forward, propelling the car across the tarmac at a similar speed to the plane I was just on. The stretch of cement is empty, allowing me to accelerate even more.

Everyone else near the private terminal gives this section of the airport a wide berth. The Morozov name carries weight in the States. Here, it's never uttered without fear.

Despite my proclivity toward driving alone, I was tempted to ride in the same car with Leo and Lyla, which is exactly why I didn't.

Today will have far-reaching consequences. And every decision I continue to make is sinking my son deeper into a life I wouldn't choose for him. My enemies have spies everywhere. The fact that I requested additional men be waiting here to escort us home from what was supposed to be a routine, quick trip won't go unnoticed or unreported.

Sometimes, things are exactly as they appear. Everyone around me—friend or foe—will take everything I've done today to mean the woman and boy in the car behind mine mean something to me.

The only living relative I have any real emotional attachment to is my mother. She's a proud, obnoxious woman in her fifties who lives in a heavily guarded home in Moscow. Hardly ideal blackmail material. Not much of a weakness.

But a woman?

A son?

I picture Dmitriy cackling with glee when he finds out. He has a high-pitched, squeaky laugh that led to plenty of teasing when we were kids. I haven't heard it in a long time. I can imagine it perfectly now along with him thinking he'll finally gain the upper hand.

I still have more men and more resources. Respect.

But now, I also have something to lose.

I quiet the chaos in my head by enjoying the feel of being behind the wheel for a while. Once I'm past Moscow, I call Alex.

He blew my phone up with unanswered messages and calls the entire flight. I owe it to him to let him know they're safe even if I'm also tempted to punch him in the face for setting off this entire mess in the first place.

I would still be in New York, not making a mental note of the best private schools in the area to call later and enroll Leo. This conflict with Dmitriy has dragged on for too many months. For his many faults, he's not a complete idiot. He also knows our operations well—*too* well. Catching and killing him won't be a quick and easy task, which means Leo and Lyla won't be enjoying a short stay.

Again, I'm conflicted. Lyla is angry with me—rightfully so. Leo has no idea why he's here. They'll leave as soon as it's safe.

But something feels…right about having them both here now.

"What happened?" is how Alex answers the phone.

There's no anger or accusation in his voice, but I hear both simmering underneath the question. He just knows better than to channel it into words.

"Bianchi."

It's not an answer to what Alex is really asking, but he doesn't press me on it.

"Where's Lyla?" he questions instead.

"With me."

"With—Roman said you just landed."

"We did."

"You—she's in *Moscow* with you?"

"Yes."

A pause.

"Why?"

"Bianchi sent men to her apartment. I need her—them—safe."

Alex's voice changes. Deepens. "You met the kid?"

"Yes."

"And…"

"And what?"

"You don't want to talk about it." His tone is dry.

Alex's father was my father's favorite *Brigadier*. He died in the attack that claimed my father and brothers' lives as well. It brought us even closer together, strengthened a bond that was already ironclad. But for the first time, there's something I don't *want* to share with him.

"There's nothing to talk about."

"*Sure*." Alex drawls the word, adding too many syllables to count. "You have a kid—a *son*. With *Lyla Peterson*. You're bringing them home with you, and we both know what the consequences of that will be. But there's *nothing* to talk about. Got it."

My patience thins to nothing. "Did you actually need something?"

Alex exhales. "I can't believe you didn't tell me you were coming. You made one trip to Philly, and all hell broke loose. You should hear the chatter on the streets right now."

I don't bother to acknowledge the first sentence. There's annoyance saturating his voice, but no genuine surprise. Because we both knew I'd show up in Philadelphia after he called me.

Anyone else *would* have been surprised by the lengths I've immediately gone to. Morozov protection is a luxury most have to beg or barter for.

If Bianchi or Dmitriy or anyone else discovered what I just did before I found out myself, I have no doubt they would have tried to use Lyla and Leo against me.

I also know they would be unsure it would work. If I'd care.

My teeth grind as I take a turn too fast. "Anything I need to know?"

"No. Mostly just speculation."

"Let me know if that changes."

"I thought you'd want me to be on the next flight."

"No."

There's a pause, and I know he'll ask to come back.

"Lyla has *no idea* what she's gotten into, Nikolaj. She must be scared and overwhelmed. I know you need to act a certain way, so let me—"

"I'm handling it. Stay in Philadelphia."

A second sigh, laced with frustration.

I have other men I could leave in Philadelphia to monitor the mess made, and he knows it. But Alex basically begged for this assignment.

Aside from his reports to me, he enjoys normalcy. He gets as sick of this life as I do, but he has a choice. I never have. Loyalty to me and his family is the only reason he hasn't left the Bratva.

But it's not just loyalty to me in his voice. He has the luxury of acting human. And I'm worried Alex will make Lyla less reliant on me.

It's selfish.

Her life was just uprooted.

But I need her to trust me. To tolerate me at the very least. And that's much more likely to happen if she has limited options of other people to turn toward.

I'm guessing Alex knows that, but he doesn't say a word.

"I called in a favor with Callahan. He cleaned up Bianchi's men and has men packing up the apartment. They'll have to stay here until I get everything sorted."

"Cleaned up? You gave a *kill order*? On *Italians*? *Here*? And now, you're relying on the *Irish* to clean it up?" Each question drips with more incredulity.

The tall gates that mark the entrance to the estate come into view up ahead. They're impossible to miss, the first sign of anything man-made in miles.

"I have to go. Keep me posted," I say, then hang up.

Press down on the accelerator harder.

CHAPTER ELEVEN

LYLA

Russia is beautiful. A harsh, wild, rugged beauty.

But it's hard to appreciate beauty when you're trapped.

And that's exactly what I am.

I stare out the car window and retrace the last few days in my head, trying to figure out how exactly I got here.

It always ends on the exact same moment.

Contemplating my decisions like a series of toppled dominoes, I can pinpoint the precise second the first one fell. Unfortunately, knowing the cause does nothing to change the outcome.

I glance at Leo, who's fast asleep. His eyes closed a few minutes into the drive, finally succumbing to an exhausting day and the cold he's battling. He stayed awake the entire flight, absorbing everything around him with wide eyes. He'd never been on a plane before. Neither had I. One of many firsts we're headed toward, I'm guessing. And not the kind you celebrate.

I focus on Leo's peaceful expression in an attempt to calm the anxiety churning in my stomach.

He's safe, I tell myself. *He's safe*.

That has to be the most important thing. Something to cling on to at the edge of this cliff of uncertainty. Ever since I found out I was pregnant, my main focus has been ensuring Leo is safe and happy and healthy.

Seizing the opportunity to let his father know he exists wasn't supposed to threaten any of that. There's no way I could have known that it would. Logically, I know that.

But there's also a part of me—a big part—that knows I toppled the first domino.

Nick left.

Nick *chose* to leave.

He wasn't the first person in my life who did. I should have learned my lesson. When people choose to leave you, let them.

I should have let him.

I did, when I had no other option. As soon as Alex pulled back that curtain, things changed.

And I can tell myself it was all in Leo's best interest that I took the opportunity to request answers to questions that should have remained in the past, but I'm not sure if that's all it was. I wanted those answers for myself, not just for my son.

And now, I'm in Russia, zooming past sharp spires and rainbow domes. Out of my element in every possible way.

Viktor is the only one in the car with us. I watch his profile as he navigates through the traffic with ease, driving at a speed that feels faster than the limit.

I want to pelt Viktor with questions, but I don't want to risk waking Leo. Or risk having him overhear what I'm wondering about.

There's a good chance Viktor wouldn't answer me anyway. I saw the way he looked at Nick on the plane—the way all the men did. It looked like the way worshippers revere a deity, tinged with awe and respect.

Whatever illegal activities Nick is involved in inspires loyalty far beyond the ordinary boss-and-employee relationship. He's a part of something big. Something dangerous. Something I'm now involved in…because of a frat party.

So, I stay silent for the drive that stretches for close to an hour. We leave the bustle of the city behind and weave through an endless maze of roads, lined with barren trees that stand like haunted sentries. There's a forgotten inch of snow sitting on the ground, frozen in place and speckled with gray in spots.

By the time the car slows, I'm fighting my eyelids. Between the long flight and the time difference, we lost a whole day.

Dusk is falling fast, bathing the scenery in shadows that grow darker and longer with each passing minute. The battle to stay awake becomes a war, but I'm determined to stay conscious. My body has burned through all its adrenaline and anxiety, leaving just exhaustion behind. I'm tired of being scared—and just plain tired.

When we stop, it's in front of an ornate set of gates, carved of dark metal. They're purposefully imposing and incredibly intimidating. If hell has gates, I'd imagine these are what they'd look like. The black metal cuts a harsh slash through the backdrop of the darkening sky. They tower over us like a warning about approaching. The men standing and holding machine guns are another strong deterrent.

Viktor talks to one of them for a minute. He climbs out of the car for the length of the discussion, but I'm assuming I wouldn't have been able to understand a word of it regardless.

Language isn't a barrier I've encountered before. All of a sudden, it's a wall caving around me. Underscoring how, by climbing on that plane, I've handed complete control over to Nick. I'll only be able to understand what he chooses to share with me.

The gates creak open slowly, Viktor climbs back inside, and the car creeps forward. Up a long, sweeping drive. We turn a corner, and all of a sudden, I can see our destination. It looks like every single light is on inside, illuminating the entirety of the massive mansion.

I'd estimate it covers a similar square footage as the apartment building Leo and I lived in. *Live* in, I remind myself.

If I lose sight of who I am—what I want—I won't make it through this. I have to believe this is temporary. That the seriousness on Nick's face when he told me Leo and I were in danger will quickly be alleviated and life will return to normal.

Viktor stops the car in front of the building. Calling it a house is a misnomer. It's a palace. A compound. Two wings flank the massive entrance, spreading far enough to each side. It's impossible to take the whole structure in at once.

The same car Nick sped off in is parked outside the wooden doors that mark the mansion's entrance. A tall, dark figure leans against the black bumper, golden shadows dancing across his impassive expression. The flame disappears, then flickers to life again.

It's a strange sensation—knowing small details about someone, but nothing big. I know that Nick carries around a silver lighter. I even remember how rough the metal felt against my fingers, marred with scratches and age.

But I don't know why Nick disappeared from my life without a word. Or the scale of what exactly he's involved in now that requires a small, heavily armed army to work for him.

The first time I met Nick, I noticed the aura of charisma that surrounds him, the way you're pulled in effortlessly by his presence alone. It never faded. And it's especially obvious now, against the backdrop of the stone mansion and the manicured grounds and the darkening sky.

I'm worried how well I ever knew him. If I can even trust this version of him, who seems so at ease in these circumstances. Who appears unfazed by the threat of violence and unbothered by having us here.

The flicker disappears again as Viktor parks the car. I open my door right away, intending to demand answers. The sooner I know what the situation is, the easier it will be to figure out some solution.

Cold air smacks me in the face. I forgot, somehow, how bitter the wind was during the short walk from the plane to the waiting car. No customs or baggage claim. There weren't even any airport workers when we landed. Just hordes of men, wearing black clothes and stoic expressions. Is it illegal to enter a country that way? Probably. The thought sends a fresh spike of anxiety through me.

I'm used to feeling alone. Not to feeling helpless. It's an emotion I purged from my system and never wanted to be reacquainted with.

I wrap my arms around myself to ward off the chill, feeling the dig of the phone in my pocket pressing against my stomach. It should be reassuring, but it isn't any longer.

At best, my outdated cell usually manages a couple of hours of battery life. I'm sure it's dead by now. Even if it is charged and the gothic castle in front of me has Wi-Fi, I have no idea who I would contact or what I would say. I've always prided myself on my independence and self-sufficiency.

And it would be one thing if it was just me taking risks.

But I'm not willing to gamble with Leo's safety.

Nick strides toward me, his long legs eating up the distance between us quickly. I open my mouth to speak, but he beats me to it. "Where's Leo?"

Everything about this moment feels surreal—including

hearing Nick ask me that question. Hearing him say our son's name.

"He fell asleep—" That's all I get out before Nick is rounding the car and opening the door.

A few seconds later, he's standing and then walking toward the front door that's swinging open to greet him, a sleeping Leo draped against one shoulder.

I'm too stunned to move for a minute. I've never *not* been a single mother. Every decision when it comes to Leo has been squarely on my shoulders. And in a matter of hours, Nick has totally taken over. Barged into our lives with the same subtlety of a bull in a china shop.

I thought he'd have apprehensions about parenting. That he would avoid Leo or act uncertain around him. I had eight months to get used to the idea of being a mother, and I still felt unprepared.

Nick found out he's a father less than forty-eight hours ago. And yet he's acting like he's carried Leo around a thousand times before.

His assurance isn't comforting. It makes me feel even more uncertain and out of control as I follow Nick inside. My feet feel heavy and my chest hollow as we walk through a soaring entryway. Uniformed staff scurry around, but no one stops to greet us. Everyone's eyes are downcast, their posture subservient. Like they're…scared.

My heart rate picks up as I watch Nick's tall frame move toward the stairs. No one speaks. Everyone silently moves out of his way.

I swallow, picking up my pace and hurrying upstairs after him. My focus is on Nick's back and nothing else, drawing on old memories to quell the panic inside of me.

I think of the way he used to kiss me. The way he used to hold me.

That's part of who Nick is. He's not just this cold, detached man everyone appears terrified of.

My eyes are bleary with exhaustion as Nick walks down a long hallway and into a room. By the time I catch up, he's laid Leo down on the huge bed and is taking off his coat and shoes. Draping a blanket over his body. Leo has always been a heavy sleeper, but I'm surprised he hasn't been jostled awake yet. He's still in his elf pajamas, curled up on the massive mattress that makes him look small.

Once he's put Leo to bed, Nick heads for the hallway. I hurry after him, like a trained dog on a leash. I wince at the unflattering comparison as soon as I think it, but it's annoyingly accurate right now.

As soon as the door to Leo's room is closed, I whirl on him, intent on getting answers.

Once again, Nick beats me to speaking. "You and Leo are safe here. Get some sleep, and we can talk tomorrow." He nods toward the door we're almost to, leading into the room next to Leo's.

I want to argue. Partially because capitulating feels like ceding the little control I have in this situation, accepting it's nonexistent. Mostly because I have so many questions—questions I've wanted answers to for years. Questions that landed me in this mess.

Nick doesn't wait around for a response or offer up a, *Sweet dreams*. He's gone in the length of time it takes my heavy eyelids to blink. Leaving me to walk into the guest room and wonder what the fuck I managed to get involved in. I'm almost relieved I'm too tired to panic about it.

CHAPTER TWELVE

NICK

A door slams upstairs, followed by a shout. Roman and Grigoriy glance at each other, then at the ceiling.

My hand finds its way into my pocket, tracing the edge of the lighter I always keep there. The metal is warm from my body heat and somewhat reassuring.

Another slam.

Another shout.

It's been like this all morning. I had breakfast brought up to Lyla and Leo first thing. American foods I specifically requested the chef prepare and haven't eaten since I lived in the States. But I've remained in my office ever since I woke from the few hours of sleep I managed to get, ensuring I won't run into either of my visitors.

Aside from my mother, no one besides me and the staff has spent the night here in nearly a decade. I keep an apartment in Moscow for female guests, preferring to keep the solitude and the security here sacred.

It's strange, hearing signs of life echo through the drafty halls. The staff stays silent and organized, working hard to stay out of my way. Based on the commotion upstairs, I'm confident the same won't be the case for Leo and Lyla.

"Bianchi didn't answer my call," I state.

"Shocking." Roman smirks. "Think it could have anything to do with the way two of his soldiers disappeared on the same day you were in town?"

I shoot him a glare that could freeze water. "I'm going to have to meet with him in person again."

Grigoriy raises both eyebrows. "That's risky. If you—"

"I wasn't asking. Bianchi will set off a shitstorm if he kills me, and he knows it."

"He can't afford to let murdering his men go unpunished either."

"Let me worry about that." And I *am* worried about it. It's one of the many things that kept me tossing and turning for most of the night.

Worry has been a constant companion of mine for years, more reliable than anyone or anything else. I've dealt with it well because I'm removed from it. They're my problems, but they've felt like someone else's. Like the *Pakhan*'s. This situation we're in now affects me directly and is tangled up in choices I made before being forced to step up to this role. There's no degree of separation from business.

"So…he's yours?"

I let Roman's question hang in the air long enough to gain substance. For it to feel like a living, breathing presence in the room.

That's when Lyla decides to burst into my office with the determination of a bull after a red flag.

Roman and Grigoriy jump to their feet, immediately on high alert. Interrupting a private meeting in my office is akin to a death wish.

I don't flinch. Just appraise her tangled hair and the clothes that are a size too large.

It's been eleven hours since we arrived at the compound. Honestly, I expected her to demand answers sooner.

Grigoriy glances between me and Lyla's annoyed expression.

Roman scoffs, looking at Lyla with a scowl that makes my temper flare. "You dare—"

"Don't finish that sentence," I instruct him. Leather creaks as I lean back in my chair. "Leave." I say the last word in English while looking at my men.

Lyla opens her mouth—to protest, I'm assuming. She shuts it as Roman and Grigoriy shuffle toward the door after exchanging an uneasy glance.

I'm certain there's been no shortage of gossip and speculation among the men since I returned from the States last night. There's the shock of me appearing to have a son—an eight-year-old American one at that. There's concern about how Leo might be used against me, how he could act as a powder keg in an already-uncertain situation.

They don't have anything to be concerned about.

Leo's existence has provided me with focus and purpose.

I've let my enemies flounder as of late. Accepted them as an irritation. An inconvenience.

I've stood on shaky ground with Bianchi for a while. Smiled at him across the table while fingering a trigger beneath it. Our truce is an uneasy one, to put it mildly.

But he's never been a threat—not until he sent men to Lyla's apartment. It doesn't matter that he did it out of curiosity. If he presses the issue or holds an unreasonable grudge, he'll die for that decision.

And then there's Dmitriy. My cousin who wants what is rightfully mine. He's a threat to Leo—because he'll see Leo as a threat to him. I have to stop putting off the inevitable and kill him.

I haven't been stalling the decision. Ever since the first warehouse was hit, I knew what had to happen. But I haven't been willing to exert the resources or risk the necessary men to make hunting him down a priority.

And it won't be a merciful death. It will be a harsh demonstration of what crossing me looks like. A warning that what I do to family is nothing in comparison to how I'd treat anyone else.

Lyla hasn't said a word since the door shut behind Grigoriy and Roman. She's staring at me like I'm a stranger. But with a burning intensity that speaks to familiarity.

I stand and walk over to the bar cart parked in the corner of the room. I direct a generous splash of vodka into a crystal tumbler, then glance at Lyla. "Want a drink?"

She approaches hesitantly, twisting the hem of the shirt that's too large on her. I wonder if it belongs to her *boyfriend*, then crush the thought.

"It's not even eight."

I drain the glass in one gulp, savoring the fiery burn as it trickles down my throat and sears my stomach. "I'll take that as a no."

Lyla takes another step closer. "Is it safe to leave now?"

There's hope in her voice. Naivete. It sparks a fresh slew of self-loathing inside of me.

My men are worried about having her and Leo here.

She doesn't want to be here.

And I—I don't know what the fuck to do or say.

I opt for honesty. "The world isn't a safe place, Lyla. Have you watched the news lately? Murders and robberies and wars and famine?" I fill my glass again. "I'm the *Pakhan* of the Morozov family. I work with a lot of important people. And I have a lot of powerful enemies. That means it will *never* be safe to leave."

Her face pales, the constellation of freckles on her cheeks mapped out as a stark contrast against white skin. She's dressed casually in a pair of jeans she's had to roll the waist of to keep up. Her hair is unbrushed and messy, and she's not wearing any makeup. She looks nothing like the dancers and models I've spent the past years fucking.

And when she bites her bottom lip, I have to turn away to will my erection away.

Lyla Peterson still affects me, and it's an unwelcome realization. I thought it was mostly teenage hormones and the thrill of freedom that made her so irresistible before. She was a little innocent, a lot jaded, and on a short list of people who I felt relaxed around.

She sinks down into the chair where Grigoriy was seated before, her fingers digging into the arms until they turn snow white. "But…those men who were in my building, aren't they…"

"They're dead. But they worked for someone who doesn't do his own dirty work. Someone who is very much alive. And even if he wasn't, there will *always* be other threats."

"What are you saying?"

I take a sip of vodka. "You know what I'm saying."

Lyla won't face me. Her eyes are fixed on the bookcase to the right, skimming over the embossed spines of Tolstoy and Pushkin. "You're in the mob."

"Bratva. There's a difference."

"I don't suppose that difference is *not* breaking the law or *not* killing people?"

I almost smile, but there's nothing amusing about the situation. "No."

Lyla exhales, and it comes out a little unsteady. "I think I will take that vodka actually."

She sounds defeated, her shoulders slumped and curved inward. The shirt she's wearing is by no means scandalous. It teeters on one shoulder, barely hanging on, but it's not showing anything. It's the memories of everything beneath that are torturing me.

I want to kiss her.

The thought strikes me suddenly as I splash some more vodka in a second glass. She's mad at me, and she has every right to be, and I want to know if she still makes that little whimper in her throat when I suck on her tongue.

I carry the tumbler over and hand it to her. Then, for the first time since I inherited this office, I take a seat on the side of the desk closer to the door.

Lyla downs the vodka like a single shot, making a face at the taste. Her expression looks like she just sucked on a lemon, and once again, I have to forcibly stop myself from smiling.

Usually, the only thing I have difficulty with is keeping my temper in check. Not containing rogue emotions, like amusement. Aside from the occasional conversation with Roman or Alex—usually vodka-fueled—no one in my life is comfortable with joking around with me.

It's so strange, being around Lyla again. Outside of my men, I don't spend enough time around anyone to learn their habits and memorize their cues.

Lyla is an exception. I memorized everything about her a long time ago and forgot far less than I thought. Looking at her is like studying a favorite painting in the dark. I don't need to be able to see the brushstrokes to know exactly what picture I'd be looking at if I turned on a light.

"Where's Leo?" I ask. I haven't heard a single *thud* since she entered my office.

"Upstairs, exploring." Her finger runs the rim of the glass. And I just know—I remember—that it's something she does when she's anxious.

"I'm glad he's making himself at home."

"He's *not* at home though." The edge to Lyla's voice could draw blood.

"He's half Russian."

"Interesting you say that. Considering how you never mentioned *you* were Russian."

I exhale, then lean forward, resting my elbows on my knees and looking down at the carpet. "I was six when I figured it out."

"Figured *what* out?" The edge hasn't dulled.

"Why grown men looked like they wanted to piss themselves around my father." Unconsciously, I trace the raised scar on my left palm. The one thing he left me, aside from the lighter in my pocket and a healthy fear of failure. "He had a reputation, and he earned it. My older brother took the brunt of it."

I hesitate, deliberating on how much to share. There's a glossy version of me taking over for my father, and then there's the rough and ragged truth.

"Does he not still?" Lyla asks. There's plenty of anger lingering in her voice, but it's mixed with some curiosity now too.

I shake my head. "No. Nine years ago, my father and brothers were murdered. It's why I left Philadelphia. I had a duty to take over everything here. To...avenge their deaths."

Lyla's pointer finger keeps running the rim of the glass. Over and over again. The repetition is oddly soothing in a way.

"Want more vodka?"

She doesn't answer. "I'm sorry about your father. And your brothers."

I clear my throat. The air in here feels like it's solidifying, slowly tightening around us. I don't want anyone's pity, but her sympathy feels nice. She's acknowledging the death of my father, not the former *Pakhan.* The latter was the root of all the other condolences I received.

"Thank you."

"Are…are the people who killed your family the ones who were in my apartment building?"

It would be easier to say yes.

An enemy is an enemy. She doesn't need the specifics. But I decide to share them anyway.

"No. They were punished a long time ago. I was in New York on business when Alex called."

"*Illegal* business?" Her tone is dry. And judgmental.

I smirk. "Legal actually. I just invested in some commercial real estate. There were a bunch of meetings about plans and building permits."

"I'm surprised you don't have people who handle all of that for you."

I do. And I don't think she meant it as a compliment, but I take it as one. I've never felt the need to impress a woman. My title—or rather, the wealth and power associated with it—has always taken care of that. But I like that Lyla has noticed where I sit on the hierarchy despite knowing next to nothing about the Bratva. Like it more than I should.

"I felt like a visit," I say. "When Alex called, I was shocked, obviously. I wanted to travel to Philly, decide what to do, and the easiest way to explain that to my men was to arrange a meeting with Luca Bianchi. He's a *capo*—part of the Italian mob. I should have anticipated he'd have men tailing me as soon as I crossed the city limits, but I didn't. The fact that I stopped at your building… it drew their attention."

"So, they weren't after me and Leo? They didn't know you're his father?"

I decide to be honest. Lyla is tougher than her slender frame and delicate features suggest. "If Bianchi knew my son lived there, he would have sent a couple dozen men. So, no."

"And you had them killed anyway." Accusation saturates her voice. Followed by more judgment.

"They might have kidnapped you out of curiosity. That wasn't a risk I was willing to take."

Lyla bites her bottom lip and looks away, clearly torn between chastising me further and agreeing Leo's safety is paramount.

"There's something else," I admit.

Her wide, worried eyes flash back to mine. "What?"

"About a year ago, my cousin defected. Well, first, he tried to kill me, and *then* he left."

I attempt to inject some humor into my voice. But like most of my life, there's really nothing funny about it.

Lyla's eyes are wide enough to see every emotion reflected in them. There's fear and anxiety, both of which I expected to see. But her eyes dart down, so quickly, I almost miss it. Almost like...she's looking me over and checking I'm okay. Like some of that fear and anxiety might be about *me*.

Plenty of people care whether I live or die. But few of them care about my safety, just the consequences if I'm killed.

"Were you hurt?" Lyla asks quietly.

"No, but other people were. Dmitriy messed the timing up." I exhale, recalling the screams and smoke. The smell of burning flesh and the realization someone I used to protect was showing their appreciation by trying to kill me. "We've been playing a game of cat and mouse ever since. He'll pop up now and again. Hit a warehouse or kill a supplier and then disappear. Lately, he's gotten bolder. He's losing patience."

"What does he want?" Lyla asks.

I hear the curiosity in her voice, even as she tries to hide it. That's the thing about Lyla. Part of what drew me to her probably. She's seen darkness. Seen ugliness. And ran from it, as most rational people would. I didn't run, but I asked for a respite that ended with me getting pulled in deeper than before. I had no choice but to face my past. I don't think Lyla has ever acknowledged how those experiences leave a stamp on your soul. She's been too busy running.

"He wants to be *Pakhan*," I reply. "His father was my father's only sibling. Blood matters."

"And you don't want him to be *Pakhan*?"

"It doesn't matter what I want. Or what he wants. It's my birthright, and this isn't a democracy."

"So, the only way he'd become *Pakhan* is if he kills you?" Lyla is fiddling with the rose charm around her neck now—another nervous habit I remember. The necklace was a gift from her mother.

"Dmitriy knows he'll never be *Pakhan*. There's a clear order of succession to avoid this exact situation. He convinced a few men to leave with him, but the rest remain loyal to me. Even if he manages to kill me and tries to take over, they'll turn on him." I sigh. "Especially now."

Lyla's brow furrows. "What do you mean, especially now?"

"*Blood matters*, Lyla. Dmitriy and I were the only two living Morozovs."

"Is your mother not alive?"

"She is. But she's a Morozov by marriage, not by blood. And women aren't considered eligible to be *Pakhans*. Leo…is."

Anger flashes across her face like a strike of lightning. "If you think that—"

"I *don't*, Lyla," I snap. I'm under no delusions she'll want our son involved in any of this. "Bianchi won't be easy to deal with, but I'll make sure we have an understanding when it comes to you and Leo returning to the States. And Dmitriy…I need to take care of him."

Lyla drops the charm, leans back, and blows out a frustrated sigh. "What are you saying, Nick? How long will we be stuck here?"

I exhale. "I'm sorry—truly, I am—that this is all happening. But I need some time. To smooth things over with Bianchi. To deal with Dmitriy. And the safest place for you and Leo is here."

"How long?" she bites out, not acknowledging my apology.

"I don't know."

Her exhale is long and heavy.

"I have men packing up your apartment. All your clothing and personal items will arrive tomorrow. And Leo has been enrolled at a private school in the city."

"Aren't you efficient?" Her tone is sarcastic. "What about my apartment? My car? My jobs?"

It's news to me that she has more than one, but I don't mention that right now. "It'll be best if you and Leo totally disappear for the time being."

"What about the men in the hallway? I'll be wanted for questioning by the police."

"They were taken care of. The police won't be involved." Assuming Callahan did his job, there won't be a drop of blood to test.

She considers that, then says almost triumphantly, "Leo's school will call them. So will my office."

I bury a smirk. It's oddly endearing—how little power she thinks I have. How much faith she has in the average person to do the right thing when it doesn't directly affect them. How she thinks a shiny badge means you can't be bought.

Everyone has a price.

"I'll handle it. Once I've dealt with Dmitriy and Bianchi, you'll be able to go back to Philadelphia. I promise."

Twin lines form between her eyes as she studies me with suspicion. "I thought you 'don't make' promises."

I told her that the first night we met. Then, I knew we were temporary. I knew the girl who was oblivious to every guy in the kitchen checking her out and who gnawed on her bottom lip when she was nervous deserved assurances from someone with something concrete to offer her.

"Because I don't make promises I can't keep."

There's no keeping Lyla out of anything now. There's just minimizing risks while doing my damnedest to keep her and Leo safe.

Lyla sighs. "I don't have a choice, do I?"

"You do. It's just not the one you want to make."

She looks away, back at the bookshelf. "I was…dating someone. And I have a best friend. Her son is the same age as Leo. They're best friends. I can't…they won't just call the police. They'll worry too. Can't I call? Or email? Or—"

"That can all be tracked or traced. But…" I sigh. "I have a private line you can use for a *brief* call. And if you want to write them something, I'll have Alex deliver it."

"He's still there?"

"Yes. His residency lasts a few more months."

"I thought he said he works for you. That he's involved in… all this."

"He is."

Her finger picks up the path around the rim again.

I'm tempted to offer her more than alcohol. An *everything will be okay* at least. But I'm not sure if she wants any assurances from me. It's certainly not a role I'm comfortable in. I dish out orders, not hugs.

Lyla and I are on shaky ground. It's obvious in how she's gnawed on her bottom lip for most of this conversation. In the anxious circles her finger is tracing around the rim of the glass.

I'm not impervious to the uncertainty between us either.

I'm just not used to considering other people's feelings. To being questioned. No one else in my life expects it or would dare attempt it.

We sit in silence for a minute. I'm tempted to pour myself another drink, more alcohol intake than I usually allow during the day. All because of the foreign feeling curling in my gut as I consider how to frame my next request.

I'm nervous.

"I want Leo to know who I am," I finally state. "To know I'm his father."

The shake of Lyla's head is predictable. It also pisses me off. "So you can disappear again as soon as this mess is sorted out? How is that fair to him, Nick?"

"I'm not going to *disappear*," I bite out. "He's my kid too, Lyla."

"You don't know his birthday, Nick. How many hours I was in labor with him for. His favorite color—his favorite *anything*. All you are in his life is a liability."

I suppress a flinch. "I didn't know he *existed* until two days ago, Lyla. Obviously, I'm playing catch-up."

"So, your plan now is to…what? Send a birthday gift every year once you learn the date?"

My jaw clenches. I have to work to unlock it before answering. "Leo is old enough to decide what role he wants me to play in his life. All I'm asking is that he knows it's an option."

And I am—asking.

For the first time in years, there is something I want that feels out of reach.

I know barely anything about kids, and my own father was a shitty example of what parenting should entail. My mother wasn't much better. Fatherhood has always been a distant, unappealing prospect.

I have no idea what me as a dad would look like. But I know it's something I want. I've known that since Alex said there was no doubt about paternity, and it solidified when I saw Leo for the first time.

"What's an option, Nick? You're going to show up whenever there's a lull in criminal activity and take him bowling? Kids aren't a partial commitment. You're in, or you're out."

"You grew up without a dad. Is that what you want for him?"

"I didn't have any other choice," Lyla snaps. "You disappeared."

"Why did you tell Alex?" I fire back.

"I—what?"

"If you don't want me to be involved in Leo's life, why did you tell Alex about him?"

"It—I didn't know who you were then!"

"Who I am?" My voice has turned dangerous, a tone grown men flinch from, but Lyla is oblivious.

"I didn't know about all this!" She sets her glass down and waves an arm around. "The blood and the guns and the enemies and the politics. Part of parenting is putting your child's interests above your own. You think fearing for his life every day is how Leo should grow up?"

I stand, her words an ugly reminder of my failure yesterday. Bianchi got men with guns within feet of my son. "That is *not* how he will grow up."

Lyla stands too, her chest heaving and her eyes blazing. "You've put us in the middle of a pissing match—"

Roman bursts into my office. He glances at Lyla, apologizes for interrupting, and then tells me Dmitriy is on the phone.

Lyla glances between us, not understanding the rapid flurry of Russian.

I sigh. "I have to take a phone call."

"Now?" Her voice is incredulous.

"It's important, Lyla."

"This is a perfect example of why you should have stayed the hell away from us, Nick. You say you want to be a part of Leo's life, but you can't even spare ten minutes to have a conversation. What am I supposed to tell Leo when he asks me how long we'll be here? Why we're here?"

"You could start by telling him I'm his father."

"You haven't earned that title," she snaps.

"I don't have to *earn* a goddamn thing. I'm his father, and all I've done since I found out he existed is protect him."

"From yourself! From choices you made!"

My jaw works furiously as she stalks past Roman without another word. He's trying valiantly to pretend like, despite being feet away, he didn't catch a word of what was just said. Then, he follows her out of the office.

I pour another glass of vodka, then answer the phone.

"Morozov." It's how I typically answer the phone, but I add extra emphasis just to irk Dmitriy.

"Wouldn't have guessed you have a thing for American girls, cousin."

Any hope that Dmitriy is slipping evaporates. I know he pays spies around the city and he'd learn I was back. I knew there was a possibility he'd also find out I returned with company.

"Or for single moms."

"What do you want, Dmitriy?" My fingers clench the glass with enough force, I could break it, but my voice is measured and cool.

I shouldn't have taken his call. It's only going to darken my mood.

"To congratulate you, of course, *nana*. What do you think Igor would say if he knew his first grandchild was a half American bastard? Would he say anything? Or would he just kill the boy and force you to fuck a Russian?"

"I don't waste time thinking about the dead," I lie.

Truthfully, I know Dmitriy is probably right. My father would have authorized hunting down Leo and Lyla and put bullets in their heads. Would have seen them not as people, not as family, but as stains on the Morozov reputation. As liabilities. As threats.

I would do anything to have my brothers back, not the least because it would take the pressure off me. But most of the time, I'm fucking relieved my father is dead. For many small reasons—and this big one.

I can feel Dmitriy's irritation through the phone. He was obviously hoping the mention of my father would hit harder. But I've always been better at schooling my emotions than he is. One of our *many* differences.

"You have weaknesses now, Nikolaj," he tells me. "We both know what will happen if you don't claim this child. And we both know that doing so will have consequences. Pavel might be incompetent, but he's no idiot. A firstborn Popov was part of the deal you struck."

"A deal you have no role in," I remind him.

"For now. He might reconsider."

"He won't," I reply. "You fucked up, cousin. And the worst part is, you know you did. Don't you? The money you stole is drying up. The men you made promises to haven't seen a promotion. You bet on a losing horse because your damn pride couldn't accept I was first in line."

"It has nothing to do with *pride*." Dmitriy spits the last word. "You're too weak. Too soft for this life. And we both know it."

"You'll die for your betrayal, Dmitriy. It's why you ran in the first place, after you fucked up a simple assassination. It could have been merciful. Quick. Not anymore."

"He's a handsome boy, Nikolaj," Dmitriy taunts. "Looks a lot like his mother. She might be American, but at least she's a hot piece of ass. The things I'll do to it after shooting your son…" He clucks his tongue. Lets out a soulless, grating chuckle. If he ever had a soul, it's long gone.

The fear that runs through me is crippling.

Debilitating in a way I've never experienced before.

Threats are nothing new. They pass as pleasantries in my world. And they're not empty either. What happened to my father and brothers was proof of that. Ronan was only thirteen, but he was murdered like a man.

Growing up fast was a requirement, not a suggestion. So was vengeance for my father and brothers' deaths. A show of strength to protect my men. My mother. Me—the final remaining male heir.

The thought of Leo ever paying for my sins the way Ronan and Arytom paid for my father's runs my blood cold, trickling through my veins like icy water. The thought of Dmitriy ever touching Lyla—ever forcing her—makes me want to throw up. I wouldn't view vengeance as a chore then—a necessity to stay in power and stay alive myself.

I'd filet all the men responsible, not just him. Butcher them like livestock and enjoy their suffering. Bring them back to life and torture them all over again.

But I'm trying to lull Dmitriy into complacency. Ease him into brash decisions.

So, I don't tell him any of that.

"You know…" I pull the lighter I always carry out of my pocket and flick it to life, staring at the tiny orange flame as I harness my anger. Try to consolidate the roaring rage down to a small flicker. "Part of me thought this was a tantrum. An attempt to prove you aren't the spineless idiot your father was. I thought you must have some secret weapon, some play to make. But you've stalled for months. Threats without action. I'm finished, cousin. The next time we speak, it'll be your final words."

Dmitriy laughs. It's a heartless, grating sound. "Speaking of final words, say hello to Belyaev from me. I always admired his loyalty."

He hangs up.

"Roman!" I shout, capping the lighter with a *snap*.

He hurries into the room a second later.

"Send Antonov and Rogov to Belyaev's."

Roman swears. "Grigoriy just got a text from Anya. Mila called her this morning, worried because Belyaev never came home last night. What did Dmitriy say?"

I don't answer. I grab my phone and head for the door. "He shouldn't have been able to get to him."

Roman hurries after me, urgently tapping buttons on his phone. "They sent a box. It just appeared outside. Mila called it in."

I say nothing, just keep striding toward the front door. How long it takes us to get there won't matter anymore though.

Belyaev is dead.

I suspected it as soon as Dmitriy said his name. He's in an inferior position, and he's not an idiot. Dmitriy wouldn't have played a losing hand.

He's escalating.

His previous hits could have killed men, but didn't. He knows as well as I do that killing me will lose him favor. It might have earned him some grudging respect, considering everyone else who's attempted to is now six feet under.

But killing a member of the family—especially an older, respected man like Konstantin Belyaev—sends a clear message. I'm not sure if it's a response to Leo's existence or if he's simply losing patience.

Either way, it heightens tensions to a new degree.

Either way, it means this needs to end.

He has nothing to lose.

But I do.

CHAPTER THIRTEEN

LYLA

Each inhale feels like a knife to the lungs. The cold here is sharp and extreme. Impossible to ignore.

In some ways, it's exactly what I was hoping for when I left the warm house. The huff of my breath and the pain of each breath remind me I'm alive. Force me to focus on nothing else besides the cold air and the struggle of my body to stay warm.

In others, it's a staggering visual reminder that I'm entirely alone here. At least the sprawling metropolis of Philadelphia provided the flimsy illusion of company. Here, snow-covered ground stretches endlessly in every direction.

My companion today is just as silent as yesterday's was. I think his name is Ivan, but I'm not sure. It's impossible to keep track of the constant flow of people in and out of Nick's estate. It feels more like living on a military base than staying in someone's home.

Nick hasn't limited my movements in any way. I have the freedom to go anywhere in the house I want and to explore the grounds as well. Nothing is off-limits.

All of the personal items from my apartment arrived, neatly

arranged in boxes, just as Nick said they would. I've hardly unpacked, holding on to hope this is all temporary. But it's been a week with no indication we'll be leaving anytime soon.

I've barely spoken to Nick since I confronted him in his office. He's always distracted and busy. The constant flow of traffic has been mostly in and out of his office, where intense conversations take place. They're always in Russian, so even when I try to eavesdrop, I can't. I've tried to pick up on key words to search on the fancy encrypted phone that was delivered to my room the second day here, but I can't get the spelling right. Unless Nick decides to get chatty, I'm oblivious.

The only times I've left the property since arriving is to ride with Leo on the trip to and from his new school.

I could leave more often, but I don't know where I would go. When we were in Philadelphia, I'd go to work and to Leo's school and grocery shopping essentially.

I'm not working, and all my meals are prepared for me now. I have nothing but free time and nothing to do. No friends to talk to. The brief calls to Michael, June, my work, and Leo's school, under the watchful eyes of two of Nick's men, were more stressful than comforting.

As expected, the conversation with June was the most difficult. She's the closest friend I've ever had, one of the few people on the planet I've ever entrusted with Leo. And I know she's already experienced more than her fair share of loss and tragedy.

That's how life often works in my experience. Life likes to strike once and then pummel away until there's hardly anything besides devastation left.

I told her I'd left to care for a sick relative overseas. That I hoped I'd be back soon and would call her once I was. Then, I claimed to be borrowing a phone running low on international minutes and hung up.

I'm not sure if international minutes are even a thing.

I left voice mails for Leo's school and at the law firm, both of which were closed. I forgot about the time difference. On both answering machines, I parroted the line about a sick relative. I'll have to find a new job, I'm sure, but that's nothing I can do anything about until I'm back.

Breaking up with Michael was surprisingly easy. Embarrassingly easy almost after dating for two months. I thought my feelings were stronger toward him than just…like. Maybe I was too busy with the rest of my life to give it enough notice. Maybe I forgot what it feels like to have strong feelings for someone. To notice when they're not in the room and feel a fizziness when they are around.

My memories aren't hazy when it comes to Nick. I clung to them, especially after I found out I was pregnant. I wanted…*something* to be able to tell Leo when he was older.

And I wanted to feel less alone.

My few friends in Philadelphia were all through UPenn. I dropped out at the end of freshman year. My scholarship paid my tuition, but I was already struggling to pay my other living expenses when I learned I was pregnant. There was no way I could afford to continue going to class and also have a baby.

I remember everything that happened between me and Nick. But I forgot—or blocked out—how I feel around him.

That I notice when he's not in the room and I react when he is.

And I can tell myself it's because things were left unresolved between us. Because there's resentment and anger about how he left and how he reappeared. Because his decisions are currently determining my life in ways I don't appreciate.

But I think, beneath it all, there's something else.

Something I'm scared to face and terrified to name.

Something that endures over time and distance and uncertainty.

Puffs of air leave my mouth as I stare out at the unforgiving landscape, watching the tiny clouds dissipate into nothing. Up until last week, I'd never left the United States. Now, I'm thousands and thousands of miles away from any familiarity. Dropped in the middle of an arctic wasteland.

It's beautiful here. I'm not too bitter to admit that.

I only got a glimpse of Moscow when we arrived. But as someone who's almost exclusively lived in cities, there's something about looking around and seeing absolutely nothing that I thought I would hate but have come to crave. My walks outside have become more and more frequent despite the freezing temperatures.

It's the one way I have to escape the mess in my head. While I'm out here, the world looks big and peaceful, and my problems seem solvable and small.

Exercise is one of those things that fell by the wayside the past few years. In high school, I loved running. I'd join all the track and cross-country practices but miss all the meets so I could work shifts at the local diner.

Running lately would require waking up even earlier or going out after dark. Either before or after the busy shuffle of getting Leo to and from school and me getting to and from work, mixed in with errands and meals.

It would have eaten into my meager free time and required being out alone at unreasonable hours. Not only would that put my own safety at risk, but it also fed into my greatest fear—leaving Leo alone.

At least that's not something I have to worry about any longer.

The frozen tundra crunching beneath my boots isn't conducive to running. Neither is the heavy parka I'm wearing.

But just being outside and moving simulate a similar experience. Feeding a freedom I didn't realize how badly I was craving until now.

I glance at my silent companion.

I go nowhere alone now. It seems unnecessary when I'm still on Nick's property, but I can't communicate with anyone to ask them to stay behind.

I've never objected to the security that travels with us to and from Leo's school. Those trips are spent holding my breath, waiting for something to go wrong. I hate them, but can't imagine sending Leo alone. And I smile the whole time, mostly in response to Leo's eagerness.

He's adapting to living here better than I am. Maybe because I've played this off as a fun and different experience, not a life-saving measure. It's difficult to think Nick is exaggerating about the level of threat, considering how his home security is set up.

One last inhale of cold air, and I turn to head back toward the house. The man follows me silently. There's not even a crunch of snow as he trails behind. It's eerie.

About ten minutes later, we reach the whiskey-colored front door. The wind has picked up, blowing strands of hair that have escaped my ponytail across my face.

Walking inside the spacious hall feels like opening an oven door. There's a whoosh of warm air that replaces the cold, the temperature exacerbated by the two extremes.

I shed the heavy coat I'm wearing quickly and step toward the coatrack. Before I can hang it up, a maid appears. I'm not sure how many people work here, but I have yet to see the same person twice.

"Thank you," I say.

She nods and gives me a tentative smile before shuffling off with the coat.

That's all I can get out of anyone. Polite nods and small shrugs. A week of it, and I feel like I'm slowly losing my mind.

Nick's English is flawless. There's not even a hint of an accent. I have a hard time believing none of his staff understands a word of it. Grigoriy and Viktor both spoke English as well, albeit with a thick accent that alluded to their native tongue. Grigoriy's was harsher than Viktor's. But I haven't seen either of them in days, and none of the other stoic men who I've seen come or go have spoken a word to me. Including the one who just accompanied me outside, who's disappeared as quickly as he appeared when I was pulling on my coat.

Everyone seems to pay attention to me to anticipate what I'll do. Whether it's walking outside or hanging up my coat.

It's unsettling. I'm used to doing everything myself. To being alone, aside from Leo.

I head upstairs, trailing my palm along the wooden banister that runs the length of the stairs.

All the furnishings are elegant and extravagant. Lots of dark wood and oil paintings. Cream wallpaper. Runners cover most of the floors, woven in bold colors. Maroon and emerald and navy.

There aren't any family photos or plants anywhere. It doesn't feel like anyone lives here. More like I'm touring an old castle.

The rooms Leo and I are staying in feel more modern. Both have hardwood floors so dark, they look black, but the walls are off-white, adding some airiness to the space. They also both have attached bathrooms, which is a luxury in and of itself. Leo and I have always shared. Taking a shower without having Leo knock and say he has to pee is a novelty for me. There's even a bathtub.

I haven't taken a bath since I was a kid. Never had the time—or a clean tub. This one is scrubbed, so it practically sparkles, just like everything else in the house. Nothing is musty or dusty.

I shower in the spacious bathroom, then dress in jeans and a warm sweater. Slowly but surely, the wooden wardrobe has been stocked with more and more clothes.

It would be a relief, if not for the underlying message. If we were able to leave soon, more clothes wouldn't be appearing daily to supplement what was brought from our apartment.

Another nameless man is waiting by the front door when I make my way downstairs. He gives me a respectful nod as a different maid from earlier brings my coat back to me. I thank them both and head into the cold.

There's already a convoy of cars waiting. Three, just to escort us to and from the school. I have no idea how many men work for Nick, but based on how many unfamiliar faces I've seen, I'd say it's upward of a hundred.

I climb into the middle car, and we set off, rolling down the long driveway and through the massive gates that have already been opened in anticipation of our departure.

Everything here seems to run on some seamless internal schedule. All of our meals are always ready at the same times in the dining room. The cars are always waiting to make the trip to and from Leo's school, as if shuttling him has always been part of the routine. No one ever runs late or looks rattled. It's such a stark contrast from how my life used to be—harried and scattered and always having a million things to do.

The quiet hum of the radio and the low chatter of the two men in the front seat, discussing something, are the soundtrack to the drive.

I stare out the window at barren, white-coated trees and industrial-looking buildings until we reach Leo's school, which is located on the edge of the city. It has a sprawling campus with an intimidating brick facade.

A long line stretches the length of the school's circular driveway. A line we bypass. There's no hesitation and no honking before we pull up to the front like it's a reserved spot.

As soon as the car stops, I step outside, wrapping my arms around my waist as I peer through the throng of students for Leo. I feel out of place and young among the other mothers braving the cold, most of who are wearing heels and fur coats. Several of them cast me disapproving, haughty looks.

Leo appears after a couple of minutes, talking with a few other boys. He's wearing the same navy coat and red backpack I bought him at the beginning of the year. But he looks different. Older, maturer. I watch him interact with the three boys he's walking with, noticing the way Leo smiles and tilts his head as he listens.

The physical similarities to Nick are obvious. But it's his expression and posture that make their relationship look obvious right now. That make me feel extremely guilty for not telling him exactly whose house we're staying in for the time being. I've pushed away thoughts of my argument with Nick, and he hasn't brought the subject up.

But he was right about one thing—the main reason we're in this predicament is that I seized the chance to tell him about Leo.

It would be one thing if Nick posed a threat himself. But dubious decisions aside, I don't think he's a bad influence. I know he would never harm Leo. And as far as I can tell, this is all a possible overreaction to a fear that someone else might.

Nick could have left us in Philadelphia. He could be sending Leo to school with no security. Instead, Leo and I are constantly protected.

Leo breaks off from his small group and heads toward me. "Hi, Mom."

"Hi, sweetie. How was your day?"

"It was good."

"Good." I turn toward the car, eager to escape the cold and the prying eyes on us. And the persistent hum of fear, wondering if one of Nick's enemies will show up at any minute and launch an attack. "Let's go home."

The last word slips out without thought.

Leo doesn't correct me, which is almost worse. He nods along, like Nick's fortress *is* what he considers home now. The guilt expands, a heavy weight in my chest.

A flurry of Russian sounds behind me. I turn to see a smiling, smartly dressed woman. She glances at Leo and then looks back at me.

"Sorry," she says. *R*'s roll delicately, her accent sounding just as effortless as her Russian. "English is best, yes?"

I nod.

"I am Raisa Maximovna, the head of the school."

"Oh." I shake her offered hand.

"It is a pleasure to meet you."

There's a reverence—an awe—in her tone that makes me deeply uncomfortable. There's only one reason I can think of why a woman I've never met before would be looking at me with obvious respect, and it has nothing to do with me directly.

I glance at Leo, who's watching our interaction closely, then back to Raisa. "It's nice to meet you too."

"If there's ever anything you need—anything at all—please let me know." There's nothing effusive in her tone. Just serious.

"Uh, I will. Thanks."

"Of course." Raisa lets out a light, twinkling laugh. Once again, there's reverence.

"Okay then. Have a good afternoon."

"You too."

I wait, but she doesn't walk away. Raisa is looking at one of the men waiting to escort us the few feet to the car. Two more appear, one opening the rear door and the other answering a call and muttering on the phone.

I give her an awkward smile and turn, climbing into the car after Leo. The door shuts behind us, and I release a sigh of relief, happy to be away from prying eyes.

"How was your day?" I ask Leo.

Immediately, he starts talking a hundred miles a minute. I listen to Leo chatter about new friends and different subjects, torn between wanting to smile and cry.

Honestly, I thought he'd struggle here, adjusting to a new school and new classmates on top of being in an unfamiliar place. That he would be seen as an outsider, arriving in the middle of the school year with an American accent without knowing a word of Russian.

But my son is happy here. *Thriving* here.

I can't remember him ever talking about his school in Philadelphia with this level of excitement. Maybe because I was exhausted and overwhelmed—juggling two jobs and still stressed about money. Here, my only concern is Leo.

But I think there's more to it. Think of Nick's words. *"He's half Russian."*

Leo's new room here is the same size as our entire apartment in Philadelphia. It's hardly surprising he'd prefer it.

And for the first time in his life, he's living with both of his parents.

Not that he knows that.

Leo hasn't run out of things to tell me by the time we return to the estate. I should appreciate it. Far too soon, I'm sure he'll reach the teenage years, where dragging out a single sentence is a chore.

I'm happy Leo is happy. But I also resent it, and I can admit it to myself at least. It stings that he's so happy and that Nick's crimes don't make him appear to be an inferior parent.

"Nick!"

I stop pulling my jacket off in the front hall to watch Leo beam at Nick, who's talking with one of his men by the stairs.

There's no mistaking the excitement in Leo's voice. More excitement than when he was talking about his new teachers or the other students at his school, which was a high bar.

His obvious enthusiasm forms a fist of dread in my stomach at the prospect of telling Leo who Nick really is. Ethics aside, Nick has much more to offer Leo than I do. He has money, connections, clout. And I have no idea what Nick's real expectations are when it comes to Leo. Sure, he said he wants Leo to know who he is. But I have no clue what that would look like. Co-parenting on different continents? Sending Leo here in the summers and worrying what could happen?

Nick walks over to us. I focus on the maid who's appeared to take my coat while subtly eavesdropping on Nick asking Leo how his day was.

Leo is chattering away again, answering Nick's questions. I cross my arms and watch them interact, that stupid pang in my heart appearing again.

Seeing them together is pleasure and pain.

A dream and a nightmare.

Bittersweet.

And it sucks me straight into what-ifs.

"Can I, Mom?"

"Can you what?" I ask, glancing at Leo.

"Go with Nick."

I missed more of their conversation than I thought. "Go where?"

Leo looks to Nick since that's a detail he didn't ask, apparently. Another pang. He *wants* to go with Nick, wherever that might be.

"I have to take a trip to a training facility," Nick tells me.

"Training for what?"

He runs a thumb along his lower lip, and I try not to focus on how distracting it is. Every time I see Nick, I'm reminded of how attractive he is. How he's undeniably the best I've ever had in one clear respect. It's inconvenient yet irrefutable.

"Defense."

My eyes widen.

He's not *serious*, right? But there's no trace of teasing on his face.

"Leo, I need to talk to Nick for a minute. Go put your backpack in your room. And make your bed, please. You forgot to do it this morning."

"Mom..."

"*Now*, Leo."

He grimaces but complies.

Nick doesn't move or react. For some reason, he looks like he expected this.

As soon as Leo is up the stairs, I step closer. "What the fuck, Nick? *Defense*? This place is part of your criminal enterprise? And you want to bring Leo there?"

Nick has the audacity to look amused. "It's a *gym*, Lyla. I just have to pick up some paperwork."

"I don't want him involved in anything you are."

A muscle tics in Nick's jaw. "Yeah, you've made that *crystal* clear. It's taking a drive. I'm not suggesting I take him to a shooting range and teach him how to defend himself."

"*Of course* you're not taking him to a shooting range! He's *eight*, Nick."

"My father started training me when I was seven."

"You're not your father."

"No, but I am the *Pakhan*. And Leo is my only heir."

"He's not an heir; he's a *child*."

"He's also a target. Aside from me, he's the only living male Morozov with a rightful claim."

I feel the color drain from my face as it dawns on me all over again—how badly I've fucked up. "His last name is Peterson."

"He's my blood. That's all anyone will care about."

"You said we're safe here. That's the only reason I—"

"The estate is heavily guarded, but nowhere is impenetrable. There's no such thing as too careful, especially when it comes to Leo."

"I want to go home," I whisper.

Nick's expression softens, then hardens again as the words hang between us. "I won't stop you."

"I wouldn't leave without Leo." And without Leo, I won't leave at all, which he knows. Just like he knows I won't risk Leo's safety by taking him anywhere else.

"He's safest here," Nick says, reading my thoughts.

I release what's meant to be an unamused huff, but it comes out with an edge of hysteria.

"I wish I could erase every threat and you and Leo could be safe to do whatever you want. But that's not the way the world—my world—works. And you can hate it and resent me all you want; it won't change anything. I'm doing the *best I can*."

I exhale. "I know."

Footfalls pound the stairs as Leo rushes downstairs. His backpack is gone, but he's still wearing his coat. And a hopeful expression as he glances between me and Nick.

Nick opens his mouth to say something, then closes it. "I need to get going."

I sigh. Beneath the horrifying realizations that have filled the last few days, underneath it all is a guy I loved. A guy who knows intimate details about me. Details I entrusted him with. Reconciling the version of Nick I met in college with this guy standing in front of me has been easier than I thought it would be.

He's the moon, and I'm the tide.

I could fight the pull.

But I look at Leo's eager expression, and I know I won't.

"If anything happens to him—anything at all—I will *gut you.*"

Rather than smile at the whispered threat—or laugh, like Grigoriy did—Nick nods. "I know."

I glance at Leo and raise my voice. "You can go. Whatever Nick tells you to do, you do. Okay?"

Leo nods like a bobblehead.

"Okay. Have fun." Reluctantly, I glance at Nick, including him in the statement.

He wants to spend time with his son. I shouldn't resent that. I'm just not used to sharing Leo with anyone, let alone the one other person who might deserve to have a say in how he is raised.

There's something soft in Nick's expression as Leo rushes toward him. "Ready, kiddo?"

Leo does another bobblehead impression. "Bye, Mom!" he calls, already following Nick toward the door.

I watch as Leo glances over and mimics his father's posture, straightening his spine and squaring one shoulder. Nick looks over one shoulder at me, catching my stare.

He holds my gaze for a minute, and I hate how right this moment feels. How much the sight of him walking with our son feels like one I've been waiting to witness.

CHAPTER FOURTEEN

NICK

Leo's wide eyes take in everything as we drive. I want him to see my homeland—his by extension—even if he has no idea the scrubbed, snowy earth has any connection to him or his ancestors.

"What does this do?" Leo asks, pointing to the seat warmer.

"Heats the seats."

"Really? Can I try it?"

"Sure."

He presses the button, then looks at me. "I don't feel anything."

"Give it a minute."

"What's that?" He points to the parking brake next.

"Doesn't your mom's car have all this stuff?"

"I guess so." Leo pauses. "She doesn't let me ride up front though."

Fuck.

No wonder the kid looked so elated when we climbed in the car. My Huracan doesn't have a backseat, and it didn't even occur to me he should ride in one. This is the first time I've spent any time alone around my son, and I'm already messing up the dad thing.

I glance at Leo. "Our little secret."

He nods so seriously, I almost smile.

I'm pretty sure telling your kid to lie to his mother is also a parenting no-no. But Lyla already has plenty of doubts about me, and it's not like I've had time to research how to be a dad. The last time I was around an eight-year-old was when I was that age myself.

"How do you know my mom?"

I hesitate before answering. I doubt Lyla has told Leo anything about me, besides that we're "friends."

I don't want to lie to him, but too much truth could cause other problems. "We went to school together for a little while."

"You did?"

"Mmhmm."

"How old were you?"

"Older than you. College."

"And you were friends?"

Friends who fucked. "Yep."

Leo considers that for a minute. "How come you never visited?"

"Because I live here."

He seems to accept that explanation and drops the line of questioning about Lyla. "Where are we going?"

"Do you remember the men who flew here with us?"

"Yes."

"They work for me."

"*All* of them?"

"Yes."

"Wow."

At that, I smile. His obvious awe feels special.

"Sometimes, we end up in dangerous situations. They all train to prepare for those in a special building."

I have no idea how to explain the Bratva to a kid. My father never sat me down and said a word. I figured out exactly what my family did by observing. By taking in bloody shirts and the way everyone cowered away from him and figuring out what it meant for the trajectory of my life.

And I don't know how much to share with Leo. How much will help or harm.

"Like what happened in the apartment?"

"Yes, exactly like that."

"What if that happens again?"

"It won't."

I park the car outside the industrial warehouse. Leo clambers out of the vehicle as soon as the doors unlock, eyes wide as he takes in the long, low building. There's not much else to see. We're in a remote, abandoned area for a reason.

"Come on."

Leo follows me inside. I grasp his shoulder and steer him along the far wall, ignoring the curious looks from the men scattered around. Some are huddled, some training. A small group is gathered around a card table, playing poker. All staring.

Me showing up here with Leo is a straight response to the speculation that's littered the past week. I'm not in the habit of huddling my men around for heartfelt speeches. I give orders and expect them to be followed. Effective, respected leaders don't offer explanations.

I didn't consult anyone about a potential alignment with the Popov Bratva. If I decide to marry Anastasia Popov, it will be my decision and my decision only.

But I know a choice to stay silent when it comes to Leo will carry a different connotation. Children conceived outside marriage aren't uncommon in the Bratva. What is common is sweeping them under the rug, usually to protect "legitimate" children.

Bringing Leo here is a clear statement.

I'm not ashamed of my son. I'm showing him off.

Roman climbs out of the boxing ring situated in the center of the open layout with a wide smile on his face, wiping sweat away with a towel and then slinging it over one shoulder.

He greets me in Russian, then gives Leo a wave.

Leo waves back, but I feel his shoulder tense beneath my hand. He shifts a half step closer to me, and my chest expands with an unfamiliar warmth.

Roman is a stranger, and I'm barely not one. But it's something. My own father was about as cuddly as a lump of coal. His only capacity when it came to affection was tepid praise for tasks performed to his satisfaction.

That's not the relationship I want with Leo when—if—he finds out I'm his father.

"Leo, this is Roman."

Leo nods, looking serious. Like he somehow realizes he's being scrutinized as a possible future *Pakhan*, not just as an eight-year-old child. "It's nice to meet you."

"You too, Leo."

Most people would describe Roman's expression as impassive. But I've known him since we were younger than Leo is now. I catch the surprise that flashes on his face.

He wasn't part of the crew that traveled to New York with me on what was meant to be a quick, easy trip. Roman has heard about Leo. But this is the first time he's seeing him in person. The first time he's seeing the resemblance between me and my son.

"Good match?" I ask, nodding toward the ring.

A broad grin stretches Roman's face. "Ask Slava. His face isn't feeling too great."

I roll my eyes. Friendly competition can be a foreign concept for Roman to comprehend.

"You were fighting?" Leo pipes in with.

Roman's eyes widen before he looks to me. He knows as little about kids as I do.

"Training," I answer. "Remember what I told you on the drive here?"

Leo nods. "Do you train here, Nick?"

Something grates inside of me every time Leo calls me Nick. It reminds me of Lyla since she's the only other person who calls me by the nickname I adopted during my brief time as an American student.

It also drives home the fact that he doesn't know he should be calling me something else. I can understand Lyla's decision not to tell Leo I'm his father. Respect it even, knowing it's coming from a place of love and protectiveness.

I know I'll never have a traditional role in Leo's life.

Lyla has made no secret that she's eager to return to the States as soon as possible, and I can't pack up and leave Russia.

She's worried I'll up and disappear the same way I did before, but she doesn't understand that's not an option.

Pandora can't be shoved back into her box. Exactly what I was trying to shield Lyla from—an association with me—has been shot to hell. She and Leo might be facing threats from my enemies now, but it's nothing in comparison to the risks if I walked away.

"Nick?" Leo prompts.

"I do," I say. "Want to see?"

The question surprises everyone in the immediate vicinity. Especially Roman.

As a general rule, I don't get into the ring.

I train plenty, but seeing your leader knocked on his ass isn't great for morale. I'm a skilled fighter. So is every man in my employ.

After seeing the excitement on Leo's face, I know I won't be losing.

"Yes!"

Roman arches a brow but climbs back into the ring. I toe off my boots and shrug off my jacket. I take my time rolling up the sleeves as I approach the ring and swing over the ropes.

"Sure you want to get your ass kicked in front of your kid?" Roman teases.

"He doesn't know."

Another eyebrow arch. "He doesn't?"

I shake my head and adopt an offensive stance.

Roman is wearing gloves, but I don't bother. He's shorter and stockier than I am.

His first punch is hesitant, feeling out how seriously I'm going to take this. I slip easily, avoiding the hit and sweeping his feet out from under him with a well-placed kick.

I don't miss the higher-pitched shout that echoes through the massive space along with the murmurs from the men watching.

Roman grimaces when he stands. "Fucking knew this was a shit idea."

I land an uppercut to his jaw. He staggers but stays upright.

Fighting a friend is an art form. It's walking a fine line before incapacitation turns to injury.

There's a determined set to Roman's jaw as he comes at me again. His pride is on the line, but so is mine.

I mirror his movements, rolling and then blocking his next maneuver.

Once he attempts an attack, I let him draw closer. Then, I use his momentum against him, darting to the side and behind. Before he can react, my arm is around his neck, choking his windpipe.

Roman splutters and kicks for a few seconds before he goes limp with defeat. "Fuck," he growls.

I grin and release him. He coughs twice, standing and glaring.

I glance out of the ring. We've captured the attention of everyone in the warehouse, but I'm only focused on one person. I climb out of the ring and return to Leo's side. His eyes are wide, swallowing half of his face.

I'm a little worried he's freaked out, but as soon as I'm next to him, he asks eagerly, "Can you show me how to do that?"

I ruffle his hair. "We can start with a few practice punches," I say. Then, I reconsider whether most children should be taught fighting. "But don't…you know you don't, uh—violence isn't—"

Roman snorts from his spot a few feet away before he sips some water.

"Let's head into my office," I say, abandoning the ironic *violence isn't the answer* speech.

"All right," Leo agrees happily and then follows me.

I might be fucking up the father thing, but it's also hard to imagine *not* being one now.

CHAPTER FIFTEEN

NICK

Roman stomps on the butt of his cigarette, then glances at me for the sixth time in fewer minutes. I keep my gaze on the shipment being unloaded and the chill slowly saturating my bones.

The air smells like snow.

Viktor ambles over, the little of his face not covered by a cap or beard ruddy from the cold.

"They short?" I ask.

He shakes his head.

Roman deflates. "*Blyad.*"

Viktor smiles at his obvious disappointment, then glances at me. "Fyodor is fond of your boy. Says he's very bright."

Something in my chest swells. Zhukovka Lyceum is the most exclusive private primary school in the country. All of my *bratoks* with families send their children there. Enrolling Leo there was an obvious choice.

"Does this mean we're discussing it?" Roman drawls.

"No," I snap, then walk away.

Until I sort out Leo's and Lyla's safety along with my ongoing role in their lives—which is looking as equally difficult as eliminating threats—I'm not going to be entertaining conversations about my son.

My Huracan is parked exactly where I left it, the six men stationed around it alert and aware. I nod at them and climb inside.

Leo jerks his hand away from the car controls he was fiddling with as I settle behind the wheel. I've never used the heated seats feature. But he turned mine on, and it's not the worst thing I've ever experienced. Warm leather instead of ice cold.

"Sorry that took so long," I tell him. The apology feels clunky in my mouth. Unfamiliar.

Leo doesn't look annoyed. I'm guessing Lyla will be another story.

"Nick?"

"Yeah?" My reply is absentminded, wondering how she'll react to us arriving back much later than I planned.

"Are you my dad?"

Any thoughts stutter to a stop. This is a moment I've imagined ever since Alex called me. I've hoped for it and dreaded it.

I don't know what I have to offer Leo.

The fact that I *am* a father is still a novelty to me.

Most people have months to get used to the idea of becoming a parent. They meet their children as babies who can't walk or talk.

Leo is a fully formed person. He's smart—smart enough to figure out what I never told him. It doesn't really matter how he found out. If it was a kid gossiping at school or if he overheard some of the men talking. Me having a child is not a tiny, inconsequential revelation—for a whole host of reasons.

Or maybe he's figured out we're related the same way everyone else seems to have—by seeing the similarities.

I won't lie to him, not when I'm not sure it's in his best interest. "Yes."

Leo nods, like the answer was expected. Like it wasn't really a question, more of a test. A challenge tossed out to see how I'd react. It's exactly what I would have done as a kid, using shock value and secret knowledge to establish if someone can be trusted, and I'm struck all over again by how much he reminds me of myself despite the fact we've only spent a sum total of a few hours together.

"Are you okay with that?"

I wish I could take the question back as soon as it's spoken. What if he says no? What if he considered the tool Lyla was dating to be his father?

"Yeah," Leo answers after some of the tensest seconds of my life. Quietly, he adds, "I've always wanted a dad."

An iron fist squeezes around my heart. There's a line of cars parked behind mine, all waiting for me to leave. Snowflakes have begun to fall, melting against the windshield and sticking to the frozen ground.

But I don't shift into drive yet. I focus on my son. "I didn't know you existed, Leo. If I had, I would have come to meet you sooner. There's nothing I want more in this world than to know you. It's important that you know that, okay?"

"Why didn't you know about me?"

I tap my fingers against the steering wheel. "Um, I didn't know your mom for very long. By the time she knew you were coming, I'd already come back here. We didn't stay in touch. She had no way to tell me about you for a long time."

"What about when we go back home? You'll stay here?"

"Yes."

"I don't want to leave. I like it here."

"We don't always get to do what we want, Leo," I tell him

gently. "But it won't be like before. You and I can talk on the phone and visit."

My son looks up at me with wide, worried eyes. "Do you promise?"

As a general rule, I hate making promises. Being the *Pakhan* isn't about accountability. It's about power and control. I'm not obligated to advance anyone's agenda besides my own.

But I look at my son, and I know, even before the words leave my mouth, what I'll say.

"I promise."

CHAPTER SIXTEEN

LYLA

It started snowing a while ago. I'm not sure exactly how long it's been. Watching the flakes fall feels a lot like all of my time in Russia has seemed—suspended in space.

I'm so far from who I used to be. The only facet of my identity that's remained the same is being Leo's mom.

I don't go to work.

I'm not in a relationship.

Other people cook and clean for me.

All I do is take up space in this big, empty house.

My foot starts to cramp. I shift, rubbing my toes against the velvet upholstery of the chair my legs are flung across.

After a productive evening, spent refolding my sweaters and eating dinner alone, I ended up in the living room.

My only company is a bottle of wine I stole from the dining room after eating. Usually, I'd be upstairs by now, helping Leo with his homework and getting him ready for bed. Then, I'll read or watch television before falling asleep.

A predictable, boring routine Nick eviscerated with his invitation to Leo.

I cast an anxious look at the clock and then drink more wine.

Five hours.

That's how long Nick and Leo have been gone for. Every second that ticks by feels like an eternity. Of waiting and wondering and worrying.

So, I've settled for drinking and watching the flakes of snow drift down from the sky. A fire crackles in the stone fireplace, each occasional *snap* of burning wood making my pulse jolt.

I lose track of how much more time passes before I hear the click of the front door opening.

I stand and rush toward the hallway, my head hazy from the sudden motion and the wine.

Nick stands in the entryway, murmuring quietly to one of the butlers. The front door is open, a line of cars pulled up outside. Bright headlights illuminate the path of the falling snow and backlight Nick.

He looks at me as soon as I walk into the entryway.

I wrap the sweater I'm wearing more tightly around my waist, buffering myself against the cold air rushing inside. And against the sight of seeing Leo fast asleep in his father's arms for the second time.

Leo grew too tall and heavy for me to easily carry years ago, but Nick doesn't look the least bit winded. He looks strong and capable as he passes me and heads up the stairs.

I stand still, debating whether to follow them or not. Eventually, I give the butler a small smile and then retreat into the living room, curling back up on the couch and sipping more wine.

Leo is home, safe and unharmed.

The fire feels a little warmer. The wine a little stronger.

When Nick walks into the living room a few minutes later, I *feel* it. Without looking away from the burning grate, I know he's walking closer. There's a soft clink as he picks up the wine bottle and sets it back down.

"Sorry, I shouldn't have helped myself."

He takes a seat in the armchair by the fire. "Yes, you should have. What's mine is yours."

I huff an uncomfortable laugh. "We're not married."

And I don't want your blood money.

I think it; I don't say it. Things between us are tense enough as it is. And I'm *already* taking it, technically. I'm not paying rent. Not chipping in on the food bill. I can only imagine how much Leo's school costs based on the fancy exterior.

"We have a child together. That's a more permanent commitment than marriage."

I clear my throat. Nick saying, "*We have a child together*," while we sit in front of a cozy fire warms my insides in a whole different way. One I struggle to ignore.

I shift uncomfortably. Sip some wine. "A commitment to Leo, not to each other. I'll pay you back for it."

Nick smiles as he leans back in the armchair. The fire's glow plays with the harsher angles of his face. Softens and smooths them. "Not necessary. It's a Domaine de la Romanee-Conti Romanee-Conti Grand Cru from Cote de Nuits, France." The French rolls off his tongue as smoothly as Russian and English do.

I glance at the cursive letting on the label. Now that I look closely, it appears embossed. "So...expensive?"

Nick shrugs as he studies the flames dancing in the fireplace. "It's meant to be drunk."

Very expensive then.

I sip some more. "It's good," I admit.

He chuckles, low and husky. A sound I feel between my thighs. "Good."

I start running my finger around the rim of the wineglass.

Everything about this should be awkward and uncomfortable.

I'm his ex, living in his house—mansion—with my son, who he didn't know existed until a week ago, because people might try to kill us if we leave.

I'm angry with him. Angry with myself—for setting off the chain of events that got us here even if it was unintentional.

But I can't seem to grasp on to any animosity right now, as I'm studying the profile illuminated by the gentle glow of the fire.

He glances over and catches me staring. The speed of my circles around the rim picks up, and I hope he doesn't notice.

Nick doesn't miss much though. I noticed that long before I learned what he does for a living. He stands and walks over to the couch where I'm sitting with all the ease and the assurance of an apex predator. Graceful and confident yet deadly.

"Do you want to be alone?"

"No," I answer honestly. I'm sick of being alone.

He looks at the empty spot on the couch next to me. I shrug, and that's all the encouragement Nick needs.

I eye him curiously as he sits less than a foot from me, trying to find some clues about where he's been or what he's been doing.

His appearance is pristine. The black button-down he's wearing looks crisp and smells freshly laundered. Same with his black suit pants. Even his boots are immaculate, shiny leather.

We sit in a silence that feels far too comfortable, me taking the occasional drink.

Nick breaks it first. "I'm sorry we're back so late. Something came up on the way home."

"Something?" There's more curiosity than panic in my voice, secure in the knowledge they both made it home safely.

"Yeah, something."

I huff and swirl some wine. "If I asked you what happened tonight, would you tell me?"

"Are you asking if I'd tell you or asking what happened?"

"Both, I guess." I start tracing the rim of my wineglass with my pointer finger again, running it in endless circles.

"I'm not proud of what I do, Lyla. Not proud of who I am. Don't confuse that with acceptance."

"So, you took him with you to do something illegal."

"I needed to meet a shipment. I had men watching the car."

Anger is muffled by knowing Leo is asleep upstairs. And probably by the wine spreading warmth through me. But I muster some irritation. "That wasn't what I agreed to. If you want to spend any more time with him, it will need to be here."

"Ultimatums, Lyla? Really?"

"Your life is *terrifying*, Nick. Do I really need to recap what has happened since you showed up?"

"Do you know a kid named Max Howard?" Nick asks abruptly.

"I—what?"

"Max Howard. He went to Leo's old school."

"Um, I…Max? Yeah, I think—"

He cuts me off, switching subjects abruptly. "What did you tell Leo about his father?"

"I—I told him it was just the two of us. That he didn't have one." I fiddle with the stem of the wineglass, fingering the delicate crystal. "I didn't know what to tell him. I figured you'd never show up, but I didn't want to tell him you were dead. And I was trying not to make you look like the bad guy. So…you're welcome."

"Max teased him about not having a dad."

I figured that was the case based on the progression of the questions. "What did you want me to do, Nick? I—"

He interrupts me again. "Leo knows I'm his father."

That sentence has its intended effect—shocking me into silence.

"He asked me a direct question. I didn't want to lie to him."

"You never had an issue with lying before."

Nick sighs. "What did I lie to you about?"

"You never mentioned any of *this*, for starters!" I wave my arm around at the plush furnishings and high ceilings. "We were together for months, Nick! You could have told me! Something. Anything. If you ever cared about me, you would have. I told you all of my family shit. Stuff I'd never told *anyone*."

Betrayal saturates into that last sentence. If we'd had a simple, surface-level fling in college, I could understand him walking away without a good-bye. But we were more than that, long before I learned Leo would be a permanent connection between us.

"I was trying to protect you."

I shake my head. "I don't want this. Any of this! I can't believe you're a part of it, and I don't want my son to know he has a *murderer* for a father."

Nick flinches. "I can't change who I am, Lyla."

I scoff. "Of course you can. Anyone can."

"I was *born* into this. It was never a choice. The only way out of this life is death. If I ever left? If I ever stepped down and walked away? I'd be hunted down and gutted. Maybe I'd be okay for a few months. Years, if I moved around and changed my identity and never trusted anyone. But that's not the life I want to lead, and going on the run isn't an option any longer."

"Why isn't it an option?"

I'm curious—about the Bratva and about his role in it, and I hate that it's obvious in my voice.

He stares me down. "I'm not just protecting myself anymore.

If I'm not *Pakhan*, I can't protect anyone else. You can hate it all you want. But the truth is, Leo is my firstborn son. I could have a dozen more kids, and he will always have the strongest claim to the Morozov Bratva. We don't elect leaders; they're born. Leo needed to know, Lyla. I told you I wouldn't tell him, and I didn't. But it's part of who he is, and he deserves to know. I was never given a choice. I wouldn't foist that fate on my own child. Not unless he chooses it."

What he's describing sounds like a mixture of cult and royalty.

"Why would he ever *choose* it?"

Anger suffuses my voice, and there's irritation in Nick's as he replies, "It's not all blood and betrayal, Lyla. It's power, authority, and family. It's an extraordinary way to live when most people only experience ordinary."

"It's also illegal," I snap. "Wrong!"

"Says who?"

"Government! Civilized people! You can't just go around killing people and making money off misfortune."

"Governments and civilized people kill all the time. Wars, assassinations, death row. They just define murder differently. They justify it so it's more palatable to the public."

"They aren't lining their pockets with other people's misfortune. The guns and the drugs and whatever else you sell *kill* people."

"Do you blame a bar for serving an alcoholic?"

"I—it's not the same thing!" I'm flustered. I wasn't expecting him to challenge me. Every other time we've discussed this, he's apologized for his choices, not defended them.

Nick tilts his head. "How? There's a demand, and I'm providing the supply. Why should I be responsible for policing other people's decisions?"

"Those decisions affect other people. *Innocent* people."

"Do you blame your mom? Or her dealer?"

I freeze for a minute. "That's not what this is about."

"Okay."

His easy agreement is maddening.

"It's *not*. She was sick. She was an addict. It wasn't her making the decisions; it was the disease."

"Okay," he repeats.

"Stop being agreeable. It's annoying."

"You'd rather I argue with you?"

"I don't know." I pick up my wine and drain the glass. "I don't know." My voice is weak and unsure, echoing the meaning of the words.

I stand and step forward, swaying slightly. Suddenly, Nick is there, the solid warmth of his body holding me upright.

Rather than move away, I make the idiotic decision to press closer. He smells like pine and leather. He feels reliable and safe, which is ironic, considering he's neither of those things. I thought he was, before he left. Before I saw intimidating men look scared of him.

My head tilts back so I can see Nick's face better. The side of his jaw is covered with a light layer of stubble. Before I can stop my brain in its tracks, I'm imagining how it would feel, rubbing the inside of my legs.

I shut down the thought as quickly as it appeared.

"What did he say?"

"Hmm?" For a few seconds, it looks like my proximity is affecting Nick the same way his is affecting me.

"Leo," I clarify. "What did he say when you said yes?"

"He said he's okay with me being his dad."

My eyes refocus on his expression. "That's it?"

"He had more questions about the warehouse. He wanted to

see all the equipment. Watch some of the matches. Watch me." Nick smiles.

"You fought?" I pull back a little so I can see him better. Nothing appears out of place.

His grin widens, realizing what I'm looking for. "Roman couldn't land a single hit."

"Arrogance isn't attractive," I tell him. But it's a lie. It looks really, really good on Nick. "Maybe he was taking it easy on you."

His smirk gains a sinister edge. "He wasn't."

Those two words are suffused with something different.

For the first time, I can see it. I can picture Nick as a *Pakhan*, barking orders that are immediately followed. It should elicit fear. Instead, I'm experiencing something that feels more like fascination.

"Good night, Lyla."

Without another word, Nick turns and walks away.

CHAPTER SEVENTEEN

NICK

Alex calls while I'm wrapping up a meeting at Landing. It's one of the premier clubs in Moscow and one of many legitimate businesses I own in the city. Sergei, the manager here, isn't involved in the uglier side of my entrepreneurship. But he's well aware of it. Every meeting we have together is spent with him looking likely to piss his pants. A healthy working relationship, in other words. I'm not worried he'll skim off the top or cause other problems. He's neither stupid nor incompetent.

I give his hand a tight warning squeeze anyway before buttoning up my coat and turning to leave.

I answer Alex's call once I'm downstairs.

Landing is divided into multiple levels, each catering to a certain audience. The ground floor is taken up by a long bar and a dance floor with a DJ booth tucked in the far corner and leather VIP booths lining the wall across from the bar. Uniformed servers glance at me, then quickly away as the call connects.

"How are they?" Alex doesn't even bother with a simple pleasantry.

"Fine," I say, ignoring one of the female bartenders as she not-so-subtly attempts to approach me.

She scurries away from my immediate dismissal, eyes downcast and cheeks flushed. My response is a reflex that doesn't really register until a waitress smiles as I pass her.

I've never fucked a member of my staff. But I've considered the idea. Indulged their flirting. It's disconcerting to realize I'm blowing past beautiful women without giving them a second glance—because of a woman I haven't slept with in nine years.

"Hello?"

"What?" I ask, realizing I missed whatever Alex was saying.

He sighs. "Fatherhood has made you even less verbose. I didn't think that was possible."

Chilly air ruffles my hair as I step outside. Grigoriy and Roman are waiting. I give them a quick nod, letting them know the meeting went without issue, before climbing into my car and zipping down the busy street. No one honks as I cut them off. You can't afford a vehicle this expensive and be someone it's smart to cross.

"Is there a problem?" I ask Alex as I turn onto the familiar road that leads back to the estate.

"No. I just wanted to check in. I haven't heard from you in over a week."

"You've become needier. I didn't think that was possible."

"Funny."

Silence falls.

I don't want to discuss Lyla and Leo with anyone, I'm learning. And it's not because I'm embarrassed they're American or ashamed I had a child outside of marriage. It's because I'm protective and possessive of both of them.

I've been too busy—actually busy, not avoiding busy—to

spend much time around them since the other night when I brought Leo to the warehouse.

But the few moments have felt different from the ones when they first arrived. They've been altered by *are you my dad* and the sway of Lyla's body when she leaned into me instead of away.

Lyla is hell-bent on leaving as soon as she can. And I have no intention of asking her to stay. Both are excellent reasons for why I should be checking in on one of my other businesses or meeting Viktor to check the latest heroin shipment personally. Instead, I'm racing home.

"I'll give you a call next week," I tell Alex. "I tried Bianchi again, and he's holding firm. I need to talk to him in person and straighten things out."

"He'll be offended you're waiting."

"He won't respect groveling."

"Fine. We'll talk soon." There's more Alex wants to say, but he doesn't.

We hang up right as I park in front of the house.

Ivan is waiting for me in the front hall when I walk inside. "Your mother is here."

Apparently, this is what I get for racing home instead of attending to the dozen other things I should have done today.

I nod in acknowledgment. "Where is Lyla?"

"She's out walking."

That doesn't tell me what I really want to know—if my mother saw her—but I don't press Ivan for details before I head down the hall that leads to the east wing.

There's already a lit cigarette dangling from my mother's mouth when I walk into my office.

No surprise there. My childhood is filled with memories of her puffing like a chimney. It's how she handles stress. Life married to my father was very stressful. And old habits are hard to break.

I greet her with a kiss on the cheek and then continue around to the opposite side of my desk.

"An *American*, Nikolaj?" She scoffs before blowing out a stream of smoke. "If you were going to bring back a souvenir from New York, it should have been designer."

I exhale—loudly—as I take a seat in my desk chair. The expensive leather creaks as I lean back. I guess that answers the question of whether my mother saw Lyla. And explains why Lyla went out walking later than usual.

"The woman was wearing *jeans*," she continues, tone dripping with disdain. "If Anastasia hears about this, she'll throw a fit."

My irritation rises at the mention of the name. "Are you questioning my decisions, Mother?"

"There's too much at stake to make mistakes, Nikolaj."

"I know *exactly* what's at stake."

"Then, you should be more careful. No one expects you to be faithful to the Popov girl. But another woman—an American—staying *here*? It's insulting." She shakes her head before taking another puff from her cigarette, muttering something under her breath as she exhales. "I'll see you for dinner."

"Wait." I lean forward, resting my elbows on the edge of the desk. "There's…" I hesitate. She's going to take this terribly. "There's a reason Lyla is here."

Another scoff. "Lyla? Common name."

"She's the mother of my child. I won't listen to you disrespect her."

The words are out before I've decided if it's the best way to break the news.

Not much startles or surprises my mother. She married a man she knew would become a *Pakhan*. Betrayal and infidelity and secrets and lies are all expected, not surprising. Bloody shirts and brandishing weapons were always her way of life. She's spent the years since the attack that wiped out the rest of our family badgering me about getting married and having children of my own.

And yet…she looks shocked by the revelation that I have one.

"How far along is she?"

I immediately realize what she's assumed. "She's not pregnant." There's a flash of confusion that quickly disappears as I keep talking. "She had the baby eight years ago. I met her while I was at UPenn. I left before she knew she was pregnant. Alex ran into her a few weeks ago. She told him…and he told me."

My mother looks away and sends another stream of smoke up toward the ceiling, silently processing. "Boy or girl?"

I should have anticipated that would be her next question. My mother isn't the soft and sensitive type. I spent more time around nannies than I did around my parents until I was deemed old enough to start training.

All she wants to know is what effect this will have on my life—and by extension, hers. Finding out the sex of a child, especially a firstborn, is a big deal.

"Boy."

She swears and stubs out the cigarette. "What does the woman want?"

"Want?"

"She's living here, Nikolaj. She must want something."

"They're here for safety. There was an incident with the Italians."

"What kind of incident?"

"The kind I'm working on smoothing over with Bianchi." Which would be easier to do if he was taking any of my calls, but

I don't mention that detail to my mother. "Dmitriy is also an issue."

"How does he know the boy exists?"

"He pays for information, as you know."

"So?"

"So, *what*?"

"So, prove to Dmitriy you have no weaknesses, Nikolaj."

"No." That's all I say and all I have to.

She arches a brow, surprised again.

"If you're staying here, you'll need to treat them with respect. I won't tolerate anything else."

She surveys me closely. "Have you trained him?"

I don't answer, which is a reply in itself.

My mother *hmms*, then lights another cigarette. A stream of smoke wafts out of the left corner of her mouth. "Igor would hate that."

"His opinion ceased to matter when he was murdered," I respond coldly.

My mother is no simpering, sensitive widow. She kept all of the perks and lost all of the pitfalls following my father's death.

"I knew allowing you to attend an American school was a mistake."

"A mistake that's resulted in you having a son as *Pakhan*," I remind her. "We both know things would have turned out very differently if I'd been in the country."

She sniffs and stands, too proud to admit I'm right. I would have died alongside my father and brothers. She would have been shoved aside like an old relic, left to remarry or fend for herself.

"Dinner is at six," I tell her.

"We always eat at eight."

"Dinner is at six," I repeat firmly. "If that's too early for you, you're welcome to eat alone. Or elsewhere."

My mother isn't one to respond to subtle cues or gentle nudges. But I've never thrown my weight around with her before. I've never had to. Our relationship is basically this: her breezing onto the estate whenever it suits her schedule, bossing her former staff around for a couple of days, until she returns to the shopping and the charity events and however else she spends her time.

We're both comfortable with the dynamic. For all her flaws, she's still my mother—not to mention, the only immediate family I have left. That used to be the case at least. Not any longer.

"Fine. I will see you at six."

I nod, and she leaves without another word.

CHAPTER EIGHTEEN

LYLA

Dinner is awkward. I didn't realize how comfortable it had become between me, Nick, and Leo until a fourth chair was filled at the table.

Vera Morozov is about as welcoming as an iceberg. Based on the very little I know about Nick's father, I'm surprised he has any inclination toward affection.

Vera seems as surprised as I am by Nick's enthusiasm as we eat, her eyes bouncing between Nick and Leo as they chat like best friends who have been separated for months. She says little while picking at the roast beef that's served with stewed potatoes and carrots, and what she does is spoken in Russian.

I'm guessing Vera must be near or over fifty, but she looks much younger. There's no trace of white or gray in her dark hair, and her pale skin doesn't show a single wrinkle. In the hour and a half I've spent in her company, I don't think I've seen her expression change once.

Maybe perpetual impassivity is the secret to not aging.

After dinner ends, Vera retires upstairs. I expect Nick to look upset by her rapid absence, but he doesn't. He appears more relieved by it. Even slightly amused.

Leo asks to be excused shortly after Vera leaves. He doesn't have any homework due tomorrow, so I'm sure he's eager to play on the tablet he has for "school" or finish reading the fantasy series he's in the middle of.

All of a sudden, it's just me and Nick. We survey each other from opposite ends of the long table that takes up most of the formal dining room, like two generals preparing for battle. Except I think we're on the same side.

"Nothing new about Dmitriy?"

Nick's lips twist into a wry version of a smile. "I won't forget to tell you when there is, Lyla. I know that's the only reason you're here."

I say nothing to that, immediately regretting the question. Because, yes, that's the easy explanation. And I don't want him thinking we're freeloading indefinitely. There are nights, like tonight, where it's especially obvious how much Leo and I have disrupted his life.

I sip some wine, just for something to do. I should have excused myself when Leo did.

"Did you finish college?"

I blink at Nick, taken totally off guard. "Excuse me?"

"Sorry," he apologizes, obviously hearing the annoyance in my voice. "I didn't mean any offense. I've just wondered...you know, where you ended up."

I don't think many—any—days have passed in the last nine years when I haven't thought of Nick at least once. His disappearance was a nagging puzzle, a mystery. And he left me with a permanent reminder of himself.

But it's never really occurred to me that Nick might have wondered about me. He chose to leave, and intentional decisions are different from forced outcomes. And now that I know the truth about why he left and what he came back to, I figured he's been too busy pulling triggers and fighting and shipping guns to give me so much as a passing thought.

There's something familiar and foreign between us. We've both changed, grown, evolved. But at our cores, we're still the same people we were when we first met.

"Um, no. I didn't finish. My scholarship covered tuition, but…babies are expensive."

Nick downs the rest of the vodka he nursed through dinner. "Have you considered going back now that Leo is older?"

I shrug. "College is expensive too."

Before he can apologize or offer to give me the money or say anything else on the subject, I decide to change it. I'm comfortable with blaming Nick for this situation. Letting go of that resentment would be healthy in some ways, but detrimental in others.

"You always said you weren't close with your parents."

His expression is so intense, it's unnerving. "What makes you think that was a lie?"

"Well, your mother just showed up. You're obviously not estranged."

"She's lonely." He sighs, studying the empty glass. "Worried."

"Worried about what?"

"She's at the mercy of my decisions."

My brow furrows. "What does that mean?"

"It means she'll pay for my mistakes." He glances at my confused expression, then sighs again. "A threat to me is a threat to her. As long as I'm *Pakhan*, she's protected. If I'm ever not…"

"She's not."

"Exactly."

"Does she see Leo as a threat?"

"She won't do anything."

"That's not what I asked."

Nick sighs. "It's not how she expected to become a grandmother."

"It wasn't how I expected to become a mother."

"I know."

He holds my gaze, something confusing and tangible arcing and connecting us. It holds until his phone rings.

Nick answers it, listening for a minute and then barking a response. It's not just the language that's changed—his tone has turned brisk and barren.

He hangs up and stands. "I have to handle something."

I nod, not interested in details. Based on the time and the way Nick's expression has hardened into a stoic mask, I'm best off not knowing.

"I know it's not how you expected to become a mother."

I still, somehow knowing I'll need to brace myself for what's coming next.

"But if I could have chosen anyone to have a kid with, it will always be you."

And then he walks out of the dining room, leaving me desperately trying to continue hanging on to resentment.

CHAPTER NINETEEN

NICK

Drops of blood drip onto the cement floor, the stream inconsistent yet steady.

I've been careful not to nick any arteries. Streams of crimson cover the naked body strung up in front of me, red rivers cutting paths through the dirt and grime covering his skin. Down his hairy stomach and flaccid cock. He's barely keeping his head upright at this point.

I flip the silver knife in my hand from side to side, watching the light glint off the unforgiving blade. The tang of metal hangs heavy in the cold, damp air, coating the air with its copper scent. It soaks into the walls and the floor, inescapable and unmistakable.

The traitor in front of me won't be the first or the last to die in this basement. The only way to remove the scent of desperation and bleach and death would be to burn the whole building down.

Dmitriy's lackey struggles, his survival instincts not allowing him to accept what his brain has already realized—there's nowhere to go. All his movements manage to do is make the blood flow faster from every break in the skin.

Dozens of droplets fall at once, staining the cement with scarlet specks.

There's something poetic and pathetic about it.

I could draw this out longer, but there's little point. The man hanging in front of me—who's refused to say a word, including his name—knew as soon as he was captured how this would end. It's a risk every member of the Bratva accepts.

There's only one way out of this life.

Dmitriy knew what he was doing when he captured and killed Konstantin. Knew it would up the stakes of our deadly game. Knew one of his loyal little soldiers would pay the price for his betrayal.

A slash of my wrist, and his throat is slit in a grisly fountain.

My stomach turns, but I force myself to watch him bleed out. Dozens of my men stand behind me, watching me execute the traitor. Many more than encompass the usual cleanup crew. They're choosing to be here, to see retribution dished out.

He's dead in seconds. It's a more merciful death than he deserved after seeing the state of Konstantin's body.

Once the blood slows to a trickle, I spin and stalk toward the doors. I pause long enough to bark a few orders to Roman and Grigoriy about dealing with the body, and then I'm outside, pulling up in deep lungfuls of freezing, fresh air. The temperature burns my lungs and makes my eyes water. I embrace both stings and the reminder they include—I'm alive.

People say life is short. But that's a subjective measure of time. A miserable existence can last forever. Happiness can pass in the blink of an eye.

My mortality has always felt tenuous. I think it's impossible to spend time in dangerous situations—to *choose* to spend time in dangerous situations—and not gain a desperate appreciation for how precious life is. To not kill someone and think about how easily that could be your flesh beneath the blade or surrounding the bullet. Your blood on the floor or your eyes turning glassy.

The feeling is nothing new, but something has changed since the last time I took a life.

I have something to live for. I have a son I want to watch grow up even if I'm not there in person to witness it.

I want to see who Leo becomes.

I want more time with him, to be the one who teaches him how to talk to girls and drive a car.

The drive back to the estate is on autopilot.

I scan my fingerprint at the gate and park just outside the front door. It's late—all the staff should be asleep.

I disable the alarm, walk inside, and set it again.

My mother always chooses to stay in the opposite wing, so I'm not worried about encountering her. Part of me wants to head to my office for a drink, but I can feel how stiff my clothing is. I'm covered with blood and need to shower. Residual adrenaline hums in my veins and heightens my senses. Usually, I'd be tempted to go to my apartment in Moscow and call for some company.

But…I don't want to. I didn't want to leave Lyla at the dinner table earlier when I got the call that one of Dmitriy's men was captured, and I was eager to return. I try not to read into either feeling, but I know exactly what they mean.

My steps up the stairs are soundless. I glance down the hall that leads to the rooms where Leo and Lyla are staying. Against my better judgment, I turn that way first. I pass Lyla's room and stop outside Leo's.

The door is already cracked. I push it open another couple of inches. The heavy cloud hanging over me lightens as I look at my son's sleeping face.

Leo is fast asleep, his mouth slightly open and his hair

sticking up at random angles as his chest rises and falls in even, deep breaths. I stare at him for a few minutes, not realizing I'm smiling at the sight until my cheeks start to hurt.

I close his door silently and retrace my steps, passing Lyla's closed door before turning down the hallway that leads to my suite.

The door that leads to my bedroom isn't closed the way I'm expecting.

It's half open, light spilling out and illuminating a sliver of the hallway's carpet.

Silently, I pull out my gun, just in case. My heart races, but not from fear. The estate might be old, but the alarm system is state of the art. I'm not worried someone broke in. I'm anticipating who would be waiting. Unless it's one of the maids—which seems highly unlikely, given how it was handled the last time one of them snuck into my room—it's Lyla.

I nudge the door open with my elbow, keeping my gun half tucked behind my thigh.

Lyla is standing in front of one of the massive windows that line the far wall, staring out at the snowy yard. It's illuminated by the floodlights that top every other post of the fence. They're bright enough, I have to close the curtains in order to sleep.

She's wearing an oversize sweater and a pair of leggings, her feet bare and her hair loose. I watch as she takes a sip of clear liquid from the glass she's holding. It could be water, but I'm guessing it's vodka.

"Exploring?"

Lyla spins so fast, she almost falls. Her hand flies to her mouth. "Nick…"

At first, I think she's spotted the gun I'm holding. Then, I remember why I came straight up to shower.

"It's not mine." I walk past her into the attached bathroom.

The tile is dark—like my mood. Lights switch on automatically, even brighter than the ones outside.

I glance in the mirror above the sinks and suppress a wince. It's not exaggerating to say I look straight out of a slasher film. Like a monster.

Streaks of crimson crisscross my arms and splatter my face. I can feel the stiff spots in the black fabric I'm wearing, where more blood landed and dried.

"Whose is it?"

I glance toward the bedroom, surprised to see Lyla is still here. Not only has she not left, but she's come closer, hovering in the doorway and looking at me with wide eyes. I can read sadness and worry in them, but there's none of the horror I expected to see. The disgust.

"Doesn't matter. He's dead." I set the gun on the marble countertop and start undoing the buttons of my shirt.

Lyla looks at the gun, but says nothing. I know most of my men hide the ugliness from their wives. We have a locker room in the warehouse for this very reason. You can shower your sins away and return home in clean clothes.

I should have done the same tonight. *Would* have, had I known Lyla would be here, waiting for me. I hurried back instead, wanting the luxury of my own space and some privacy for my thoughts. Whenever I come home, it's usually to an empty house. I've never had to worry or even think about encountering anyone else, especially not in my bedroom.

My shirt drops to the tile. I glance over at her. "What are you doing in here, Lyla?"

Lyla ignores my question, stepping closer and leaning against the marble counter surrounding the sink instead of the doorway. "Did he deserve to die?"

"I wouldn't have killed him if he didn't."

She grows bolder. "What did he do?"

"How much vodka did you drink?" That's the one and only time we've discussed any details about the Bratva—when I found her in the living room, drunk on wine worth a half a million rubles.

"What did he do, Nick?"

I stare down into the sink. "He captured one of my men, tortured him, then sent him home to his wife and two daughters in a box."

When I look over at Lyla, she hasn't moved. And when she does speak, it's not what I'm expecting her to say. "This is part of the war with your cousin?"

I'm impressed she put the pieces together so quickly, but I don't say so. "Yes. He killed one of my men; I had to retaliate."

"You're playing defense, not offense."

"I thought he'd come to his senses. I thought the men who left with him would defect back. I thought this would have been over months ago. I'm doing everything I can to end it."

I'm not sure that's true though. I could have married Anastasia by now and had Pavel's support.

The marriage was supposed to be a power play. A show of strength to scare Dmitriy into compliance. I already have more money, more men, and more support than he does. Gaining even more resources from the Popov family would have lopsided everything further.

Now, I'm not so sure it would work. Dmitriy is escalating, growing bolder the longer this defiance goes on. It doesn't matter if no one believes he can actually challenge me as *Pakhan*. The mere fact that he's still breathing is proof I'm not in complete control.

That's dangerous—for me and for the people I'm protecting.

If I marry Anastasia now, I'll have to deal with the pomp of a

Pakhan's wedding, which hasn't taken place since my parents got married decades ago.

I'll have to deal with a nosy father-in-law, desperate to stay relevant.

I'll have to deal with taking over all the business ventures included in our arrangement and folding them under the Morozov umbrella, stretching myself even thinner.

And looking at Lyla, I'm not sure if inconvenience is the only reason marrying Anastasia is becoming increasingly unappealing.

"You're going to kill him," Lyla states. "Your cousin."

"We shouldn't be discussing this."

"Because you don't trust me?"

"Because the more you know, the worse off you'll be." I pull off my undershirt, also soaked with blood, and toss it in the corner of the bathroom.

Lyla's looking.

I'm not sure if she realizes it—or knows I can tell. But her eyes trace my abdomen, then widen when my pants fall to the floor.

Modesty has never been a consideration of mine. I kick off my boxer briefs, my cock already half hard under the phantom weight of her gaze as I walk toward the shower and turn on the water. It starts cold but becomes warm quickly, washing away the blood and sweat from my skin.

I keep waiting for Lyla to leave. But she doesn't. She keeps coming closer, and it fills my mind with dangerous thoughts.

I should turn the faucet to cold. My body is reacting to not only her proximity. It's also responding to the desire in her eyes. To the energy that crackled between us in the kitchen where I first saw her and has never entirely disappeared, it seems.

The water glides down my skin, washing away everything, coating the surface and swirling the drain.

And she takes another step.

There's no barrier between the shower and the rest of the bathroom. Just a pane of glass that covers half the opening, yet shields nothing. It's steaming up slowly, the hotter the water gets.

I'm stuck somewhere between lust and incredulity as Lyla steps into the shower. She's fully dressed, but it doesn't matter. Her nearness is all it takes for me to get fully hard.

She drops to her knees and memories I thought I'd successfully buried assault me.

Something about Lyla always affected me differently. A buzz in my blood and a hum under my skin. A chemical reaction that hasn't been altered by time or distance.

Her touch is light and tentative, like a seductive whisper. Her fingers cup and trace my balls. Her mouth brushes the tip of my dick, and then her tongue darts out to taste the flared rim of the head.

I can't contain the groan that spills out of my lips. Amped up on adrenaline, the rush of bliss is almost excruciating.

Desire—lust—is something you're supposed to be able to control. To manage what you display at least. Just like pain or happiness. You can choose what you allow others to see.

It's a measure of will, not a matter of truth.

The closest Lyla and I have had to an intimate moment since she and I were reunited on the sidewalk outside of her apartment was when she leaned into me in the living room.

That was mostly hopelessness. A reluctant agreement that Leo needs to know some truth about his background.

This feels nothing like that did.

I showed her more ugliness than I've ever chosen to display to anyone.

Everyone wants the power and prestige of being a leader, but few people comprehend all that goes along with it.

It's lonely at the top. Especially when the decisions being made have life-or-death consequences.

There are a few men—Alex, Roman, Grigoriy—who I grew up with and trust entirely. But I don't discuss decisions with them. I give orders.

The wet heat of Lyla's mouth envelops more of my dick, and my mind goes entirely blank. She sucks on the head, then relaxes her jaw and takes me deeper into her throat.

I should stop her. I'm sure she'll regret this in the morning. This unexpected turn of events is likely fueled by vodka and boredom, neither of which are great decision makers.

Everything between us is already complicated enough.

But, *fuck*, does it feel good.

And if I were a good man, I wouldn't be in the shower, washing blood away.

I'm not gentle as I take what she's offering.

Lyla is layered. She's not as delicate as her expressive eyes and elegant features express. Especially when it comes to sex. She always preferred it rough and desperate. She loved it when I talked dirty to her.

Memories of our time together haunted me for years after leaving Philadelphia. There were lots of nights when I was alone —and nights when I wasn't—when I thought of her.

But no memory compares to the reality.

Leftover adrenaline swims through my system. My senses are heightened, and my emotions are a mess.

I rest my head back against the cool tile, watching my cock slide in and out of Lyla's mouth. I don't guide her, letting Lyla choose how much of my erection she takes. I can already feel the build of heat at the base of my spine as she takes me deep enough to hit the back of her throat and swallows.

I groan her name.

Her mouth is tight and hot and wet. I fight off the impending orgasm so I can savor the sensation for longer. My hips jerk automatically, thrusting once.

She doesn't pull away, just sucks harder. I come without further warning, my breathing ragged and my heart racing, audible over the spray of water.

My body blocks most of the spray, but there are spots of water darkening sections of her sweater. When Lyla stands, her knees are wet from the floor.

Water patters around us like rain.

"You didn't have to kill him," is the first thing she says to me.

My jaw works, irritation eating away at the remnants of bliss still flowing through me. "Yes, I did. There's only one way out of this life."

"What about me and Leo?"

"You're the exception."

I step forward. I'm dying to touch her, too, to see if she's just as wet as she used to get from sucking me off.

But Lyla steps back. "Your hands aren't clean," she tells me.

My fingers clench into fists as those words collide with my chest. Water sluices down my arms and swirls around the drain. For a long stretch of time, there's just the sound of falling water as I stare at her and she stares back.

There was a brief moment—just now—where I let myself forget everything. Where I let myself imagine what a life with Lyla and Leo would be like. Where it felt like she understood instead of resented.

I can't even blame her for it.

I'd resent me too. I'd reject me too.

Which is why I don't understand what the hell just happened. Why she opened the door of possibilities, just to slam it back shut.

Why she initiated intimacy—got me off—and is now refusing to let me do the same to her.

But I don't ask questions, and I sure as hell don't offer an apology. I don't react at all, just look at her. If she wants to paint me as a heartless bastard, then that's the part I'll play.

Lyla turns and walks away, leaving me standing here. The remnants of pleasure are still warming my blood. I just came harder than I have in years from a simple blow job. And in the mouth of a woman I told myself I got over a long time ago.

I stand under the shower until it turns cold, wishing my sins would wash away with the water.

CHAPTER TWENTY

LYLA

B*lame it on the vodka*, I tell myself as I walk downstairs. *Blame it on the vodka. Blame it on—*

I step into the dining room, and Nick is already there. My heart picks up in double time. He's dressed in his usual black attire, his hair neatly combed and his cuff links glinting as he sips from a coffee cup and then sets it back on the table.

All I'm focused on is the flex of his forearm. Lust pools in my stomach. I can recognize what happened last night was a mistake all I want. But I still want him too. Want a hell of a lot more than what took place between us.

Already standing, Nick ruffles Leo's hair and then walks toward me. "I've got to head out early," he tells me.

"O-okay." I study the lines of his face, and they're nothing but smooth and impassive.

"My mother already left. She had a luncheon to get back for."

I explore his smooth expression, trying to decipher any details he's not sharing. One tense dinner is not much of a visit. I wonder if the brevity has something to do with me and Leo. If he asked her to leave or if she decided to.

I can't discern anything at all. There's no sign of the hunger that was there last night either. The broken or the bloody.

Nick is looking at me the way you approach an unfamiliar work colleague—with polite indifference.

"Okay," I repeat. "Have a good day."

He nods and keeps walking past me, out into the front hallway. I hear the front door shut a few minutes later.

I paste a smile on my face and turn toward Leo, who's eating his cereal. "Morning, bud."

"Hi, Mom."

He's focused on a thin paperback, folded next to his bowl. I help myself to some toast and coffee. If—*when*, I remind myself —we return to Philadelphia, it will be a rough transition back to our old morning routine.

Leo

The day passes slowly and uneventfully. I go for my daily walk, drive with Leo to and from school, and spend an uncomfortable dinner avoiding eye contact with Nick as he talks to Leo.

After we finish eating, I wander into the living room, which has become part of my predictable routine here. There's a small selection of English titles in the library. Most of them are heavy volumes on heavy subjects. One of them is a collection of Sherlock Holmes stories. I got halfway through the book this afternoon.

There's a fire in the fireplace, same as there's been every evening. I curl on the couch with the book, surprised when Nick and Leo follow me in here. Leo usually heads up to his room after dinner, and Nick typically retires to his office. They have a planned task in mind, both of them settling at a table to the right of the fireplace.

Nick pulls a deck of cards out of the drawer and begins shuffling them. The crackle and pop of the fire muffles some of what they're saying. I think they're also talking softly so I can read. But I'm more focused on them than the words on the page. On watching their profiles shift as they exchange cards. Seeing how Leo beams and the way his brow furrows as he stares at the fan of cards.

They play for over an hour. There's a lightness around both of them that I don't ordinarily associate with either of them. Nick is rarely lighthearted or playful. And Leo is what his teachers have always called an "old soul." Thoughtful and serious, focused and responsible. I thought it was because of me, because of the financial stress I tried to hide and how it was always just the two of us. But maybe some of it was genetic.

As soon as the game ends, Nick says good night to Leo. I catch his glance in my direction out of the corner of one eye, but he leaves the room without speaking a word to me.

After a cheerful good night to me, Leo scampers upstairs. It's past his usual bedtime—something I've been strict about since coming here, mainly because it's felt like one of a very few things I can control.

I sit and stare into space for a while. Someone usually comes in to freshen the fire when I'm in here, but no one entered tonight. It's not hard to guess why.

All that's left are embers, glowing softly amid piles of gray ashes.

Rather than head upstairs, I walk down the hall toward Nick's office. The door is shut, a strip of yellow light visible beneath it.

I knock on his office door softly. I should be ignoring Nick the same way he seems to be avoiding me. Instead, I'm seeking him out.

Aside from Leo, he's the one person I *know* here. The one person I trust. I have nothing to do and no one to talk to. I blame that isolation on what happened last night as much as the vodka I helped myself to after he left me sitting alone at the dinner table.

And also…I'm attracted to him. I've never been drawn to anyone else the same way I'm pulled to him. No guy before or since has ever compared. Admitting that, even to myself, makes me feel weak.

Nick's response to my knock is in Russian. I know that means he's not expecting me. I push the door open anyway.

He glances up, irritation transitioning into surprise. "Hi."

"Hi. Are you busy?" I know it's a stupid question as soon as I speak it.

Documents are spread across the desk, most with neat notes in the margins. His hair is messy from running his fingers through it.

"No, it's fine." Nick sets down the pen he was holding and leans back in his chair. "What's going on?"

"It's—forget it. I'll let you get back to it."

I turn around, intent on rushing back out the door.

"Lyla. Sit."

Instead of leaving, I listen. I spin back toward him and take a seat in one of the two chairs that face the imposing desk.

Nick says nothing, just stares at me.

"I was just wondering, has there been any—"

"I would have told you." He cuts me off before I can even get the whole question out.

I wasn't going to ask about Dmitriy. I was curious if there had been a response to what Nick left to do last night. That, I don't think he would tell me.

"Okay." I chew on my bottom lip, choosing not to correct

him. Bounce my knee and glance out the window. The floodlights are all on outside, suspending the yard in a twilight zone, where it's dark but you can see everything.

I'm basically waiting around for Nick to kill someone—kill another person—which doesn't sit well with me.

I feel dirty and complicit. I feel like I'm dragging Leo into a darker world I escaped and swore I'd never expose my own child to. There's plenty I know I'm not able to offer Leo. But I thought, at the very least, I could provide a normal, stable life for a child. No corruption. No guns. No drugs. I'm failing at that now too.

But I have no other options as far as I can tell.

If I leave with Leo, I'm threatening his safety. No moral high ground is worth that consequence. I would never be able to forgive myself.

I have to trust that Nick has our son's best interests in mind and deal with the consequences of that choice.

Leo is old enough to grasp some idea of what is going on, which is a good and a bad thing. He also knows Nick is his father now. This won't be a chapter that's easy or neat to close.

I sigh and meet Nick's gaze. "I just…I'm bored. Leo has school, and you have…work, and I'm used to having an endless list of things to do. Can I help cook? Or clean? I've tried, but—"

Nick interrupts. "I can arrange for you to volunteer somewhere local, if you'd like. An orphanage or a women's shelter. Wouldn't you prefer that?"

"I told you, I never finished my degree. I'm not licensed to—"

"It won't be an issue." He sounds confident about it.

"Because of…" I'm not sure how to finish the sentence. *Because of who you are? Because of what you do?*

"It won't be an issue," Nick repeats.

"You get the red-carpet treatment everywhere, huh? Must be nice."

There's a beat of silence before he answers. "It's easier to appreciate from a distance, I guess. If you don't consider the cost."

And suddenly, all I can picture is him standing in the bathroom, splashed with blood. So much red, none of it artificial. All I can hear are the words I said before I left.

Nick swirls the liquid in the glass set next to the documents he was reading, and we both watch as the liquor drips back down the sides.

"Most things look better from a distance."

He makes a *hmm* sound in response. "I'll make some calls in the morning."

"You don't have to do that, Nick. I'm sure you're...busy."

He chuckles, but it lacks any amusement. "Yeah, I am."

"Did he retaliate about last night? Dmitriy?" I finally ask, too curious not to.

Nick runs a hand across his jaw, studying me. Weighing how—or if—he's going to respond, I assume.

"Yes," he finally answers.

Anxiety spikes my blood. "You lost more men?"

"No. He did. I had all the warehouses fitted with new alarms after the last round of break-ins. They were set to self-detonate if the codes were tampered with."

"How many people died?"

"I don't know. There wasn't anything left to count." He swirls the liquid in his glass again. "Red mist, they call it."

I swallow. Nick's voice is steady, his gaze level. Last night, his honesty felt raw. Right now, it feels purposeful. Level and unaffected.

He's trying to scare me. To intentionally push me away.

"You lost a warehouse?"

"Yes," he replies, picking up a pen from the table and spinning it around one finger. "This is becoming an expensive war."

We're both silent, and it's a heavy one. A charged quiet, where a lot is being said while nothing is spoken at all.

"You should be focusing on that then. I'll be fine here."

"I said I'd take care of it, Lyla."

I hate that he's making an effort. Hate that he's making a dream I let go of a while ago seem like a possibility.

I never felt like I was making a difference, working as a secretary at the law firm. It was a paycheck.

The possibility of getting to help others fills me with a joy I try to block out. Maybe I'm drawn to social work because it allows me to focus on others' problems instead of my own. Being here has removed all my choices and responsibilities. There's something freeing about it as well as constricting.

"Won't the fact that I don't speak Russian be a problem?" I finally ask instead of saying *thank you.*

"No. They'll speak English."

"No one here does."

Nick's lips quirk—the first break in his serious expression since I entered his office. Rather than satisfying me, it makes me crave more. "Yes, they do. They're just not sure what to make of you."

"What do you mean?"

"There hasn't been a woman living here since my father was *Pakhan.*"

"Why didn't your mother stay here after he died? It's not like there isn't room." I backtrack in the resulting silence. "Sorry. It's none of my—"

"We both needed space. And she was trying to encourage me to get married as soon as possible."

I hesitate, holding back the question that wants to escape. Curiosity wins over willpower once again. “Why haven’t you?”

This time, I get a whole smile. “My relationship with my mother isn’t your business, but that is?”

I flush, but don’t backtrack. Truthfully, it’s a question I’m way more interested in the answer to.

“There are a lot of factors,” Nick finally says. “My father was supposed to be in control for much longer than he was. My older brother was going to be the next *Pakhan*, not me. I was never expected to inherit this position and definitely not when I was eighteen. After my father and brothers were murdered, it was chaotic for a while. Rival families jostling for power. Internal unrest. Whispers about whether I was up to the job. Getting married is a political move. The most powerful tie besides blood. Making a hasty decision will do more harm than good.”

I tilt my head, considering. “It sounds like you’re stalling.”

“I am,” Nick replies. “Once I agree to an arrangement, I lose leverage. Not to mention, Pavel’s problems will become mine.”

“Who is Pavel?”

I catch a slight grimace that makes me think the name was a slip. “He’s the *Pakhan* of another family.”

“And…he has a daughter for you to marry?”

Nick takes a sip of his drink before answering. “Yes. I was hoping to resolve things with Dmitriy first, on my own. That’s delayed things, but I was close to accepting his offer. Until…”

“Until Alex called you,” I realize.

“Right.” Another sip.

I’m not sure how to feel. Relieved? Remorseful? Jealous?

Annoyingly, the last emotion is the strongest.

“How old is she?”

Nick looks amused, but he doesn’t call me out on my focused line of questioning. “Nineteen.”

"Just a little older than Leo then."

He laughs, and I hate how much I love the sound. It's rich and deep. Uninhibited and genuine.

"I'm just saying, she's a *teenager*. Makes me feel like an old spinster."

"Old spinsters don't suck cock the way you do." He says it so seriously, so matter-of-fact, that it takes a few seconds for the words to sink in.

I feel myself flush, hoping he can't tell.

As what normally happens when I'm caught off guard, I blurt the first thing that pops into my head. "I haven't had much practice recently." Silence. "Um, you know, aside from last night," I add in an attempt to make it less awkward, but it has the opposite effect, making it even more so.

I focus on Nick's hand instead of his face. It's clenched tight around his glass. The color has fled from his knuckles, leaving pale skin behind.

Because he's uncomfortable? I doubt it.

Because the thought of me with someone else bothers him? I'm not sure that's plausible either.

I'm sure he's had *lots* of practice in the past nine years.

He didn't go through pregnancy and childbirth alone. Didn't spend sleepless nights staying up with a screaming infant. Didn't work late into the night, juggling two jobs.

None of that was conducive to dating.

Neither was living with a permanent reminder of him. I never let a single guy I dated meet Leo.

I told myself I would only do that when it felt right, when I saw a future. I would rather have Leo grow up without a father or any father figure, like I did, than have him see his mother run through a rotating door of men, the way I also did.

Not that there was ever a rotating door. More like a dead bolt that rarely opened.

"It was a mistake. I shouldn't have…"

He inclines his head, studying me like a riddle to solve. "Why did you?"

This. This is why I was relieved Nick and I haven't been alone since the moment in his bathroom. Because I was worried he'd ask this question, which I have no good answer to. Part of it was lust. Part of it was boredom. Part of it was bravery, tossing inhibitions away like confetti. And part of it was an admission—that I'm still attracted to him despite knowing the full, ugly truth.

Nick looks down at his documents when I don't answer. "It's late. Leo will be up early."

I stand in response to the not-so-subtle dismissal that is also him letting me off the hook, but I don't walk toward the door. I round the desk instead, not stopping until my legs brush against the stiff fabric of his pants.

Nick doesn't move. Doesn't touch me. Doesn't push me away. He sits and stares, eyes unreadable and expression serious.

This is stupid. I'm not drunk or naive or unaware of the consequences. Sex with an ex—sex with your child's father—is rife with messy complications. Add in the fact that I'm here because leaving means risking my life, and I'm looking at a recipe for disaster.

Nick is a *Mafia boss*. He kills people. Tortures traitors. Sells guns, like the one that killed June's husband. Sells drugs, like the ones that killed my mom.

Rationally, I know all of that.

Compare Nick to any other guy I've dated, and the contrast is laughable. He's the total opposite of the safe, steady, reliable guy I swore to myself I'd end up with. Someone who sticks around and shows up.

Nothing like my father or the other men my mother kept company with.

The problem is, I can't seem to care about anything I *should* do or *should* want right now.

It's been nine years since I felt this magnetic pull. This reckless excitement. This wild abandonment.

I hold eye contact with him as I take a seat on the edge of the massive desk. Right on top of the papers that must be related to his criminal empire.

Nick still doesn't move.

I spread my legs a little, embarrassed by how wet my underwear is.

My sex life since him has been nice. Enjoyable. And…forgettable.

I told myself passion has a less prominent place in mature, responsible relationships. Maybe there's some truth to that.

But Nick hasn't touched me, hasn't even *suggested* he's going to touch me, and thrills of anticipation dance across my skin. It feels like standing at the edge of a cliff, staring at the dark water below, letting the nerves build until you gather the courage to leave solid ground. The last time I swam with Nick, I nearly drowned.

In one smooth motion, he stands.

The leather chair squeaks as it rolls away, shoved back by his body as he presses against me instead.

Adrenaline floods my system, sharpening my senses. My breathing is ragged. Harsh inhales and hurried exhales.

"Am I allowed to touch you this time?" There's a dry, dangerous edge to his voice, sharpened with a hint of irritation that tells me he wasn't as unbothered by last night as he's acted until now. That there's been a lot lingering under the surface on his side, not just mine.

"Yes," I whisper. "*Please*."

His callous palm lands on my thigh. A possessive, heavy weight. All I can focus on is that one spot. On the *heat* his touch incites and how it spreads. Like a lighter sparking to life and starting a fire.

"Won't your boyfriend mind?"

There's a rough, seductive edge to Nick's voice that makes me think he knows the answer. His men eavesdropped on my conversation with Michael, I'm sure.

"Adultery isn't on your long list of sins?"

One corner of Nick's mouth quirks.

I exhale and admit, "I ended it with Michael when I called him."

Nick's hand slides up my leg, between my legs, and inside my underwear. All I can hear are my rapid breaths and the wild thrum of my heart as it beats.

I can't swallow the moan before it escapes, spilling out into the silent office, bathed in shadows.

Nick says something in Russian. I can't understand a word of it. But it sounds low and dark and dirty.

It should be a reminder of what a mistake I'm making.

How different we are.

How weak I am right now. My legs wantonly spread on his desk, like he didn't break my heart by leaving years ago and return, only to uproot my entire life in a matter of minutes.

The callouses on his palm as he fingers me are another reminder. I should be horrified by their roughness. Should be picturing pink-hued water circling the drain and thinking about all the damage they've done.

But I can't focus on anything I *should* be doing.

My reflexes and my instincts—my morals—are stripped away, defenseless against the sensations building inside of me.

The pleasure is so intense, I can't feel anything else. Can't see or think past it. It's a powerful rush—a *burn* that eats away at everything else—searing through my veins and confiscating my thoughts.

It was always like this with Nick, and I purposefully forgot this feeling.

I hate addiction.

My whole life, I've battled any instinct that suggested I might be similar to my mother in any way, shape, or form. We look alike. There was a reason she was able to coax man after man into her destructive web. But everything else—everything important—I thought I'd disinherited.

I've never sampled a drug in my life. But I'm worried this is my addiction. That *he* is my addiction.

I was proud of myself for walking away last night, even though I felt guilty about my choice of parting words. But here we are again, and nothing in my body says this will end the same way.

Nick murmurs more Russian.

I tilt my head back, drunk on desire. We feel suspended in time. Unworried about consequences.

"What did you say?"

"I said, your pussy is awfully wet for someone so disgusted by me."

He rubs my clit, and that's all it takes. A peak that usually takes me a while to reach is here in seconds. I tumble, spiral, and fall.

It's been a while. But…it's him. Based on the smirk Nick is wearing, he knows it too.

I'm not disgusted by him. I wish I were.

I can see everything in black and white. But I *feel* the gray when I'm around him. Right and wrong are two extremes with a lot of space in between. Are they subjective instead of set in stone? If you kill a killer, are you saving lives in addition to ending one?

Maybe my childhood screwed me up even more than I thought.

Maybe love is a verb, an ongoing action that overtakes obstacles.

I don't want to love Nick. But I'm worried I never stopped.

"Are you sure?" he asks.

I wait for the second-guessing. But all I'm experiencing is anticipation. "Yes."

Certain moments matter more than others.

I'm worried this one means the most.

CHAPTER TWENTY-ONE

LYLA

I wake up slowly. Consciousness cuts through the fluffy clouds of dreams. The peaceful state, where there's nothing to worry about, fades to nothing, reality taking its place.

I roll over, scrunching my eyes tighter closed in an attempt to cling to the relaxation for a little while longer.

Except, instead of colliding with cool fabric, I hit a warm, muscular body.

My eyes fly open, memories assaulting my brain in a rapid rush. Hot skin and heated whispers. Dirty kisses and filthy words. Loud moans and deep groans.

When I flip on my back, there's a satisfied ache between my thighs that reminds me I had sex last night with the one guy I never thought I'd fuck again—twice.

With the father of my child.

With the man I literally watched wash blood off his hands two nights ago.

Nick is already awake. He's watching me wake up with a lazy indifference, one arm tucked behind his head. The sheets cover everything from the waist down, but the carved ridges of his abdomen are fully visible in the morning light streaming in through the cracks in the curtains.

I take my time tracing the view of Nick shirtless, skimming over the ridges of his abs and taking in the few silver scars that mar his skin. The longest one runs from his collarbone and across his shoulder, partially covered by a nautical star tattoo.

Finally, I make it up to his eyes, which are studying me.

"Hi." I chew my bottom lip, trying to decide what else to say.

"Stop doing that." Nick's voice is raspy, rough with sleep.

I shoot him a questioning look. He tugs my bottom lip with his thumb, freeing it from the grasp of my teeth.

"Unless you want to get fucked again," he adds.

"I'm sore," I admit, as if he's not aware of the size of his dick.

It's a delicious ache at least. A pleasurable pain.

"Are you?" Nick smirks.

With his bicep bulging and his hair messy, he doesn't look like a killer. He looks obscenely gorgeous. He looks like the guy I fell in love with. The confident freshman who could make me melt with just one look.

Lying in bed together doesn't help. I have many—*too many*—old memories of doing this same thing. It doesn't matter that those were in an extra-long twin bed, and this is in a king-size bed with thousand-thread-count sheets.

I feel eighteen again, ecstatic to be living life on my own terms and overwhelmed by spending time with him. Having the attention of someone so much larger than life after years of being shoved to the side was like feeling the sun after endless nights.

I've grown up. I've changed. But Nick still makes my heart race and my stomach flip, and that's even more dangerous than the reminder of how consuming our physical connection is.

"I didn't think you'd still be here."

Honesty is my best strategy, I decide. We're not the teenagers we met as anymore. I don't regret sleeping with Nick even though I probably should. I've spent too much time sitting back and simply surviving. If there's anything being here has taught me, it's that you should aim higher than survival.

Nick isn't looking at me. His gaze is on the row of picture windows that line the far wall. "I'll have new curtains put up in here today. I don't know how you sleep past sunrise."

I stare out the windows too, not bothering to point out how he could have slept in his own bed. We ended up in my room mostly because it's closer to the stairs. I didn't expect him to stay the whole night.

I try again. "No early morning today?"

"No."

I shift a little closer. Nick surveys me curiously as I turn on my side and trace a scar on his ribs. He didn't have any in college, except the one on his hand.

"How did you get this one?"

"Knife fight."

"Did you kill him?"

Like most of the conversations I have with Nick, this feels surreal. I never thought murder might be included in pillow talk. Never thought that's a question I might ask.

"No."

"Why not?"

"He wasn't mine to kill."

"Because you're the *Pakhan*?"

"No, I don't ask my men to do anything I won't do myself. And as you mentioned the other night, my hands aren't clean, Lyla."

My cheeks warm as I keep focusing on his chest. It's the truth, but I still regret stating it so baldly. They were words designed to maim someone I didn't think would be affected, much less wounded, by them. But this is the second time he's brought what I said up, which makes me think they might have at least grazed.

"I delivered him to Dmitriy," he says almost absentmindedly.

"Your cousin?" I ask, surprised. "Why? I thought you hate each other."

"We didn't use to. He was like a third brother to me."

I trace the scar again. "What did the man do?"

"He raped Dmitriy's girlfriend."

"Is she…okay?"

"She killed herself right after it happened."

"Do you think that's why he's…"

"No. The only reason he sought revenge was his ego. He didn't care about her."

"Do you think he'll kill another one of your men?" I ask after a beat of silence.

"No, I don't."

"Why not?"

"They're not easy to kill. He stumbled across Konstantin by chance. He was drunk at a club with his mistress. He was an easy target."

"I—I thought you said he was…returned to his wife and daughters."

"I did."

"Oh."

"They're employees. I don't police their personal lives, so long as it doesn't interfere with the job."

"Right." I know there's disapproval in my voice, but I don't comment further.

My surprise seems silly, the longer I think about it. My mother wrecked plenty of marriages. I'm under no delusions that most people are faithful to their significant others. Not to mention, someone who tortures and kills and thinks they're above the law probably doesn't see infidelity as much of a sin.

We're both silent as I continue tracing paths across his chest.

Nick's left hand is resting on his abs, just above the thin trail of hair that disappears under the sheets. I flip it, tracing the raised ridge that bisects his palm. It's the one scar he *did* have the last time we lay like this.

I don't believe in fate or destiny or any cosmic power. But this irony isn't lost on me as I flip my left palm upward next to his, revealing the pinkish scar that disrupts the natural lines. It's shorter and newer than Nick's, the stitches freshly dissolved, but otherwise, it's almost identical.

We match. When it comes to one short stretch of scar tissue, we seem meant to be.

Not to mention, it's a permanent reminder of the knife slip that's the reason I'm here.

Nick stares at the healed cut for a beat too long to be a cursory glance. "Alex did a good job."

That's all he says before climbing out of bed, pulling on his discarded clothes, and walking out of the room.

When I walk downstairs, Nick is talking on the phone. Leo is kneeling down on the carpet, petting a pile of black-and-brown fur with a wide smile on his face.

As I draw closer, I realize it's a dog. A very big, very sleepy dog.

Leo looks up at me, a huge smile on his face. "Mom! Look!"

"I'm looking," I say dryly, crouching down beside him. "I see the dog."

"Dad said I could play with him today."

Dad.

I want Leo to know his father. I knew, when I climbed on that plane, there was a good chance Leo would learn who owned it. But hearing it spoken so matter-of-factly is different.

"He did, did he?" I cast a look at Nick, which he misses, too busy barking orders into the phone. "Did you eat breakfast?"

Leo nods, completely focused on the dog, who's wagging and drooling, thrilled with the undivided attention.

I stand and walk into the formal dining room, where breakfast is already waiting. One of the maids is clearing an empty plate I assume is Leo's. She gives me a nervous smile and then hurries through the swinging door that leads into the kitchen.

I fill a plate with toast and eggs and take a seat at the table. I alternate between sipping coffee and chewing, staring out the glass doors that lead to a patio.

Gray stones peek through the blanket of snow here and there, melted in spots the sun has hit. Aside from that, the rear view of the house looks the same as the front. The tree line doesn't start for a half a mile, the fence that surrounds the property just past it.

Without asking, I know it's a tactical choice. There's no way to approach the house under cover, not even in darkness, thanks to the floodlights.

I'm finished with food and sipping on coffee when Nick walks into the dining room. I watch him fill a mug and drink from it without flinching, the coffee straight black and steaming hot.

"A dog?"

"You mentioned Leo wanted one."

I should be surprised Nick remembered such a small detail

from a long rant, but I'm not. It must help his criminal empire succeed.

"If you play good guy, I'll always have to be the bad guy."

"According to you, I'm always the bad guy."

I let that comment slide. "Whose dog?"

"Roman's. My dad used to keep hunting dogs here. After he died, Roman took a puppy. I asked to borrow it for the day."

Leo rushes into the room. "Are you ready, Dad?"

Something soft and warm settles in Nick's expression. I wonder if this is the first time he's heard Leo call him that. It feels surreal to me, so it must be strange for him.

"I'm ready," Nick responds, taking one final sip of coffee and setting the cup back on the table.

"Are you coming, Mom?"

"Um…" I stall, not sure what the right answer is.

I'm not sure if Leo realizes this would be our first outing as a threesome, as something similar to a family, but *I* certainly do.

And after last night, it feels like lines are blurring everywhere I look. Like leaving is growing further and further away instead of any closer. When I broached the topic of Nick being his father the morning after Nick told me Leo knew the truth, he was nonchalant about the revelation.

Rather than feeling relieved, it worried me.

We accept the things we want easily. With open arms and wide smiles.

Leo *wants* Nick to be his dad.

It fills me with mixed emotions. I'm grateful Nick knows he has a son and Leo knows who his father is. If anything positive is to come out of this snarled mess, it should be that.

But I'm hyperaware it will also contribute to the messiness. That Leo knowing who Nick is, getting attached to Nick, will make leaving even more difficult.

"You should come."

The sound of Nick's voice, deep and husky, stirs up memories I'm trying to bury. Serves as a reminder of the fact that Leo isn't the only one I need to worry about getting attached.

"Okay," I agree.

There's nothing for me to do here. And I'd be lying if I said there wasn't a part of me that wants to see this—to *experience* it.

An unintelligible conversation takes place in the front hall between Nick, one of the maids, two butlers, and a bodyguard. I eye them curiously as I shrug into my coat, trying to figure out what is being said based on body language. Leo is holding the dog's leash, patting its head with a big smile on his face.

I kneel down to pet the dog as well. My refusal to get a dog had everything to do with time and space, nothing to do with not liking animals or not wanting one.

"Is it a boy or girl?"

"Girl," Leo answers.

"Do you know her name?"

"Darya."

"Darya," I repeat, petting her soft fur.

A gust of cold air streams in from the open door, chilling the front hall. Everyone but Nick has disappeared. He's walking toward the car that's parked outside. It's sleek and fast-looking. Somewhere between the tiny sports cars I see Nick drive most days and the tank-like SUVs that escort me and Leo. I don't recognize the car's logo, but that means little.

Briefly, I think of my worn Honda. It must have been towed and impounded by now. It's an inanimate object, nowhere near as important as Leo's safety. But it's an inanimate object that I worked hard to buy and ran reliably. When I return to Philadelphia, it will be with even less than I left with.

No job, no apartment, no car. I'm sure Nick will offer money, and I'll be forced to take it until I can get a new job. Not only will I feel indebted to Nick, but I'll also be stuck with more reminders of him.

"Something wrong?"

I glance at Nick, who's watching me stare at the car like an idiot. Leo has already climbed into the backseat with Darya. She's panting against the window, fogging up the glass.

"We're not taking security?" I blurt the first question that occurs to me because it's better than sharing what I was really just thinking about.

"No."

"We've always left the property with security," I tell him in explanation.

Nick smirks, and fuck if I don't feel it between my legs. "You doubting me, Rose?"

I hesitate—and not because I don't know the answer. I can't form words because it's another boundary between us that's been smashed.

It's a reference to our past, to my past, to the necklace that hangs around my neck. A reminder of the fact that he knows more, has seen more of me, than anyone else ever has.

The rose around my neck has always hung as a symbol of weakness to me. I've never viewed it in any positive light. It's the last remnant of my mother. All she ever gave me besides life. The fact that I've never gotten rid of it, that I've worn it around like a talisman ever since she gave it to me on one of the few birthdays she remembered, has always bothered me more than I'm willing to admit.

Nick is the only one who's ever noticed the necklace. Who's ever asked or cared what it meant. When we were together, it felt special. Now, it feels too intimate. Like a layer he wasn't supposed to reach.

I focus on the first half of his question and shove my feelings about the nickname away. "I'm not doubting you," I say before walking around the front of the car and climbing into the passenger seat.

For the first time, I'm sitting up front and leaving the estate without a multi-car escort. I *should* be feeling apprehensive. I'm in a foreign country with a wild imagination that pictures threats around every corner. I usually white-knuckle my way through the school drop-off and pickup runs. But there's no trickle of fear as we pass through the front gates and start rolling onto the road.

He's familiar, I tell myself. Of course I trust Nick himself more than the many men who work for him. It doesn't mean anything.

"Where are we going?" I ask. The irony I forgot to ask isn't lost on me. And I don't have the excuse of being eight and easily excited.

"The park," Nick replies.

I glance over at his profile as he turns onto another road, surprised by the casual, normal answer. "The park," I echo.

"Mmhmm."

"Um, okay."

Without looking at me, one corner of Nick's mouth curls upward. I roll my eyes before looking out the window for the rest of the drive.

The trip takes about twenty minutes. We park in a quiet, tree-lined lot. Like Nick said, there's a park. It's a compact layout with paths that crisscross the grass and a small playground at one end with a climbing gym, swings, and a slide. Old trees with gnarled, bare branches stretch over most of the space, shading from the sun that occasionally peeks out from behind clouds.

Leo heads for the open middle section with Darya. Nick keeps up with them, pointing around and talking. I watch Leo laugh at something Nick says, gazing up at his father with hero worship in his eyes.

I think of all the reasons Nick listed for why men join the Bratva. He didn't include himself. But he's a natural leader with the sort of charisma and confidence that make people believe and miracles seem possible. And I think Nick would be right at the top for Leo, over money or power or family or any other reason.

I've always made it clear to Leo that my love isn't conditional, and since becoming a mother, I've found it more and more difficult to believe my own mom chose to make *me* feel that way.

But I'm worried Leo will think Nick's love is.

I take a seat on one of the benches and snuggle into the layers I'm wearing. I try to shut off the part of my brain that never stops stressing and instead enjoy the morning. To appreciate this moment, which is both surreal and real.

The air is cold, but the sun is warm. Leo found a stick that he's tossing for Darya, smiling as the dog runs and retrieves it. Nick stands next to him. I can't see his expression, and I'm glad. I want Leo to have this memory, but I'm not sure I'm emotionally equipped to have any more details from this outing engraved in my brain.

Russian sounds to my right.

I glance over to see an older man has taken a seat at the bench next to mine. He's bundled in wool and fur, a black-and-white newspaper settled on his lap, waiting to be read. His gaze is fixed away, so I follow it to the two figures and the dog.

"I don't speak Russian," I say awkwardly.

The man smiles. "I asked if that is a borzoi."

Nick is watching us. I give him a small nod, letting him know I'm fine.

"A what?" I'm getting better at registering Russian accents, but this man's is thick.

He smiles kindly when our gazes connect. "That's the breed. I had a dog just like it, growing up. Very smart. Very loyal. You can rely on it to take good care of your boy."

His expression is soft and wistful, lost somewhere decades ago. I decide not to correct him on the dog's ownership. Right now, Leo is probably pretending Darya is his too.

"My son has wanted a dog for years."

The man chuckles. "He looks very happy. What a beautiful family you have."

I smile at him. "Thank you."

"Your son looks just like his father."

I glance at the two of them. "I know he does."

I don't sound proud. I sound…wistful.

"All the ups and downs balance out eventually."

I hold my smile, feeling embarrassed that I'm so transparent. I've spent most of my life hiding fears and concerns. A stranger shouldn't be so attuned to them.

"We might have trouble getting Leo out of here."

I glance up to see Nick approaching, his hands shoved deep in the pockets of his coat.

I spend too long focused on his saunter and his smile and the flip in my stomach. None of which I can ignore and none of which I want to be noticing. I'm so wrapped up in Nick, I don't notice the old man standing until he's already hobbling away with his newspaper tucked under one arm.

Nick watches him hurry away as well. His expression is sanguine, but I feel like there's something beneath the surface.

"That was…weird," I state as Nick sits beside me. "He didn't even say good-bye."

Nick is silent, staring at where Leo is still playing with the dog.

"He recognized you."

It's more of a statement than a question, but Nick answers anyway. "Yes."

I wonder—worry—what sort of reputation would cause an elderly man reading a newspaper in a park to rush off.

"Better to be feared than loved," Nick murmurs.

I swallow and nod.

"Are we going to talk about last night?"

When I look over, he's still staring at Leo playing. There's something about darkness that lets secrets seep out and honesty intrude. Last night, I whispered words against his skin that make me blush in the light of day. That bravery faded at sunrise.

I clear my throat, loudly enough, it's almost a cough. "It doesn't seem necessary. You must do that sort of thing all the time."

"Are you asking or assuming?"

I think there might be a smile in his voice, but finding out for sure would require looking over at him. Instead, I focus my gaze on the same spot where his is—on our son. "I don't want it to complicate or confuse anything."

"It won't."

"Okay."

"I'm going to Philadelphia tomorrow," Nick says after a beat of silence.

"For…work?"

The park is almost empty now that the old man is gone. Aside from us, there's just a group of teenagers crowded down by the playground end.

"Does anyone travel to Philadelphia for pleasure?"

"It's a nice city. Don't knock it!"

When I look over, he's smiling.

"I'm not. I have a lot of fond memories of Philadelphia."

I swallow. "Of Philadelphia? Or of me?"

"You." He drops the word simply, like it's a syllable, not one of so many casualties.

Then, Nick stands and calls Leo's name. Leo runs over with Darya, his cheeks flushed from happiness and cold.

"We have to leave already? We just got here!"

"I have to make a trip to the warehouse in a little while. I'll talk to Roman about borrowing Darya again soon. We can come back."

Leo's disappointment is short-lived. "The warehouse? Can I come?"

"Your mom and I will talk about it. Come on."

Nick starts for the car with Leo right behind him. I linger in place for a second, watching the two of them walk together. I feel like a third wheel in my own family. But I'm not sure how else to act. I want Leo to have this time with Nick. I want Nick to have this time with Leo.

And I'm not sure how to act around Nick, honestly. We're not a couple. We're a step removed from strangers almost. Familiar in a few ways and so distant in most.

A burst of Russian distracts me.

The group of teenagers I spotted earlier are walking past on the path that runs along the far edge of the park, next to the parking lot. I can't understand a word the guys are saying, but I can guess based on the suggestive gestures one of them makes. They're older than I thought, probably early twenties. College age in the States. I'm not sure if the university system here is the same.

I've dealt with obnoxious men before. But maybe it's the fact that I can't understand exactly what they're saying and speaking will let them know that, that has my tongue glued to the top of my mouth.

Suddenly, the smirks slide off their faces. I know, without

turning around, what they're looking at. Especially once the color leaves as well.

Nick barks something that makes them all jump, then hurry away.

As much as I never want to be the woman who doesn't fight her own battles, I can't deny the way I move closer to Nick. I'm drawn to him like a magnet seeks its opposite pole. It's a chemical compulsion I have no control over.

"You okay?" His voice now is the complete opposite of whatever he said a few seconds ago. Summer's thaw after winter's freeze. Sunshine after a storm.

"What did they say?"

Nick shakes his head. He won't repeat it.

"What did you say?"

"To watch their mouths if they wanted to keep their lives."

"Death threats weren't necessary," I mumble.

"Yes, they were."

That's all he says as we walk back to Leo.

When most men say they would kill for you, it's a figure of speech.

Coming from Nick, it's a bloody promise.

It should terrify me, and it does.

But there's also a part of me that likes it, and that scares me even more.

CHAPTER TWENTY-TWO

NICK

Just past one a.m., there's a creak outside my door.

I tense, but don't otherwise react. I listen and wait, my body still but my heart and mind racing.

Rationally, I know sex with Lyla is a bad idea. She's been explicit about her eagerness to get home, her distaste for living here and for the Bratva. Letting her—letting them—go will be difficult. I've gotten used to living in a house with noise and liveliness. To not eating meals alone and to finding random action figurines lying around the house. To Lyla's walks and to Leo's school routine.

Instead of rushing home, I should be spending some nights in my Moscow apartment. Entertaining one of the women eager and willing to do whatever I want, who get wet because I'm the *Pakhan*, not despite it.

But when the door finally opens, I know I won't send her away. Just from the sound of her soft steps across the hardwood, my dick stirs. Anticipation courses through me. With Lyla, it feels familiar and new. Like we've done this a hundred times before, but it's also the first time.

"Are you awake?"

The curtains are drawn, so I can't see anything but her basic shape in the dark. But it sounds like she might be biting her lip.

"Yes."

There's a quiet rustle of fabric, and then her steps draw closer. I shift away from the side of the bed and fling the sheets to the side in a silent invitation. The mattress dips slightly under her weight as she slides in beside me. There's nothing but soft, warm skin against mine. She's naked, and I hear a surprised inhale when she realizes I am too.

My hand slips down her side and explores her back, feeling her skin react to my touch. She shivers and presses closer, her puckered nipples rubbing against me. I slide one hand between her legs and discover she's soaked. One finger pushes inside her wet entrance. Lyla lets out a breathy moan that goes straight to my cock. Her hips wriggle, trying to stimulate more friction.

"You shaved."

My thumb brushes her clit, and Lyla moans again.

"I thought you might…prefer it."

Fuck if knowing Lyla did this for me, thought about me, and is trying to please me doesn't turn me on even more. "I prefer whatever you prefer."

My dick is hard and impatient, but I don't want this to be a quick fuck. I'm in the mood to draw this out, to make her scream and beg and come multiple times. With Lyla, it comes naturally to prioritize her pleasure over my own. Seeing and feeling her shatter are what gets me off.

I roll us so she's on her back beneath me. I indulge in a kiss, sucking on her tongue while my fingers stroke her pussy. When my lips move to her neck, she gasps my name. I work my way down to her chest, teasing and licking and sucking while still slowly sliding my finger in and out. She writhes beneath me, trying to ride my hand.

"Impatient?" I slow the speed of my finger to an agonizing pace.

"*Fuck*, Nick." She arches against me. You couldn't slide a piece of paper between our bodies.

"I want your pussy wet, Lyla. I want you begging for my cock."

She blinks at me like I'm joking as I push a second finger inside, her muscles pulsing against my fingers and her hips rocking against my thigh. Every time my erection brushes against Lyla, her pussy clenches tighter, like she's imagining my cock is inside her instead.

Her fingernails dig into my back. "I want you so badly, Nick. I need you to fill me. I need you to fuck me. Please." She clenches around me again, and this time, I know it's on purpose. "*Please*."

I roll off her and reach into the drawer of the bedside table to grab a foil packet.

"Can I do it?"

I pass the condom to Lyla, watching her shape shift beside me. She leans over my dick, her long hair brushing against my stomach. I'm so hard, it's painful, my cock engorged and throbbing. Teasing her was torture for me too.

She sucks the flared tip into her mouth, licking away the pre-cum that's leaking before sucking me into warm, wet heaven. A long series of swears falls out of my mouth as I grip the sheets. Her tongue traces the pulsing vein that runs the length of my shaft.

"*Blyad*."

"Now, who's begging?" Lyla whispers as she finally rolls the rubber on.

I'm too worked up for verbal foreplay. As it is, I'm worried I won't be able to last longer than a few minutes.

"On your hands and knees, *malysha*."

The endearment falls out of my mouth without intention or permission. Lyla doesn't seem to notice as she rolls on her stomach and raises her ass in the air. I move into position behind her and grab the base of my dick, rubbing it through the slickness twice before slowly feeding my cock into her pussy. The sight of it pushing inside of her is almost enough to make me come.

There's something so primal and sexy about it, a claiming that seems more than physical. Once I'm finally fully inside of her, I slide a hand up her rib cage. I pinch her nipple, hard, and she gasps.

My hand moves lower, rubbing the spot just above where she's stretched around me. Her inner muscles clench tighter. I push as deep as possible, ensuring we're as connected as two people can be. Making sure she's feeling every inch.

Then, I start to move, sliding out before pumping in hard and fast. Lyla pushes back against me, meeting every thrust. Her breathing turns harsh and erratic, her moans into pants. She's close. I can tell as her pussy flutters and her legs tremble. With a lengthy groan, she comes, spasming around me and sinking into the mattress.

I keep pounding into her, prolonging her orgasm and then pushing her toward a new one as she keeps pulsing around me.

"Nick," she moans.

"You're going to come for me again. Look at you, taking my cock so well."

She arches her back, and all of a sudden, I want to see her face. I pull out and flip her over, then shove back in with a sudden thrust from a different angle.

"Oh my *God*." Her head tilts back, exposing the elegant

column of her throat as her legs wind around me. She pulls me closer, running her hands down my back.

I pound into her, losing any finesse or rhythm. It's raw and animalistic. Desperate and unhinged.

I feel her come, tight, hot spasms that make it impossible not to let go. Heat races down my spine and settles in my balls as I fill the condom, a devastating, mind-numbing sensation that wipes everything else away for a minute.

The delay from when I finish to when I pull out is too long. We both linger, savoring something that shouldn't matter after we've both come.

I stand and walk into the adjoining bathroom, relying on memory to navigate my way across the dark room. I flick on the bathroom light and pull off the condom, tossing it into the trash can before taking a piss.

Lyla appears in the doorway right as I flush. She's still completely naked, her hair tousled and her skin marked by my mouth. She walks past me and uses the toilet while I wash my hands. It's incredibly domestic and insanely erotic.

I can feel her eyes on me the whole time we move around one another. The bathroom is big, but it feels small right now.

Lyla saw me naked in here before, but this is the first time I'm really able to see her. She's conscious of my eyes on her body, almost knocking my cologne off the counter and rinsing her hands twice as long as is necessary. Her fingers are probably pruned by the time she's finished the process.

I walk back into the bedroom first, sliding under the covers that have cooled in the absence of any body heat. Lyla fidgets. The bathroom light is still on, backlighting her profile as she glances between the bed and the door.

"Stay," I say, then roll onto my back so I'm staring at the ceiling.

I don't sleep with women.

It's not about them. It has nothing to do with preserving feelings or avoiding clinginess. My reasoning is tied to trust and safety.

You're most vulnerable in sleep.

It's how my father was killed. His favorite mistress, Anna, planted a bomb on the yacht in the middle of the night and then jumped ship—literally. It was a cruel twist of fate that my uncle and two brothers both went on board the next morning for a meeting. The rival family who paid Anna off got more than they paid for, wiping out almost the entirety of the Morozov bloodline in one go. Unfortunately for them, I was on another continent.

"I don't have to…"

Even without looking over, I know Lyla is chewing on her bottom lip. Based on how surprised she was to find me still in her bed this morning, she has hang-ups about sleeping together in a nonsexual sense as well.

"Stay," I repeat, firmer.

She says nothing. But I feel her approach. Relax as her body settles into the space beside mine.

We lie there, side by side, in the dark, and it's almost as intimate as the sex was.

"Should I keep shaving?" Lyla whispers after a few minutes of silence.

I hesitate before answering. I'm not sure if she's asking to suss out if I'm hoping to see her pussy again or if she's honestly asking my body hair preferences.

"I'll want to fuck you either way," I finally say.

"I wanted to try something different," she mumbles. "Sometimes…I don't know. It can be harder to feel sexy as a mom, I guess."

"I find you very sexy, especially as a mom."

"Well, I had *your* kid."

Something about that statement settles right. *"I had your kid."*

"Yeah," I murmur. "You did."

"How long will you be gone for?"

"I'm not sure. Bianchi can be prideful and unreasonable. But he's also smart enough to know when it's worth cutting ties and when it's not."

"All right."

"Everything is going to be okay, Lyla."

She's silent for a beat, and I think she'll say something logical, like I couldn't possibly know that.

Instead, she whispers, "You promise?"

Something cracks in my chest, silent and permanent. "Yeah. I promise."

"Okay." She rolls over. After a couple of minutes, her breathing evens out.

But I lie wide awake. Talking to Bianchi is an essential part of ensuring Lyla's and Leo's safety. It's also a step closer to them leaving. I can't advance one of those goals without pushing forward the inevitable as well.

I want them to be safe. That's more important than anything else.

But…I also want them to stay.

CHAPTER TWENTY-THREE

NICK

Alex is waiting when I step off the plane, arms crossed. The wind ruffles his blond hair as it tears across the open space. "Hey, boss."

I answer his smirk with a smile. "Hi."

We didn't cross paths during my last unexpected trip to Philadelphia. It's been months since I saw him in person, and our phone calls have been less regular as of late.

Alex broaches the reason for that immediately. "How's Lyla doing?"

Freshly fucked. Just thinking about last night gets me hard. "Good."

Alex studies me, then shakes his head. "You're sleeping with her?"

He doesn't sound surprised, mostly disappointed.

"None of your business."

"It is if you're going to do something stupid."

"I'm here to do something smart."

"*Smart*? We both know you wouldn't have issued a kill order for anyone else."

"Leo's safety isn't negotiable. And she's his mother. What did you want me to do?"

Alex whistles, long and low. "Leo, huh?"

Figures he'd remember the stuffed lion I carried around as a little kid.

I look away at the gray stretch of tarmac.

Memories of the last time I was here haunt me. The panic. The fear. The terror.

"That was big of her. For a guy she thought hit it and quit it."

I fiddle with the lighter in my pocket. "We should get going."

"You're still in love with her."

"Still?" I scoff. "We were kids."

"And now?"

"She wants to get back here as soon as possible," I say.

We start walking toward the waiting car.

"Have you asked her to stay?"

I stop and fix him with a stare. "I didn't come here to discuss Lyla. I came to settle things with Bianchi. You can help with that, or you can stay behind."

Alex stares at me, then nods. "You got it, *boss*."

I grit my teeth and keep walking.

Twenty minutes later, we pull up outside one of Bianchi's legal establishments around the city. I avoided them all, even as a college freshman with a fake last name. The Italians had no idea a Morozov was living in their territory, but I knew I was living in theirs.

The Italian restaurant we park outside is cozy and homey.

More than half full when we walk inside and completely stuffed with lively chatter. It smells delicious inside, like tomatoes and warm bread and oregano. But we're not here to eat.

I blow past the hostess stand, where a brunette wearing a revealing white button-down is batting her eyelashes at a guy in his early twenties. I'm guessing he's one of Bianchi's soldiers.

I stride toward an empty table and take a seat, flinging my arm over the empty chair beside me in an exaggerated show of casualness.

The lighter in my pocket gets pulled out and tossed on the white tablecloth. If I have to burn this place down to get Bianchi's attention, I will. Based on his radio silence since that fateful afternoon, he's enjoying playing hard to get.

For the first time since we were elevated within our respective organizations, he has an advantage over me. Or at least he thinks he does.

All the chatter has dimmed considerably. When I glance toward the front of the restaurant, the kid up there is no longer focused on the hostess's cleavage. He's staring straight at me, his expression tense and disbelieving.

Some of Bianchi's legal businesses are nothing but a front. This place has been in his family for generations. It's where he hosts birthday parties for his kids and eats spaghetti with his *nonna*. There are a few dozen places I could have shown up to force a meeting with Luca, but this sends the most direct message.

If my family is fair game, so is his.

Alex leans back in his chair across the table from me, an excited smile stretching across his face.

An older woman approaches our table. More strands of white than brown thread through her bun. She glances between me and Alex with an apprehensive expression. She recognizes me or senses danger. Her knuckles are white as she clutches the ordering pad. "Can I get you anything?"

"A cappuccino, please," I order.

Alex shakes his head. "Nothing for me."

She nods, then hastily hurries away.

As soon as she's gone, Alex raises an eyebrow at me. "You're not worried they'll poison it?"

"No. That would be a very stupid decision."

"Not their first," Alex mutters. I smile, but it dies when he adds, "Late night?"

"Act less interested in my sex life," I tell him.

The woman returns only a few minutes later with a white cup and saucer. None of the other patrons around us have been served yet, all of them here before we arrived. She knows.

China clatters as the cup is set down. "*Prego*."

"*Gratzie*," I respond, lifting the cup and downing most of the cappuccino in one gulp. It's frothy and scalding, the steamed milk and espresso burning my tongue before sliding down my throat. "Wait."

The woman freezes, the pink leaving her cheeks like rain sliding down a window.

"Luca Bianchi. He owns this place?"

She nods once quickly. Then again, slower.

"I want to speak to him. Make sure he knows Nikolaj Morozov is waiting. And pass along that I don't like to be kept waiting as well."

She nods again, then rushes away.

Alex smirks. "Subtle."

I lean back in my chair and drain the rest of the coffee.

I *am* exhausted. I only managed a few hours of sleep before leaving for the airport to fly here. Most of the trip was spent catching up on work I've been neglecting in favor of spending more time with Leo and Lyla. I've spent most of the past twenty-four hours awake.

"So…what's he like?"

I glance at Alex, brow raised.

"Not asking about her. I'm asking about Leo."

"He's…" I exhale. "He's amazing. So smart. I'm teaching him poker. And he's super thoughtful. Always excited. He loves coming to the warehouse, wants to see everything. We took Roman's dog to the park yesterday, and he never stopped smiling. He's started calling me Dad. The first time he did…fuck, I'll never forget it."

Alex smiles. "Look at you, all domestic and shit. I want to meet him."

"He'll be back here soon enough." I say the sentence as a reminder for myself, more than anything.

There's a reason I'm here.

The silence stretches until a new voice speaks. "You've got a pair, Morozov. I'll give you that."

I glance to the right at Luca Bianchi. He strolls toward our table in a three-piece suit, hair neatly combed back. Both his hair and his suit are black, like an oil slick.

"Consider it a compliment. I hate house calls."

Luca lets out a dry chuckle before sliding into the seat across from me. Alex moves away subtly as one of his hands disappears beneath the table. There's no way Bianchi missed it, but he keeps his eyes focused on me.

"I don't invite Russians into my house. And this isn't where I conduct business."

"I'm not here on business."

"No? What are you here for?"

"Pleasure."

Luca taps his fingers on his table. His right hand is nowhere to be seen. Probably holding his gun, just like mine is.

"And here I was, thinking you might be here because the county coroner fished a Russian bullet out of my favorite *capo*."

Fucking Irish.

I hold Luca's gaze. "I don't know what you're talking about."

"I'm sure you don't."

We continue staring at each other, the din around us sounding muffled. I'm not sure if it's because the customers are aware of the fact that they're sitting next to a couple of powerful, pissed off leaders or if it's my body's response to the revelation that I came here with even less leverage than I thought.

The timing of what went down in Lyla's apartment building is suspicious at best. I was in town, I have a connection to two of the building's residents that is obvious with a little digging, and I have the means to cover it up. But I didn't think Bianchi would have proof. It puts me in a perilous position.

"This favorite *capo* of yours, do you have any idea where he was when he died?"

Luca stares at me, and I stare back, locked in a stalemate. I won't admit I issued a kill order, unprovoked. He won't admit he had men trailing me, who followed into Lyla's apartment building.

I lean closer. "I'd rather be friendly than foes, Bianchi. But make no mistake, I have no issue making enemies. Whoever killed your favorite *capo* might be trying to give you a warning about trespassing in a residential building you have no business with."

After a *long* pause, Luca nods. "I've made worse than a bullet disappear. As long as we avoid future incidents."

"As long as we avoid future trespassing."

"I own this city."

"Not the parts that belong to me."

Luca's lips tip upward. "So, you're claiming the bastard? And sending him back here?"

I say nothing.

Luca's eyes glint with mirth as he leans forward. My grip on the gun tightens.

I don't think he'll provoke me here, but I don't trust him not to.

"I want a favor."

"I don't work for anyone."

His smirk grows. "So, what's the deal with you and Lyla Peterson? A druggie's daughter was good enough for you to fuck, but not to keep around? I suppose Igor would have had some issues with it. Convenient excuse for taking no responsibility for your kid."

I'm sorely tempted to pull the trigger on the gun I'm aiming at Bianchi under the table, but I don't. Doing so will set off a shitstorm I'm not prepared to handle. Cost me money and men in addition to delaying Lyla's and Leo's return to normalcy, possibly indefinitely. Not to mention, a reaction is exactly what Luca is looking for. I'm too proud and too stubborn to give him one.

"I want protection for them while they're here. Your word they won't be harmed."

Bianchi sneers, "We don't shield Russians."

"One favor."

His poker face is excellent, but I still catch the flicker of surprise before it disappears. Despite making the demand, Luca didn't think I would meet it.

"Never thought I'd see the day." He taps a few fingers on the table, the pattern regular and irritating. "Nikolaj Morozov folding. Over a woman no less."

Alex eyeballs me, clearly worried I'm close to losing my shit. I'm not.

I hold out a hand, eager to make the agreement before Bianchi changes his mind. This isn't exactly a lucrative deal for either of us. Bullet or not, Luca would have a hard time proving my men shot his, unprovoked. He had no good reason to have men in that building.

There's nothing to be gained by trying, and it would lose him a powerful ally. He's gaining a favor in exchange for not pursuing something he already wouldn't have and controlling what happens in Philly, which he is already doing. Me agreeing is evidence of how far I'll capitulate when it comes to my family, and I know Luca will exploit it. Unfortunately, since they *are* a priority for me, I have no other option.

"Like I said, I don't do business here. You gentlemen thirsty?"

Luca loves games. He's not a straightforward businessman. I can see this unfolding, and I don't love the direction it's going in. But I have no choice. Leaving here without an arrangement isn't an acceptable outcome.

"Do you have vodka?" Alex asks, joining the conversation for the first time.

"Yes," Luca replies, looking at me.

I stand, not bothering to hide the gun I've been holding as I tuck it into my hip holster. "After you."

I know where we're headed. Bianchi owns a gentlemen's club one street over. On paper, it's a legal entity, but I have no doubt there's plenty of dirty money funneled through.

Three of Bianchi's men join us at the door. I'm unsurprised he's called in reinforcements, but it still makes me uncomfortable to see the numbers more than evened. Alex is tense by my side.

Walking into the club doesn't help. It's dark inside, muted, flashing lights reflecting off the shiny bar top and exposed skin.

Alex lets out a low whistle as we walk farther inside. The atmosphere is sultry and dim. The scent of smoke tinges the air along with sex and sin.

Bianchi leads the way into a private back room. It has its own bar and its own stage.

All but one of his men disappear. His attempt to tell me an ambush isn't imminent, I guess.

And then the women appear. All scantily dressed, showing off endless stretches of smooth skin. Big tits spill out of tops, and high heels show off long legs. I'm basically sitting front row for a lingerie show, and my dick doesn't even twitch.

Bianchi beckons a redhead over. "Bring over a bottle of Stolichnaya Elit for my Russian friends."

She complies immediately, returning quickly with three glasses and a brand-new bottle of the expensive vodka. Luca's attention is on the show taking place onstage, but I watch closely as each glass gets filled with a couple of inches of clear liquid and then distributed.

Luca raises his glass and tips it toward me. "To keeping secrets."

I'm not sure which secret he's referring to—the bullet or my son.

Leo isn't much of a secret. I've done nothing to hide our relationship, opting to protect him with association instead of attempting anonymity, like I'm ashamed or indifferent. My son is what I'm most proud of. The title of *Pakhan* was handed to me because of nothing but the family I was born into and unfortunate circumstances. At least when it comes to Leo's existence, I played a small role.

Bianchi laughs when I tap his glass. He watches while I down it, then gestures toward the group of women like a game show host displaying prizes. "Take your pick."

My jaw works. I've been waiting for this moment ever since we arrived. "I'm good."

Luca sips his drink and leans back. As if on cue, the redhead returns to his side. All she's wearing is a seductive smile and a G-string.

Bianchi is paying no attention to the naked woman who is now gyrating on his lap. His gaze is focused straight on me, intense and unwavering. "It's rude to refuse a gift."

I lean back as well, adopting a relaxed posture even though I'm anything but. "Rudeness is one of my more redeemable character traits. Trust me."

"Along with performance anxiety?"

"Women come to me willingly. They're not fucking for a paycheck."

Luca's lip curls as he studies me over the rim of his glass. "You're not even married to the American bitch, Nikolaj. Yet you're loyal."

"Loyalty is an interesting ideal to be lectured on by a man who has a wife and three kids waiting at home," I muse.

Bianchi slides a palm up the redhead's bare thigh. There's nothing tender or even eager about it. It's a purposeful movement, and it tells me a lot I already know about the Italian seated across from me.

It's one thing to keep family separate from business. I work with plenty of associates who act cold and indifferent. Never mention their children, if they have any. I respect that approach, especially since becoming a parent myself. But it's another thing to flout a disregard for it, to revel in acting superior.

Luca is putting on a show to test if I'm willing to do so, and he isn't happy with the answer. In his mind, I failed.

He thought I came here to preserve our uneasy understanding.

He considered Lyla and Leo easy weaknesses to bring up because I have few of them.

I pour more vodka into my empty glass, hoping it will keep some of Luca's fickle favor. He doesn't care if I fuck one of his women or not. He's playing with me, trying to assess what our previous limited interactions haven't revealed. The meeting with him after seeing Lyla was short, centered around weapon exports. He'll brag about this interaction—me drinking in a Bianchi establishment—to every Italian who will listen.

I drain my glass again and hold a hand out. "We have a deal."

Luca studies my extended palm for a minute.

It feels like hours pass.

When he finally shakes my offered hand, I have to swallow the sigh of relief. He can play all the games he wants. But now, if he breaks his word, no one will do business with him. Luca might be a snake, but he isn't stupid.

I stand, glancing at Alex, who's distracted by a blonde.

"There an alley to smoke?" I ask Bianchi.

He jerks his head toward the door behind the bar, exploring the redhead's body while she continues to grind in his lap.

I stand and head toward the door. It connects with a short hall, and that leads outside. The alley is narrow and dark. Also quiet and empty.

The only sound is the muffled music emanating from inside the club, probably from the front section open to those without deep pockets or connections.

I pull the lighter out of my pocket and flick it to life, watching the tiny flame dance in the small opening. There's a pack of cigarettes in my pocket, but I don't bother to pull them out. I mostly picked up smoking as some combination of an intimidation tactic and stress relief. I'm not addicted to the habit or the nicotine.

Hazy warmth from the ounces of alcohol I just downed swims

through my bloodstream as I lean against the hard exterior of the building. Bored, I pull a cigarette out and light it, inhaling a long pull and then blowing the smoke out at the sky.

I pull my phone out, taken aback by the amount of notifications. I scan the first dozen, surprised by the number of them and who they were sent by. Then, I tap on the number for the phone I gave Lyla.

I'm not expecting her to answer. I've never seen her use the phone, though I know she's taken possible threats seriously enough to carry it with her.

Lyla answers on the third ring.

"Hey, it's me." Distantly, some part of my brain is disturbed by the fact that I chose to start the conversation that way. *It's me* implies an intimate level of familiarity. Where you memorize a voice, to the point that it needs no introduction.

"Hi." She breathes the word, exhaling it with oxygen. It sounds like relief until her voice pitches with concern. "Is everything okay?"

I snuff the cigarette and flick the lighter on again, watching the flame dance for a few seconds before extinguishing it. "Everything is fine. I'm just ending your game of Telephone."

"I don't know what you're talking about."

I smile. In a dark alley that smells of garbage and sounds like scuttling rats, I *smile*. Every single man who I left guarding the house let me know she was asking about me. "Don't lie to me, Lyla. Your ten accomplices ratted you out."

There's a silence that sounds like her deliberating about what to say. "I didn't want to bother you," is what she decides on.

"You wouldn't have bothered me."

"I figured if there was anything to say, you would have texted me."

I read between the lines.

She *wanted* me to reach out, which is why she went through a chain of my men. And calling her didn't occur to me until I saw the other messages.

I'm here on business even if it's closely related to something more personal. Relations with the Italians—and with the Bianchi family in particular—are crucial in many ways unrelated to Philadelphia and having my son live in his territory.

I'm also entirely naive when it comes to anything even resembling a relationship. The last time I was in one was…her. It's rare for me to even have sex with the same woman twice. When it's happened, it's been interspersed with months or even years. Not hours.

"It's early there." I crap out on commenting anything deeper.

"It feels late. I didn't get much sleep." She yawns, as if to emphasize her point.

Miss me? hovers on the tip of my tongue. But I don't speak it, not even as a tease.

There's no good answer. Either it will be what I want to hear or what she doesn't want to say.

I've been gone for less than a day.

I think there's more than impatience about leaving factoring into her curiosity about what's happening here, but I'm not sure. And it will be better for the both of us if that's all it is.

"I'll be back tomorrow," I state, making plans up as I speak.

I left my return open-ended. It's a long flight to make for one day. Depending on how long discussions with Bianchi took, I planned to go to New York next and finish up the business my last visit cut short. Or visit Boston to coordinate with the Irish.

Rather than do any of that, I'm rushing home.

Maybe Alex is right to be concerned.

"Leo will be excited. He misses you."

Just Leo? is what I think. But once again, I don't say it.

I can't recall a time where I didn't say as much as I did. When I chose tact over bluntness. But I'm well aware Lyla and I are balancing on a knife's edge right now. Wavering in an uncertain space with certain, separate futures.

"I miss him too," I say and wonder if she's analyzing my words the same way I'm digging through hers.

We sound like divorced parents. Like *my* parents, who had little in common besides their children.

And then there's a silence that stretches, one that isn't uncomfortable, but *is* noticeable, where we could exchange the same sentiment.

Neither of us does. But we don't fill it either. It stretches like the space between a beginning and an end that could be filled in lots of different ways.

"I'll see you tomorrow," I finally state.

"I'll see you tomorrow," Lyla repeats.

It's not until I hang up that I realize…she never even asked how it went with Bianchi.

Maybe she's assuming it went well since I'm not staying longer.

But I can't help but consider other reasons.

CHAPTER TWENTY-FOUR

LYLA

I stretch my arm into the cold side of the bed, hating just *how* cold it feels. The air temperature isn't that chilly. I can hear the radiator hiss as it heats the huge house. And there's a thick comforter over the bed, draping me in down.

The number of mornings I've woken with Nick versus the number that I've woken up alone is comically lopsided. Yet, somehow, waking up without him feels cold and empty when it should really just be familiar.

It's not the warmth I miss.

I miss *him*, and that's dangerous.

For my heart. For my future. For my kid. For my safety.

I toss an arm over both eyes and chew my bottom lip, willing the feeling away. Instead, *I'll see you tomorrow* echoes around in my head.

I give up and get up, showering and dressing before heading downstairs. Breakfast is already laid out at the long table. Leo is in his usual spot. He's not reading anything today. He's just staring into space as he eats his cereal.

I kiss the top of his head as I pass to grab some coffee.

He startles. "Mom!"

"Morning, sweetie. Did you sleep okay?"

"Yeah." Leo plays with his spoon.

I drink some coffee and serve myself a plate.

Once I'm seated across from Leo, he asks the question I've been dreading. "Do we have to go back to Philadelphia?"

He's asked me some close relative of this question for the past week or so, ever since he learned Nick is his father. But this is the blatant version, the *I want to stay.* The start of resentment. Leo has never really fought me on a decision before. But I can see this being the battle he chooses, and I'm dreading it more and more every single day that passes.

"Philadelphia is where we live, Leo."

"It's a long way away," he tells me, as if I might have forgotten the hours we spent on a plane to get here. And that was flying private, not dealing with the delays and inconveniences of flying commercial.

I eat my yogurt instead of replying, like a coward.

"My friends here will all forget about me."

"*No one* here will forget about you, Leo. Especially not your father."

I don't tell Leo Nick might be returning today. Part of me isn't sure whether to believe it myself. He flew all that way to spend a few hours.

"Some kids used to make fun of me for not having a dad."

"They shouldn't have done that. But, Leo, that had nothing to do with you. They were upset or angry about something else and decided to be mean instead of dealing with it. I can talk with the school when we get back and—"

Leo huffs, annoyed. "Don't say anything. I just go to the nurse's office when I don't feel like dealing with it."

I think of his last day at school—our last day in Philadelphia.

That's why he went to the nurse's, I realize, and it makes it hard to swallow all of a sudden.

"Everyone here wants to be my friend as soon as they hear Nick is my dad," Leo adds. "But Dad told me to only trust people who want to be my friend, no matter what."

In addition to everything else, Nick has eclipsed me when it comes to giving advice, I guess. That's better than what I would have come up with in response to Leo telling me kids wanted to be his friend because of me.

"Philadelphia is home, Leo," I say gently. "What about AJ? He's your best friend."

"I could visit AJ. He'd want me to be with my dad. He misses his."

I'm not sure what to say to that. I know what Leo means. AJ had no say in losing his father. And Leo feels like I'm forcing the same outcome on him.

I'm distracted for the rest of breakfast and for the ride to school, worrying about how Leo will handle our departure and wondering whether Nick will really be back today. I don't snap out of it until I walk back inside the mansion after dropping Leo off and spot a figure standing by the stairs. My heart stalls for a second—until I realize it's not who I thought it was.

Vera Morozov is exactly as tall and intimidating as I remember her being. She strides past me and toward the door I just entered with nothing but a barked, "Come!"

I cast a glance at Valentin, who drove this morning. He doesn't appear concerned by Nick's mother's presence, which I take as an encouraging sign. Not a cause for panic at least.

I hurry after her, back out into the cold. The convoy of cars from the school run is still parked outside.

"Is everything okay? Is Nick okay?"

Vera doesn't appear concerned, just impatient, but she also doesn't strike me as the type of mother prone to excessive worrying.

"Nick." In her heavy accent, the word sounds strange. "Nikolaj is fine. Just stupid."

"Stupid?" I echo.

Vera waves a glove-clad hand toward the row of black cars. "How many men you travel with? Stupid!"

Does she think I requested them? "I didn't ask for this many men. Nick—Nikolaj just had them sent with me, and I wasn't sure —I mean, I was happy for Leo to have as much protection as possible."

Vera makes a show of looking around. "I do not see Leo."

Then, she climbs into the first car, leaving me standing here.

A few seconds later, her door opens again. "Hurry!"

I walk over to the car and climb in on the opposite side. There's a flurry of Russian between Vera and the driver, and then we set off, back down the long, winding driveway. Every time I glance at Vera, she's studying me through narrowed eyes, so I mostly keep my gaze outside the car.

"Where are we going?" I eventually ask.

She's Nick's mother, and these are Nick's men. I'm not concerned about my safety, but I'm definitely apprehensive about what's to come.

"Women's shelter."

"Really?"

Nick hasn't mentioned his offer to set up a volunteer arrangement since that night in his office, and so I haven't brought it up either. I'm elated to realize he didn't forget even if I'm uncertain about it involving Vera.

Vera's harsh expression softens slightly as she registers the excitement in my voice. She studies me without the irritated scowl, which is somehow more unsettling.

"Maybe just dumb," she decides.

It's far from praise or approval. But it's a little from someone who seems accustomed to giving nothing, which somehow seems like a lot.

CHAPTER TWENTY-FIVE

LYLA

"What are you doing?"

I startle and glance up from the tangled mess of yarn. Nick is leaning against the opening between the hall and my bedroom, an amused smile playing across his lips. There are dark circles beneath his eyes, but otherwise, he looks the same as before he left.

I inhale, sharp and surprised. "You're back."

He nods. "I'm back."

We stare at each other for what is really seconds but feels much longer.

"Your mom is here."

"I know. She's downstairs, teaching Leo how to play chess."

"We went to a women's shelter today."

Something in Nick's expression tells me he already knew that. Confirms he had a hand in it. "How was it?"

"It was good. Sad but good. I helped peel potatoes and iron. A few of the women have job interviews tomorrow. One of them hasn't seen her kids in a year. They've been staying with her sister."

"Are you going back?"

I nod. "Next week. As long as that's okay?"

"You don't need my permission, Lyla."

"I know." I play with the yarn, avoiding his gaze.

"What is all the string for?"

"Leo needs a new hat."

"So, buy him one."

"I'm knitting him one."

Nick raises one eyebrow. The longer he stands there, the faster my heart races. "I'm going out tonight."

"Oh. Okay." I continue avoiding his gaze and untangling a knot in the yarn, not wanting him to see the disappointment in mine.

"Do you want to come?"

My hands still in the strings, and my head snaps up. "Where?"

"It's a dinner. An engagement party, I guess."

That takes a few seconds to sink in. I'm not sure which is more shocking—that Nick is going to an engagement party or that he invited me to come along.

"Um…" The invitation is unexpected, but that's only part of why I'm hesitating. I want to go, and I'm unaccustomed to indulging those impulses, honestly.

Nick half smiles. "I'll see you tomorrow."

"Wait." I stand, tripping first over the yarn and then banging my shin on the bedframe. "It's just…" I approach where Nick has paused. "What about Leo?"

"My mom wants to stay with him."

I don't miss his choice of phrasing. *Want* isn't can or could. "She does?"

He nods.

I inhale. "Okay. I'll go. What time are we leaving?"

"Whenever you're ready. Just come downstairs, okay?"

I'm assuming that means we're already running late. "Okay."

Nick smiles and disappears.

I head into the bathroom to wash my face. For the first time since we arrived, I open the makeup bag that arrived with the rest of our belongings.

My daily routine used to consist of a little concealer beneath the eyes and a quick slick of mascara. Since I've been here, it's begun and ended with a heavy layer of moisturizer to combat the bitter cold. The lengthy routine of foundation and bronzer and blush and eye shadow and eyeliner is a rarity.

It gives me something else to focus on instead of uncertainty about the party we're attending.

When I finish with my makeup, I head for the wooden wardrobe that takes up half of one wall. I have one option for a dress. It's a black velvet one with a tassel sash, plunging neckline, and short sleeves, which I bought on sale for the office Christmas party at the Curtis Atrium two years ago. That was the last time I wore it, so I'm relieved it still fits. I don't have any tights to go with it. I simply slip on a pair of black heels and head downstairs.

I can hear Leo's voice as I descend the staircase. He's chattering away, cheerful and excited. And I just enjoy the sound instead of worrying about the consequences of him loving living here so much.

The world Nick is involved in, the organization he leads, is not something I'm comfortable with. But it's no longer as scary and overwhelming as it once was. The men who travel with me to and from Leo's school every day are intimidating. But they also hold the door for me and smile at Leo. And every one of them is risking their life to protect my son. It's hard not to appreciate that. To not sense the camaraderie Nick spoke about when he was discussing the reasons men choose to pledge lifelong allegiance to the Bratva.

When I reach the living room, I spot him immediately. Leo is bouncing on the couch opposite from Vera, who's scrutinizing the black-and-white board resting between them.

Nick is leaning against the wall by the fireplace, studying the two of them. I watch him watch them, seeing some of the emotion he's trying to hide. He looks wistful and happy, standing handsome and tall in his tuxedo. It's all black, which is basically all he wears. But there's something polished about his appearance tonight that reminds me of what waking up in an empty bed felt like.

After a few seconds, his gaze snaps to mine.

As long as I live, whether it's years or decades, I'll never forget the look on Nick's face. I'll never forget how the way he's looking at me makes me feel. It sears into my mind, leaving a permanent mark.

I don't think it has anything to do with the way I'm dressed. He's seen a lot more of me than this dress teases at.

There's lust and fascination and relief and interest and hope and protectiveness. Some I understand and some I'm not expecting to see.

And it makes me feel cherished. Appreciated. *Seen.*

"Wow. You look pretty, Mom."

I tear my eyes away from Nick to smile at Leo. "Thank you, love."

Wobbly steps bring me closer to the chess setup. It's been a while since I walked in heels.

"You're learning chess?"

"Yes." Leo beams. "Grandma is teaching me."

"Grandma sounds old," Vera states, moving a pawn.

But she doesn't tell Leo to stop calling her that, I notice, and he seems undeterred. "You said English doesn't matter anyway."

"I did say that," Vera replies. "Your move, *vnuk*."

"We should get going," Nick says.

My pulse pauses and then picks up at the sound of his voice.

Stupid, I tell my heart.

I bend and kiss the top of Leo's head. "Be good. I'll see you in the morning."

Leo nods, mostly focused on the board. "Night, Mom. Night, Dad."

Two sentences I never thought I'd hear my son say.

Nick bends down to whisper something to Leo. Whatever it is, it makes him smile. He straightens and says something to Vera, louder. But that exchange takes place in Russian, so I once again have no idea what is being said.

I give Vera a small smile before walking out of the living room. She doesn't return it exactly, but she doesn't scowl either, which I would call progress.

A maid is waiting with my coat in the front hall. I shrug into it and thank her before heading out into the cold. The wind nips at my bare legs, brutal with no barrier at all. Thankfully, there's a car pulled up and waiting, exhaust winding from the rear into the void of night air.

I settle into the passenger seat as Nick adjusts the driver's. And then we're zipping away from the estate and toward the front gates.

"Who got engaged?"

"Leonid Belyaev."

"He works for you?"

"Yes."

"I wouldn't invite my boss to a party."

It's hard to tell in the dim car, but I think Nick smiles. "I doubt he's expecting for me to show up."

"Why are you going then?"

"You said you're bored."

"You made it sound like you'd go without me."

"I lied." Nick rolls down his window to talk with the gate guard.

The metal swings open, and then we're moving again, zipping along dark roads.

I should ask him how things went in Philadelphia. Whether it's safe to return once Dmitriy is handled. But instead, I say, "What did your mom call Leo? Vr-nik?"

"*Vnuk*."

"Right. What does it mean?"

Nick hesitates before answering. "Grandson. It means grandson."

I swallow. "Oh."

We pull up outside a stone house a few minutes later. It's not as large as Nick's estate, but still is impressive. Nick steps out of the car first. Uniformed men are already swarming the car, literally falling over themselves in an effort to be the one assisting Nick.

I'd categorize Nick as confident, but not cocky. I'm not sure how his ego isn't the size of Russia though, seeing the reverence on the faces of a dozen men. Maybe it's part of the traditional respect for the *Pakhan*. And I'm biased. But I think it's mostly Nick. The way he carries himself that makes him someone you want to be around.

He mostly ignores the men, tossing the keys to one guy with a flurry of Russian I assume is a warning not to damage the car. But then he's by my side, resting a hand on my lower back. Somehow, that slight touch is enough to warm my whole body despite the freezing temperatures.

"Too bad no one noticed you're here yet," I comment as we walk toward the front door.

The sound of Nick's chuckle trails behind as I gain confidence in my heels with each step. The smooth velvet rubs against my skin as I walk, whispering like a lover's caress.

The front door opens as we approach, as if on cue. Music and voices spill out.

"Stay close to me."

I glance up at Nick. There's no trace of amusement in his expression now. I'm looking at a different version of him, a harsher and crueler version than the man who trails kisses across my skin and whispers dirty words. Who teaches Leo card games and plays with him in the park.

He guides me through the front door into what is essentially a ballroom. A packed ballroom, crowded with men in tuxedos and women draped with jewels to accompany their fancy dresses.

Not a single person misses Nick's entrance.

There's an audible hush that falls, even mirrored by the live music being played in the corner. It feels like there's an invisible spotlight trained on us, hot and bright.

I stay close to his side, just as Nick requested. I can tell every time he introduces or mentions me. The eyes of whoever he's talking to will dart my way, assessing and often confused. Mixing in with the lustful expressions of the women and the awed, jealous looks from the men.

All the conversation is in Russian. I entertain myself by people-watching as the rapid flow of dialogue passes by like a river I can't dam, sipping on glasses of the champagne being passed around.

Eventually, I excuse myself to use the restroom. It's off the ballroom, easy to access and just as ostentatious. Nothing is dark and old. The bathroom is all marble and cream-colored tile, shined to a blinding brightness.

I'm washing my hands when a petite blonde woman sweeps into the restroom. I study her in the mirror. The top of her head barely reaches my shoulder. Everything about her is delicate and doll-like, down to the sleek updo and silk gown. Rather than walk into one of the stalls like I'm expecting, she simply strolls past them, checking each door to make sure it's unlocked and empty.

Apprehension uncurls in my stomach as I continue watching her in the mirror. I shut off the tap and dry my hands on one of the fancy towels.

She turns and approaches me slowly, like you would a wounded animal. Then whispers something so softly, I doubt I would understand it even if it were English.

I raise and drop a shoulder. "I don't understand."

The blonde takes a deep breath. Casts an anxious look at the door. "Is he cruel?" she asks, hardly louder than before. I barely catch the words before they drift away like leaves dancing in the wind.

I stare at her, confused. "Cruel? Who?"

"Nikolaj Morozov. My father means to marry us, and the tales I've heard…" Her voice trails off, as if she's too terrified to continue.

I'm horrified for another reason altogether.

Because I'm looking at this girl—this girl who I now realize is the nineteen-year-old Nick mentioned—who looks scared and alone and desperate, and I'm *jealous*.

I'm envious.

The fate she's so scared of? Marrying Nick?

It's what I want for myself and will never have. I'm not part of this world, and I don't want to be.

But I *do* want Nick.

And looking at the woman who will likely become his wife, who will have kids he'll hold as babies and spend nights beside him, makes me want to throw up.

Or throw something.

Or both.

I find my voice. “He’s not cruel.”

That’s all I offer her, and it’s not much. A lack of cruelty doesn’t make someone a good person.

But it seems to be enough. Relief softens the worried lines of her face, making her expression even more radiant. And me even more bitter.

“Thank you.” Fervent with gratitude, her response makes me feel even worse about my ugly thoughts.

I only have time to nod before she sweeps out of the restroom as gracefully as she appeared.

She cornered me, I realize. She was watching me and followed me in here.

The sensation doesn’t sit well with me, but I can’t do a damn thing about it. I leave the restroom before anyone else enters, resisting the urge to look around for the delicate blonde.

When I spot Nick, he’s already looking at me.

I grab another glass of champagne off a passing tray and down most of the fizziness in one go, irritated with no other outlet. I scan the dance floor that’s been set up in the center of the room. All the couples are maintaining a polite distance, most of them sharing awkward smiles. It makes me sad. Witnessing love—especially romantic love—is a rarity, it seems.

And then Nick is at my side. “Everything okay?” he asks, speaking English for the first time since we arrived.

“Do you want to dance?”

His brow furrows, his expression intense as he studies me.

I roll my eyes. “Never mind. Is there food—”

He grabs my hand and yanks me toward the dance floor, barely allowing me time to get rid of my glass.

Nick has never treated me like I’m breakable, and I hate how much I love it. Most people seem to see me as delicate, which has always felt like a close cousin to pathetic. I might be a single parent, and I might be poor, but I think those have made me tougher, not weaker.

Lots of people stare as we join the small group on the dance floor, but I've had just enough champagne not to care.

"I met your fiancée," I tell him after two spins around.

Nick's hand tightens around mine. "She's not my fiancée. Nothing has been decided."

"She's terrified."

"I expect you two got along splendidly then."

"I'm not scared of you."

"You're not." There's something sardonic in his tone, in the words that waver somewhere between a statement and a question.

I lift my chin. "No, I'm not."

I mean it. I'm not scared of Nick. I know he'd never hurt me physically or purposefully.

Emotional scars are another matter. I'm afraid of his life, of the situation I'm in simply because of a frat party.

"Don't forget about my dirty hands."

"I shouldn't have said that, Nick. I'm sorry."

Surprise, then annoyance crosses his face. "Don't apologize, Lyla. About anything, but especially about that."

"You killed a killer, not an innocent person. It's not for me to judge you for it."

Nick's lips twist into a smirk. "I thought you were an atheist."

"I am. I'm not talking about God. I'm not saying you *will* be judged by anyone." I take a deep breath. "Just that it wasn't my place to."

I don't share the real reason I said it in the first place. I *wanted* Nick to touch me that night. The thought that his hands had been covered in blood a few seconds earlier didn't bother me, and the realization it didn't bother me terrified me. Because if I couldn't reject him in such an extreme moment—a clear example of why we would never ever work—everything else would be quicksand.

And here I am, sinking.

"You're a good dancer." I say it as a distraction.

Nick eyes me before he responds, letting me know he realizes that. That's the problem—he always notices far too much. Sees what most people miss.

"I'm good at a lot of things," he finally replies.

I roll my eyes. "Not modesty."

A tiny smile plays on Nick's lips. "My mom loved dancing. She was a ballerina. After she married my father, she stopped performing. But I'd see her dance sometimes, when my father wasn't around."

"He didn't like her dancing?"

"He didn't see any point to art."

"That's a sad way to live," I say softly.

"You're right. It is."

"So, dancing reminds you of your mother?"

"It reminds me of the etiquette lessons my mother forced on us to make up for the disappointment of not having a daughter."

"Does that mean you don't like dancing?"

Nick is a puzzle. I shouldn't be trying to put the pieces together, to understand the whole picture instead of judging the parts I've seen.

"I hate it," he answers. Then, his arms tighten.

I can feel the tendons in his forearms flex through the thin material of my dress, and I shiver without meaning to.

"Are you cold?"

"No." My reply comes without thinking.

I feel him tense as my response registers. "I don't hate dancing with you," he says, glancing down so I can see the sincerity on his face.

I pull in a deep breath, flooding my lungs with oxygen I hope will chase away everything I'm trying to ignore. "Don't say stuff like that," I whisper.

We're in the middle of a crowded room, but it feels like the world has narrowed to the two of us and nothing else.

The tenderness in Nick's expression melts away, replaced by frozen stoicism. "Don't ask questions then. I told you I wouldn't lie."

We spend the rest of our dance in silence. When it ends, Nick spins and stalks toward the bar.

I want to shout at his back. To ask him why he's making this so difficult. Why he says perfect things yet comes home, covered in blood. Why he's the villain and the prince in my fairy tale.

CHAPTER TWENTY-SIX

NICK

I can't look away from her.

This was supposed to fade.

I'm not sure when, but it was definitely supposed to. No women besides her has ever held my attention. And the last time she did was under very different circumstances.

I gave the circumstances more credit than they were owed. The only overlap between my time with Lyla in college and now is her, and it feels the same. I can barely focus on the conversations I'm supposed to be carrying.

Everyone here is hoping to curry favor. These are valuable people to talk to, and I honestly couldn't care less what a single one of them has to say. I'm focused entirely on Lyla, who has thankfully shifted from champagne to water.

There isn't a drop of alcohol in my blood, and it pisses me off. I opted for no driver so I would be alone with Lyla in the car. And I'm realizing now I won't drink and drive with her. So, I'm stuck staying sober and battling an erection every time I catch a glimpse of her cleavage in the low-cut dress she's wearing.

People are talking. About the fact that I'm here when I never show up to meaningless social events. About the American I came here with when I never show up with a date. About the scowl on my face when I'm usually somewhat pleasant.

Pavel Popov sidling up to me does little to improve my dark mood. He's been trying to get ahold of me for weeks—ever since rumors about my son started to spread.

"Nikolaj."

"Pavel."

"Lovely party, isn't it?"

"Delightful," I drone.

Popov is smart enough not to make enemies out of powerful friends. Even if he didn't want to marry his daughter off to me, he wouldn't chide me for poor manners.

"I hoped we'd be celebrating a different couple's engagement by now."

"I've been busy, Pavel."

"So I've heard. You must have taken quite a hit in that warehouse explosion." Pavel leans closer, and I can smell the alcohol on his breath. "Sign the agreement, and I can help."

My phone rings in my pocket.

"Excuse me," I say, then step away.

"We caught Maxim Golubev," Roman tells me as soon as I answer the phone out on the freezing terrace.

"Where?"

Of the eight men who left with Dmitriy, Maxim is the one I expected. He and Dmitriy are close. Dmitriy relies upon and trusts him, and Maxim is quite possibly the only person that applies to.

"At the Troitsk warehouse. You were right about them hitting it next."

Pride is unmistakable in Roman's voice, and some of it hits me as well. This is a victory, the closest thing to capturing

Dmitriy himself. Not only is it a moral blow, but Maxim will know his plans. His hideouts. His weak points.

"Should I get him strung?"

"No," I answer. "Put him in one of the cells. With food and water. He'll be expecting us to torture him right away. Let him imagine it for a few days. Let Dmitriy wonder about what he's telling us."

"You got it, boss."

When I walk back into the room, I spot Lyla by the bar. I watch the bartender ogle her cleavage, then knock a bottle over. She laughs, and that's when I lose it. I stalk over, wrap a possessive hand around Lyla's waist, and pull her out of the room. From past events that were hosted here, I know there's a private bathroom down the hall by the kitchens.

I guide her inside and lock the door.

"What are you doing?"

I unbuckle my belt. "What does it look like?"

"Maybe I don't feel like fucking you."

"Then, leave."

Lyla doesn't move.

"Turn around," I instruct, pulling a condom out of my pocket and unrolling it on my hardening dick.

Lyla raises a brow but listens, gripping the marble counter and steadying on her heels. She looks over one shoulder, watching me toss the wrapper and give my erection a couple of quick strokes. My blood is hot, fueled with anger and lust. A volcano waiting to explode.

"What if I get pregnant?" she asks.

I freeze. "Are you?"

"No."

"Then, why are you bringing it up?"

"Because it's a possibility."

"We're using protection."

"We were using protection when I got pregnant with Leo."

I scan her face. "Where is this coming from?"

"It's a possibility. I'm trying to be responsible. Realistic."

"Do you want more kids?"

"Not on my own."

"No one said anything about doing anything alone."

"We're not together, Nick."

"We live in the same house. We sleep together. We eat together. We have a child together. What do you call that, Lyla?"

She spins around so I can see her annoyed expression. "I'm here because of Leo. Because you made choices that put his life at risk and I'm stuck dealing with the consequences!"

"Oh, is that what you tell yourself when you're coming on my cock? That you're doing it for Leo?"

I see the slap coming, but I don't stop it. I embrace the sting.

"I'm not my mother," she hisses. "I won't put Leo through the hell I grew up in."

"What hell would that be? He has everything he could possibly—"

"There's more to parenting than money, Nick. I know you can provide for Leo financially. I'm talking about where that money came from. What kind of example you're setting for him. You can't possibly want this for him. You said you never had a choice, and maybe that's true. Leo will have one."

I shake my head. "Stop pretending he's the only thing we have in common. If that were true, you'd be home with him. You wouldn't be here with me. You wouldn't be dripping"—I sneak a hand between her legs, tracing the drenched lace wedged there and then tugging it roughly—"at the thought of me fucking you. I'm not lying to you, Lyla. Extend me the same fucking courtesy."

I pull my hand away and wait for another slap. For her to walk out. Instead, she rises up and kisses me. It starts out gentle, mostly because I'm too shocked to reciprocate.

Slowly, the surprise melts away. Our kiss turns greedy and desperate. Filthy and angry.

I jerk away and study her. Our ragged breathing is the only sound in the bathroom. "The emotional whiplash is getting old, Lyla."

"When it's safe to leave, I will. While I'm here"—she raises a delicate shoulder, covered with black velvet, then lets it drop —"I'd rather fuck you than fight with you."

My jaw flexes as she turns around, facing the mirror. Her eyes meet mine in the reflection as she leans forward and rests her hands on either side of the sink. Her gaze holds mine as one hand gathers the hem of her dress and tugs, revealing inch after inch of smooth, creamy skin. My cock comes to life with a jerk, lust overtaking irritation.

I'm pissed at Lyla. Furious with myself. And so hard, it's physically painful.

The black strip of lace between her legs comes into view. My hand strokes my cock without permission, attempting to alleviate some of the pressure. "Tell me no, Lyla."

She bites her bottom lip in response.

"Last chance, Lyla." I growl the words. I've never been this worked up about sex. The hunger and the rage are consuming. Thrilling. I crave Lyla like an addictive high. An indescribable rush.

She stays silent. I slap the right side of her ass, and it's not a light swat. It leaves a pink mark against her creamy skin. Still, she says nothing.

Her back arches when she feels the tip probe her wet pussy. "Oh my *God*."

"He's not the one inside this tight pussy, Lyla. Who's fucking you right now?"

"You. Fuck—you. I can't. Nick, I *can't*."

I smile. If this is all I get with her, these memories of the whimpers and the wet clasp of her cunt wrapped around me, it will have to be enough.

CHAPTER TWENTY-SEVEN

LYLA

I never thought I'd be drawn to the darkness like a moth seeks a flame. Never thought arousal would smell like smoke and look like sin. But I can feel it tightening and tugging low in my belly, my body reacting to the feel of those dark green eyes on me.

A stream of smoke leaves his lips as he rolls the orange-tipped stick between his fingers, lazy and unbothered.

My tongue prods the inside of my cheek. We both know why I'm here. Both know it's a bad idea. Both know it will happen anyway.

I'm just as enthralled by Nick as I was when he fucked me in the bathroom at the party last night. Everyone stared at me for the rest of the night after I returned with mussed hair and puffy lips, some combination of judgment and awe on their faces. I've simply accepted he's a web I can't crawl out of until there are thousands of miles between us.

Nick stabs out the cigarette and cracks the window, letting a blast of cold air wash away the lingering smoke.

I shiver, and he opens the window wider, swirling the clear

liquid before swallowing a large sip. Those green eyes remain on me the whole time, seeing too much and too little.

My nipples pucker against the wind as cold creeps across my skin. I'm icy and warm at once, like jumping into a hot tub after lying in a snowbank. I only know because I went skiing with Kennedy at her family's chalet once, over winter break, just before that fateful night I met the guy currently studying me like a science experiment. Like he's not sure what to do about me standing here.

I mourned the loss of the happy, carefree guy I met freshman year twice.

Once, when he left.

And again when I found out his real identity a few weeks ago.

But now, I wonder if the lightness was what I was attracted to. I saw glimpses of his moodiness then—when he'd finger the silver lighter, when his family would come up—and it fit well with my melancholy. Made me feel seen and less alone.

Any comfort from that is fleeting and bittersweet now. We might be the same two people in some ways, but everything else has changed.

I should go back to my room and face the inevitable hours of tossing and turning.

But I know I won't.

When he's inside of me, it's the only time I can pretend. The only time I admit to myself I'm drawn to the darkness too.

"You were gone for a while."

Predictably, I'm the one who speaks first. Nick's only response is a callous raise of one eyebrow and shutting the window. The air that lingers between us is cold, in more ways than one. He disappeared after dinner and only returned a few minutes ago. The creak of the top stair has become a Pavlovian cue for me.

I take a couple of steps closer, closing what feels like a massive distance but is actually less than ten feet.

"Were you at the warehouse?" I try again with a direct question.

"No." He takes another sip of his drink.

I smell the sharp burn of vodka, followed by a floral, expensive aroma that isn't emanating from the glass.

Nick smells like perfume—something heady and expensive.

Betrayal slashes my chest before it slithers inside of me, dark and ugly and consuming.

I'm not jealous, like an outsider seeing someone else with something I want. I'm mad.

He doesn't owe me anything, least of all loyalty. We're not a couple, like I argued last night.

But all I feel is betrayal.

"Not a fan of your new cologne." There's bitterness and judgment in the words, and I wait for him to call me out on both.

Instead, Nick looks at me with what could most easily be described as indifference. But I know him well enough—or maybe I just want to *think* I know him well enough—to catch the glimpses of other emotions. For a second, his eyes will dart to my breasts or my mouth or my legs and darken with lust. His knuckles will turn white around the glass, or a muscle in his jaw will jump.

Yet he doesn't move. Doesn't say anything.

I want to shake the indifference like a bottle of champagne until it explodes everywhere.

I step closer and closer until I can feel the heat emanating from his body. I take the glass from his hand and sip from it, forcing myself to keep a straight face as the alcohol sears a trail down my throat and scalds my stomach.

Nick looks out the window, away from me, and that hurts too.

Meanwhile, I inhale his closeness. His scent, buried beneath smoke and vodka and perfume.

I feel like my mother, relying on a man for what I should manage myself.

I don't want Nick for his money or protection though. I just want him.

In some ways, that's worse.

I'll get a new job. Carry pepper spray.

But I won't be able to replace him when I return to my old life.

"Which are you worried about, Lyla?" he asks, looking outside at the bright yard. "Whether I fucked someone or whether I killed someone?"

I swallow. "Both."

"Neither happened tonight."

The slew of relief is staggering. And concerning. I shouldn't care. I should be praying he'll come home, covered in blood and with a wet dick. It would make leaving easier.

But I think leaving will hurt like hell, no matter what, at this point.

"Get naked and get on the bed."

I blink at his profile, still staring out the window.

Eventually, he glances at me. "Isn't that why you're here?"

Nick looks away immediately, not expecting an answer. He thinks it is a rhetorical question, and I hate that he's right. Sex is not the only reason I couldn't fall asleep until he was home, but it's the only one I'll admit to.

I walk over to the four-poster bed. It looks less imposing and more inviting than it used to. The cotton shorts and t-shirt I am wearing fall to the floor, followed by my underwear, before I climb onto the mattress. The luxurious material of the comforter is cold and soft against my bare skin.

"What next, *boss*?"

I say the boss bit to annoy him. But as I say it, I'm reminded that plenty of people call him that with no flippancy at all.

"Spread your legs and touch yourself."

The words are cool and detached. Clinical almost. Like me naked on his bed is a nonevent. An inconvenience even. He'll do the bare minimum to fuck me *after* I've warmed myself up.

I roll my head to the side so I'm staring at his broad shoulders. My eyes keep moving down the taper of his torso. I wish he were shirtless.

My eyes close, and my hand skims down my stomach, between my legs. My fingers aren't warm, and they're not long and callous like I'm craving either.

I squeeze my eyelids tighter and pretend they are. This isn't the first time I've fantasized about Nick. It won't be the last time either.

I move my fingers faster, gathering the wetness that's started to appear and stroking myself with quick circles. I picture Nick pumping into me from behind in the bathroom. Looking in the mirror and seeing the expression on his face as he fucked me. The feel of him inside me, hard and thick.

The warmth of pleasure starts to trickle and spread. The comforter beneath me is no longer cold.

I moan, getting lost in the sensations.

And then, suddenly, he's here. My fingers are pushed away, and Nick's tongue replaces them, wet and warm and a thousand times more erotic. A possessive palm lands on my hip, holding me open.

I open my shaking thighs even wider and lift my hips, shamelessly asking for more. My eyes are wide open now, focused on watching him pleasure me.

The sight alone is enough to get me off. When he sucks my

clit into his mouth, my back arches, and I cry out as the pleasure explodes. I clench around nothing, grasping the sheets and tipping my head back as the flood of euphoria rushes through me.

Aside from my ragged breathing, the room is completely silent. Rather than satisfied, I feel restless. I want him to fuck me. I want *him* so, so badly. The urge aches inside of me, throbbing persistently, like a fresh bruise.

Nick rises onto his knees and exhales. His expression is tight and irritated as he unzips to free the bulge pressing against the black fabric of his pants. His erection bobs free, the flared head flushed red and the vein that runs the length raised. I only get a glimpse of his hard cock and dark pubic hair before he's stroking himself, fisting the length that's already long and hard.

I reach for his penis, wanting to feel the hot, taut skin for myself.

"Don't."

I flinch before dropping my hand, but I'm not surprised by the harsh command. Moments like this are how we punish each other. And also how we express everything we won't actually say.

He reaches for a condom and rolls it on, the crinkle of the foil wrapper the only sound in the room. Most of the curtains are closed, but the outside lights are bright enough, the exposed windows illuminate the room with enough to see.

Nick sighs again. This time, it's less aggrieved and more conflicted.

"*Fuck.*"

All of a sudden, he's hovering over me. And then he kisses me, his tongue invading my mouth urgently. I can taste myself on him, and it turns me on even more. It makes him seem more like mine, if only for this fleeting moment.

The heavy weight of his erection rubs my thigh and brushes

my clit. I moan and writhe beneath him, trying to force his dick inside of me.

One of Nick's hands pulls my wrists up above my head while the other moves to his cock, guiding it between my legs. He teases me for a few seconds, nudging, but not entering. Anticipation crawls across my skin, consuming and overwhelming.

With a sudden thrust, he pushes all the way inside of me. I've barely accustomed to the stretch before he's moving, fucking me with deep, rapid strokes. Rough and desperate, so far from indifference, I can't help but smile.

Wrong things shouldn't feel this good.

Nothing should feel this good.

It's too easy to get lost in. So hard to stay afloat and stay vigilant.

To remember exactly what this is and everything it isn't.

I'm close to coming when he pulls all the way out and rolls onto his back. I blink at him, the haze of pleasure slowly fading and confusion appearing instead.

"Ride me." Nick's voice is gruff, roughened by need and annoyance.

I'm too horny to argue. I want to come around his cock, and as long as that happens, I honestly don't care which position I'm in.

I shift until I'm straddling his thighs. He pulls me above him and fists his cock, guiding it to my entrance. I gasp when I feel the head push into my pussy, expecting him to slam inside me again. I'm unprepared for his hips to barely lift, for him to only slide in another inch.

"Please," I whisper. "*Please*, Nick. I want you so badly." The words spill out of me in a flood of naked honesty. I know I'm not just talking about now, about sex. I'm admitting what I've been avoiding.

I want Nick.

I want to fuck him. But I also want to kiss him and sleep next to him and buy birthday gifts. Dinners and dates and more kids and Christmas cards and vacations. I want to be happy and normal and whole. The white picket fence, golden retriever, minivan family.

And that's something I can't have with Nick.

Life with him would be looking over my shoulder and fear and armed guards.

He can't walk away.

I can't stay.

It hurts. It hurts so much. And it mixes with the maximum of bliss.

He slips in another inch. Then two more. I close my eyes and focus on the delicious stretch as gravity pulls me down and Nick pushes deeper.

"You take me so well," he praises.

I open my eyes. There's something tender in his expression, something that makes me think he knows exactly what I'm thinking.

He smiles, and I smile back, and then he spanks me, fracturing the poignant moment.

I hiss and rock against him as he slips out a couple of inches and then pounds back into me.

His hands roam my body, lingering on my breasts before sliding down my waist to my hips. He grips me tightly as he thrusts upward, pushing even deeper inside of me. His thumb finds my clit, rubbing tiny circles that drive me closer and closer to the edge while he watches his dick disappear inside of me.

We fall into a familiar rhythm as we crash together, the slap of skin and moans and grunts filling the room. I hold on for as long as I can, pushing the pleasure away, because as much as I crave the orgasm, I hate the end. I hate the distance and the reality and the finality.

But it's too much. Too consuming. Too powerful. Too commanding. My inner muscles convulse, tightening around the cock filling me. My release explodes inside of me, a surge of heat that spirals and spreads.

Nick's hold on me tightens. I watch his eyes close and his jaw tighten and his abs clench. Feel him swell and jerk inside of me as he comes.

Blissful remnants are still swimming through my bloodstream when I move away and lie down beside him.

A few seconds later, I hear the rustle of him moving. Probably taking care of the condom, deciding how to deal with the aftermath. My eyes flutter closed, shutting out everything. They fly back open when Nick scoops me up off the bed and starts walking, carrying me bridal-style. I think he's heading to the hallway, intending to deposit me back in my room. But instead, he walks into the bathroom.

The lights flicker on automatically.

Nick walks straight into the shower. He sets me down slowly. Unwillingly. Then, he turns on the spray, blocking the water until it runs warm. I lean against the cool tile, watching him with some mixture of fascination and wariness, until he puts a hand on my waist and tugs me toward him.

He has one of those fancy showerheads that feels like a waterfall or the perfect amount of rain. Warm water saturates my hair and begins dripping down my face. Pelts my skin and warms my body. And then Nick is massaging something that smells like rosemary and mint into my hair before washing my arms and my breasts. My stomach and between my legs.

Despite the fact that we're both naked and he's touching me

intimately, it's more sweet than sexual, which wreaks havoc on my heart.

The darkness and the moodiness excite me. Arouse me. But it's not real or sustainable. This thoughtful care—the kind I've always craved and never received—isn't supposed to come from the man who I watched wash off blood in this very spot.

I've met plenty of people who I felt I could rely upon—kind, trustworthy people, like June and Michael—but I've never had anyone I could lean on the way Nick is supporting me right now.

I don't think Nick is a bad person. But I know he's done bad things. And any attempt to parse out a difference between who he is and what he's done would be a disguise for selfishness.

But it doesn't keep me from filling my palm with the rosemary-mint shower gel and covering him with suds.

I've never really had the time or the presence of mind to admire Nick's body. The closest I've come the night he came home, covered with blood. Which was obviously distracting. Not to mention horrifying.

There's no trace of crimson now. Just an endless stretch of smooth skin and defined muscle.

Looking at him is like gorging on a decadent dessert after eating a full meal. You know you should resist, but you want to indulge. I soap his hair, his arms, his shoulders. Move down the center of his chest, over his abs. Trace the V and the thin trail of dark hair, both of which point straight at his cock.

I take my time, not leaving any inch untouched, until I fist his penis. It hardens under my touch. Nick hisses as I move my hand, the silky soap making my motions slippery.

"Ignore it," he tells me as his dick grows stiff and engorged again.

I smirk and stroke him faster.

Nick's Adam's apple bobs as he swallows. His head tilts back to touch the tile wall, but his eyes stay on me. I hold eye contact, dipping down to massage his balls before returning to his erection. His breathing picks up as he swells in my hand.

He reaches out and strokes my jaw with his thumb. Then, his fingers thread into my hair, gently tugging at the wet strands. Our faces are closer together now, mine tipped up and his angled down.

We don't kiss. He doesn't say anything. I don't stop stroking him until his release spills into my hand and washes away.

Neither of us moves away.

It's intimate.

It feels like he's seeing me, *really* seeing me, beneath skin and muscle and bone and blood and what physically makes up a human being. Past the defenses I raise with everyone else.

Truthfully, I don't really have a safe place. I act strong and brave and organized and independent.

And I'm some of those things sometimes.

I'll admit to being tired or too busy. I don't try to make it seem like my life is picture-perfect.

But I've never told anyone I often wake up in the middle of the night, panicked I might have forgotten to pay a bill or lock the door. That I bring flowers to the cemetery where my mother is buried every year on her birthday—July 7. That most mornings, Leo is the reason I get out of bed. That I never left Philadelphia, not because I love the city, but because I hoped there would be one day when Nick reappeared. That my greatest fear is leaving Leo alone.

It's incredibly ironic—I'm only just comprehending *how* ironic—that I feel safest with Nick, who is undoubtedly the most dangerous person I know.

"You still wear it." He's looking at my rose necklace.

I nod. "It's stupid."

"It's not stupid." His finger traces the thin chain and touches the small charm.

"It couldn't have cost her much. It'll probably break soon. It's just…hard to let go of things you know you should, I guess."

"Yeah, it is." His voice is soft. Knowing.

"She could have chosen something a little more interesting. Like a falcon or a moon."

Nick half smiles in response to my attempt at levity.

"Roses are cliché. Common. Boring. Exactly what she thought of me, I guess."

"They're also bold," he says. "Resilient. Fierce. Most flowers don't have thorns."

I exhale. "It's easier for me to see the ugly than the pretty. When it comes to my mom. When it comes to most things maybe."

"It can be pretty *and* ugly, Lyla. Anything can be. Even regrets."

We share a bittersweet smile before he shuts off the water.

Nick turns to step out of the shower, but I grab his wrist before he can move away. I graze my thumb against the pulse point, feeling the steady thrum of his heartbeat.

"You're not a regret. And not just because of Leo. Maybe it would have been easier if you'd told me the truth when we met. But I get why you didn't, and I know I've blamed you for a lot that wasn't really your fault. Plus…I was pretty much a goner from that first night. Even if you had told me…" I shrug.

I'm still holding his wrist, so I hurriedly drop it. The slow *drip, drip, drip* from the showerhead is the only sound.

"We captured one of Dmitriy's men last night. *The* man. He'll know operations. Plans. Hiding places. This will all be over soon."

"You're going to torture him?" I whisper.

"Yes." Nick holds my gaze without flinching.

I swallow.

He grabs a towel from the rack and hands it to me before he uses a second one to dry off himself.

We're both silent as we finish getting ready. I go pee, brush my teeth, finger-comb my hair, and then crawl into bed. Nick shuts the remaining curtains and then climbs in beside me. He doesn't reach for me. Doesn't say anything.

I fiddle with the rose around my neck, rubbing my finger against the rough outline of the petals.

Sometimes, I see it as a symbol of strength. A reminder of everything I've overcome.

But it's also a sign of weakness. Proof I've clung to the memory of a woman who barely cared about me. Evidence that part of me is hoping to rewrite the past.

"This will all be over soon."

The sentence should sound comforting.

A threat to Leo's safety—extinguished.

A trip back home to familiarity—imminent.

But I don't feel relieved or excited.

I've gotten used to life here. More than *used to*. Comfortable.

I love working at the shelter and feeling like I'm making a difference in people's lives. I love walking around the estate and soaking in the solace. I love when Nick gets home and we eat dinner as a family of three. I love looking forward to sleeping with him—both in the literal and the sexual sense—all day long.

Tears slip silently down my cheeks into the pillow that's already damp from my wet hair, mourning the loss that's about to take place.

And at some point, I fall asleep.

CHAPTER TWENTY-EIGHT

LYLA

"Mom?"

"Yeah?" I glance at Leo, who's sitting beside me and studying me with a curious expression.

"Are you okay?"

"Of course. Just tired." I manage a smile.

Leo has a book in his lap. I didn't think he was paying any attention to me, so I zoned out for the first half of the trip to school.

I look at the front of the car, trying to figure out how close we are to Leo's school. Valentin is driving us today. I'm not sure when that happened—when I discovered I know most of Nick's men's names. The ones who I interact with regularly at least.

Valentin is one of the friendliest and therefore one of my favorites. He's chatting with Egor, who's usually more reserved. All of a sudden, Valentin's tone changes. He's speaking Russian, which I still can't understand more than the occasional word. Before it was eager, almost playful. Now, it's sharp with a repressed edge. Like worry he's trying to hide.

Something slams into us from behind. There's commotion all

around. Screeching tires and shouts and the distinctive echo of gunfire.

The car stops. I'm focused on Leo. His eyes are wide and locked on mine.

"Leo—"

The car door opens, and I'm pulled off the seat, surrounded by the scent of sweat and smoke. I don't struggle, deciding it's better to seem like less of a threat. My eyes blink, taking in the carnage of two damaged cars. And the dozen men holding guns.

They're all familiar faces.

The one attached to the man holding me isn't.

"Drop them, or she dies!"

A new voice joins the melee, one that's cruel and commanding. Even before he steps right in front of me, I know it must belong to Dmitriy.

If I look closely, I can find traces of the Morozov genetics. He's a crueler, uglier version of Nick.

When Dmitriy looks at me, I know exactly why he spoke in English. He wants me to know what's happening. To feel as helpless as possible. To know my life hangs by thin threads and he's holding the scissors to snip them.

"Nikolaj is not the forgiving type," he adds.

For a wild second, I think he's speaking to me, and I'm trying to figure out what offense he thinks I've committed.

But then I realize he's looking at Nick's men. That he's talking *about* me.

I want to scream and tell them no. That the guns they're pointing at me are the only things protecting Leo, who's still in the car. He's too old and too aware not to understand what's happening. I can't shield him from this, pretend it's a game with minimal consequences instead of life or death.

But every gun pointed at Dmitriy and the man holding me falls.

Dmitriy smiles, then walks toward the car. Everything inside me freezes. Even the flow of blood through my veins slows to a lazy trickle.

Valentin is closest to the car. I watch him say something to Dmitriy. Watch Dmitriy laugh. Watch the gun he's holding fire and a red hole appear in Valentin's head.

I gasp, seeing him crumple to the ground.

Someone joking and smiling moments ago gone.

I'm stuck somewhere between terror and disbelief.

I've seen dead bodies before. I was the one who discovered my mother's. But I've never seen someone *die*. The transition from living to gone that's so fast, you could blink and miss it.

Nick's words echo in my head.

"There's only one way out of this life."

Dmitriy disappears around the opposite side of the car. Tears pool in my eyes because I know exactly what he's doing, who he's getting.

This would be my best chance to escape the grip of the man holding me. But even if I managed to get away, I know that Nick's men won't risk Leo's life by firing. His life is far more valuable than mine, and the stakes are way too high.

Dmitriy reappears. I'm relieved to see his gun is pointing at the ground, not at Leo, who's walking along willingly.

I scan my son, terrified I'll find some sign of injury. But he looks healthy and alert, taking the scene in with a grim determination that makes him look much older than eight. That makes him look like Nick.

There's a quick exchange of Russian between Dmitriy and his coconspirator before we're pulled away, leaving the smoking cars and the stoic men and Valentin's body behind. I know they'll call for reinforcements—call Nick—as soon as we're out of sight.

It worries me that Dmitriy *doesn't* appear worried about that inevitability. He could have killed every man there while they stood defenseless, but he didn't. He's banking heavily on assurance that Nick won't risk us as collateral.

Dmitriy has us wait by a van while the other man ties our hands behind our backs. He's competent in the task. I'm disappointed to find them tight, no sign of sliding or fraying the way you sometimes see in action movies.

"You okay?" I whisper to Leo.

He nods. "Dad will come for us." Leo's voice is filled with complete confidence in Nick.

It cuts through the panic crushing my chest. Because I know he's right.

Unfortunately, Dmitriy hears Leo too.

He reappears to look at us with a leer that makes my skin crawl. "I'm counting on it, kid."

CHAPTER TWENTY-NINE

NICK

I rub my forehead, trying to ignore the headache forming. I got a paltry few hours of sleep last night, going over everything that happened with Lyla in my head while she slept beside me.

She's leaving.

I'm staying.

I've known those two facts all along, but they've become harder and harder to accept with each kiss. Every conversation.

"What about next Thursday?" Dean Wilkerson asks.

He's one of the managing partners at Wilkerson, Thompson & Owens LLP, the big-shot law firm that handles all my legal business in the States. Ever since my last trip to New York was cut short, he's been trying to pin me down on a date to deal with the remaining paperwork.

"I'll see—" I stop talking when Roman bursts into my office. "I'll call you back," I say, then end the call and stand. "What is it?"

Two things concern me. For one, Roman—everyone—knows not to enter my warehouse office when the door is closed. And secondly, Roman was the one who came to Philadelphia to let me know my brothers and father were murdered. It was sensitive information to share by any other means, and he offered to be the one to tell me. I can still picture the look on his face, grave and furious.

All I see now is fear.

"What?" I bark.

Roman swallows, looking like he'd rather be waterboarded than tell me whatever he rushed in here to say. "He hit them on the school route. Valentin and Lev are dead, and he took—"

I'm already out the door and heading down the hall. I enter the basement code into the keypad and take the stairs two at a time. Damp mustiness and the scent of chemical cleaner, heavy and bitter. Panic attacks me like a thousand paper cuts, barely visible but destructive.

My pulse thunders in my ears as I stride across the cement, scan my fingerprint, and yank the cell door open.

Maxim is lounging on the cot, staring up at the ceiling like it's the fucking Sistine Chapel.

His head turns when I enter the cell.

His body tenses as I approach.

He's a trained killer, same as me. It takes a lot for us to react, and the fact that he did is a testament to whatever expression the rage and terror rushing through me is displaying.

I grab the torn shirt he's wearing and jerk him upward. "Where did he take them?"

A smile slowly unfurls across Maxim's mouth. "So, he actually—"

"You've barely been rotting in this cell, but you've had time to imagine what was going to happen to you." I barely recognize the sound of my own voice. "Imagination can be a man's worst enemy. The unknown, his worst nightmare. But I'll swear to you one thing, Golubev. Whatever you thought I might do to you, it will be worse. I'll cut out your tongue. Snip off your balls. Strip all your nails. Burn your skin. Carve your flesh. And then? I'll call a doctor and get you stitched up. Hook you up to a feeding tube, let you heal, and start all over again. There are a lot of ways to maim and not kill. To push someone to the brink and then yank them back. You know that as well as anyone. I'll save you and ship you back to Dmitriy, piece by piece. He'll know exactly where you are, and he won't save you because it would be a suicide mission, and the only person Dmitriy cares about is himself."

I grab my gun out of its hip holster and press it to his temple.

"Tell me where they are, and this ends now. You'll die either way. It's a fate you chose when you disrespected the oath you swore. You'll die when I want and how I want. The only decision left is *when* you die, Maxim. And this is your one and only chance. You knew he was planning to take them, which makes me think you know where he took them. Whenever you talk—and you *will* talk—I'll make sure you suffer until death sounds like the best option. Or you can talk now, and it ends quickly. Ten seconds to decide."

I start counting down.

Maxim's eyes dart around the cell, looking for a way out. But there isn't one. There's just me and him and the rage that takes up all of the surrounding space, suffocating us both.

When I hit four, Maxim spits out an address.

I study him, my grip tightening, aware this could cost me more than him. The putrid scent of urine fills the cell.

I smile, then pull the trigger. Blood blooms from the hole in Maxim's head, spreading in a crimson stain that spills down his neck and soaks into his shirt.

When I let go, his body slumps against the stone wall. I spin and walk out of the cell, not bothering to shut the door. There's no one to contain any longer.

"He could have been lying."

Until he speaks, I hadn't realized Roman followed me down here.

"He wasn't." I have to believe that. Maxim swore loyalty to me, same as his father swore to mine. Rebellion usually reaches a point. Especially when you chose the losing side. "And if he was, I'll burn this whole fucking city to the ground."

Drawing out Maxim's anguish would have been satisfying, but it wouldn't have accomplished my main goal—getting to Lyla and Leo as quickly as possible. It's unlikely he would have cracked after weeks or months of torture. And by then, I don't want to imagine what could have happened.

Maxim was the only leverage I had.

Dmitriy's whereabouts were the only leverage Maxim had.

Either those interests worked together or I'll have to pick this city apart piece by piece until I find them. If Dmitriy isn't where Maxim said he is, I'll use every resource I have to find him. Unlike Dmitriy, I'm not hiding in the shadows. There isn't a person in this city who will protect him if they know it will come with the lash of my wrath.

Roman nods. "Dmitriy won't have more than twenty trained men, at most. We'll have triple that."

I nod. "I'm going in alone."

"You know I have to tell you that's a stupid fucking idea, boss."

"You know I'll do it anyway."

Roman sighs. "Yeah, I know."

"The odds are in my favor," I remind him.

Growing up, I was always stronger and faster than Dmitriy

despite just being a few months older. It probably fed into this penultimate moment, but there's fuck all I can do about that now.

"Get Grigoriy here and update him on the situation. Once I know if they're there or not, I'll be in touch. And if I don't make it out and they do—"

"They'll be safe and taken care of. You have my word," Roman says, his expression grim.

I head upstairs without another word. Time is of the essence now, especially with so many unknowns.

The warehouse is emptier than it was when I arrived this morning, but a dozen or so of my men are around, most of them huddled and talking. I'm not surprised word has already spread about what happened. Attacks on a *Pakhan*'s family are rare and rarely successful. For the most part, it's a suicide mission. Perpetrated by someone hell-bent on revenge with no care for the consequences.

I'm slightly mollified by the knowledge Dmitriy *does* care. He wants something more than revenge. Simply killing me won't accomplish what he's aiming for. He needs to do it in a way that impresses and proves he's superior.

Kidnapping an innocent woman and child won't do him any favors. Even among criminals, there's a moral code. He decided to involve Lyla and Leo because he knew it would be a guaranteed way to draw me out. And I was stupid enough to think twelve men would be enough. I should have been the one driving Leo to and from school.

It takes me ten minutes to speed to the address Maxim provided.

The building is nice. By a Morozov's standard's, it's a hovel. I ignore the elevator and take the stairs. Dmitriy will have taken the top floor.

There are two units to choose between when I exit the stairwell. I veer left first, debating on whether to kick the door in or not. In case I chose wrong, I don't want to give Dmitriy any extra warning. If I chose right, it will save time.

I close my hand around the brass doorknob and send up a silent prayer to a greater power I'm not sure I believe in. There's also a chance this is a trap Dmitriy set up weeks ago and I'm about to set it off. I'd rather put a bullet in my brain than abandon my family. So, I twist the handle.

To my shock, it opens. As soon as a crack appears, I realize why. The sickening scent of decay hits me first, followed by a pair of legs that turn into a male body when I push the door fully open.

As twisted as it is, hope springs in my chest. Killing for sport has often been Dmitriy's style. This suggests there is a chance he's actually in the building.

I close the door and creep down the hallway, trying to ignore the rush of blood in my ears and the deafening decibels of the metronome in my chest.

If they're not here, I don't know what I'll do.

But I do know it won't be pretty. People that say they aren't capable of violence are liars. Everyone is capable of it. It's a matter of learning what will push you to that point.

I've spilled plenty of blood. Out of duty.

This crusade is fueled by love. A pretty, sparkling, soft emotion, capable of wreaking more havoc than hate.

Hate can't dig under the skin the way love does. It doesn't alter your cells or spark chemistry. You'd bleed for someone you love, never someone you truly hate. But hate holds a dark power of its own. And right now, both hate and love are driving my decisions.

I'm volatile and angry.

Terrified and nervous.

I kick down the door. Everyone inside jumps. And there *are* people inside.

"Hate what you've done with the place."

Dmitriy's head jerks toward me so fast, I hear a *crack*, his expression lost somewhere between disbelief and fury. "Fucking Maxim," he growls.

I nod, like I have some sympathy for his plight of betrayal. "Loyal men are hard to find these days, aren't they?"

My eyes scan the room. He only has the one man with him. Stupid and reckless.

I take the opportunity to steal a second glance at Leo and Lyla, who are both looking at me. Leo's expression is lit up like a Christmas tree. I don't meet Lyla's gaze, just look over her body to make sure she's unharmed. I'm not sure what I'll see in her expression, and a distraction is the last thing I need right now.

"So are women," Dmitriy responds, switching to English. "Your American slut offered a fuck for her freedom." He smirks, then glances at Lyla to catch her reaction.

I know it's the best opening I'll get. I fire twice in rapid succession. Head. Heart. The bulky man stumbles once, then falls.

I don't recognize him. I'm sure Dmitriy made plenty of promises in exchange for his assistance. Instead, he's paying with his life.

That's why I hate making promises. They're easy to make and even easier to break. No debt will ever be collected.

Dmitriy no longer looks amused. His fists are clenched with barely restrained anger, looking at his accomplice with no trace of sympathy and a whole lot of rage as he realizes his advantage just disappeared.

I anticipate his next move, raising my gun at the same time he does. Except Dmitriy isn't pointing his gun back at me.

He's aiming straight at Leo.

"Drop it, Nikolaj. Or your son dies."

It's my worst nightmare, playing out in high definition. It's worse than pacing the tarmac in Philadelphia felt. I knew then that Lyla was important to me. I knew I had a son, but I didn't even know his name. I didn't know what it would feel like to have a family. To love two people more than you love anything else.

My father's choices are what got him killed. And I've often wondered if he would have done anything differently, knowing he was risking a lot more than his own life. He was an excellent *Pakhan* and an abysmal father. I always swore I would be different.

I'm an excellent shot, as I just demonstrated. "Let them go. They have nothing to do with this."

Dmitriy clicks his tongue. "I have this theory you'll be more cooperative if they stay."

"I'll stay."

I glance at Lyla, but she's focused on Dmitriy. "Let Leo go. I'll stay."

Dmitriy tilts his head, considering.

I don't think there's a chance in hell he'll agree.

I'm the one he wants. Leo is also valuable to him, as my heir. They were both bait when he could have just taken Leo. That tells me Dmitriy knows—or at least suspects—Lyla is just as important to me as my son.

After a long deliberation, Dmitriy agrees. "Fine. The boy can go."

His gun swings from Leo to Lyla, which does little to decrease my anxiety. I'm distracted by Leo running to me instead of the door. I lean down to hug him, banking on the fact that Dmitriy would find it distasteful to gun me down while talking to my child. He has one of the worst traits in a potential leader—craving approval.

I only hug Leo for a few seconds. Dmitriy can change his mind quickly, and I don't want my son anywhere near if that happens.

"At the end of the hall, there's a door. Take the stairs all the way down. There are men there, and they'll protect you."

Leo nods, so stoic and so determined, it cracks something in my chest. Kids shouldn't have to be this brave. They should laugh and play and stay woefully ignorant to the ways the world can be a strange and scary place.

"I love you, Leo," I tell him. Three simple words my father never told me. "Remember that, always."

Another nod, just as serious.

"Go."

He listens, darting out the door and into the hall. And for a split second, I feel relieved. Then, I look at Dmitriy. Look at the gun he's holding, and all I feel is dread.

I'm going to do everything I can to get Lyla out of here. But there's a good chance I'll fail. She's entirely expendable in Dmitriy's eyes. American, not Russian. Poor, not rich. I could do everything he asks, and there's still an excellent chance he'll kill her.

Part of me—the detached *Pakhan* part that's a duplicate of my father—knows I should turn around and walk out of here. I'm risking my life for a woman I owe no loyalty. We're not married. We're not even a couple. And I'm still armed. It's a move Dmitriy won't be expecting.

But my feet don't shuffle so much as an inch.

"Now, her." I revert to Russian.

Dmitriy laughs. "Drop the gun, and I'll think about it. Keep it, and she dies."

Fuck.

His expression is all triumph. He loves games like this. Loves that he finally has the upper hand.

It's a terrible deal. Nothing close to an assurance. But I flip on the safety and toss the gun on the floor—because if I don't and he kills her, I'll never be able to forgive myself.

Dmitriy's expression is all surprise. And I realize he had no idea if this would work. Maybe it's just too difficult for a narcissist to comprehend prioritizing someone else above yourself.

Surprise melts into glee. "Take a seat."

He finally moves the gun away from Lyla, but I don't dare look at her. I walk toward the chair he's pointing toward, hoping obedience will lull him into a false sense of complacency until I figure out some sort of plan.

Once I'm seated, Dmitriy dangles a set of handcuffs in front of my face. The metal glints in the fading light. "Put these on."

I smirk as I take them. "I didn't know this is what you were into, cousin."

"It's not," he sneers. "Maybe I'll rape the slut and let you watch."

I wasn't entirely surprised when I found out Dmitriy had left. I knew he wasn't content as the supporting act, that he was temperamental and impulsive. But this is the moment I realize the person I might consider family is truly gone. Because the man I delivered a rapist to wouldn't have suggested sexual assault as an intimidation tactic.

"Just like Natasha?"

Dmitriy's ugly expression falters, just for a moment. I know revenge for his former girlfriend wasn't driven by love. She was a model he liked parading around on his arm. But her assault and death bothered him, probably more than anything else ever has.

"Let her go, Dmitriy," I plead. "This is between us."

I don't dare look at Lyla. We're still speaking in Russian, so she can't understand what we're saying. I hope she's planning an escape. Dmitriy is totally focused on me, which makes this her best chance.

"Not so high and mighty now, Nikolaj? What happened to my last words and tearing me limb from limb?"

"I won't do anything with her in the room."

Lyla—and Leo—already saw me kill one person today, which I'm trying not to dwell on.

Dmitriy shakes his head. "Always so fucking principled. There's no point to having power if you don't use it."

"That," I say, "is why you'd make a terrible *Pakhan*."

I predict the hit coming. I don't move to avoid the butt of the gun as it slams into my cheek. The metallic tinge of blood fills my mouth, which makes me think I must be bleeding externally as well.

I could lift a hand to feel since I haven't put on the cuffs yet. But that would draw Dmitriy's attention to the fact that I haven't, which I'm trying to avoid doing.

He's too invested in this moment he's spent almost a year chasing to think critically. To treat me the way you should treat a dangerous opponent.

I gauge the distance between us and the angle he's holding the gun at, deliberating on what to do. I've never had to calculate the risk of having an innocent person involved in a volatile situation like this. It's always been trained men beside me who would face the consequences if I made a decision that backfires.

Lyla could die if I decide wrong…and she could die if I cooperate.

And then a shot goes off. Confusingly, it's not from Dmitriy's gun. I stare at the firearm he's holding for a couple of seconds, confirming it's still pointed at the floor. And then I realize it's not the only weapon in the room.

There's a bizarre delay in my mind as the pieces slowly fall together, like I'm watching this unfold from a distance instead of up close. Everything seems to be moving fast and slow.

Dmitriy lets out a choked gurgle, glancing down in shock, just as perplexed as I am. Blood is beginning to flow from the wound in his stomach, slow yet steady.

His hand begins to rise. Not the empty one, the one holding a gun.

That's when I react. I lunge forward and twist the gun from his grasp.

Ever since I walked into the flat, Dmitriy has had the opportunity to kill me. He hasn't acted. But I don't hesitate.

I raise the gun and fire twice, killing him instantly.

I stare down at his still, bloody body, a maelstrom of emotions swirling inside of me. For the first couple of years after I became *Pakhan*, he was right by my side, as close a confidant as Alex or Roman.

We drifted apart gradually, bitterness building up when he made suggestions and I acted differently, which culminated with him committing the ultimate betrayal. I knew it would end this way ever since I heard he left. But it's different to see it.

The sound of heavy breathing cuts through the haze of adrenaline and disbelief.

I glance at Lyla. She's looking at Dmitriy's dead body. Her face is completely white, devoid of any color. Even her lips look pale. My gun hangs limply in her hand.

I approach her slowly, taking the gun out of her loose grip and using my free hand to tilt her chin up. Her skin is cold, her eyes dull and unfocused. My thumb moves along her jawline, but she doesn't react to the touch. She keeps inhaling quickly and exhaling shakily.

"Lyla."

Nothing.

"Lyla!"

She still doesn't react, just keeps hyperventilating.

I should slap her. Instead, I kiss her.

It takes a few seconds for her to respond. For her open-mouthed breaths to turn deep. I doubt any doctor or psychiatrist would consider this a recommended method for coping with shock and trauma, but it seems to work. The kiss is sweet with relief. Filled with the intoxicating essence of being alive.

"Are you okay?" I whisper as soon as our lips separate.

"I killed him."

"*No*. You didn't. I did."

"I shot him, Nick."

"People survive gunshot wounds all the time."

It's a stretch, and we both know it. Based on how quickly he started bleeding out, she hit an artery. He could have been hit in a hospital, and I'm not sure he'd make it. But Dmitriy's death is a burden I don't want Lyla to carry. He kidnapped her. Intended to kill her. There are deaths to mourn, and his isn't one of them.

I tilt her chin up, forcing her to look at me. "You didn't kill him. I did. It's on me, Lyla. Let it be on me, okay?"

My eyes bore into hers, trying to force her to hear me. To accept what I'm saying.

Finally, she nods.

I release her, pulling my phone out of my pocket. Something Dmitriy should have taken from me. Another rookie error on his part.

That was always part of the problem between us though. He never wanted to treat me as a worthy opponent. He thought being a similar age and having similar backgrounds made us the same. That because I was the *Pakhan*, he could be. And in my experience, the people who think they'll make the best leaders are often the worst.

Roman picks up on the first ring. "Thank fuck you're alive."

"Leo?"

"He's safe. Talking with Grigoriy right now about the layout of the building in case your ten minutes ran out."

I exhale. "Good. I need a crew up here to take care of Dmitriy."

"Done."

"Send Viktor up too."

"You got it, boss."

"Leo is safe," I tell Lyla as soon as I've hung up.

She closes her eyes and exhales shakily. I place a hand on her lower back, so lightly that I'm barely brushing the fabric of her jacket, and guide her out of the apartment's living room into the hallway.

It's dim, chilly, and narrow, but there's no dead body in sight. My eyes flicker to the door at the opposite end of the hall, recalling the horrors it hides.

Lyla is quiet beside me, wrapping her arms around her midsection and staring blankly at the white plaster wall. Part of me wishes she'd cling to me or seek out some comfort. But I know she's used to being independent. And this is all my fault, so I can hardly blame her for not running into my arms romantic movie–style.

Viktor and a crew of five men appear a few minutes later. They all give me respectful nods, and I'm surprised when Lyla receives one as well. It's rare for anyone outside the family to receive that sort of acknowledgment. I'm not sure if Lyla notices the gesture. She still looks dazed.

"Take her down to Leo," I tell Viktor. "And get them back to the estate."

Viktor nods, serious. Dmitriy was the brains and force behind the revolt, but he never worked alone. It would be foolish to think killing him is the equivalent of safety. I still have plenty of enemies.

"Viktor will take you downstairs to Leo," I tell Lyla.

Her gaze jerks from the wall to me. Her mouth opens, but then she looks at Viktor and the other men and closes it. "Okay," she says, her voice barely louder than a whisper.

I watch them walk down the hall, then turn to the rest of my men. "Put Dmitriy in the bathroom to be found. Everything else gets wiped. No trace left behind."

Most of the local *politsiya* are in my back pocket. But there are always a few who decide to be heroes, who think that the whole system isn't rotted and fighting corruption isn't a futile task. Who would love to see me behind bars.

We head back into the apartment. I can already smell the rot of death, the aroma of the undead permeating the still air. It's probably in my imagination, but my stomach curdles anyway.

"What about him?" one of my men asks, nodding toward the corner.

Up until now, I'd completely forgotten about the burly, bearded man who helped Dmitriy with the kidnapping.

"He disappears."

The crew nods, already pulling out chemicals. I force myself to look at Dmitriy's body until it's carried out of sight and the cleaning begins. Bleach burns my nose.

I keep waiting for the satisfaction to appear. The triumph and sense of victory. Despite his lack of resources, Dmitriy was a threat. He knew our operations, our warehouse locations, our protocols. That's dangerous information for an enemy to possess. The nature of this business requires constantly being on alert, but rarely to the level we've had to maintain lately. Loyal lives were lost.

It's more bitter than sweet.

Dmitriy was technically family, which I can't say for anyone else I've killed. But it's more than that. Dmitriy was an inconvenience, true.

He was also keeping Leo and Lyla here.

I pull out my lighter and start flicking it. None of the men look up. They're used to me doing this. Not to mention working under conditions worse than this. It doesn't take long for them to finish.

"Make the call to the *politsiya* from a burner," I instruct.

Then, I walk away.

CHAPTER THIRTY

LYLA

It's dark out by the time we roll through the gates that now look more safe than scary.

Viktor and Roman are in the front seats. Leo is curled up next to me. He seems remarkably calm. Relaxed even.

Maybe kids are hardier than we give them credit for.

I think of everything I tried to protect Leo from in Philadelphia.

Things like overdue bills and doing something special on Father's Day seem silly in comparison to being kidnapped at gunpoint by a deranged mobster. My childhood wasn't unicorns and rainbows, and I wanted Leo to know nothing but love and safety.

I feel like a failure for everything he's been exposed to, but I also feel proud. He handled everything today better than most people would have, regardless of his age.

He's half Nick and half me. He's tough.

We stop in front of the house, and everyone climbs out of the warm car. I give Roman and Viktor tired smiles before walking inside.

"We'll be down here if you need anything," Viktor says.

I nod. I think he and Roman are waiting for me to fall apart, but I feel calm. I know I'm in some state of shocked disbelief. Not about the kidnapping or the fear for Leo's safety though.

I *shot* someone. And no matter what Nick says, it would have killed Dmitriy. I saw the way blood started pouring out of him like a cork popping out of a bottle. The bullet hit something vital.

The fact that I didn't intend to kill him, didn't aim to kill him, doesn't matter. I *would* have, and I had no idea I was capable of that kind of violence. I saw my mother get slapped around by some of her boyfriends and always wondered how anyone could purposefully inflict pain on someone else that way. It's disturbing to realize I have that capacity even if I can use drastic circumstances as an excuse.

What also terrifies me is that Leo was gone. I had no idea what Dmitriy planned to do with me. Based on the story Nick shared, I hoped Dmitriy wouldn't rape me. There was a good chance he would kill me.

But I didn't pull that trigger because I was scared of what might happen to me.

I pulled it because I knew he was planning to kill Nick.

When we enter the house, there's more staff around than usual. At this hour, they're usually gone for the night. I assume it means they know what happened.

"Are you hungry?" I ask Leo as we walk deeper into the house.

He shakes his head. "No. I'm just tired."

"Okay."

We head upstairs. It's strange, being back somewhere familiar. Like waking up from a nightmare to realize it was all in your imagination and you're actually in your own room. It's unsettling, realizing this looks familiar. Looks like home.

I help Leo get ready for bed even though he's been old enough to do it himself for years. After he's in his pajamas and tucked into bed, I take a seat on the mattress and blow out a long breath.

"Today was scary. And I'm so, so sorry it happened. All I want to do is protect you, Leo. So does your dad."

"I know," he says, playing with the hem of the sheet.

"I'm sure you have a lot of questions. Some, I might not have the answers to. And there are others…I don't want you to worry, sweetheart. When your dad found out about you, so did some of his enemies. One of them was the man who took us today."

"What happened to him?"

I swallow. "He's dead."

Leo is silent, processing that for a minute. "Okay."

I study his serious expression, trying to figure out what else to say. Leo's eyes dart behind me, excitement lighting up his expression. I swallow for a second time, not needing to look behind me to know who must have entered the bedroom.

I lean forward and kiss his forehead. "I'm sure you want to say good night to your dad. We can talk more tomorrow. I love you, Leo. So much."

He smiles at me. "I love you too, Mom."

I smile back, then turn and pass Nick without making eye contact. The pieces I'm holding together feel more brittle around him.

Once I'm in my own room, I get ready for bed on autopilot. It's a couple of hours earlier than I usually go to sleep, but I feel mentally and physically drained. I'm too nauseous to contemplate dinner.

A hot shower and slipping into pajamas help. I'm combing my wet hair when there's a knock on the door.

"Come in," I call, hearing the hitch in my voice.

I know it's Nick.

When he walks into the room, he's changed as well. It's the first time I've seen him in anything but black slacks and a black dress shirt, which seem to be his daily uniform.

I'm disappointed in my gaze—how it lingers on the gray sweatpants and white t-shirt Nick is wearing. Apparently, he owns no color. My libido doesn't care.

"Thought you could use this." He holds out a wineglass, half full of maroon liquid.

Disturbingly, my first thought is how it looks like blood.

"Thank you." I take it and take a sip. The wine tastes familiar, and the realization Nick brought me my favorite wine—that he even *noticed* what my favorite wine is—warms me more than the alcohol.

"I'm sorry, Lyla." Earnestness leaks from every syllable.

"I don't blame you."

"You should."

"It wasn't your fault, Nick." The long chain of events that ended in Dmitriy kidnapping me and Leo is one thing. But I know Nick would have done anything—absolutely anything—to prevent it from happening if he had any idea it might.

"Yes, it was." His jaw clenches. "I should have ensured Dmitriy was taken care of a long time ago. If I'd had every man combing the streets for the past ten months, we would have found him by now."

"Unless you knew where he was and decided not to do anything about it, you couldn't have done anything."

"I should have done more."

"Don't hold yourself accountable and then tell me not to."

"That's different. He kidnapped you. You had every right to take that shot."

"Well..." I look away and take another sip of wine. "I can't change it."

"I never wanted this for you, Lyla. I didn't want you to even know this life exists, much less live it. That's why I never said good-bye. I knew you'd ask why I was leaving, and I couldn't tell you the truth. Couldn't promise you anything."

"I know." I drink more wine, then pull in a shuddering breath. Dread eats at my insides. "I need to go home, Nick."

"You can leave whenever you want."

I can't look at him yet, but his voice sounds indifferent about it.

"I need a few days. To figure out flights and an apartment and a car—"

"It's all been taken care of."

I look at him. Nick looks unruffled, one hand tucked into his pocket as he leans against the wall.

"What?"

"You have a fully furnished apartment waiting for you. It's two minutes from Leo's former school. Although if you want to send him to a private school, I'd be happy to pay for it. There's a car for you in the garage. I think it's a Volvo. I had Roman do some research on what was safest. And you can take my jet whenever."

"You…you really didn't need to do all that."

He raises one shoulder, then drops it. "It's done."

"I-I guess we should leave tomorrow then. There's no reason to…we should get settled as soon as possible."

"That's fine. I'll let the pilot know. Pack whatever is essential. I'll have the rest shipped in a few days."

I nod. "Thank you."

He's making this so…easy. Part of me has dreaded this departure for longer than I'd ever admit. Has hated the idea of packing up our lives here and returning to Philadelphia. To have to apartment hunt and find a decent used car and search for a new job.

And it's all done. A new life waiting for me.

"Also, I think you should go back to school. If you want to."

A kernel of hope sprouts in my chest. I crush it as quickly as possible. I'm not surprised Nick has realized or guessed I want to get a degree. It would open up my job prospects and allow me to get the credentials to make social work a realistic possibility.

"I'll pay for it, obviously," he adds, misreading my hesitation.

I smile, my facial muscles tight and stiff. I once read getting everything you want in the world is the worst thing that could happen to you. At the time, I thought it was some happy sap's attempt at making the rest of us feel better. Now, I think *this* is the worst thing that could happen to you: having everything you want in front of you and having to walk away.

"I can't, Nick."

A muscle in his jaw jumps, betraying irritation. "Why not?"

"It's…it's way too much money."

"I have plenty of money."

I half laugh, half sigh. "I know you do."

"Not all of it is dirty. I have real estate holdings and clubs and—"

"It's not about how you earned it either," I tell him. "I mean, yeah, you know it bothers me. But I can't take that much money from you, Nick. I just…can't."

The jump in his jaw turns into a pulse of annoyance. "You're taking the car and the apartment."

"For *Leo*. It's how I'll get him to school and playdates and appointments. And it's where he'll live. I know whatever you've arranged is better than I could do on my own, and I'm not too proud to admit that. But school…that would be for me. There's a difference."

"I haven't paid child support in eight years. You've had to handle everything. It's not a fucking handout, Lyla."

I sigh. "I'll think about it."

He studies me for a few seconds, then nods and straightens. "Good night."

My mouth opens.

Stay, sits at the tip of my tongue.

I don't want to be alone right now. Specifically, I want to be with him. I want sex and snuggles and the intimacy I've only ever experienced with Nick.

This is our last night. My last chance.

"Good night."

He half smiles. "Let me know if you want more wine."

I see it so clearly—what staying here would be like. How easy it would be. But then I hear the clank of the gun hitting the floor in Dmitriy's apartment. I feel the terror of being tied up on that couch with my son next to me.

I never want to be in that situation again. I never want Leo to be in that situation again.

And I don't want Nick to ever have to make that choice again. He was ready to die to save us, and I'm not sure I would be standing upright if he had. I'd be in a fetal position on the floor, falling apart.

Nick left Philadelphia nine years ago to protect me.

This is me leaving to protect him. And Leo.

"I'm just going to pack and go to sleep."

His half smile dies a hasty death as soon as I say the word *pack*.

"Sounds good," he says.

Then, he leaves.

CHAPTER THIRTY-ONE

NICK

Bianchi calls just after five a.m. I'm sitting in my office, sipping on vodka.

I never went to sleep. My eyes feel gritty and dry, but I'm not tired.

For a while, I thought there was a chance Lyla might appear. Hoped she might show up the same way she did that first night we slept together. But I know it's for the best she never did. Letting her go is going to be hard enough as it is. I don't need fresh memories.

"What?"

"You're awake. Excellent."

I sigh. "What is it, Bianchi? I'm in the middle of something."

There's a pause.

"You and Callahan have an agreement?"

"I don't know what you're talking about."

Bianchi chuckles. "Of course not. It's quite an accomplishment, you know. The Irish are notoriously temperamental. Your old man would be proud."

"Once again, I don't know what you're talking about."

"Fine. I need you to call the Irish and sweet-talk them. First time you'll have talked in ages, I'm sure."

"And why would I do that?"

"My favor, Morozov. Or are you breaking your word?"

I grit my teeth. "I'm not breaking anything. It's a delicate situation, as I'm sure you can appreciate."

"Of course." I can hear him smiling. "Look, my brother is in Dublin."

"Business?"

"No. He was there, visiting a friend. Got involved in a skirmish in a pub and—"

"They realized who he is," I finish.

"Yes."

"It will likely cost you."

"That's not much of a favor."

I flex my jaw. It hurts like a motherfucker, thanks to the butt of Dmitriy's gun. The skin didn't break, but I can feel one hell of a bruise forming. "I'll see what I can do."

"Good." Luca hangs up before I can, which is annoying and predictable.

The timing is either terrible or fortuitous—I can't decide. I won't be here when Lyla and Leo leave.

Delaying the slew of phone calls I need to make, I stare out the window until the sun rises. Most of the snow has melted. We're creeping toward the end of March, so it's possible there won't be any more this winter.

I've never noticed how *empty* the grounds are. There's nothing but open land until the tree line and the fence. I'm sure my father saw it as ideal for security purposes. But I think it's also one of the many symbols of how he never bothered to make this estate feel like a home. Growing up here was like living at a boarding school. Set schedules and more time spent with staff than family.

When I walk into the dining room after spending an hour on the phone, making arrangements, Leo is already there, munching on a bowl of cereal.

"Hey, Dad."

"Hey, buddy. You feeling okay this morning?"

I study him carefully. His coloring is good. No dark circles suggesting he didn't sleep. And he's munching away at the cereal like he hasn't eaten in weeks.

"Yep. I was actually wondering…could we maybe go to the park with Darya this morning? Mom said I can skip school today."

I swallow, my heart sinking like a stone. "Did she say anything else about plans for today?"

Leo's brow wrinkles. "No. Why? Are we doing something?"

His face is alight with excitement at the idea. I wish I still had his curiosity and optimism. I hope he always has it. Yesterday, an outing resulted in a kidnapping. But here he is, hoping we have some expedition planned.

"You and your mom are headed home today," I tell him, holding his gaze, even as his expression falls. "Back to Philadelphia," I clarify, as if that needs explaining.

"You aren't coming with us?"

I shake my head, walking over and taking the seat next to him. "I have to stay here, Leo. This is where *I* live."

Leo plays with his spoon. "I don't want to go," he says quietly. "I like living here."

"It's what is best for you," I tell him. "You'll be able to go back to your old school. See your friends again. You said AJ is your best friend, right? You'll get to play with him again."

"I don't care." His jaw sets stubbornly.

"Leo, your mom and I just want what's best for you. The plan was always for you to stay with me for a little while and then go back home. I'll always be a phone call away. It won't be like before."

Leo looks at me. "You promise?"

I swallow the lump in my throat. "I promise."

He nods. "I love you, Dad. I forgot to tell you yesterday."

The lump grows. "I love you too, son."

Leo slides out of his chair and walks over to me. His small arms wrap around me, and I inhale his scent. He smells like a kid, which sounds stupid. But there's something innocent and earnest about it.

He pulls back, and I ruffle his hair.

"You should finish your breakfast. You never had dinner last night, right?"

"No. I wasn't hungry."

"Well, if you're hungry now, you should eat."

"Okay."

Once Leo's back in his seat, I sigh. "I have to go now, Leo. Something came up with my work. And when I get back, you and your mom will be back in Philadelphia. This is good-bye—for now."

He looks down in his bowl, then nods.

I stand and kiss the top of his head. "Have fun on the jet, okay?"

"Can you really fly it?" he asks.

I smile. "Yes. One day, we'll fly it together, okay?"

"Okay."

He doesn't ask me to promise again. But if he had, I would have.

When I walk out of the dining room, Lyla is standing on the bottom step, holding the banister. Her hair is in a messy bun, she's wearing an oversize sweatshirt, and I'm not sure she's ever looked more beautiful.

"You heard?"

"Yes."

I don't ask how much, just nod. "I need to leave now. Egor will take you to the airport whenever you're ready. The plane is on standby. And there will be another car waiting in Philadelphia to take you to the apartment."

"Egor?"

"He'll keep you safe."

Her hand slides up and down the banister. "Why isn't Viktor or Roman taking us?"

"They're coming with me."

"Oh." She pauses. "Where are you going?"

"Ireland."

"For work?"

"Yes."

I'm not sure if she's asking because she truly wants to know or just doesn't know what else to talk about. There's nothing left to say between us really. Just vestiges of the past.

I start to roll down the sleeves of my shirt. "If you need anything once you land, you can still use the phone I gave you. It's set up for international service. Call if you need anything at all."

Lyla clears her throat. "Okay."

I'm not sure what else to say. Anything I think of seems too insignificant or too monumental. And I'm flying commercially since she and Leo are using my plane. So, I don't have the flexibility of leaving whenever I want. "All right. I already told Leo."

I smile at her even though it feels tight and tense, then turn toward the front door.

"Nick." Lyla has taken the final step. "Or should I call you Nikolaj? I never asked…"

"Nick is fine."

She and Leo are the only ones who call me Nick, and I like that they do.

"Be careful, okay? Don't…don't drop the gun."

It's the first time she's referenced the moment that happened yesterday.

I didn't think she would.

At all, ever.

"Unless you or Leo is in the room, I'll never drop a gun." I pull my gun out of my hip holster. It's the same one she used yesterday, but I don't tell her that. I hold out the handle to her, gripping the barrel. "You can bring it with you or leave it. Up to you."

She cracks a smile as she takes the gun. "What a romantic farewell gift."

"I want you and Leo safe more than I want anything else in this world. Call that whatever you want."

I turn and walk away, not waiting to see her reaction. Masha, one of the maids, is waiting by the door with my coat. I shrug it on and then step outside. Roman, Grigoriy, and Viktor are all waiting in the car. I climb in the driver's seat and set off at a pace that has Viktor and Grigoriy exchanging a loaded look in the backseat. I glimpse it in the rearview mirror and then focus on the road.

"Are we talking about it?" Roman asks.

"Talking about what?"

"Egor mentioned he's taking Leo and Lyla to the airport later."

"And?"

"Not talking about it. Got it."

"There's nothing to talk about."

"Your son is leaving, Nikolaj."

My fingers tighten around the leather steering wheel. "That was the plan all along."

"And nothing has changed?"

I don't answer, and the rest of the drive is silent.

When we land in Dublin, I have four missed calls from Alex. I call him back immediately, worried about what might have happened in Philadelphia.

Not even bothering with a hello, he says, "You're letting them leave?"

I exhale, regretting calling him back so hastily. I'm on the friendliest terms with Bianchi that a Morozov *Pakhan* has ever been on, as evidenced by the fact that I just flew thousands of miles to save the life of a man I'd otherwise torture and execute myself.

"Who told you?"

"Better question: why didn't you?"

I rub my forehead, eyeing Roman. He's my best guess at over-sharing. "Everything with Dmitriy just went down yesterday. Then, Bianchi called to cash in his favor. I'm dealing with a lot."

"*Avoiding* a lot, you mean."

"You're overstepping, Alex."

"This is *Lyla*, Nikolaj. You've been hung up on her since you were eighteen, and you know it. You fuck women and forget about them. You haven't gotten married even though you need an heir and you could have anyone you want."

I stare at the dreary gray landscape. "They're better off without me."

"That's bullshit."

"They were *kidnapped* yesterday. My son had a gun to his fucking temple!"

"Life has risks. You know that better than anyone. They could get in a car accident. She could get mugged one night. Do you have any idea how many school shootings happen here each year?"

"At least it wouldn't be my fault."

"And that would make it easier to deal with?"

No, it wouldn't. The thought of anything happening to either of them while I'm on the opposite side of the world carves a pit of fear in my stomach. But… "She chose to leave. She doesn't want anything to do with this life. There's no future between us. I knew it when we left Philadelphia years ago, and it's still true now. Leo isn't old enough to make his own decisions, and even if he was… I'm not going to fucking fight her for custody."

Alex sighs. "I still think—"

"We're about to meet with Callahan," I state. "If you call me again, it had better be about business."

Roman glances over at me once I've hung up. We're still a few minutes from the pub where I'm meeting with Liam, but he doesn't call me out on the lie. He apologizes instead. "Sorry. We meant well."

I slip a hand into my pocket, turning the silver lighter over and over. "Just keep your opinions to yourself."

Roman nods before looking back out the window.

CHAPTER THIRTY-TWO

LYLA

Philadelphia looks the same. Smells the same. Sounds the same.

But *I* feel different.

The apartment where we live now is in Rittenhouse Square, one of Philadelphia's nicest neighborhoods. There's a park across the street and no sound of sirens at night. The building is old but tastefully refinished, exposed brick walls, crown molding, and shiny appliances. All the furniture is fancy and color-coordinated. The Volvo SUV that was waiting in the heated garage retails for sixty thousand dollars. I looked it up.

I can't pretend the time in Russia never happened.

I miss the drafty castle.

I miss walking through the snowy yard.

And I miss Nick. A lot.

It's funny how right and wrong can become nuanced.

Maybe it's because I grew up seeing the way people looked at my mom, looked at me, but I always thought they were clearly defined. Obvious. That it was easy to tell what you should do and what you shouldn't. Of all my worries about being a single parent, setting a good example for Leo was never one of them.

I pay my taxes on time. I hold doors for strangers. I don't speed.

And I shot someone. Someone who wanted to kill me and my son.

It's harder to see the black and the white when you're in the middle of the gray.

I finish wiping the counters—for the third time—and shut out the lights in the kitchen. Leo is gone for the night, spending the night with AJ at his grandparents' house. I'm supposed to meet June for drinks at the bar down the street.

It's been surprising how few people have questioned my and Leo's disappearance. I'm not sure if it's a testament to whatever Nick might have handled behind the scenes or if most people are just too wrapped up in their own lives. Leo's school reenrolled him without question. The law firm wrote me a glowing recommendation, saying they wished they could hire me back but already filled my position.

Part of me was relieved since it means I won't have to run into Michael every day. I have an interview at a different law firm on Monday. As much as I'd love to do something different, it's where my experience is. And I need a steady paycheck more than I can afford to be picky.

I know June will have lots of questions tonight.

I lock up and head outside. It's still chilly, but it feels like there's a warmer undertone to the temperature. A distant hint of spring. I wonder what the estate looks like in warmer months. With green grass and leaves on the ivy.

Forcibly, I shove the wondering away. June is waiting at the front of the bar when I walk inside.

"Hey! How are you?"

"Good. It's nice to be back," I lie.

June smiles and gives me a hug. "I missed you."

"I missed you too," I say, squeezing her back.

The bar is crowded. It's a struggle to push through the crowd. And a wait to order drinks. June gets a cabernet while I deliberate.

"Do you have…" I try to remember the French words that flew so effortlessly off Nick's tongue. I can't remember. Moments are already beginning to feel distant. I'm sure it's an expensive wine anyway. "I'll just have a vodka soda. Thanks."

We make easy chitchat as we wait for the drinks. AJ's ninth birthday is coming up soon, and June is starting to plan the party. She fills me in on the disastrous bake sale at the elementary school a couple of weeks ago.

Once we have our drinks, we snag a free table tucked alongside the wall.

"So now that we have alcohol…how are you *really*?" she asks.

I smile wryly. It's a little reassuring, knowing someone knows me well enough to tell when I'm lying. "I'm okay. It's nice to be back in some ways. Just…weird too."

June sips on the red wine she ordered. "Your call was vague, but it was a relief. I was sure something happened to you."

"I would have thought the same thing. I'm sorry for worrying you. It was sudden and hard to explain. Even now, I'm not sure what to say."

"We don't have to talk about it," June says. "I'm just happy you're back and everything is okay."

I nod, and she smiles.

"Have you talked to Michael since you've been back?"

I shake my head. "No. I think that's over. We weren't…it never felt right, you know?"

June raises both eyebrows. "I remember saying that. You said, and I quote, 'He's the perfect guy.' What happened?"

"I fell in love," I admit.

June's eyes widen. "What? When? With *who*?"

I exhale. "It doesn't matter. It's not going to work out."

"Why not?"

"It's complicated. He just—he's not a good guy."

"Did he hurt you? Hurt Leo?" With each word, June's voice pitches higher with alarm.

"No. *No*. He would never. He just…he's hurt other people."

"Dangerous people?"

There's something in June's expression, something in her voice, that makes me think she understands more than I meant to tell her. "Yes."

She nods and takes a sip of her wine, gaining a distant, haunted expression. "Carson didn't die in a supermarket. He died in a supermarket parking lot because his friend thought he could get away without settling a debt. Life is short, Lyla. If this guy is good to you, good to Leo, good in the ways that matter, that's what is most important."

"He's Leo's father."

June's eyes widen even further. "Really? I've always wondered…"

"I know. He—I—it's…"

"Complicated," June finishes.

"Right."

"Does he love you too?"

"He's never said it." I replay the *clank* of a gun hitting hardwood. A terrible sound, yet somehow, it gives me comfort. I start running my finger around the rim of the glass in endless circles. They're soothing and depressing. Endless. They never go anywhere.

June studies me, then purses her lips. "That's not a no."

I lift a shoulder, then drop it. "I'm here. He's…not."

Her nod is slow and unconvinced, but she changes the subject. We talk for another couple of hours before paying the check and then heading outside.

"Lyla?"

I turn to see a shocked Michael standing on the sidewalk a few feet away. He's wearing the wool coat I'm convinced is the only jacket he owns and holding a grocery bag in one gloved hand.

I give him a small, awkward wave before we share a brief hug. "Hi."

"I'll let you two get caught up," June says, shooting me a questioning look.

We give each other a farewell hug.

"I'll text you in the morning about getting the boys," she tells me before flagging down a taxi.

Michael is studying me with a disbelieving expression. "You're back."

I fiddle with the zipper on my down coat. "Yes."

"You requested a reference? I just assumed it was…somewhere else."

"I should have called or texted. I just wasn't sure what to say. I…I wasn't expecting to be gone for so long. It was a lot to figure out. My phone didn't work overseas."

Michael's smile gains a bitter edge. "There's no need to explain, Lyla. I had one of the firm's PIs look into your disappearance. They asked me if anything unusual had happened right before. All I could think of was that doctor. Dr. Ivanov. I had them dig. He is a doctor. But he didn't go to Harvard. And his family is notoriously tied to the Morozov family. Some of what comes up when you search that name…" He shudders.

"What are you saying, Michael?"

There's an edge to my voice, and the emotion driving it isn't one I expect to feel. I'm defensive, and it's not just because he's calling me a liar. Because everything he's insinuating about Nick pisses me off even if it's accurate.

He studies me. "I don't want to know anything. Just be careful."

Michael is an attorney. An upholder of the law. He's supposed to fight for what is right, not flee from what is wrong.

I thought my taste in men improved after Nick. I thought I was picking men who were solid and reliable. Who had principles and morals and convictions. Who were *good*.

If Leo and I ever disappeared without a trace, the way I vanished from Michael's life, I know Nick wouldn't let the police handle it. He wouldn't launch a half-baked private investigation that ended at the first sign of trouble. He would burn buildings and spill blood.

The thought should terrify me. I should flinch from such madness, from the obvious depravity. Instead, there's some sick comfort in it.

"I will be," I say because I know that Michael's words, while cowardly, come from a place of caring.

He nods, then glances at the bar. "Are you driving home?"

"I had one drink, Michael."

I used to find Michael's responsibility reassuring. All of a sudden, I'm finding it overly restrictive. Like a child who isn't trusted to handle anything. Nick let me fly thousands of miles away from him the day after being kidnapped and shooting a man.

"I'm just worried about you, Lyla."

"I know," I allow. "I actually moved. I'm walking."

"You moved? To Rittenhouse Square?"

I nod, pretending not to hear the judgment and curiosity in his tone.

"I'll walk with you," he says. "I parked down the street."

"Okay," I agree because I can't come up with a polite excuse. And I'm quite certain this will be the last time I see Michael. There's no reason to end things on a negative note.

We set off down the street.

"How are things at the firm?" I ask.

"Busy. I'm headed to Phoenix for a deposition next week."

"That sounds warm."

Michael nods enthusiastically. He hates the cold.

"Um…this is me."

Michael glances at the building. It's an older brick building but obviously well-maintained. I haven't looked up exactly how expensive housing in Rittenhouse Square is, but I can make a good guess that it's pricey.

Instead of impressed, he appears worried. It makes me wonder what exactly comes up when you look into the Morozov family. My internet access was limited when I was in Russia. And I've done my best to avoid anything directly related to Nick since being back. Forgetting him has been difficult enough without looking for reminders.

"Take care of yourself, Michael. I'm sorry about…well, I'm sorry."

Sudden disappearance, followed by a cryptic breakup call, isn't a conventional way to end a relationship. But Michael doesn't appear to be the least bit surprised that I'm not interested in picking our relationship up where we left it now that I'm back in Philadelphia. It makes me wonder what exactly he's assumed about what my disappearance meant. And if maybe I was the only one who idealized our relationship into something it wasn't.

We never talked about him meeting Leo. Moving in together.

Marriage. More kids. All the things you're supposed to picture with someone at a certain point.

"Take care, Lyla." Michael smiles and then keeps walking.

I watch his tall frame until it disappears from sight, lost in the shadows cast by the streetlights.

It feels like the end of something. My quest to live differently from my mother maybe. And if I really think about it and look back on it, I think I accomplished that a long time ago. Leo's life is very different from mine was, and that was true long before Nick came into his life and back into mine.

I pull my keys out of my purse, brushing against the hard metal of Nick's gun. I never ever thought I'd be the person who walked around with a loaded weapon. I'm not even sure it's legal, and concerningly, it's not the first law I've broken without a second thought lately.

For better or worse, I see the world differently now. I see the gray. I'd think it's a bad thing, but I also know that there's always been something between black and white I just chose not to look at. Becoming aware of something isn't the same as it never having existed in the first place.

There's also some sentimental value I never thought I'd associate with a weapon capable of killing someone.

I unlock the door and flick on the kitchen light, surveying the empty space with something close to disappointment. This will become a more and more frequent occurrence, I realize, as Leo grows older and more independent.

I keep walking through the kitchen and toward the living room. Sweatpants and a glass of wine are calling my name.

A glimpse of movement in the corner of the room captures my attention and stalls my heart.

I swallow the scream that crawls up my throat, dropping the keys and pulling out the gun. My grip is steady as I raise and aim the weapon, removing the safety before I point directly at the dark shadow sitting in the armchair next to the fireplace.

"Late night at the office?"

Relief hits me in a staggering wave at the sound of the familiar voice, making my fingers shake. I lower the gun, worried I'll accidentally pull the trigger. "What are you doing here?"

"I had some business in New York. I thought I'd come see how you're settling in."

Nick stands, strolling over toward me slowly, like a predator approaching prey. He takes the gun and flips the safety back on before setting the firearm on one of the side tables.

"Nice draw."

He manages to make the compliment sound like an insult. Annoyance fills the words instead of pride.

"Leo isn't home. He's at a sleepover."

"Okay," he replies. And then he keeps walking toward the front door.

It takes me a few seconds to realize he's leaving. "Wait. Where are you going?"

"Not sure."

"Nick!"

He keeps walking.

"Nick! What are you doing? You break in and then walk out?"

He spins, his expression a thundercloud. I can feel the anger rolling off of him, an intense, dangerous buzz that vibrates through the air like a silent storm. "Breaking and entering is defined as the act of entering a building using force with the intent to commit a crime. I used the key I have as the building's owner, and the only thing I've done since I arrived is sit in this damn chair."

Some anger of my own sparks in response to his haughty tone.

"Of course you'd be well-versed in criminal codes and their loopholes."

He scoffs and starts walking again.

"Nick!"

His shoulders stiffen, and he stops, but he doesn't turn around.

"What are you doing *here*?" I ask again, hoping I'll get an actual answer this time.

"Are you fucking him?"

"I…" I flip through a carousel of emotions. Shock, annoyance, confusion, uncertainty. "I-I thought you've been sitting in the chair."

Another scoff. This time louder and angrier. "I didn't damage the curtains. Don't worry."

"I wasn't worried." I spit the words, irritation hurtling them out like sharpened arrows.

"You weren't?" He tilts his head, expression dark and mocking. "Well, isn't that a fucking first?"

My molars grind together. "Why. Are. You. Here?" I enunciate each word, hoping it will keep him from evading an answer for the third time.

It doesn't.

"The jet is here. Flying out of Philadelphia was better than commercial through New York."

Or maybe that is the real answer. Maybe, at most, his showing up has something to do with Leo and absolutely nothing to do with me.

Nick starts walking again. Something inside me recognizes this as a defining moment.

Fight or flight.

Sink or swim.

The easiest way to mask love is with hatred. The opposite extreme. But, by definition, the true opposite of love is indifference. Utter apathy is the furthest you can flee from love. Caring the most versus not caring at all.

Apathy isn't, *"Are you fucking him?"*

Apathy isn't tense shoulders and unspoken words.

He could have called or texted to announce his arrival in town. He could have taken his jet and left immediately. He could have said he was happy to see me settling in.

Instead, he's striding away like being around me is painful.

"I miss you." The admission comes out without permission. Desperation coats it, and I hate that. Hate how Nick is *always* the one in control. Hate how even here—in my country, in my condo, which he pays for—he pulls the strings.

Nick is almost to the door. I don't think he'll stop.

But he does.

"You can't just appear in my living room, Nick. Legal or not. You told me this is my apartment. Owning the building doesn't give you the right to barge in here and scare the shit out of me."

Impossibly, Nick's shoulders tense even more. "You're right. It won't happen again." His tone is as stiff as the suit he's wearing.

"I don't want you to leave."

I'm not sure if he hears me. The words are soft. A secret spoken aloud. I say them so they'll stop bouncing around in my head, expelling the truth like sucking poison from a rattlesnake bite—in some desperate attempt to heal.

When Nick doesn't move, I know he did. He's inches from the door, and then he's suddenly much closer—near enough I can smell the spicy musk of his cologne and feel the heat of his body.

"You don't want me to leave? What do you *want me* to do? You decide, like usual."

"Like usual?" I echo, disbelieving. "I didn't decide *anything*, Nick!"

"No? Then, how the hell did you end up back here? Because that wasn't my fucking call, Lyla. It was yours."

"It wasn't—I needed—"

Half-formed sentences fall out of my mouth.

I can't decide how much to tell him.

That when I wake up in the middle of the night now, I see Dmitriy's blank eyes?

That I was worried if I didn't leave right away, I wouldn't be able to?

"I'm not fucking him." I finally answer Nick's earlier question about Michael. I know doing so will appeal to his overbearing nature and the alpha possessiveness.

Sure enough, his eyes flare. "What do you want, Lyla?"

I hate how much I love the sound of him saying my name. How his accent peeks out when he says my name, like he's leaving some special stamp on the syllables.

"I want you to fuck me." I step closer, inhaling his scent and letting it flood my veins with fire. "Hard." My head tilts back, meeting his stoic gaze without flinching from the flint. "Rough." I tuck a piece of hair behind one ear and swallow. "I want you to fuck me like you hate me." As soon as the words are out, I bite my bottom lip.

Nick chuckles, a dark sound that wraps around my lungs and squeezes. "Won't be hard."

"I know," I whisper.

"We could have been brilliant."

His use of the past tense stings, but I keep what I hope is a seductive smile plastered on my face.

He's here. Now. Right in front of me and too tempting to resist. And at this point, I'm not sure it can hurt any more. I might as well take the pleasure as well.

Nick's presence is a jagged knife stuck in my chest. Painful but also keeping me from bleeding out.

"Are you staying or leaving?" I bite out the question because I can't keep holding my breath.

Nick exhales, long and irritated. "I need a fucking drink." He steps away, yanking at his tie like it's become a noose and tossing it onto the table by the front door. He unbuttons the top of his shirt next, revealing the smooth skin of his throat and the top of his chest.

I trail behind the broad line of his shoulders as he walks away from me and into the kitchen.

I head for the cabinet next to the fridge. "I have…wine?"

When I glance over, Nick nods. "Wine is fine."

I grab two glasses, set them on the kitchen island, and uncork the bottle. "So…how was Ireland?"

Nick pauses in the middle of rolling up his shirtsleeves. My stomach flips at the sight. There's something about him that's just so…virile.

"It went fine," he answers, his tone slow and measured. Maybe a little confused, like he forgot he ever mentioned it or is surprised I'm asking.

"It's supposed to be beautiful there."

"We didn't do much sightseeing." He leans his forearms on the counter and studies me more intently than I'd like.

I slide one of the glasses toward him and take a long sip from the other, ignoring his piercing gaze.

Most of our anger seems to have dissipated into thin air, leaving other confusing emotions behind.

Fifteen minutes ago, I was actively working on forgetting Nick with no expectation to see or hear from him in the near future. And now, he's standing three feet away from me, dissecting me with his eyes.

Finally, he looks away, taking in the white walls and marble countertops and walnut-colored cabinets. There's no towel on the stove handle or any magnets on the fridge. The few decorations are all staged, like a show home. I shift, wondering if he notices.

Leo was gone for most of the day. I told myself I'd do some unpacking, and all I did before meeting June was submit job applications, clean, and paint my toenails.

"This place is great," I say. "Thank you again."

Nick nods, then drains the rest of his glass. "This wine tastes like shit."

I scoff at the rudeness. "It was on sale."

"I'm sure it was."

I roll my eyes. "Do you want more? I'm sure it tastes better, the more you have."

"I'm good. Thanks."

Awkwardly, I smile, then study the brick wall behind him. This was easier when we were yelling at each other.

"Should I go?"

My eyes dart to Nick's. His head is tilted to the side, watching me.

I shake my head. Dread fills me at the suggestion. Having him here is the first time this condo has felt complete. And since I'm unwilling to delve into why that is, I want to enjoy the feeling for as long as possible.

Nick stares at me, deliberating. I wait for the, *This is a bad idea*, or, *We shouldn't do this.*

But he doesn't speak either of those obvious truths. He stands and circles the island until he's right in front of me, crowding my space and stealing my oxygen.

He stares at me like he's mesmerized by the sight. Like it's the first time he's seen me. Like all the tiny details matter, not just the full picture. The tip of his thumb slips under the hem of my sweater and glides along my waist, sending sparks of heat spiraling through me. It's basically an accidental brush, but it sets me on fire because *he's* the one touching me.

"This isn't why I came."

Oof. That comment slaps like an insult, but he's matter-of-fact.

Nick isn't trying to hurt me. He's letting me know him being here is temporary. This isn't the start or continuation of anything. It's an addendum, tacked on after what was supposed to be the ending, because no matter what state our relationship—or lack of one—is in, the sex is always phenomenal.

He left, and I left, and we've always taken different paths when the road splits, either by choice or circumstance. That hasn't changed. Won't change, even as he rubs the sensitive skin just above the waistband of my jeans.

"I know." I breathe the words, barely louder than a whisper.

Knowing it's selfish.

Knowing the person I'm hurting is myself—and maybe him.

I'm too cowardly to ask Nick if I matter to him. As Lyla, not just his son's mom.

That's been an easy excuse for some of what's taken place between us. And I've embraced the fuzziness because it's allowed me to enjoy this without taking responsibility. Without assigning meaning. Without analyzing that *clack* of gun hitting wood.

"I miss you too," he whispers.

And then he's kissing me, capturing my bottom lip between his teeth and sucking on my tongue and making it very difficult to think or to breathe or to remain upright.

One of his hands moves between us, unbuttoning and unzipping my jeans. He jerks at the lace of my underwear, the textured lace rubbing against my clit.

I gasp, arching against him. Liquid pleasure runs through me languidly, dripping like warm honey.

"I lied earlier," he says, still jerking the lace.

"About what?" My voice is raspy and rough. Like sandpaper soaked with desire.

"I don't hate you, Lyla. I *can't* hate you."

I pull his lips to mine instead of answering. Nick is dangerous. Dangerous for my heart and dangerous, period. He's like stepping into the eye of the storm and simply hoping you don't sustain any damage.

Emotions aren't logical. They're messy and unpredictable. And I feel like I have to sort through them once for myself and once for Leo.

Nick gets on board with talking with our bodies. He lifts me up onto the counter and tugs my jeans the rest of the way down. I part my legs, and he steps between them, simply tugging the soaked lace to the side. I whimper, a breathy, desperate sound that probably conveys how much I missed this. Not just the pleasure, but the closeness, the intimacy.

I'm not embarrassed around Nick. I *want* him to see me bare like this. On display in front of him, I feel revered. Cherished. Sexy.

He looks his fill, then rolls on a condom. The head of his cock notches into place, nudging into my pussy an inch before he stops moving. The anticipation builds until it becomes a presence between us.

I wonder if he's thinking the same thing I am. That this is probably the last time we'll be in the position. The last time that we're in the before as opposed to the after. The last time that there will be *another* time.

He pushes inside slowly, giving me a chance to adjust to his size. We stay like that for a moment, and then it shifts. Slow turns frantic. Skin slaps. Sweat builds.

Nick's thrusts are rough, not gentle. There's nothing considerate or loving or romantic about it.

I'm supposed to be purging him from my system. But with each thrust, it feels like the opposite is happening. Like he's sinking into me more than in the physical sense, embedding himself so deeply, it will be more than painful to remove. Right now, it feels impossible.

Tears sting my eyes.

I lose control over everything.

He pulls me in like the persistent tug of an undertow.

So, I close my eyes and get swept in the current.

CHAPTER THIRTY-THREE

LYLA

When I wake up, I feel relaxed. For the first time since I moved to this apartment, I don't open my eyes to the sight of a gun. I forgot to even carry it into the bedroom.

I was...distracted. After fucking me on the counter, Nick carried me into the bedroom, and we immediately fell asleep.

The doorbell rings. I glance at Nick's face, smooth in sleep, and slip out of bed, pulling on a robe and hurrying through the apartment. I only pause to slip the gun into a drawer in the living room before opening the front door to June, AJ, and Leo.

"Hey," June says. "I'm so sorry. Did we wake you up?"

"No," I lie. "It's fine."

I'm externally calm and internally panicking. I don't want Leo discovering Nick in my bed. Don't want him to have any hopes about me and his father having that sort of relationship.

"My mom forgot about a brunch. When you're over seventy, I guess brunch begins at nine a.m." June rolls her eyes. "I called, but you didn't answer. Is...is everything okay?"

"Yep!" I tighten the knot of my robe and run a hand through my hair.

I follow June's gaze to the tie draped on the table. "Did something happen with..." She mouths Michael's name even though the boys are oblivious, both looking at a toy AJ is holding.

"No. He just walked me—"

I *feel* Nick's presence a second before Leo shouts, "Dad!"

I turn to watch as he launches himself at Nick.

Leo's voice contains more excitement than I've heard from him in the few weeks we've been back in Philadelphia.

It cracks something in the very center of my chest, watching Leo embrace Nick, only pulling back to say, "AJ, this is my dad."

Pride fills Leo's voice as he introduces Nick to his best friend. The crack widens, filled with the heartbreaking realization that Nick will always be able to offer Leo something I can't—himself.

I can provide Leo with everything I never had—the unconditional love of a mother, security, support, a reliable home—but I'll never ever be able to fill the father-shaped hole in his life. Especially now that he knows the exact size and shape of it.

June takes Nick in. He's dressed in last night's clothes at least, but it does next to nothing to hide his impressive physique. His dark hair is messy, and stubble coats his sharp jawline. He looks like the fantasy of the guy you wake up to, not the reality.

"Nice to meet you, AJ," Nick says, leaning down to shake the boy's hand. The sound of his voice, deep and rumbly, stirs something in my stomach. Ignites memories of him saying other things. Nick stands and offers a hand to June next. "I'm Nick. It's nice to meet you."

"June," she says. "It's very nice to meet you too."

Once introductions are out of the way, there's a beat of silence.

"How long are you staying, Dad?"

Nick ruffles Leo's hair, giving him an affectionate smile. "I have to leave tonight, buddy."

I'm pretty sure my face is wearing the same disappointed expression as Leo's.

"We'll have the whole day together, all right?"

Leo nods, his face losing some of the sadness. "Are you going to fly the plane back?"

Nick grins. "Not this time. I'll probably try to catch up on some sleep."

My cheeks warm, and the ache between my legs tingles. Leo is oblivious. I don't check June's reaction. I'm not even sure if that's what Nick meant. His sleep schedule seems to be haphazard at best. Maybe I'm projecting the way I had the best night's sleep since I left Russia, marathon sex and all.

"Well, we should get going," June says. "Let you guys have some family time."

I smile at her, absorbing how those two words sound. Something so simple and so meaningful. "Thanks, June."

"Anytime." She smiles at Nick and then gives me a loaded look I'm not ready to unpack before the front door shuts behind her and AJ.

"How come you're here so early?" Leo asks Nick as they walk into the kitchen.

I hold my breath and tighten my robe, hyperaware I'm not wearing anything under the terry cloth.

"I came from New York. I thought you'd be home and I could say hi to you and your mom. When she said you were at a sleepover, I decided to wait until you got back."

"You were in New York?"

"Uh-huh. You want breakfast?"

"Sure." Leo climbs up on one of the island stools, watching Nick as he starts rummaging through one of the drawers and emerges with a frying pan. "What were you doing in New York?"

"I bought a building there recently."

"Really?"

"Yep." Nick pulls the carton of eggs out of the fridge, making himself at home in the kitchen.

"How come?"

"It's an investment. Real estate tends to hold its value. You pay a lot of money up front to buy a property, and then over time, you earn it all back, plus more."

"How much did it cost?"

"Leo," I chide. "That's rude to ask."

He looks down. "Sorry."

"You don't need to apologize. Just remember, sometimes, people get offended when you ask them how much they spent on something. It's up to them whether they choose to tell you."

Leo nods.

"I'm going to get dressed. Can you help your dad with breakfast?"

Another nod. Some of the excitement he wears so effortlessly around Nick disappeared as soon as I spoke, and I wonder if this is the role I'm destined to play forever.

Nick will always be the cool parent who appears on his private jet with stories about places Leo has never been. I'll be the one who enforces bedtime and reminds him about homework and makes dentist appointments.

It's not Nick's fault either, which makes it even harder. I'm the one who moved Leo thousands of miles away. I'm not the one with commitments to a certain place. I might be mostly ignorant to the workings of the Mafia—by choice—but I do know it's not an operation you can pick up and move. There are territories and traditions. Warehouses and routes.

Nick is tied to Russia. I'm choosing Philadelphia.

Once I'm around the corner, I pause.

"Thirty-four million."

I hear Leo's gasp. "For real?"

"Uh-huh."

There's a cracking sound that must be an egg.

"How do you have that much money?" Leo wonders, then hastily apologizes. "Sorry. Mom said I'm not supposed to ask about money."

I bite my bottom lip hard enough, it hurts. Maybe I was too hard on him. I'm not sure how much to encourage when it comes to Nick. It seems inevitable he'll discover the real source of Nick's wealth eventually, if he hasn't surmised enough already.

"Your mom is right. Some people get uncomfortable, talking about money. But you can ask me anything, Leo. If I don't want to talk about it, I'll tell you."

"Okay." Leo's voice has brightened, undoubtedly compiling all the things he can ask Nick about now that he's been given free rein to ask. "Did you talk about a lot of things with your dad?"

I hover even though I should walk away because Leo is asking questions I'm not sure I have the right to ask. I'm curious about Nick's childhood. His parents. How someone gets molded into who he's become—a ruthless killer who kisses tenderly and hugs tightly.

"No." Nick's voice has changed, taking on a somber tone. "I didn't."

"How did your dad die?"

Another question I never asked. I never told Leo his paternal grandfather is gone, so Nick must have.

"He was betrayed," Nick answers. "By someone he shouldn't have trusted."

"Do you miss him?"

"I wish he were still alive. I wouldn't be…as busy if he were. I could spend more time with you."

"I wish you lived closer."

"I know, buddy. Me too. But let's have fun today, okay?"

"Okay."

I keep walking down the rest of the hall even though I want to stay and eavesdrop. Leo hasn't asked me many questions about his father. He's a perceptive kid who has undoubtedly figured out that the situation is complicated. I'm just now realizing that I thought he would ask me any questions, not Nick directly. I somehow missed how close they got. How comfortable Leo is around Nick. How he doesn't just revere him. He trusts him.

I'm worried he'll resent me for moving thousands of miles away from his father. He already knows leaving was my choice, not Nick's. And he has picked up enough on Nick's business to understand it's not a mobile business, that Nick needs to be there for his work.

Leo's quiet disappointment on the plane ride back here was difficult to endure. I thought being back in Philadelphia would help. Returning to his old school, seeing AJ and his other friends. His room down the hall is twice the size of the one in our old apartment with its own attached bathroom, just like in Russia.

None of that put the massive grin on his face this morning. That was all Nick.

Back in my room, I take a long, hot shower. The warm water pounds my skin and relaxes my muscles. But it does absolutely nothing to soothe the turmoil in my head.

I went to Russia, planning to leave at the first possible opportunity. It was something to cling to through the terror and uncertainty, a proverbial, familiar light at the end of an unfamiliar tunnel. When the barrier keeping us from leaving was lifted, it was easiest to leave. To avoid the confusing feelings and the complications and the fear by retreating into the known. By following the plan that was in place and returning to the life I created as a single mother.

But the problem with change is, you can't revert to your former self.

Change is irrevocable.

Irreversible.

I'll forever live with the memories of the six weeks of living in that big house. They passed so slowly, and yet all but a few hours from that final day are ones I wish I could rewind and relive all over again.

Leo is everything to me. The only blood relative I have left. We feel incomplete without Nick now. Like part of a family rather than two halves of a whole.

When I finally step out of the shower, a swirl of steam informs me I stayed in longer than I meant to. The mirror is fogged, to the point I can only make out a rough outline of my face. I got lost in a labyrinth of my own thoughts, looking for some new path to appear.

Nick's presence in the condo feels like it changes things. But it doesn't, not really. It's just muddying murky waters.

He never asked me to stay. Never indicated there was any *us* in the future. Even the sex was usually initiated by me.

Nick is probably happy to have his house to himself again. He's probably screwing his way through the women who were eyeing him at that party and possibly planning to marry Anastasia Popov.

And if he isn't…that would be heartbreaking in other ways. If he cares, if he has regrets, this will be even harder.

I towel off and get dressed, my eyes drifting toward the unmade queen bed over and over again. For once, the tangled sheets aren't tangled from tossing and turning all night.

There's a Nick-shaped hole in my life too. And the problem with knowing what you're missing is that it's impossible to replace. There's only one Nikolaj Morozov in this world, and I think I knew that the second I saw him in that red kitchen.

A knock sounds on the bedroom door as I'm tugging a brush through my hair.

"Come in," I call, my voice a little throaty and a lot nervous.

Leo wouldn't knock.

Nick opens the door and steps inside. There's a flash of… something in his expression as he looks me over, wet hair and bare feet. "We finished breakfast," he says. "Is it all right if I take him for the day?"

"Oh. Uh, yeah. Of course."

I feel like I was just rocked back on my heels. Surprised and off-kilter. I should have been expecting this. Of course Nick would want to spend time with Leo, just the two of them. I want that—for both of them. I just didn't think I would be cut out of the picture quite so seamlessly. I'm *jealous of my son* and humiliated by the realization.

I make a show of picking my phone up off the dresser and checking the time. "You guys ate fast," I tell Nick because he's still standing here and I'm at a loss for what else to say.

I want to ask where they're going. If he's taking security. What time they'll be back. But I'm trying not to come off as a helicopter parent, and I don't want Nick thinking I don't trust him with Leo's safety—because I do. There's no one I trust it with more, honestly.

"You took a long shower," he replies, a small smirk creasing one corner of his mouth like a comma.

I look away, blushing, but not for the reason he probably thinks. I was thinking about him in the shower, just not in a sexual sense. I'm flushed because I know this playful, teasing side of Nick doesn't appear often. And it's a glimpse of something I want so badly, the desire is practically acute with pain. The guy flashing me a boyish grin doesn't look capable of any of the crimes I know Nick has committed. This version of him—carefree and lighthearted—is impossible to resist.

"We should talk," he tells me, the smile falling away and his expression shifting to serious.

I nod, my heart galloping in my chest.

"About Leo," Nick adds. "I want to know what to tell him."

My head stops moving. I'm no longer sure what I'm agreeing to.

"I was thinking twice a week to start. I'd like to get him his own phone, if you're comfortable with that. It will be encrypted and set up for international calls, just like yours. You can keep it on days we're not scheduled to talk, but I'd prefer he keeps it at all times so he can contact me if there's ever…" He exhales. "I would also like him to spend a few weeks with me this summer. There's…I won't be able to travel back here anytime soon."

I try to ignore the pang in my chest, but it's persistent, like a ball bouncing against the same surface over and over again.

"I have a job interview on Monday," I tell him. "Once I know my schedule, we can figure something out."

"Have you given school any more thought?"

"It's the middle of the semester, Nick."

Some bitterness leaks into my voice, and I hate that it's there. Nothing I'm upset about is his fault. And that makes it even more difficult to swallow.

I'm on this path because of choices I made, and I can't figure out where I chose wrong. All along, I thought I was making the right decisions. But I somehow ended up in this place I don't want to be, with thoughts I don't like.

His eyes scan my face, looking for something I probably don't want him to find. I need to shut it all down when it comes to Nick. The lust and the longing and the rancor.

"Okay," he says softly.

We stare at each other, and my mind is blank.

"Dad! I have my shoes and coat on!" The eagerness in Leo's voice is unmistakable.

"He'll be safe," Nick tells me, holding my gaze.

I chew on the inside of my cheek. Nod. "I know. Have fun."

He lingers for a minute. Then, he nods, turns, and disappears. There's a burst of chatter from the entryway. The front door opens and closes.

I'm alone.

And I feel it.

CHAPTER THIRTY-FOUR

NICK

For the first time ever, I spend a full day with my kid, just the two of us. No bodyguards. No trips to the warehouse or checking on drug shipments.

It's a snippet of what my life could look like if I was born with a different last name.

It's wonderful and terrible.

The perfect day, tinged with the bitter aftertaste of reality. Because outings like this with my son will be rare and far between, going forward. Time with him the exception, not the norm.

I missed eight years, but I didn't *know* I was missing them. Had no idea Leo existed. Now that I do, there's a clock planted in my brain, continually keeping track of all the days we're apart.

It's not just the worst-case scenarios I'm envisioning. I'm realizing I'll miss out on the happy moments too. I won't get to go to the state fair Leo spent half the morning talking about. He's hoping to do his project on Kansas, simply because his teacher said it's the most boring state. That's the exact sort of thing I would have done as a kid, and it sparks this weird mixture of pride and nostalgia.

Lyla is trying to provide Leo with the best possible childhood, and I respect her for it.

I know it's partially driven by all the ways in which her own was lacking, but it's a noble intention, no matter the impetus. One I can hardly find fault with.

I sure as hell can't argue with the fact that the Mafia isn't the best environment for a kid.

But it's hard to ignore the pinch in my chest every time Leo mentions something I'll miss out on.

We spend the morning at the zoo. It's obvious Leo's animal obsession extends far beyond dogs. He rattles off random facts about every animal we pass—from the hippos to the pythons. Makes sympathetic faces at the bored-looking giraffes and the lion that's sprawled lazily in scraggly grass, uninterested in calls from the crowd to stand up.

Leo looks horrified by the callousness. I can't help but think of my father, whose idea of sympathy toward any living creature was firing his Glock in its forehead.

I told Leo earlier I wish my father were still alive, but I'm not sure that's true. *Pakhan* is never a responsibility I wanted. Oddly, I know I was always my father's favorite for the position. It's why he let me leave for the States, hoping I would come back and step up. Pulling the strings from behind the scenes, like always.

After leaving the zoo, I take Leo to lunch at a steak house. Despite being a Saturday, it's filled with plenty of corporate suits, picking at salads and making polite small talk. Our waitress is blonde, young, and overly attentive.

Leo asks why she keeps stopping at our table, and I have to muffle the snort that wants to escape.

Kids are blunt. It's refreshing, hearing unfiltered thoughts.

Most people are scared to say what they're thinking around me. Leo has no such qualms, and it's a relief.

I know I can be intimidating. I know my father tried to intimidate me.

Honestly, I'm winging the whole parenting thing. There's no blueprint to follow or manual to read on how to parent a son you just met while also juggling your responsibilities as head of a massive criminal organization. But I think Leo saying what he's thinking around me is a good start.

After lunch, we go to the natural history museum. Leo is just as enamored by the butterfly room and the dinosaurs as he was by the zoo. By the time we leave the museum, it's dusk out. The sun is rapidly sinking, dimming the natural light. Streetlamps flick on as we walk toward my rented car, casting shadows.

Leo is clutching the book and T-shirt he picked out in the gift shop, marveling at the ocean exhibit that was our last stop, when my phone buzzes in my pocket.

I let it ring twice, delaying the inevitable. I texted Lyla throughout the day, knowing she will be worrying about Leo. She responded to each text almost immediately, simply liking it in acknowledgment. Either she didn't want to disturb my time with Leo by asking questions or she didn't know what to say.

Whoever is calling me knows I asked not to be disturbed. If they're calling from Moscow, it's the middle of the night there. It's urgent, and it's going to pop the bubble I lived in today, where I can spend a day with my son and not worry about anything else.

I open the door for Leo to climb in the car—in the backseat because this car has one—and answer the call.

Answer, but don't speak.

There's a half beat of hesitation before Taras, one of my *bratoks*, speaks. "Nikitin just called. CKP is planning to raid the Savyolovskaya warehouse."

I pinch the bridge of my nose. “Fuck. When?”

“He didn’t have details. Top level only. Zakharov said there has been chatter ever since the Tekstilschiki incident. Guess a building has to have a working gas line to actually explode that way.”

I growl, not in the mood for jokes. I’m mentally weighing the risks. Everything stored in the Savyolovskaya warehouse is untraceable. The building itself is owned by a shell company that leads down a rabbit hole of fake names, none of which can be traced back to me. Leaving everything there will mean losing out on a payday and scrambling to replace the stock for buyers. Moving it will mean tipping off we have a mole feeding us information—something I’m sure the CKP knows, but I’d rather avoid confirming it.

“Move it. And redirect the liquor shipment. Let them test two hundred bottles of Beluga Noble.”

“Got it, boss.”

Taras lingers on the line, and I sigh.

“What else?”

“Alarms went off at Penthouse an hour ago. They shot out the cameras, but nothing is missing.”

“You’re sure?”

“It’s been checked over twice.”

“What about surrounding cameras?”

“Nothing clear,” he replies.

“Did you let Roman know?”

“Yes. He’s worried Dmitriy had plans in motion.”

I rub my temple, certain he’s right. “Double the security and sweep it for explosives.”

“Will do.”

Taras hangs up, and I’m left staring down the street. The sun has dropped even lower, partially covered by the tall buildings downtown. Warmth fades with the light. It feels fitting. The closing of a chapter.

Leo has climbed into the front seat. He's fiddling with the center controls when I climb into the driver's seat. Kid has a thing for cars in addition to animals, both living and extinct. As soon as the door opens, he's clambering into the backseat like he's worried I'll scold him.

I smile at him in the rearview mirror. "The driving age is eighteen in Russia, you know. Living here, you'll be able to drive at sixteen."

That's eight years, I realize. A time that sounds long but will feel short.

Leo smiles, but it has a forced edge to it. He's smiling to make me feel better, and it has the opposite effect.

I start the car and pull away from the curb. Rather than head toward Rittenhouse Square, I turn in the direction of UPenn's campus. It's quiet, even for a Saturday. I realize it must be the university's winter break.

The empty parking lot serves its purpose exactly.

Leo looks out the window, confused. "What are we doing here?"

"Climb out of the car," I tell him, shifting my seat back and opening my door.

Leo listens, an adorable furrow appearing between his eyebrows.

"Come on," I tell him. "This is your first driving lesson."

Confusion turns into elation as Leo settles into my lap and grabs the steering wheel with his smaller hands.

If my own father had ever suggested doing this, I would have felt rife with worry. It would have been a test—or worse, a trap.

Leo's lack of hesitation eases some of the worry I'm fucking up the parenting thing. The weight and warmth of his body in my lap is comforting, not claustrophobic. Not many people touch me. My immediate family begins and ends with my mother, who is far from affectionate. Unless I'm training or fucking, no contact is made with anyone. I'm hard to land a hit on, and I'm not a snuggler—with one exception, I guess, considering how I woke up this morning—so those are brief occurrences.

We drive in circles around the parking lot until it's completely dark out. I glance at the clock. Everyone will be waiting at the tarmac by now.

"We've got to go, buddy."

Leo doesn't argue, but I feel his disappointment hovering like a tangible thing. All the questions I ask on the drive back to Lyla's condo are answered briefly until I give up.

A curtain flutters in the window as I park outside the brick building. I smile to myself, unsurprised Lyla is anxiously anticipating our return. Leo sees it too.

"Mom worries too much."

I squeeze his shoulder. "She loves you, Leo. That's a good thing."

Leo heaves a sigh that makes him sound like a teenager.

The front door opens before I have a chance to knock. Lyla's wearing the same outfit as earlier under a plaid apron, her hair up in a messy bun that's more messy than bun.

"Hey. You guys are back! Long day." She aims for a casual tone and falls somewhere around curious.

"We saw you spying, Mom," Leo states.

I have to bite the inside of my cheek to keep from grinning.

Lyla's cheeks flush. "Did you have fun?"

"Yeah, we did. It was great. Right, Dad?"

Leo looks up at me, and my stomach knots.

"It was great," I confirm.

"I'm, uh, I'm making dinner," Lyla states. I can smell it—

roasted meat and fresh herbs. "If you want to stay…" Her voice trails off, leaving the invitation open-ended.

I watch Leo's expression fill with hope at first, then disappointment when I reply, "I can't stay."

"Right. Of course." Lyla's reply is hasty.

I think I catch of trace of disappointment on her face, too, before she schools her expression to nonchalance. Her arms cross like armor.

"Something came up with work. It can't wait."

"Of course," Lyla repeats, dismissing my explanation.

I catch the wry twist to the words, the subtle disapproval. But she still doesn't look eager for me to leave.

I hate it, and I love it.

It's a lot harder to walk away from someone when you're not sure they want you to.

That's the problem though. Lyla *isn't* sure. She doesn't want this life—for herself or Leo—and I can't blame her.

I bend down and hug Leo. "We'll talk soon, okay? You can tell me all about Kansas."

"You promised, right?"

I brush my lips against his hair. "Right."

"All right."

I give him one last smile after I straighten, then glance at Lyla. Her knuckles are white as she clutches her elbows, everything about her body language screaming, *Stay away*.

I don't listen. I step forward and kiss her cheek, another gentle brush. The way you'd kiss a grandmother.

Lyla inhales sharply, like I shocked her. I pull away, avoiding eye contact like a coward. Then, I turn and retrace the path to the car, answering the call buzzing in my pocket. It's Roman.

"What?"

"Penthouse just went up in flames."

I won't be sleeping on the plane after all.

"I'll be at the airport in ten minutes," I tell him before hanging up.

I allow myself one glance in the rearview mirror as I drive away.

They're gone.

CHAPTER THIRTY-FIVE

LYLA

The car behind me has to honk twice before I realize I'm sitting at a green light. I tap the gas too aggressively to compensate. My old Honda would have barely moved. The Volvo lurches forward like a pouncing cat spotting easy prey. My spine flattens against the seat, and the seat belt cuts in below my chin as I cross the intersection and pull into June's driveway.

There's a stone bunny perched on each side of the stairs and a glittery egg hanging on the front door.

Leo informed me three days ago that a bunny delivering eggs is silly and I shouldn't hide them this year. It broke my heart a little bit, realizing he's growing up so much faster than I would like. Knowing he's already seen ugliness in the world and lost innocence makes it harder. So is seeing him wake up at five a.m. every Saturday, bursting to tell Nick about his week when he calls at ten.

We're limping along, Leo and I. Going through the motions. The law firm I ended up getting a position with is even smaller than where I was working before. I hole up in my cubicle all day, filing forms and sending reminder emails. Pick up Leo from June's or after-school club and go home to make dinner. Clean or do a load of laundry if the hamper is overflowing. Leo will play with his figurines or ask to play video games while I sip wine on the couch and watch TV. He goes to sleep, and I'll usually follow not long after, only to wake up early and start the routine all over again.

Leo isn't the only one who looks forward to Saturday mornings. I'll usually hover in the kitchen, conveniently choosing to clean or bake something, just so I can catch the rasp of Nick's deep baritone on the other end of the line.

It's pathetic, eavesdropping on my son's conversations because I'm too much of a coward to pick up the phone and call his father myself. Our exchange coordinating his calls with Leo was via text, short and to the point.

And I keep waiting for this ache to abate. For the wondering and the second-guessing to stop. For Leo to smile more than he frowns.

I'm not sure if we were missing something before and didn't realize it or if those weeks with Nick easily bulldozed years of routines. Maybe both.

Both of June's eyebrows climb her forehead when she opens the front door and sees me standing on her porch. "Everything okay?" she asks carefully.

I gave June the condensed version of Nick's visit. No mention of the sex or the argument or the gun. Just that he showed up unexpectedly and spent the day with Leo. But I'm pretty sure she saw right through me.

Pretty sure I'm still transparent.

The worst part is, I'm not wallowing. I'm not trying to be miserable. I'm trying to be grateful for all the important things. For safety and health and having a home.

I still have to force a smile on my face. It doesn't want to come naturally. "I'm fine!"

Rather than invite me in like I'm expecting, June steps out on the porch. "What are you doing, Lyla?"

"Uh, picking Leo up?"

She rolls her eyes. "I mean, with your life."

I roll my bottom lip between my teeth. "Well, that's a broad question."

June laughs, then shakes her head. "Have you talked to Nick since he was here?"

"We've discussed his calls with Leo."

"Saturday at ten, I know. Do you know how I know that, Lyla?"

I don't answer, assuming it's a rhetorical question.

"Because the only person more in love with that guy than *you* is Leo. So, what are you doing, Lyla? Why are you here while he's there?"

"It's complicated."

"I know it is, and I'm not trying to belittle that. But I wouldn't be much of a friend if I didn't ask."

I look away at one of the happy bunnies. "I don't know if it's best for Leo."

"We're all figuring out the parenting thing as we go, sweetie."

"I don't know if Nick…I don't know…" I can't even put it into words, but June figures out what I'm trying to say.

"I think you should tell him you love him and want to be with him and go from there."

"What if it doesn't work out?" I whisper.

"What if it does?" she counters. "What if saying something means you're not stuck wondering *what if*?"

I exhale. "I don't know. I'll think about it."

All I've done for the past three weeks is think about it, and June calls me out on it. "Be open."

"I *am* open."

"No, you're open about being closed off. There's a difference."

I stay silent, conceding she has a point. My social circle is basically just June at this point. I haven't gone on a single date since being back in Philadelphia. I haven't spoken to any of my "work friends" since starting at the new firm. I've always been guarded and quiet, and the effort I'm making each day is already exhausting.

"I'll watch Leo," June says softly.

My eyes fly from the rabbit to her. "You mean, go *now*?"

She shrugs. "Why not? You don't have work tomorrow."

"I…"

I try to come up with a reason for why I can't pick up and fly to Russia tonight. There are lots of reasons. But not a single one that's actually standing in my way. I have the money. Nick had passports made for both me and Leo that I was handed when we landed a month ago. I'm not due back at work until Monday, and I could take a sick day if I had to. I trust June to care for Leo.

"I'm scared. I'm *so* scared, June. He's…he's always been *that guy* for me. Even if I hadn't gotten pregnant with Leo and had never seen him again after college, I know I would still wonder about him. And I *like* having the possibilities even if they're really what-ifs. If I try and it doesn't work out, I'll have nothing."

She hugs me. It eases some of the anxiety locking up my muscles. So does the shuddering sigh I exhale, resting my chin on her shoulder.

"I saw the way he looked at you, Lyla. I wouldn't be pushing you unless I thought you were headed toward a happy ending. Life is unpredictable and short. It doesn't always have to be planned out and responsible. If you want to see him, you should go see him. Simple as that."

Uncertainty spirals and tangles in my stomach, spiked with excitement. Because I'm realizing I will do this. That I will go see Nick, and I'm not sure how to process it. It feels like I've spent years wondering how he feels about me, that I've drawn the uncertainty out so far that it's become this behemoth of an unknown. Partly because I never thought I'd ask for an answer.

"I need to pack Leo some things."

June smiles. "He and AJ are the same size. I have plenty of spare toothbrushes. Just go before you talk yourself out of it."

I roll my eyes. She knows me too well.

"Fine. Let me talk to Leo."

I head inside, finding him and AJ playing a card game in the living room.

"Hi, boys."

"Hey, Mom," Leo answers, not looking up from his game.

"Hi, Ms. Peterson," AJ adds.

"Leo, can I talk to you in the kitchen for a minute?" I ask.

He looks up, brow furrowed. It's the expression that reminds me most of Nick. "Okay," he says carefully, setting his hand of cards down and standing up.

"Can we finish the game before leaving?" Leo asks once we're facing each other in the kitchen.

"Actually, June offered for you to stay the weekend," I reply. "Is that okay with you?"

"Why? Where are you going?"

I hesitate before answering. "I have a work trip. They need me to go to a conference this weekend."

I hate lying to him, but I can't tell him the truth. If this trip ends poorly between me and Nick, I never want Leo to know about it.

Leo's expression falls. It's a bit of an ego boost until he says, "Does that mean I won't get to talk to Dad tomorrow?"

"I'll figure out a different day for you to talk with him, all right?"

"Yeah, okay," he replies, visibly working to smother his disappointment.

I lean down and kiss the top of his head. "I love you, Leo."

"I love you too."

Leo

When I land in Moscow, it's just past six p.m., local time.

I almost changed my mind about this trip a dozen times. Packing a bag and my passport back in the condo. On the drive to the airport. Paying an obscene amount for a last-minute seat at the ticket desk. Going through security. Sitting at the gate. During the two-hour layover in London.

But I'm here. Surrounded by commotion and a language that no longer sounds so foreign even if I still can't understand more than a dozen words of it and can speak even less.

The British woman who sat next to me on the plane is in front of me in the customs line. She aims a worried look my way, probably because she watched me pick at my lunch and shred through two napkins. When she sees I noticed, it turns into more of a pitying smile.

Nerves ricochet inside me like pinballs in a machine.

I don't regret coming here, but I'd be lying if I said I felt confident about this decision. I only packed what would fit in my carry-on. I didn't call or text Nick.

This is the hastiest, most impulsive thing I've ever done in my life. The realization is freeing—and terrifying. Because I'm not some free spirit who goes with the flow and is content to float around. I wish I were, and I know exactly why the thought horrifies me.

Chasing a man across thousands of miles is something my mother would have done.

So is falling for a guy who doesn't make an honest living.

But falling is an ongoing action. It's difficult to stop and continues for an indeterminable length of time.

Since I only have a carry-on, I head straight for the exit after getting through customs, bypassing the crowd around baggage claim.

This is the moment when I should turn around, but I've come too far now. I'm sleep-deprived and starving, disbelieving I'm really and truly here. Now that I am, it seems very obvious this is a visit that should have been predated by a conversation. A simple phone call would have given me a little insight at least into what Nick is thinking.

I walk through the automatic doors and outside the airport. A row of cabs lines the sidewalk, waiting to ferry passengers. I scan the row of cars, deliberating. I don't really want to waste precious hours here in a hotel, but I'm not sure what else to do. Every time I traveled to or from the Morozov estate, I was shuttled by Nick's men. I never took public transit or memorized an address.

I have Alex's number, and I could call him to ask. But that feels cowardly, and the point of the trip is facing fears.

Based on the way people are hurrying past, getting a cabbie could be a challenge. So, I decide to focus on that problem first, then decide where I'm going.

I approach the line, glancing across the street at the fancier row of cars waiting for particular passengers.

And then freeze, my heartbeat pounding in my ears like a percussion drum.

My fingers loosen on the strap of my bag. I almost drop the small piece of luggage, barely clenching my hand in time to keep it from falling.

Nick is leaning against the side of his favorite car, watching the flow of traffic leave the airport with his arms crossed. There's an invisible bubble around him. Despite the busy street and sidewalk, the hustle and bustle of activity, no one walks near him.

I glance around for an omnipresent SUV, for Grigoriy or Roman to be standing around on standby or as security.

Nothing.

Nick is here, alone, and I'm confused.

I approach him cautiously, half worried this is a prank sleep deprivation is playing on me.

But the closer I get, the clearer Nick becomes.

"*Privyet.*"

One dark brow arches, followed by a rapid flurry of Russian.

"That's all I know," I admit.

Nick looks like he's fighting a smile.

"Yet."

"Yet," Nick repeats, rolling the single syllable.

I don't know what he's thinking. I don't know if I'm making the right decision. And all that not knowing has coalesced in the pit of my stomach, dragging me down every day like an anchor. I need to stop assuming and start asking.

Wind blows, the cold cutting through me like a sharp blade. It's frigid and dark, no trace of anything but frostiness in the air. Or emanating from the man in front of me.

He does shrug his heavy coat off though and drapes it around my shoulders. It smells like his cologne, spicy and expensive.

"*Spasibo,*" I say, using up the rest of my Russian vocabulary.

"Are you hungry?"

"I...yes."

I'm waiting for Nick to ask what I'm doing here, but he doesn't. He nods and takes the bag from me before getting in the driver's seat.

I steal glances at his profile as we drive away from the airport and into the city, inhaling the scent of his spicy cologne. He's acting like this was a planned visit, like this was an expected arrival. It's thrown me for a loop, to say the least.

Since I've put as much planning into what I'll say to him as I have into the rest of the trip—none—I stay silent as we drive. If he wants to act like this is normal, maybe some of the knots in my stomach will untangle themselves. I focus on the sprawling architecture of the city instead until we stop in front of a stone building with carved archways and scrolling accents.

Based on the way the valet starts fumbling and tripping over himself, he recognizes Nick. The same is true for the hostess who meets us inside the glass doors, although her appraisal is more appreciative than fearful.

"I'm not dressed for this," I whisper to Nick as we weave through the center of the restaurant. Not only am I wearing jeans, I'm wearing jeans that have been through fifteen hours of travel and a black tea spillage. Most of the women here are wearing silk evening gowns and fur wraps.

"You look beautiful," Nick tells me, placing a palm on my lower back and guiding me toward the back of the restaurant.

He sounds like he means it, and it flusters me. So does the fact that it feels like everyone is looking at us. I can't understand any of the chatter or even the soft music playing in the background. I'm especially attuned to the body language and the atmosphere, noticing every head that turns our way. Each tilt and whisper.

Nick ushers me into a private room, and I feel like I can properly breathe again. The sense of comfort is leached away though once I realize we're alone, tucked away, out of sight.

"This place is nice," I say, eyeing the framed prints on the walls so I don't have to look directly at him.

He makes a noncommittal hum.

"You own it?"

"Yes."

A beat of silence, where I fiddle with my napkin, wishing it were paper instead of cloth.

"Leo is okay?"

"Yes. He's with June. She offered to watch him for the weekend." I inhale. "I lied to him about where I was going. And told him you couldn't call this weekend."

Another hum that reveals nothing.

A uniformed waiter appears before either of us says another word. I exhale, trying to let out some anxiety with the carbon dioxide and breathe in some courage with the oxygen.

Watching the waiter doesn't help. He's more nervous than I am. His hand shakes as he fills the glasses with water, tremors that nearly soak the tablecloth. Under other circumstances, I'd find it amusing. Distract Nick so the poor guy can do his job without being scrutinized.

But I'm not ready for that piercing gaze to be aimed at me. I'm having enough trouble gathering my thoughts as it is. I know what I want to say to him, what I came all this way to say to him.

Getting there is proving to be difficult. I'm lost in a maze of my own thoughts, trying to find the right path to get to where I want to end up.

Another waiter appears, delivering a glass of amber-colored liquid and placing a charcuterie board in the center of the table, next to the candles burning.

I stand so suddenly that I knock the table with my knees, realizing the waiters are about to depart. I need a minute to myself before being alone with Nick.

"I'll be right back. Restroom."

I barely catch Nick's nod before I flee down the hall and into the restroom. The long sink has multiple faucets, illuminated by flattering lighting. I wash my hands and use one of the fluffy towels, patting my face as well. The soap smells like lavender, a supposedly soothing scent. I'm not sure it's doing a whole lot for me right now. My heart feels like it's trying to run a marathon in my chest.

Heels clack against tile, announcing the arrival of another woman in the restroom. She's willowy and imperious, wearing a silk dress and a haughty expression. She looks my outfit over and sniffs with disapproval before sweeping out of the restroom dramatically, as if my presence is offensive.

I decide to follow her since standing at the sink indefinitely isn't much of an option.

There's a gush of colder air that greets me when I step out of the hallway. I look to the left. A door is cracked open at the very end of the hall, letting in a sliver of chill through the opening.

I walk left instead of right, the way I came, inhaling deeply. The cold smells fresh and pure. Refreshing.

I wander outside without really thinking about it. In the bathroom, I could hear muffled chatter from the restaurant and clatter from the kitchen. The alley the door led to is empty aside from a few trash cans, dimly lit by the streetlamps and excess light emanating from surrounding buildings.

Traffic whizzes past in the distance, but it's otherwise silent. Not the same as the surrounding landscape of Nick's estate, although it is still more peaceful than I'd expect the center of a city to be.

I tilt my head back to stare up at the stars, relieved to see the silver pinpricks sparkling against the backdrop of black sky. Russia isn't dark and gritty the way I pictured it to be before I'd ever been here. It's fathomless and sprawling. Even the cold is something I've come to appreciate.

A creak announces the opening of the door. I glance over hurriedly, preparing to explain why I'm loitering out here to one of the kitchen staff.

But Nick is the one who steps out. The reaction is instantaneous. My stomach flips, and awareness spikes my system. Impossible to ignore, like a charge of electricity, commanding attention.

He doesn't ask what I'm doing out here.

He doesn't question my sanity for standing in a dark alley, shivering because I left my coat inside.

He strolls over to my side, head tilted back to take in the view of the sky. His silver lighter appears, the flicker of a flame setting the end of the cigarette ablaze. The butt glows orange, casting more shadows over his face.

Silently, he holds it out to me.

I take it, noticing he doesn't pull away when our fingers brush. "You're a bad influence," I tell him.

I'm not just talking about the cigarette.

One corner of Nick's mouth—the side I can see—hitches upward. "I know."

I take a small puff of the cigarette, then hand it back to him. The ashy taste is terrible, and the tobacco smells like burning newspaper. I cough. Nick hands me a piece of gum. I take it without looking over, feeling his eyes on my face as minty flavor fills my mouth.

It's disconcerting, as is the realization that the moment is here. This—standing under the sky, sharing a cigarette—feels like a more appropriate setting than a crowded airport or fancy restaurant.

Right as I'm inhaling to speak, Nick finally does. "What are you doing here, Lyla?"

I bite my bottom lip. It's a nervous response, not meant to be a seductive one.

"Long way to fly for a fuck," he comments, flicking the cigarette to the ground and carelessly crushing it with his boot. I hope it's not a metaphor for my heart.

"You're one to talk," I retort.

I wait for him to tell me that trip was just to see Leo and I was just a convenient pit stop along the way. But he doesn't say that. Doesn't say anything.

"Leo misses you," I state. "I'm worried moving him so far away from you was a mistake. He didn't know what it was like to have a dad before. Now, he does, and aside from Saturday mornings, he still feels like he doesn't. That's my fault, and Leo knows that. I'm worried he'll resent me for it. And…I'm worried you will too."

When I glance over, Nick's jaw has tightened. His profile is harsh. He looks like a statue of an emperor. Or an avenging god. Still, he says nothing.

"But I'm not here because of Leo. I know he'll be okay. I know we can figure it out. It just feels…it feels like I've been driving along for a while, not really noticing the scenery, just focused on what is ahead. Then, I was here, and I had to stop. I saw the scenery. And now, I'm trying to look ahead again and just keep driving, but I can't stop noticing everything."

I laugh a little, then shake my head.

"Does that—does that make any sense? I'm sleep-deprived. What I'm trying to say is that—"

Nick opens his mouth. "Lyla, I—"

"Wait. Let me finish." I take a deep breath. Admitting this feels like preparing to rifle around in broken glass. There's a good chance I'll get cut. "I'm in love with you, Nick. I tried to avoid it and ignore it and pretend that it was just sex. Being back in Philly, I hoped it would fade. But it hasn't. And honestly? I'm scared it's never going to. Because nine years was plenty long enough to move on…and I never really did. I know it's complicated with Leo and with everything that's happened. And maybe you're engaged now and I—"

"I never made an agreement with Popov."

I'm relieved by the revelation, and I let it show with a long exhale. But it turns to apprehension when it becomes clear that's *all* Nick is planning to say in response.

"You never asked me to stay," I whisper.

His jaw tics with irritation. "You made it very clear what the answer would be."

"What if the answer has changed?"

He stares at me, eyes stormy and expression grave. "Lyla… nothing else will change. There will be more bloody shirts. If you're telling me this, thinking it will be the push I need to walk away…it's not."

I nod and swallow. "I'm not going to lie and say I'm suddenly okay with it all. But so long as Leo isn't involved, not unless he chooses to be once he's eighteen, I can handle it." I pull in a deep breath. "And I'd rather have you with all that comes along with it than not have you at all."

His hand rises. His thumb traces my cheek, the touch featherlight. "Are you sure?"

I nod. "I've thought about it a lot the past few weeks. And… it's not like my hands are clean either."

"The situations aren't comparable, Lyla." Nick's tone has

changed from soft to sharp. "Don't say you shooting a dangerous man in self-defense is the same as what I do."

"It gave me a new perspective, Nick. That's all. We all do what it takes to survive."

"You don't want this life."

"I don't," I answer. "But I want you. I can hate what you do and still love you. You said you don't have a choice, that you never had a choice, and I understand it better now. I know I do… and I want to choose you."

"You never—"

"*You* never, Nick. You never said good-bye. You never came back. You never said you *love* me. You never acted like I meant anything to you at all, like you wanted us to last longer than was necessary."

He's silent for a few seconds.

"My father was a cold, miserable bastard. He could find fault with someone's breathing. And no one took the brunt of his abuse more than my mother. Anything that went wrong, he'd find some way to blame her. The party she threw distracted his men. If she was off shopping, she was ignoring her responsibilities. If she spent time with me and my brothers, it was coddling.

"I swore to myself my marriage would never be like that. But I never thought I'd marry for love. Even if I was never going to be *Pakhan*, I knew my father would leverage my marriage to advance his interests."

Nick's hand moves down my cheek, cupping my jaw and tilting my face so I couldn't look away even if I wanted to.

"And then I ended up at a frat party in Philadelphia. I was standing by the fridge when I saw a girl walk into the room. It felt like I'd been waiting my whole life just to look at her."

I inhale but say nothing.

"I know I left, Lyla. I left because I didn't think I had another choice. I left because I was trying to protect you. If I had to do it all over again, I'm not sure I would do anything differently. Ever since you've been back in my life, I've still tried to protect you. I'm not what's best for you. I never will be. But don't you dare think you're not all I want. Don't you dare think it's because I don't want you or because I don't want you to stay. Don't you *dare* think I don't love you. I love you more than I thought I was capable of loving someone."

Something inside of me releases like a valve when he says those last two sentences. Something sweet and satisfying and heady floods my body, like a powerful drug.

"Really?"

Nick smiles. "Really."

He takes a step closer, caging me against the wall of the restaurant. I'm no longer cold, cocooned by his body heat. He smells like smoke and spicy cologne.

Like sin and temptation.

He startles me by speaking. "I really want to kiss you."

The gravel in his voice forms goose bumps on my skin. But that's the only way I react. I'm too stunned by the admission. It's at total odds with his usual assuredness.

"So, kiss me."

Nick smiles. "I'm going to."

But some of the amusement trickles from his expression as he looks at me, his handsome face turning severe with emotion.

"What?"

"I'm worried you'll change your mind." He brushes some hair away from my face, his touch lingering and leaving a trail of heat in its wake. "I'm worried it's going to be too much and—"

I kiss him. His mouth is warm, the heat almost too much after the numbness of the cold. I expect him to taste like ash, but his lips have an oaky, malty flavor. He must have sipped some scotch while waiting for me to return.

My back rubs against the rough exterior of the building, my sweater not much of a buffer. But I'm aware of nothing beyond the sensual glide of his tongue against mine. The warm grasp on his palm on my hip as he pulls me flush against his body. His other hand weaves into my hair, tugging gently to angle my mouth exactly where he wants it.

Everything fades away—the garbage bins, the starry sky, the cold air.

Nick pulls away first, then leans back in for a softer, more chaste kiss. "What about marriage?"

"Is this your idea of a proposal?"

He half grins. "No. But it will be expected, especially since we already have a child. The Bratva can be…old-fashioned. Not following tradition is seen as disrespectful, not progressive. And having my last name is the best form of protection I can give you."

I nod. "Marriage sounds good."

"More kids?"

"Yes," I whisper.

His smile morphs into a full one before he grabs my hand and starts tugging me along, just not in the direction I'm expecting. I thought we'd head back into the restaurant, but he's pulling me toward the street.

"Where are we going?"

Nick glances over and answers as if it's the most obvious answer in the world, "Home."

CHAPTER THIRTY-SIX

LYLA

I blink. When I open my eyes, they're still there, laid out in a perfectly symmetrical row on the marble counter that surrounds the sink.

The last time I took a pregnancy test, it was hunched in a tiny stall of the student center's bathroom, which always smelled like burned coffee. I was too embarrassed to take it in the dorm bathroom, worried one of the other girls who lived on the floor or one of the women who cleaned might see it.

I was ashamed too.

I had a far from traditional upbringing. I wasn't raised to believe sex outside of marriage was a sin or you needed to be married to have a child. But I knew the judgments of women with a baby but not a ring, and the part of me that felt like I was finally overcoming the shitty hand life dealt me was furious with myself for sabotaging it.

My parents weren't married. I didn't want to be like them. I wanted to give my kids a family. A home.

I don't feel shame or embarrassment now. I feel…happy. This is what five months of unprotected sex were *supposed* to result in, but it still feels surreal to be standing here, looking at the lines on five plastic sticks that are all positive.

There's a knock on the door.

"Lyla!"

I quickly sweep the tests into the top drawer and turn on the faucet to wash my hands. "Yeah?" I call back.

"Your hair and makeup need to be done."

"O-okay." I assess my appearance in the mirror. My cheeks are flushed, my eyes wide. Both can be attributed to wedding jitters, not pregnancy.

I walk over and open the door.

Katerina, the wedding planner, is waiting, assessing me critically. "You're not running, are you?"

"No. I'm not running. But I do need to talk to Nick."

Katerina studies me incredulously. "There is no way that—"

Vera claps her hands. Everyone in the spare bedroom that's been transformed into my bridal suite jumps. "*Ubiraysya*!"

Katerina is the last to leave after pointedly looking at the silver watch on her elegant wrist and wincing. But a few seconds later, I'm standing alone.

I walk over to the window, fiddling with the tie of my robe as I look outside. What used to be snow is now lush grass, splashed with colorful flowers and bustling with activity.

I went to a handful of weddings in Philadelphia as a plus-one or for coworkers. I never expected the most glamorous, ostentatious wedding I'd attend would be my own. Even Andrei's, which I thought was over the top when it took place a few months ago, pales in comparison. I know who I'm marrying, knew what I was getting into when I said yes, but it's staggering to look at.

The door opens and shuts. I glance over at Nick, who strides in and looks around until he spots me. His steps quicken as he hurries over to the window, his expression pinched with concern.

"Is everything okay?" he asks, low and urgent.

I stare at him for a few seconds, soaking everything about this moment in. The sun streaming in through the window. The muffled commotion downstairs. The way Nick looks in his tux, deadly and handsome. And increasingly anxious.

"I'm pregnant."

"You–you're…"

It's somewhat reassuring that Nick looks as stunned by this news as I felt while staring at the sticks.

"Yes."

"Wow. I wasn't—I mean, I just…wow."

"You're happy, right?" I whisper. "I mean, we've been…"

Nick closes the distance between us, tugging me into his arms and resting our foreheads together. "I'm thrilled, *malysha*."

I exhale, relief and happiness making me dizzy. "Good. It's not returnable."

He chuckles lightly, then kisses me. It starts out sweet and soft. Like a breeze rustling blades of grass or embers in a fireplace. Then, it shifts. The wind picks up, and flames grow.

Nick tugs me closer and then spins me around so my back is against the wall. Most of the furniture—including the bed—was moved out of here for today. All that's left are the chair, where I'm supposed to be getting my makeup applied, and the long table, covered with every beauty product imaginable.

Nick's mouth moves to my throat, then even lower. The slit in my robe parts easily, drooping down to reveal the strapless bra and thong, which is all I'm wearing underneath.

He says a stream of rough Russian. I'm getting better at understanding the language, but I'm so overwhelmed by the pulsing between my legs that I'm not sure I'd comprehend *any* language right now.

I buck against his hand, now resting on my thigh. "Please."

I feel needy and desperate. Maybe it's pregnancy hormones. Maybe because it's my wedding day. Maybe it's the intimacy of being able to tell the father of my child I'm pregnant minutes after finding out myself.

"We'll be late," Nick says as his hand is already moving between my legs.

The lace of my underwear is impatiently tugged to the side, and then one finger fills me, quickly followed by a second.

I moan, rocking against his hand and riding his fingers. "You're the boss. They can wait."

He flicks my clit, making me yelp. "*Eto moye*, Lyla."

"*Da*," I breathe.

His fingers slip out of me, and something much thicker takes its place. I arch against the intrusion and moan as his cock slides deeper. Nick groans as I wrap my legs around his waist, pulling him even closer.

He fucks me fast and hard. I come with a muffled cry, feeling the warmth of his release fill me seconds later.

There's a loud knock on the door.

"We should have eloped," I whisper.

Nick chuckles. He kisses me, slow and sweet. "I love you."

"I love you too."

Another impatient knock sounds.

Nick kisses me once more, then heads for the door. I walk into the bathroom again to clean up. My cheeks are flushed and my hair mussed. But I look *happy* as I fix my hair and straighten my robe.

I grasp the rose charm hanging from my neck, rubbing the metal between two fingers. Rather than a reminder of the past—than a warning—I look at it like a symbol of strength. A sign of fierce beauty.

I doubt that's what my mother was trying to tell me when she gave me it. More likely, it was the first necklace she saw or it was the one on sale. But that doesn't bother me as much as it once did. I've left my mother and her mistakes in the past, where they belong. Accepted her life wasn't black and white, and mine isn't either. That I don't have to look for the contrast in my decisions compared to hers in order to make the correct choice.

When I reemerge into the bedroom, there's a team waiting. My hair is brushed and curled. My skin is wiped and painted. And then I step into the white gown that's hung in this room for the last few weeks.

Leo is waiting in the hallway when I walk outside, clutching a bouquet of roses.

"You look really pretty, Mom," he tells me.

"Thank you, sweetheart." I kiss the top of his head because I have a feeling this is one day he'll indulge me.

Leo holds out a hand to me. We walk down the stairs side by side, out the front door and into the yard that's alive with color. Rows and rows of seats line the aisle, mostly filled with unfamiliar faces. I'm only focused on the familiar one waiting at the end of the aisle.

Nick watches me and Leo approach him, his expression severe with emotion. I wonder if he's seeing our whole future stretched ahead of us the way I am.

It's not what I thought my life would look like.

It's better.

EPILOGUE

NICK

As soon as I register the knock on the door, I'm standing and striding over to it. Alex still has his hand raised when I turn the knob and pull it open.

"Is it time?"

"Yep. They're on their way."

Alex's answer is what I'm expecting—hoping for. But my body reacts like it's a surprise, my heart pounding and my mind racing.

"Okay. I need—I need…" I glance around my office, blankly registering stacks of papers, trying to think through *what* I need.

"Keys would help with driving," Alex suggests.

Ever since he returned three months ago, he's thoroughly enjoyed watching me approach parenthood for the second time with a strong mixture of excitement and unease. I'm thrilled. I'm also terrified.

Shooting him a glare to make my feelings about the sly smirk on his face clear, I return to my desk. I power off my computer and grab my leather jacket off the chair. Once it's shrugged on, I pat my pocket, making sure I can feel the metal shapes inside before heading into the hallway.

Alex follows. "Labor is a long process. There's no big rush."

"Women give birth on the side of the road because they don't make it to the hospital in time," I say, quickening my steps to the fastest pace possible.

I should have worked from home today. *Would* have, if Lyla hadn't told me I was driving her crazy with my hovering.

I've been overprotective her entire pregnancy, and it's gotten worse, the closer she's gotten to her due date. I can't help it. The first time around, I missed everything. I never got to see Lyla pregnant with Leo or hold him as a baby. This feels like a gift I never expected to receive on top of everything else Lyla has given me.

"Statistically, that's very unlikely," Alex tells me, still trailing behind.

"I don't give a fuck about statistics." I shove open the metal door that leads straight into the parking lot.

Winter air smacks me in the face, cold wind raking through my hair and cutting through the fabric of my clothes.

I barely register the chill, hustling toward my car. And then I freeze. Whirl on Alex, who's spotted the same thing I have and now appears more worried than amused.

My wife is in labor, and the Aurus I drove today has a flat tire. Expensive, irritable, *useless* hunk of metal. Maybe this is karma for all the tires I've shot at.

There's no visible mark on the rubber. I probably picked up a nail, driving through the industrial area where the warehouse is located.

The how doesn't matter now. The only question is, what to do now?

"Did you drive?"

"No," Alex replies. "Viktor drove after we finished with the Babanin shipment. I can call—"

I'm already striding back toward the warehouse.

"You heard what I said about no rush, right?" Alex asks, jogging after me.

I don't answer.

"What would I know anyway, right? I'm only a *doctor*."

I ignore Alex's heavy sarcasm in favor of focusing on typing the code in at the door. The warehouse is emptier than usual. We received a big shipment last night, and so most of the men are at home, sleeping.

"Viktor!" I bark, spotting him over by the entrance to the locker room.

He hurries over. "What's up, boss?"

"I need your keys."

Viktor's brow crinkles as he digs them out of his pocket. "Okay? I—"

Whatever else he says fades into the background as I head for the exit a second time. Mentally, I'm tracing the route from here to the hospital. We have a safe house, where injured men go to get treated, so I'm not as familiar with the building as most people in dangerous lines of work probably are.

"It's the black Mercedes at the end." Alex appears beside me again.

I say nothing but pass him the keys. My thoughts are slippery and spiraling. Probably best not to get behind the wheel.

Usually, I'd push straight through any uncertainty. But Lyla is my Achilles' heel. Risks I normally wouldn't think twice about are unfathomable where she's concerned.

Alex reads the worry I'm trying to cover up.

"Hey." He grabs my arm, pulling me to a stop. "You don't have to be *Pakhan* right now."

"I'm always *Pakhan*."

"She'll be fine. Lyla is tough."

"I know she is. I just…" I exhale, attempting to let out some of the worry as well.

"She'll be fine," Alex repeats, gripping my shoulder and squeezing it tightly.

I let out another deep sigh and nod. Because there's no other outcome I can comprehend, and worrying about worst-case scenarios won't help anyone.

Minutes later, we're racing along roads, streaked with white from salt. It hasn't risen above freezing in weeks, which is reflected in the frozen heaps of snow piled on either side of the highway.

Alex stops right in front of the hospital's main entrance, recognizing I don't have the patience to park.

I rush through the automatic doors, not really registering any of the looks I'm receiving.

It's chaos inside. Screaming children. Shouting adults. An endless rush of activity.

At the first opportunity, I turn. The hallway is lined with numbered doors. Not a one of them gives me any indication of where I should be heading to find Lyla.

"This is an authorized personal area only."

I turn in the direction of the female voice. A woman in scrubs stands with her arms crossed.

"Where is labor and delivery?"

The woman's lips purse. "You're here to visit a patient?"

"Yes."

Her eyes flicker between the bulge of my gun beneath my jacket and my face before she lifts the tablet she's holding. "What's the patient's name?"

"Lyla Morozov."

The nurse pales but holds my gaze, obviously recognizing the last name. Under other circumstances, I'd admire her bravery. Right now, I'm seconds from losing my shit.

"Are you family?"

"She's my wife."

"Fifth floor. There's an elevator at the end of the hall."

I thank her and continue down the hallway. When I reach the end of the hallway, I hurry toward the stairwell instead of the elevator.

It takes me less than a minute to climb the ten flights. Ivan is waiting by the desk in the center of the floor.

"Room 516," he tells me before I can say a word.

I nod at him appreciatively before continuing down the hall to the right room.

Lyla is lying in bed and staring out the window, her right hand splayed over the hill that's her stomach.

"Good view?"

She glances over, relief washing over her face as she registers my presence. "You're here."

"Of course I'm here." I walk over to the bed, leaning down to brush a kiss across her forehead. "Where else would I be?"

Lyla inhales, her hand circling around my wrist as she soaks in my proximity the same way I'm savoring hers. "You should have stayed home today."

I chuckle, rubbing my thumb over the subtle drum of her pulse point. "That's not what you said this morning."

"I know." Lyla sighs, then winces, rubbing her bump. "What time is it?"

"Almost three."

"Leo needs to—"

"His security detail will pick him up, like normal. Don't worry about it."

"He'll want to come here."

"I know." If anyone could give me a run for my money when it comes to levels of excitement about Lyla's pregnancy, it's Leo. Kid walks around, telling every person he sees that he's going to be a big brother. "We'll see if he's able to convince them."

"Nick." Lyla's voice gains the same hard edge that always appears when Leo's future and the Bratva comes up.

She doesn't want to see what is obvious to everyone else—Leo is a born leader. He has the intensity and the focus and the intelligence to be a successful *Pakhan.*

But it will be his choice whether he pursues that path, like I promised her.

The door opens, and a white-coat-wearing doctor enters, flipping through forms. He starts speaking Russian, a lackluster spiel of bored drivel about patience and pain management.

I cut him off with a flat tone and instruct him to speak English, already contemplating requesting a different doctor and weighing whether it will be worth annoying Lyla. She hates it when I emphasize the treatment most Bratva wives expect to have handed to them.

Lyla glances between me and the doctor, not understanding a word.

I'm the one who speaks the most Russian to Lyla. And the majority of what I say around her are swears or dirty talk, neither of which are useful right now.

The doctor glances between the form—which I'm betting has Lyla's last name listed—and the bed, all color rapidly draining from his face. Mumbles something incoherent and then turns and flees the room.

Lyla's accusing eyes land on me. "What did you say to him?"

"I told him to speak English."

I might have also called him a moron and threatened his life. But she'll have to learn Russian to call me out on that.

Her eyes narrow anyway, guessing I'm excluding. But then another contraction hits, and she's entirely distracted.

Four hours later, I become a father for the second time. The second time—when it comes to anything—is supposed to be easier than the first. More predictable at least.

But for me, it's new.

I look down at the perfectly miniature face of my daughter as she sleeps in my arms, then to her mother's sweaty, exhausted, glowing one. Lyla beams, watching me hold Rose.

I lean down and kiss her, the worry and anxiety melting away, leaving happiness and relief behind. I whisper how much I love her, the words more for me than for her. Saying them feels good. It's the same giddiness of watching someone open a present you picked out for them.

Lyla and I are a love story with an obvious ending. I would burn the world or rebuild it, just for her.

We might have an obvious ending, but we had unlikely chapters. We met by coincidence. Overcame odds. Escaped horrors. Reconnected randomly.

There are so many ways in which we could have not ended up here. If her friend Kennedy had led her to the right party the night we met. If she hadn't gotten pregnant. If my father and brothers weren't murdered. If she hadn't cut her hand and seen Alex. If Bianchi hadn't sent men to her apartment.

But here we are.

The door opens, and Leo walks into the room. I catch a glimpse of two of the members of his security team in the hall before the door shuts again. They both look exasperated.

I glance at Lyla and grin. She's not too exhausted to roll her eyes at me.

Honestly, I have mixed feelings about Leo joining the Bratva. Your instinct as a parent is protecting your child from everything. But I'm damn proud Leo has all the traits of a *Pakhan*.

He looks like a kid now though, staring at Rose with wide, amazed eyes.

"Come here, sweetheart," Lyla says.

Leo rushes to the side of the bed, climbing onto the mattress and snuggling next to her.

"Do you want to hold your little sister?" I ask.

Leo's head bobs wildly in response to my question. I smile, then lean down and carefully transfer the sleeping baby from my arms to his. Leo's expression is serious and focused as he tightens his hold on the bundle of blankets.

Leo looks at Rose, and Lyla looks at both our kids, and I look at all three of them. Stare in wonder at my family.

For me, family was always a bargaining chip and a hierarchy.

For Lyla, family was absent.

Together, our family is perfect.

THE END

ACKNOWLEDGMENTS

Like always, this book was a team effort. I'm so grateful to the amazing women who helped shape and polish *Pretty Ugly Promises* into its best possible form.

Mel, thank you for all of your insight. This was a different direction for me and hearing your valuable feedback from a reader perspective was incredibly helpful.

Tiffany, THANK YOU! I truly will never be able to say those two words to you enough. You contribute so much to every book you work on and I will never take it for granted.

Jovana, thank you for fitting me in and for another meticulous job! It's always a pleasure working with you.

Kim, this cover is absolutely perfect. I'm constantly blown away by your talent and excited to see what you come up with next!

Autumn at Wordsmith Publicity, thank you for helping Lyla and Nick reach as many people as possible.

Finally, thank YOU for reading. Every book sold, every review written, every post or TikTok, all of it makes a huge difference. It's what enables and inspires me to keep writing. I never thought I'd be sitting here writing the acknowledgments for my *seventeenth* book. Thanks for making this dream a reality!

ABOUT THE AUTHOR

C.W. Farnsworth is the author of numerous adult and young adult romance novels featuring sports, strong female leads, and happy endings.

Charlotte lives in Rhode Island and when she isn't writing spends her free time reading, at the beach, or snuggling with her Australian Sheperd.

Find her on Facebook (@cwfarnsworth), Twitter (@cw_farnsworth), Instagram (@authorcwfarnsworth) and check out her website www.authorcwfarnsworth.com for news about upcoming releases!

www.ingramcontent.com/pod-product-compliance
Ingram Content Group UK Ltd.
Pitfield, Milton Keynes, MK11 3LW, UK
UKHW040910241125
9137UKWH00045B/1114

9 781088 171806